Dick

WH... YOU HIDE...

WHEN THE ONLY SAFE PLACE...

IS AT 35,000 FEET?

Praise for
HEADWIND

"Retired Air Force pilot Nance shows the same skill at guiding a thriller through white-knuckle weather as he did as a civilian landing a 737. . . . Hugely entertaining: a gripper that not only battles heavy headwinds while fuel runs low but plunges you headfirst into a meat-grinder of international legal complexities." —*Kirkus Reviews*

"Peppered with [Nance's] trademark razor-edge escape scenarios and death-defying aviation theatrics . . . Hair-raising near-disaster in the air, high courtroom drama and a strong international cast of characters make this surefire bestseller a nonstop read." —*Publishers Weekly*

"Fans of suspense fiction and aeronautical thrillers in particular will find much to like in Nance's latest . . . white-knuckle flying sequences . . . authentic technical details . . . sparkling dialogue; a relentless pace; and an exciting courtroom drama in Ireland, where the legal jousting reaches its climax. . . . After the first one hundred pages, which crackle with tension, the reader is hit with another jolt that lasts just as long, with more thrills yet to come. Highly recommended." —*Library Journal*

"Harrowing . . . *Headwind* is his most exciting novel yet as a former U.S. president evades his would-be kidnappers by leading them in a whirlwind chase around the world in a hijacked jet." —*The Stuart News/Port St. Lucie News*

"Fast pacing . . . brisk dialogue . . . fun to read." —*St. Louis Post-Dispatch*

"[Nance] masterfully puts you in the world of aeronautics, whether in the cockpit, at the control tower, or in the passenger seat. The ending, thrilling both in the air and in a Scottish courtroom, brings this page-turner to a satisfying landing." —*Booklist*

Strap yourself in for more praise . . .

"A nail-biting thriller . . . It's hard to put down, and more power to anyone who can read this on an airplane. Delivers one of the scarier pieces of thriller fiction to date." —Copley News Service

"*Pandora's Clock* is an unnerving flight."
—*St. Petersburg Times*

"Exquisite suspense . . . the ultimate flying adventure. If you read this on an airliner you're a lot braver than I am." —Stephen Coonts

"Nance's riveting thriller is a fast, fun read that never lets up." —Phillip M. Margolin

"The one you don't want to miss." —*The Orlando Sentinel*

PHOENIX RISING

"Harrowing . . . Nance delivers suspense and smooth writing. A classy job." —*The New York Times Book Review*

"A superb novel." —*Library Journal*

SCORPION STRIKE

"Terrifying . . . white-knuckle flight scenes."
—*Kirkus Reviews*

"Nance brings insider knowledge to this military adventure." —*The Seattle Times*

"Gripping." —*Seattle Post-Intelligencer*

"Exciting . . . a good read." —United Press International

continued . . .

FINAL APPROACH

"A taut high-tech mystery that could have been written only by an airline insider." —Stephen Coonts

"Convincing . . . a fine work of fiction."
—*San Francisco Chronicle*

"Fasten your seat belts! John Nance turns an air disaster into a gripping investigative novel." —James A. Michener

"Compelling." —*The Seattle Times*

THE LAST HOSTAGE

"A thrilling ride . . . [Will] keep even the most experienced thriller addicts strapped into their seat for the whole flight."
—*People*

"Nance . . . knows how to keep his readers turning the pages."
—*Booklist*

"Slam-bang special effects . . . right up to its startling . . . climax." —*Kirkus Reviews*

MEDUSA'S CHILD

"So compelling it's tough to look away." —*People*

"A high-flying thriller . . . Nance delivers plenty of punch."
—*Orange County Register*

"Gripping." —*The Indianapolis Star*

"Fast-paced and exciting." —*Detroit Free Press*

"The nonstop ride of your life." —*Rocky Mountain News*

"Nance puts the thrill back in 'thriller'."
—*Statesman Journal* (Salem, OR)

"Will leave readers breathless." —*Montgomery Advertiser*

Other books by John J. Nance

FICTION

BLACKOUT
THE LAST HOSTAGE
MEDUSA'S CHILD
PANDORA'S CLOCK
PHOENIX RISING
SCORPION STRIKE
FINAL APPROACH

NONFICTION

WHAT GOES UP
ON SHAKY GROUND
BLIND TRUST
SPLASH OF COLORS

HEADWIND

JOHN J. NANCE

JOVE BOOKS, NEW YORK

This is a work of fiction. Names, characters, places, and incidents either
are the product of the author's imagination or are used fictitiously,
and any resemblance to actual persons, living or dead, business
establishments, events, or locales is entirely coincidental.

HEADWIND

A Jove Book / published by arrangement with
G. P. Putnam's Sons

PRINTING HISTORY
G. P. Putnam's Sons hardcover edition / April 2001
Jove edition / March 2002

All rights reserved.
Copyright © 2001 by John J. Nance.
Cover design by Marc Cohen.
Cover photo by Tony Stone.
This book, or parts thereof, may not be reproduced
in any form without permission.
For information address: G. P. Putnam's Sons,
a division of Penguin Putnam Inc.,
375 Hudson Street, New York, New York 10014.

Visit our website at
www.penguinputnam.com

ISBN: 0-515-13262-4

A JOVE BOOK®
Jove Books are published by The Berkley Publishing Group,
a division of Penguin Putnam Inc.,
375 Hudson Street, New York, New York 10014.
JOVE and the "J" design
are trademarks belonging to Penguin Putnam Inc.

PRINTED IN THE UNITED STATES OF AMERICA

10 9 8 7 6 5 4 3 2 1

*Dedicated with love and respect
to my aunt, my father's sister,*

Virginia Nance Maccabe,

*a fellow Veteran of U.S. Military Service
who served her country with honor during World War II
as a female United States Marine.*

✈ ACKNOWLEDGMENTS

While the world of aviation is my domain, I am also a lawyer, and *Headwind* gave me an extraordinary opportunity to meld both the aeronautical and legal worlds together in an exciting romp that has many dimensions, all of them needing the research help of numerous people in Europe and the Americas, some of whom I'd like to thank publically and specifically.

First, as always, the evolution of this story was helped immensely by the constant and patient editorial and developmental assistance of my wife, Bunny Nance.

I want to express my appreciation to my prime advocate at Putnam, Senior Editor David Highfill, whose top-flight abilities at fine-tuning the manuscript always make a good story even better. And my thanks, as well, to my publisher, Leslie Gelbman, and to my long-time agent and friend Olga Wieser of the Wieser and Wieser Literary Agency in New York.

Here in Washington State, the demanding day-to-day task of line-editing, polishing, and helping to shape this work was performed again with indefatigable energy by Patricia Davenport, who is also my business partner, an

English Master, and my world-class *in-house* editor who never seems to run out of red pens.

I could not have rendered an accurate description of how Irish justice would have handled this international crisis without the learned assistance of a world-class Barrister named Patrick Dillon-Malone of Dublin, Ireland, who spent time instructing me and assisting the editing process, as well as directing my visits to the historic Four Courts building and appropriate pubs. My thanks also to Dubliners Mike Rogan of Parc Aviation at Dublin Airport, Feidhlim O'Seasnain, and Peter Donnelly (a member of the Shelbourne Hotel's management staff), and to my daughter, Dawn Nance, who lives in Ireland and whose suggestions sparked the idea to bring the "circus" to town.

In London, I want to acknowledge also the kind assistance of Solicitor Leslie Cuthbert, who helped significantly in understanding the Bow Street Courts, and the assistance of Mr. John Coles of Metro Business Aviation at Heathrow.

And back home in the States, a hearty "Thank You" to Gary and Elizabeth Rhoades, Jim and Kelly Watt, Kirk T. Mosley, and Msg. Jerry Priest, and fellow attorney Ross Taylor for helping proof the results.

The year 1999 was marked by many things, but the passing of my longtime friend George Wieser was especially difficult. George was there in the beginning of my authorship with an indomitable optimism, and an infectious pride when we reached the bestseller lists with both nonfiction and fiction. He was a gentleman and a scholar and a fighter and that rarest of commodities: an honest man. I shall miss him in this life.

✈ ONE

"Captain, I think you'd better get back here!" the chief flight attendant said as she burst into the cockpit.

Captain Craig Dayton snapped his head around and began reaching for his seat belt as soon as he saw the worried expression on Jillian Walz's face.

"What's the matter?" Dayton asked, aware that his copilot had shifted around in the right seat to look at her as well.

Jillian shut the door and stood in the tiny space aft of the center console, breathing hard and signaling him to wait. She watched a police car pull up on the ramp of the newly opened airport and stop in front of their Boeing 737, its blue lights flashing. Dayton followed her gaze and spotted the patrol car.

"We're about to get in the middle of a diplomatic crisis," Jillian said. "The gate agent—"

A voice on the overhead speakers cut her short. "Flight forty-two, operations."

The copilot lifted his handheld microphone. "Go ahead, ops."

"We will have to hold you at the gate for a while, forty-two."

"Why?" the copilot asked sharply, noting the arrival of a second police car on the ramp.

"Forty-two, there is an official order . . . ah . . . wait, please . . ."

The microphone in the operations office remained on while urgent voices conferred in the background. "Ah . . . we will have to remove some of your passengers."

Jillian nodded rapidly, her words tumbling out. "Craig, they're here to arrest President Harris!"

Craig Dayton clasped Jillian's right elbow as he searched her eyes. "Slow down, Jillian, and tell me precisely what you're talking about."

The day had started in Istanbul with the exciting news that a former President of the United States would be riding with them in first class through Athens to Rome. Fresh from delivering a speech to an international conference on hunger, President John B. Harris had come aboard with an attractive young female aide and an appropriately dour Secret Service agent, greeting the crew warmly at the door and even sticking his head into the cockpit to say hello. Impeccably groomed, and wearing a well-tailored dark business suit that made him seem taller than his five-foot-ten height, Harris had proven to be as friendly and gracious as the Washington press corps had always described him during his almost legendary single term in office.

"Our agent . . . gate agent . . . I know her," Jillian was saying. "She came down the jetway all upset and said the Greek government has a warrant for his arrest."

"Why? What for?"

She shook her head, creating a moving blur of chestnut hair. "She didn't know."

First Officer Alastair Chadwick whistled and inclined his head toward the ramp, where a third and fourth police car had parked, all with their top lights flashing frantically. "Something's definitely up, mate."

"This is a foreign-flagged airliner," Dayton said. "No

one's removing any passenger without my permission." He motioned to Jillian to reopen the cockpit door as he moved the captain's seat back on its tracks and prepared to get up, filling the air with the aroma of peanuts as the contents of an opened snack pouch scattered on the metal floor.

"Damn."

"I'll take care of that," Jillian said.

The copilot caught his arm.

"Craig, you remember I'm a solicitor in my other life in England, right?"

"Yes, I know," Craig said, his eyes on Jillian as she stepped out.

"A little free legal advice, okay? You're an American national with a European work visa, you're the master of a German-flagged airliner, and that airliner is currently sitting on Greek concrete. You're not the U.S. ambassador. They could arrest you for getting in the way."

The captain shook his head impatiently. "This is Greece, Alastair. They've been civilized for at least a few years now. About two or three thousand, in fact."

"Craig?" Chadwick tightened his grip on the captain's arm, and Dayton responded with irritation.

"WHAT?"

"Be careful, okay? I know he's your President, but you can't protect him."

"No?" There was a flurry of movement as Craig Dayton resumed the process of hauling himself out of the seat. "Just watch me!"

✈ TWO

Rome, Italy—Monday—1:00 P.M.

The Presidential Suite of the Metropole Hotel in the center of Rome was designed for kings and presidents and captains of industry, but despite the opulence of its decor, the most valuable feature to its occupant was a portable phone and plenty of floor to pace.

"Dammit, man, where *are* they? You are still in Athens, are you not?"

Sir William Stuart Campbell, a Scot by birth and a knight of the British Empire by deft political maneuvering, reversed direction without warning and strode briskly toward the ten-foot-high windows opening onto an ornate balcony overlooking the Via Veneto. The doors to the balcony stood aside as a warm breeze flowed in, redolent with the essence of fresh flowers and the fragrance of a busy nearby bakery, but leavened with a hint of exhaust fumes from the midday traffic—all of it lost to the intensity of Campbell's concentration.

"*Mister* Kostombrodis!" Campbell barked, his polished accent worthy of an Oxford don, which he had been at one time in his endlessly distinguished legal career. "My dear sir, I was under the distinct, but apparently misguided impression, that we had retained you to keep track of them moment by moment, and that was to include the moment they left the court and headed for the airport. Is it really so difficult to follow instructions?"

A conservatively dressed young woman wearing a sexless gray suit and a worried expression entered the room, her eyes tracking the imposing hulk of the six-foot-four international lawyer with the wariness of a jackal. She calculated his next trajectory across the forty-foot expanse of the vaulted room and waited.

"You are virtually certain, are you not," Campbell was saying into the phone, "that they have a certified copy of the Interpol warrant in their possession?"

Campbell turned and caught sight of the secretary, who signaled him with a nod of her head. He nodded in return and raised an index finger in a wait gesture.

"Yes. Yes. I understand. The second you're certain they have him physically off that aircraft, ring me back. Is that perfectly clear? Whether he's arrested in Athens or here in Rome is a small matter, but having up-to-the-second information on what is happening is a very large matter. Yes. See that you do."

He punched off the phone and collapsed the small antenna in a controlled gesture of disdain, rolling his eyes as he looked at the woman and smiled. "Yes, Isabel?"

"The foreign minister has arrived, sir."

"Show him in, please," Campbell said, gesturing toward the door as his distinctive features melted into a broad smile, the effect similar to opening a curtain on a sunny day.

A short, rotund man in a dark suit scurried through the ten-foot-high double doors at the far end of the room and moved across the eighty-year-old Persian carpet as Campbell came to greet him, clasping his right hand and clapping him on the shoulder in a seamless gesture only a larger man could use with such practiced grace.

"Giuseppe, how good of you to come. It's wonderful to see you again."

Giuseppe Anselmo, the foreign minister of Italy, managed a thin smile as he returned the greeting and accepted a proffered chair next to an ornate couch. A waiter materialized silently with an elaborate silver service of coffee and tea as Campbell inclined his eyes toward the door.

"Close the balcony doors and leave us now, would you?" Campbell instructed. "And be good enough to secure the main door."

The waiter sealed off the balcony, muting the traffic noise as a previously drowned background track of classical music swelled into prominence.

Campbell reached for a remote control and lowered the volume.

When the waiter was gone, Anselmo shook his head and leaned forward, keeping his voice irritatingly low.

"Giuseppe," Campbell smiled, wagging a finger at him, then tapping his ear. "Sorry, old boy, but I think I might be growing a bit deaf in my dotage. May I ask you to speak up? There are no other ears around, I assure you."

"I was saying," Anselmo repeated in a louder voice as he scooted forward to the edge of the chair, "that this puts us in a very difficult position. Unofficially, of course."

"Of course. Treaty obligations are often inconvenient, but are you aware of what Peru's complaint against Harris really contains?"

Campbell poured the steaming coffee into one of the expensive gold leaf cups, making mental note of the rich aroma of the special blend he always specified. British or not, he loved rich coffee.

"I have read it, Stuart. Yes."

"Excellent. Then you realize that the Peruvian government made a substantial case to the Peruvian judge who properly issued the arrest warrant under Interpol procedure. President Harris is directly, criminally, personally responsible."

Anselmo was shaking his head. "We do not believe that, and I doubt you do either."

"Let's look at the facts, Giuseppe. We know there was a clandestine intelligence operation eighty miles from Lima during Harris's presidency. We know the targeted building contained some sixty-three men and women, and that regardless of what they were alleged to be making in there, they were, in fact, tortured and, three days later, burned alive."

"Stuart, I . . ."

"Wait, please. Permit me to finish. We also know the American CIA commissioned the operation with local thugs, and we know that commission was the result of a covert operation that could have only been authorized personally by the President of the United States."

"But you have no direct proof of that, Stuart!"

"Giuseppe, as a lawyer, you know we've got a rock-solid prima facie case under the Treaty Against Torture. The warrant is valid. It will be up to a trial court to decide if the proof is sufficient. And by the way, we *do* have the proof, though I'm not prepared to discuss it at this time."

Giuseppe Anselmo reached out and tapped Campbell's forearm with his index finger. "Why are *you* representing them, Stuart?" His eyes were riveted on Campbell's. "You have a thriving practice in Brussels. Your firm represents half of the truly successful companies in Europe. You're very wealthy now. Why take on the United States in a crusade you can't win?"

"Is that what you believe this to be?" He smiled. "A crusade?"

"Isn't it?"

"Of course not! Giuseppe, the only point is that no one on this planet is above the law when it comes to this treaty and the hideous crimes it seeks to prevent. No person may escapé universal jurisdiction. No peasant, no king, no president . . ."

"Please, Stuart! Save your speeches for television," Anselmo snapped. "I am quite aware that you wrote the majority of the treaty and were the driving force behind passing it and getting it ratified. I am aware of your role in trying to extradite Pinochet."

"I am Peru's lawyer in this matter," Campbell interrupted, "because they have a valid case, as horrifying as that may be to our American friends."

"But Stuart . . . *Peru?* No one's going to take this seriously."

"Peru is not the issue, Giuseppe. The United States is the issue. You and I are rather familiar with the American attitude that they're only subject to international jurisdiction when it's convenient."

"Yes, but . . ."

"Need I remind you of the U.S. Navy's flight through the ski lift cable?"

"No."

"Or the arrogant legal response to your requests to try the pilots under Italian law?"

"Of course I am aware of all that!" Anselmo answered with a scowl. "That's one of the many reasons my government finally collapsed last year and we had to go through elections. It is rather ungracious of you to remind me."

Campbell sipped his coffee and glanced through floor-to-ceiling windows at blue skies beyond the balcony, purposefully letting silence hang between them for a few moments before looking back at him.

"I would never mean to be ungracious to you, old friend," he said, shifting to flawless Italian. "But the fact is, if I were representing the United States and asking Rome to enforce a warrant for the arrest of Slobodan Milosevic, you would not hesitate."

"Now, look here, Stuart . . ." Anselmo continued in English.

"Giuseppe, the fact is, about thirty minutes ago my associates left a magistrate court right here in Rome with a signed warrant for the police to arrest President Harris when he lands at Da Vinci Airport. The judge is prepared to hold immediate hearings tomorrow on our petition for expedited extradition to Peru."

"What?"

"There will be a plane waiting, you see."

"What are you doing, Stuart?"

"Why, being a good lawyer for my client, of course."

"But . . . extradition hearings take months, if not longer! How did you convince . . ."

"There will be appeals by the U.S., of course, but we're

going to demand immediate extradition to Lima for trial. We would appreciate your government's assistance in cutting through any official delays. Otherwise, under the treaty, I will be forced to insist that Italy try Harris itself."

Anselmo made a short, rude, staccato sound as he shook his head. "In your wildest imagination, Stuart, can you imagine the government of Italy putting an American President on trial for alleged crimes committed in a backwater of South America?"

Campbell shook his head slowly, a smile on his lips. "No, Giuseppe, which is why you do not want this problem in town any longer than necessary. If it comes here, I will help you make it go away, as the Americans say."

"Excuse me," Giuseppe said, his eyes lighting with the possibility of deliverance. "*If?* His itinerary is uncertain?"

Stuart Campbell nodded. "I'm managing this from Rome, but at this moment, Harris's flight is being detained at the Athens Airport pending the arrival of the proper authorities. If they succeed, they'll relieve you of this potentially vexatious burden. If the Greeks fail, however, John Harris will be arrested on arrival here."

"And what if he elects to go somewhere else?" Anselmo asked with undisguised sarcasm.

The senior partner of Campbell, Chastane, and McNaughton smiled.

"Giuseppe, have you ever known me to take inordinate risks? At this moment, I have associates with certified copies of the Peruvian Interpol warrant waiting with cell phones in virtually every nation in Europe in anticipation of just such a possibility. But I'm fully expecting to hear good news from Athens any minute."

As if on cue, the portable phone at his side began ringing.

✈ THREE

All the baggage had been loaded and the passengers boarded by the time seven Greek police officers gathered in the jetway outside EuroAir Flight 42 and Captain Craig Dayton appeared in the doorway of the airplane.

"Who speaks English?" Dayton asked, keeping his voice controlled and calm.

One of the officers stepped forward, brushing past the wide-eyed gate agent, who was somewhere between panicked and helpless. The officer motioned to quiet down the other policemen who were in animated discussion behind him, then turned back to the captain, carefully noting the four-stripe epaulets on the shoulders of his white uniform shirt. "Captain, we are ordered to . . . hold everyone aboard your aircraft. There are others . . . government officials . . . coming here with papers."

"What for?" Dayton asked.

The officer shook his head. "I do not know. My orders are to keep everyone on board at the gate."

"How long before they get here?" Craig asked.

"A half hour, perhaps."

Dayton said nothing for a few seconds, then pointed to the 737's forward door, which was folded back along the forward fuselage.

"All right. Here's what I'm going to do. As captain, I'm responsible for these passengers. So I'm going to close the aircraft door to keep everyone on board for you, as you ask. Okay?"

The policeman thought it over quickly and nodded with a fleeting smile.

"Okay."

"I'm also going to start one of the engines to keep the air-conditioning on."

The officer looked concerned. "Start . . . engines?"

"I have to. It's part of our regulations. If we keep people on board, we have to start an engine. Standard procedure. Rules."

The officer smiled and nodded, understanding the last word. "Okay."

"Stand back, now," Craig said as he worked the small latch on the upper hinge arm and pulled the door back through the opening before using the single lever to lock it into position.

He leaned forward and peeped through the small, round window on the door, assuring himself the delegation of police had not been alarmed by his actions. They'd stepped back obediently and were waiting, hands in pockets, convinced they were doing precisely as their superiors had ordered.

Craig turned to Jillian and took her by the shoulders, his eyes finding hers, but his words betraying nothing of their long-term off-work relationship.

"Listen to me! Tell President Harris what's happening, then get his Secret Service man up here to the entryway, strap him in your folding seat, and have him hold this door handle in place so no one can open it."

"What are you planning to do, Craig?"

"What I'm sworn to do. Don't ask. Just go." He turned and disappeared into the cockpit, launching himself into

the left seat and scrambling for his seat belt, aware of the
questioning look from Alastair in the right seat.

"Before Starting Engines checklist," Dayton barked.

"I say, my ears must be going," Alastair replied, his
eyebrows raised. "I could have sworn you called for the
checklist."

"I did. Checklist, please. Now! We're getting out of
here."

Alastair hesitated, then took a short breath. "Forgive me
for pointing out the obvious, old chap, but we're still attached to the jetway and there's no tug in place to shove us
back."

Craig looked at him suddenly. "That's precisely what
I'm counting on, Alastair. We're going to start engines and
get out of here."

"This is an American thing, isn't it?"

"You're damn right it is. No one's going to arrest a U.S.
president on my watch."

"May I remind you this is a German airline?"

Craig nodded without looking as his eyes scanned the
forward instrument panel. "So noted."

There was a hesitation from the right seat, and Craig
looked around at Alastair. "What?"

"You're going to get us both sacked, aren't you?" Chadwick said quietly.

"I got you this job," Dayton said, "and I'll make sure
you keep it. It's my authority and my neck. I made you do
it. So do it! Checklist, PLEASE!"

Alastair read the deadly serious expression on his captain's face and quietly pulled the laminated checklist into
his lap, beginning the challenge and response litany immediately.

"Brakes?"

"Set."

"Hydraulics?"

Jillian Walz had gone immediately to brief the Secret Service agent who moved without hesitation to the front to
hold the door handle immobile. She returned, then, to brief

President Harris—unprepared for the message to be taken lightly.

"Wait a minute, Ms. Walz," President Harris said, leaning toward her with a smile. "There's obviously a mistake somewhere in translation," he chuckled, "or someone's pulling your leg. To the best of my knowledge, I haven't started any wars or overthrown the Greek government in the last few days, so there's really nothing to arrest me for. I'm sure that delegation is just some sort of welcoming committee. We get a lot of them. They probably found out belatedly I was coming through town, got a late start, phoned ahead, and inadvertently got everyone excited."

"Sir!" Jillian interrupted. "Our agent out there was told they were coming to arrest you. Not greet you. She mentioned an arrest warrant."

President Harris exchanged looks with the woman beside him, thirty-two-year old Sherry Lincoln, a Rhodes scholar and his assistant for the previous two years. Before she could say anything, the boarding music playing over the PA system shifted to a fast-paced instrumental more suited for the sound track of a movie chase scene. Sherry Lincoln glanced at the overhead speakers in irritation before looking back at her employer.

"What do you think, Sherry?" he asked with a wink. "A bunch of angry Democrats back home manipulating relatives in the old country? I've always been told to beware of Greeks bearing gifts or warrants, but . . ."

She wasn't smiling, and it stopped him. "Sir," Sherry Lincoln began, "if the word *warrant* was used . . ."

"It was," Jillian interjected, realizing the 737's auxiliary power unit had just started up, a small jet engine in the tail section that provided electricity as well as compressed air to start the engines. She could hear the distant whine.

President Harris was shaking his head. "Oh, come on, Sherry! Our allies don't make a habit of arresting former U.S. presidents. They throw formal dinners and bore us to death with welcoming speeches. Far more effective punishment. Anyway, there's still such a thing as sovereign immunity for any parking tickets I might not have paid while in office."

Another sound of rising frequencies reached Jillian's experienced ear. One of the engines was at idle and the second engine was winding up. There was a momentary flicker in the lights as one of the pilots switched over electrical power from the ground unit to the engines, and the sound track went off-line for a few seconds, then resumed, the rhythm almost matching her accelerated heart beat.

"Look," President Harris was saying in a soothing voice. "When they get here, whoever it is, I'll talk to them and take care of it."

Jillian raised her hand to stop him. "Sir, for right now, please, the captain wants you to stay seated and keep your seat belt on. I'll report back shortly."

"Are we leaving on schedule?" John Harris asked.

She shook her head. "I don't know."

The scream of the 737's two CFM-56 jet engines starting up had forced the police officers to shove their fingers in their ears and retreat up the jetway, where they missed the significance of the slight movement of the fuselage against the accordion-like padding that encased the doorway of the Boeing. Thrust reversers were an unknown concept to them, so the fact that both sets of reversers had just come open was meaningless.

A sudden, unexpected lurch threw all seven against the wall of the jetway, instantly garnering their undivided attention. The lead officer scrambled to his feet and went flying back toward the airplane in time to see the cockpit of the 737 sliding backward in his field of vision. It looked as if the jetway were being moved, but when he reached the end and braved the scream of the engines to peer around to the right, he realized that the jet was moving on its own, a maneuver that had not been covered by his orders.

"Careful, Craig!" Alastair had yelped as the captain yanked the thrust reverse levers up to a high-power setting, causing the 737's nosewheel to jump over the single chock in its way and roll backward. Dayton cocked the nosewheel to the left, tracking the front end of the jet to the right and clear of the jetway. Just as quickly, he centered the nosewheel, rechecking the reflection of the area behind them in the windows of the terminal. They were clear as far as he could see. He held the reverse thrust at a high setting, knowing he was probably damaging the engines with debris from the ramp.

A roiling cloud of dust and dirt and a few stray papers boiled up in front of them and billowed angrily up the side of the terminal. Craig could see startled faces just inside the glass of the waiting area as people turned at the sound, wondering why Flight 42 had decided to leave ahead of schedule, and without a push-back tug.

The ground crewmen had turned in wide-eyed surprise and had stood in confusion as Craig had started the engines, but the sudden movement backward caught them unprepared. One by one they began running after the jet, waving their arms frantically at the cockpit.

Flight 42's baggage compartment doors had already been closed, but there was an entire train of baggage carts parked on the right, and the jet blast overturned them now, spilling the contents, which skittered away, accompanied by an upended baggage handler who was rolling end over end toward the terminal.

There was a loud *thwang* as the ground power cable snapped loose from beneath the nose and snaked back toward the building, barely missing one of the ground crew chasing after them but doing no other harm.

The 737 was suddenly clear of the jetway and backing rapidly into the middle of the airport ramp, an area they couldn't see from the cockpit.

"Craig! Stop!" Alastair yelped. "We don't know what's behind us."

"It was clear," he said. Craig could see several of the startled police officers leaning out of the end of the jetway, while two others spilled through the door to scramble down the metal stairway to the ramp with no clear idea what to do to stop the retreating jetliner.

The 737 was rolling backward at five to six knots. Craig stowed the reversers and waited what seemed like an eternity.

"Don't touch the brakes!" Craig cautioned. "We'll rock on our tail."

"Right," Alastair responded.

When the interlock had cleared, Craig shoved the thrust levers forward, waiting for the engines to come up to speed.

Slowly the big jet halted its rearward motion and transitioned to moving forward. Craig cranked the nosewheel to the left and guided them out of the ramp area toward the taxiway, aware that the ground crew was still giving chase and several police cars on their right were now moving cautiously, keeping pace, but maintaining a respectful distance.

"Call the tower for immediate takeoff clearance," Craig barked.

Alastair complied, getting the response he expected. "EuroAir Four-Two, hold your position, sir! You were not cleared to taxi."

Craig punched the transmit button for his headset before the copilot could reply. "Negative, tower, I'm declaring an emergency at this time. Clear us please for immediate takeoff on Runway Two Seven."

Alastair turned toward the left seat shaking his head. "What?"

"An emergency takeoff."

"There's no such thing that I'm aware of. You're going to cashier both our licenses. Come on, Craig. Stop this."

"No. Finish the Before Takeoff checklist. We're rolling as soon as we get to the end."

"Craig," Alastair replied, his voice deep and serious, "I beg you, don't take off without clearance!"

"We have the air traffic control clearance?"

"Yes, but no takeoff clearance, as you well know," Alastair said, keeping his eyes ahead and calculating the distance to the end of the runway. There were no other aircraft in the way, and the cars giving chase were behind them now. "If we take that runway without a takeoff clearance, we're both in serious trouble, and I'd rather keep my ticket. This is insane!"

Craig punched the transmit button again. "Tower? Are you going to clear me for takeoff under my emergency authority? We do not have time to explain, and lives are at stake."

"Ah . . . I . . . this is most irregular, EuroAir. Are you being hijacked?"

"I can't answer that. Understand?"

There was a telling hesitation as the tower operator found the right slot for the problem. Hijacking! That must be the answer. This must be a hijacking!

"Roger, Four-Two, you are cleared for immediate take-off on runway Two Seven."

"The checklist is complete," Alastair said, his voice tense and urgent as he watched Craig take the 737 at a higher-than-normal taxi speed around the end of the taxiway and onto the runway.

"Setting power. Autothrottles engaged," Craig said.

"Roger. Airspeed alive." Alastair waited, watching the airspeed leap to life. "Eighty knots, looking for one hundred twenty-seven."

Craig glanced to his right, past the copilot, half-expecting armed vehicles to be chasing them down the taxiway, but they were leaving unopposed.

The powerful thrust of the engines pushed them back in their seats as the airspeed needle moved against the dial.

"Vee One, and Vee R," Alastair stated, reporting the commit speed and the rotation speed as the terminal flashed past in the distance on their right.

Craig pulled gently on the control yoke, lifting the nose, feeling the jet come off the runway as a flying machine and accelerate even faster, freed of the constraints of wheels on concrete.

"Positive rate, gear up."

"Roger," Alastair replied. "Gear up." He moved the lever to the up position, monitoring the sequence of red lights and then no lights before moving the gear handle to the off position, his mind racing through the possible trouble they had just created for themselves. At the very least, EuroAir management would be apoplectic. At worst, he and Dayton would be fired and possibly prosecuted. He was the copilot and a British subject. Why had he permitted this to happen for the likes of an American President?

"Flaps One, Level Change, N1, Two Ten, Heading Select."

"Flaps . . . One, Level Change . . . all done," Alastair replied. "May I ask a question?"

"Yes, if you put the flaps up now."

"Flaps . . . up. Very well. Where, exactly, are we going, now that we're fugitives?"

Craig glanced at the copilot. "Rome. As scheduled. I'm going to deliver my former Commander-in-Chief safely to his destination."

✈ FOUR

Rome, Italy—Monday—1:40 P.M.

Word that EuroAir Flight 42 had blown its way out of the gate in Athens and departed with former President Harris aboard came as the Italian foreign minister prepared to leave Campbell's suite. Stuart Campbell bade Anselmo good-bye before ordering his car to the front door.

"Notify everyone as planned, Isabel," he instructed his secretary as he headed for the elevator, "and ring me with the expected arrival time of the flight."

He slid into the backseat of the new Mercedes, quietly pleased that the showdown was going to be in Rome after all. He much preferred the Italian capital city to Athens, not to mention the fact that he spoke no Greek. Too bad for Anselmo, of course. Giuseppe and the entire Italian government would be twisting in the wind under excruciating pressure from the United States to quash the warrant and refuse extradition. But the international spotlight and the need within the European political arena to resist American arm-twisting would keep Italy from caving in.

And, of course, there was the basic strength of the case.

Stuart Campbell smiled to himself, imagining the impending legal battle that in some ways he'd been preparing for—spoiling for—for nearly two decades.

EuroAir Flight 42, Airborne, Fifty Miles West of Athens, Greece

The satellite phone in the cockpit of Flight 42 had begun ringing almost as soon as the 737 reached cruise altitude. EuroAir's operations center in Frankfurt had been informed by Greek authorities that the flight was being hijacked, which would explain their damaging departure from the gate as described by Athens operations.

"Is that true, Forty-Two? Are you being hijacked?" the dispatcher wanted to know.

"I can't talk right now," Craig replied. "I'll call you on the ground in Rome."

The response had puzzled the man thoroughly. Rome? Why would someone hijack an airliner and force the crew to fly to their scheduled destination?

Craig disconnected the link before more awkward questions could be asked.

All Mediterranean air traffic controllers had been notified of the presumed hijacking, and despite the fact that Flight 42 wasn't squawking the right transponder code to confirm an act of air piracy, they were giving the pilots anything they asked for.

Craig pulled the PA microphone from its bracket and glanced at Alastair as he pushed the transmit button.

Folks, this is your captain. I apologize for the sudden and . . . unusual departure back there in Athens. We . . . were not able to get a push-back tug, and the airport was going to close and prevent us from getting to Rome on schedule, so I elected to go a bit early and use reverse thrust to get us backed up. I'm sorry if we startled you. None of the bags you saw blowing around the ramp were yours, by the way.

Yours were already loaded. Thanks, and we should arrive in Rome on schedule.

He repeated the announcement in German and a shorter version in passable French before replacing the microphone.

"I'm going to go back and talk to Harris," Craig said, watching Alastair's response as the copilot winced and looked to his left, a haunted expression on his face.

"I truly am worried, Craig," Alastair said. "We made a real hash of it back there, legally."

"I know."

"May I ask why?"

"Why?"

"Yes. Why?" Alastair asked. "Why on the mere strength of a rumor and the presence of a few policemen you elected to imperil an aircraft full of passengers and blow through a half dozen regulations, including the registering of a false hijacking report?"

"I never said we were hijacked. The controller said that."

Alastair was shaking his head, his face reddening as his anger rose against the background of fear and confusion. "Don't split hairs! You used that, and we're still using it. There will be hell to pay when they find out no one's forcing us to do anything!"

"I am. I'm forcing us."

"And I'm your culpable copilot. Good heavens, man. Why?"

"I'm an Air Force officer, Alastair."

"Well, bloody hell, so was I, for the Royal Air Force and the Queen, of course, but that doesn't make me a guard at Buckingham Palace."

"I'm a reservist. I'm still a commissioned officer sworn to protect the President of the United States."

"I hate to break it to you, Craig, but the gentleman in the back isn't President any longer."

"Doesn't matter. Once and always."

"We'll never explain this to Frankfurt. You know that? They're operating on a shoestring with this upstart airline as it is. If they don't hand our heads to the Greeks on a pike, they could be denied future landing rights in Athens. We're . . . what's that phrase you use? We're toast."

Craig shook his head energetically. "Don't count on it. As I said, it was all my idea." He slid the seat back and climbed out, patting Alastair on the shoulder as he opened the door. "Be back in a few minutes. Keep us flying."

"Indeed," Chadwick said, sadly. "I'd better enjoy it. Could be my last time at the controls."

Sherry Lincoln saw the cockpit door open and was already on her feet and moving forward to catch the captain as he came out. She intercepted him by the forward galley, introducing herself and Matt Ward, the Secret Service agent who'd remained by the forward door on takeoff.

"You're President Harris's aide?" Craig asked Sherry.

"Aide, assistant, advisor, and secretary," Sherry said, "and we want to thank you for getting us out of there in time."

Craig looked at them in turn. "You . . . understood what I was doing?"

Matt Ward nodded. "I know that seven thirty-seven's don't back out of gates under their own power, Captain. Jillian told us about the arrest warrant."

"That was quite a show with the baggage carts." Sherry Lincoln chuckled. "You took one heck of a risk for him."

Jillian appeared beside them. "I told them about your Air Force background, Craig," she explained.

The captain nodded, inclining his head toward the chief flight attendant. "This is a German airline, by the way, but Jillian is a U.S. citizen, too."

A smile flickered across Jillian's face as she glanced at Craig.

"Ms. Lincoln," Craig said as he touched Jillian's arm in response to her smile, "who, exactly, might have been trying to arrest the President? All we were told was that a government delegation was on its way to the airport to take him into custody, and I couldn't allow that. They wouldn't tell us why."

Sherry took a deep breath and leaned back against the

forward bulkhead, shaking her head. "I don't know for certain, Captain, but I strongly suspect you just earned a medal. I think you just prevented what some at the State Department call the *second-tier* nightmare scenario for an ex-president."

"Second-tier?" he asked.

"The first is a kidnapping. The second is a Pinochet warrant."

"Pinochet, as in the Chilean dictator?" Craig asked.

"Absolutely. The general who personally ordered thousands of Chileans tortured and killed for political reasons."

"Wait . . ." Craig interrupted, smiling and holding his hand up. "What does Pinochet have to do with President Harris?"

"In the eighties," she replied, "most nations signed a treaty that made the infliction of torture in any form by any official of any country a borderless crime. In other words, you can be tracked down anywhere on earth and prosecuted by any country. Pinochet was one of the first major challenges for that treaty."

"I do recall some fuzzy details about that case," Craig said.

Sherry stopped and looked at her watch. "How long do we have before landing?"

"A little over an hour and twenty minutes," Craig replied. "But please finish what you were saying about Pinochet."

"Okay. I've got some urgent calls to make, but in a nutshell, a Spanish judge issued a warrant for the general's arrest and they snagged him when he came to London for medical care. But it took the British courts over a year to rule that Pinochet must be extradited to Spain to stand trial."

"But . . . he was sent back to Chile," Jillian said.

"True," Sherry agreed, "but only because he was finally judged too sick to stand trial anywhere. The key British ruling, that a former head of state has no protection from criminal responsibility, no sovereign immunity, was a great step forward with a big problem attached. What happens if the bad guys use it against the good guys?"

"You mean," Craig began, "someone like President Harris?"

"Exactly. Instead of having a bloody dictator arrested, suppose country Y misuses the treaty's legal procedures to capture an innocent government official from country X, because country Y is angry with or at war with country X?"

"Who, though?" Craig asked. "Who was country Y in Athens? The Greeks?"

She glanced at Matt Ward and shrugged. "I doubt it. I haven't a clue which country was responsible back there. There are a lot of countries in the so-called family of nations that still hate us. Fidel doesn't have a corner on that market."

They all fell silent for a few moments as the sound of the slipstream outside filled the small entry alcove with white noise. The aroma of warmed sweetrolls wafted from the galley, along with the pungent scent of fresh coffee.

"The nightmare," Matt Ward interjected, "is that someone like Saddam Hussein or Milosevic or Muammar Gaddafi could trump up a warrant based on accusations that U.S. military strikes authorized by the President tortured their people, or other such garbage."

Sherry was nodding agreement and looking at her watch again as she spoke. "Under the treaty—which Greece ratified, by the way—they could theoretically have John Harris arrested in Athens and extradited to face a kangaroo court, and a gallows, in Baghdad."

Jillian's hand went to her mouth. "You're kidding!"

"No, I'm not. It's a real threat, and thank God, Captain, you were thinking fast. President Harris doesn't want to believe it, but I'll bet that's what almost occurred, although Iraq's probably not behind it."

"Any country can issue a warrant, then?" Craig asked.

"Any one of them," Sherry affirmed. "Any judge in any obscure corner of the world could come up with a list of charges and issue an international arrest warrant, and once issued, that warrant can be used virtually anywhere to apprehend anyone, even if the name is John Harris, Jimmy Carter, George Bush, or Jerry Ford."

"Good Lord!" Craig replied.

"At the very least," she continued, "they could keep an American ex-President under arrest for a year or two, causing the U.S. great embarrassment." She paused and checked her watch again. "I've got to get on the phone. My GSM cellular doesn't work in flight."

"Me, too," Matt Ward added. "All of my cell phones are inoperative."

Craig let his eyes wander to the third row of seats in first class to President Harris, who had his reading glasses on. He was studying something intently. One hundred eighteen other passengers were aboard, most of them reading or dozing.

Craig turned back to Sherry Lincoln. "You *can* find out when we get to Rome what that was all about, can't you?"

He could see the sudden cloud drift across her face as she thought about an answer.

"Rome is your destination, isn't it?" he pressed.

She looked staggered and he could see the blood drain from her face.

"I'm sorry . . . what?" Sherry asked.

"You folks did want to go to Rome, right?"

She nodded, licking her lips and looking at Matt Ward. "Yes, but . . . oh my God, I hadn't had time to think this through!"

"What?" the Secret Service agent asked.

"If there's a warrant in Greece," Sherry Lincoln replied, "there could be a warrant waiting in Italy, too. Italy also ratified the treaty."

"Are there any countries that haven't ratified?" Craig asked.

"None we'd want to fly to," she said. "Of course the United States didn't get around to ratification until nineteen ninety-four." She turned to Jillian. "Is there a satellite phone aboard? I need one desperately, and I've got to get my Palm Pilot out of my purse."

"Any of the seat phones," Jillian replied. "They'll automatically switch to satellite if they can't get a normal signal. But . . . wait, use the phone up here."

Sherry started to turn, but Craig gently caught her arm.

"Ms. Lincoln, wait a minute. Are you . . . are you saying he could be arrested in Rome, too?"

"Call me Sherry. I don't know. How much time did you say until we land?"

"About an hour and ten minutes."

"If I can reach the right people . . ." She hesitated, looking him in the eye and sighing. "I'm very much afraid I already know the answer. If some country's gone to the trouble to issue a warrant for the arrest of an American President, you can bank on the fact that they won't give up easily. Yes, they'll be waiting."

"And you've no idea who's behind it?"

"No."

"Maybe we should land somewhere else," Craig said. "Of course we have the other passengers to consider . . ."

"Where else could you land?" Sherry interrupted, her tone suddenly hopeful.

Craig shook his head. "I don't know. We have enough fuel for Switzerland, France, maybe Spain, and Germany. Of course, I'm already in serious trouble with my company. Everyone thinks we've been hijacked. There will be hell to pay when they find out otherwise."

"Really?" She shook her head again. "Oh, man! That could make one thing easier, though."

"How so?"

"You say air traffic control thinks we've been hijacked?"

"Yes. And my company does, too."

"Then Washington will already know about it."

Jillian was holding out the telephone receiver, and Sherry Lincoln almost lunged for it.

"Excuse me, Mr. President?" Craig Dayton was leaning over from the aisle.

"Ah! Captain. I know Sherry was talking to you, but I want to thank you for . . . well, getting me out of there."

"You're entirely welcome, sir."

"I seriously doubt it was necessary, but she seems to think so."

Craig squatted down to meet Harris at eye level. "Sir,

they told us a delegation was on the way in from town with a warrant for your arrest. There were no minced words, and we had seven cops on the jetway."

John Harris chewed his lower lip for a second as he looked Craig in the eye. "There is a concern we've all had . . ."

Craig nodded. "I know. The Pinochet warrant. She was briefing us."

"What degree of trouble have you created for yourself?" Harris asked.

"Don't worry about it, sir," Craig replied.

"Well, I am going to worry about it. And if they try to come down on you, I'll do my very dead level best to halt the process."

"Thanks, Mr. President."

"If you're laying over in Rome, would you let me take you and your crew to dinner tonight?"

Craig smiled. "If it works out, sir, we'd be honored."

✈ FIVE

The White House—Monday—8:05 A.M. Local

News that a commercial airliner carrying a former President of the United States had been reported hijacked in Athens, Greece, arrived almost simultaneously at the Federal Aviation Administration's command post in Washington and the Central Intelligence Agency just across the Potomac in Langley, Virginia. In another five minutes, the Defense Intelligence Agency, the FBI, and the National Reconnaissance Office had also independently received the same report.

The routine intramural scramble to be first to notify the White House with the most correct information sent staff members scurrying in each agency, but the first call received in the White House Situation Room came from Langley—a fact that the CIA staffer duly noted with both pride and premeditated intent to brag.

The President's daily briefing had been printed and sent from Langley to the White House overnight, so the late-breaking report was quickly reduced to a couple of paragraphs and hand-delivered to the Chief of Staff's secretary, who brought it into the Oval Office during the first few minutes of the President's 8 A.M. meeting with the Chief of Staff and the Press Secretary.

"What's that, Jack?" the President asked, noting the sudden silence.

Jack Rollins, the Chief of Staff and a former senator from Maine, had put down his coffee mug, scanned the paper with rising eyebrows, and whistled under his breath before handing it to his boss.

"It appears that John Harris, in the process of running around Europe and giving speeches, has gotten himself hijacked."

"Hijacked?" The President took the report and read it before handing it to Diane Beecher, the Press Secretary. "What do you think, Diane?" the President asked.

"I think . . . ," she began, "that this will divert a lot of attention from the Vice President's little problem this morning. This will be the lead on all the networks tonight, especially if it goes on for a while."

"And what do *we* think?" the President prodded.

"Well, sir," Diane said, "I think that we think that we're monitoring the situation very closely and with great concern . . ."

"Right. And?"

"And . . . ," she continued, "we're standing by to provide the appropriate authorities any necessary assistance to get our former President back safely."

"Guarded alarm, in other words?"

"Yes, sir, but 'guarded alarm' is *your* pet phrase. Sir."

"I like my pet phrase. I'll let you use it."

"Frankly, Mr. President, I don't *want* it," she said, with a smile. "And I know you're pulling my chain, but I do pray quietly every evening that you will never, *ever* use it in a press conference."

The President smiled easily and turned to Rollins. "And privately, Jack? What do you think?"

The Chief of Staff shook his head. "Well, fact is, we do owe that overgrown Boy Scout a lot. Like, for instance, your election."

"Wait a darn second!" the President said with mock indignation. "That's an excessive statement. The fact that the Republican Party couldn't find a better candidate in time doesn't mean I won by default, which is what you're trying to say."

"Well, Mr. President, somewhere along the way we need to acknowledge the fact that if John Harris had not screwed his own party by refusing to run for a second term on the strange concept of principle, we wouldn't be sitting here. Do I have to remind you he was twenty-eight points ahead in the polls?"

The President scowled. "I don't have to acknowledge that."

"That's true, sir," the Chief of Staff replied with a grin. "You don't have to. History will do it for you."

The President laughed and flipped to the next page in his briefing book.

"No kidding, Jack. Keep me informed on Harris's flight. I see in this note that the hijacking hasn't been confirmed. Let's pray it's a false alarm."

EuroAir Flight 42, Airborne, Southeast of Milan, Italy

Sherry could feel the time ticking away and her stomach contracting with every wasted second.

"Hello?" she said again into the receiver, wondering when the White House operator was going to come back on the line. There were certain phrases she was supposed to use to get the operator's immediate cooperation. Sherry had all the direct numbers to the White House staffers she needed to contact from time to time, but she hadn't located the list and the wrong words had tumbled out of her mouth. She was struggling to bring up the right page in her Palm Pilot as she balanced the receiver against her ear.

"White House Comment Office."

"*Comments?* Jesus! She gave me the wrong extension. Can you connect me to someone in the Situation Room?"

"Who's speaking, please?"

"This is Sherry Lincoln. I'm assistant to former President John B. Harris. Hurry."

"Well, Ms. *Lincoln* . . . first, if you insist on cursing, I'll break the connection. Second, we cannot connect just anyone to the Situation Room. Now, what would you like to tell the President?"

Sherry was rubbing her forehead frantically. "Okay. Please, just reconnect me to the White House operator. Can you do that? They gave me the wrong extension."

The sound of a dial tone filled the earpiece and a long list of expletives raced through her mind.

For the second time she dialed the lengthy combination of numbers and waited for the White House operator to come on the line.

"All right, please listen. This is a staff-related emergency, a Signal Zulu. I have a call from former President John B. Harris for . . . Jack Rollins, Chief of Staff. Please put me through to his office immediately."

"Yes, ma'am. Please hold."

Over a minute passed before a suspicious female voice filled the other end of the phone.

"Mr. Rollins's office."

Quickly and carefully she explained who and where she was, and her immediate need to speak to the Chief of Staff. At the same moment she found the listing of code names she could never remember.

"And, for authentication, President Harris's Secret Service designation is 'Deacon.' Mine is . . . um . . . 'Magpie.' "

Within thirty seconds Jack Rollins came on the line. He listened intently to her before asking a few quick questions.

"So you're not hijacked?"

"No. The captain just let them believe that to get us out of Dodge. Athens, to be precise."

"Understood. And you're headed for Rome?"

"Affirmative. And the key question, Mr. Rollins, is this: can we land safely in Rome, or do we run the risk of encountering this same arrest attempt there? And, naturally, the other question is, who is trying to nab him, and why?"

"I don't know, but we'll find out. They called it an arrest warrant?"

"Yes, Mr. Rollins. I have no details other than that. The Greek government will know."

"You mean a warrant such as a criminal warrant?"

"I suppose. Why else would we have heard the word *arrest*?"

"That leaves me completely puzzled. He wasn't visiting in Greece, was he?"

"No. Just passing through from Istanbul. We weren't even going to leave the aircraft."

"Which means this is definitely something international. Okay. How do I call you back?"

"I'll have to call you," Sherry said. "Is there a direct number?"

He passed two private lines and a cell phone number. "Call me back in ten, no more than fifteen minutes, okay?"

"Absolutely. And on behalf of President Harris, thank you."

"No thanks needed."

More than 4,200 miles distant in his compact office in the West Wing, Jack Rollins replaced the receiver and hesitated for a few seconds, thinking through the irony of his comments to the President a half hour before. The fog cleared and he bellowed for his secretary at the same moment he snatched up the receiver and pressed a memory dial button.

After disconnecting, Sherry Lincoln moved quickly back into first class to find Matt Ward still on the line with Secret Service Headquarters in Washington. He motioned her to wait while he finished and disconnected.

"What are they telling you?" she asked.

"Sit tight. Violate no laws."

"I figured they'd have to say that," she replied.

He grimaced. "This is really delicate, Sherry. I can do almost anything to protect him physically, but I can't protect him from this legal document or a legal arrest. How about you?"

She turned to check on the President, who was still

reading, then sat next to Matt and relayed the details of her call. "I've got to phone back in a few minutes."

"If it's what we were discussing, an arrest warrant, they can't block it, can they?"

She shrugged. "I don't know, Matt. That's . . . a lawyer question, I suppose."

"Does he have one?"

She stared at him. "Not for this sort of thing. You think I need to line one up?"

"Wouldn't hurt. Provided there's a chance of arrest."

She checked her watch once more, watching her hand shake slightly in the process. There would be just enough time to brief the President before calling back, and she moved to her original seat to fill him in before pulling the seat phone from its cradle and redialing the appropriate numbers.

Jack Rollins answered personally.

"Hold on, Ms. Lincoln. I'm connecting a conference with Rudolph Baker, Assistant Secretary of State, and Alex McLaughlin at Justice."

She repeated the names out loud for the President's benefit and felt his hand on her shoulder. "Let me talk to them, Sherry," he said. "You've paved the way nicely."

John Harris took the phone, his distinctive rumble of a voice filling the transmitter, instantly recognizable to the men on the other end.

"So, folks, what are we dealing with out here?" he asked.

"Mr. President, Rudy Baker at State. Sir, I spoke a few minutes ago with my counterpart in Athens. The . . . for want of a better term, legal instrument . . ."

"Call the damn thing what it is, Rudy!" someone interjected. "It's an arrest warrant, Mr. President, and this is Alex McLaughlin, Assistant Attorney General."

"Thank you, Mr. McLaughlin," John Harris said. "Mr. Baker, you were saying?"

"Yes, sir. I was saying that this *arrest* warrant was issued by a court in Lima, Peru, on a complaint filed by the Peruvian government, and specifically, the current president of Peru, Alberto Miraflores. It charges you under the

Treaty Against Torture for violations of . . . well . . . Alex?"

"Mr. President, there was apparently a raid on a drug factory in Peru during your term that ended very badly."

"I remember it all too well," John Harris said, picturing the gruesome photos of charred corpses in a burned-out building. "It was a tragic mistake. Langley went off on an unauthorized crusade and hired a bunch of criminals."

"They're trying to hold *you* criminally liable for that, Mr. President."

"That's absurd, Alex."

"Yes, sir. I'm sure it is, but that's what the warrant alleges, according to Greek authorities."

The Assistant Secretary of State spoke up. "Sir, the Greeks sound very relieved your pilot got you out of there. They weren't interested in arresting you and sending you off to Peru, or trying you there, or anything else. But my counterpart emphasized that they had no choice legally but to honor the warrant when they received it."

"And, gentlemen, what about Rome?" Harris asked.

There was a telling silence from Washington before Baker spoke.

"Sir, Peru's counsel took the warrant . . . which is now called an Interpol warrant . . . before an Italian magistrate earlier today and had it, in effect, certified. The Italian Foreign Ministry tells me that, just like the Greeks, they will have no choice but to execute it. In other words, they'll have to arrest you as soon as you arrive."

"I see," John Harris said, quietly drumming his fingers on the armrest of the plush leather seat. "Gentlemen, those charges are nonsense. I don't mind hanging around Rome a few days if I can get some help clearing this up. Is that feasible? Can State help?"

"Sir, Alex McLaughlin again. Let me be perfectly frank, Mr. President. What they will do is place you under some sort of house arrest. I'm sure no one's going to try to dump you in a cell. Britain didn't even do that to Pinochet. But what undoubtedly will happen is this. Peru, through their lawyers, will ask whatever Italian court they're using to immediately extradite you to Peru. Now, we haven't had

time to study the ins and outs of their extradition procedure, but as you may know, under the Treaty Against Torture, they really only have two basic choices in the absence
of letting you claim sovereign immunity, and Britain's
pretty much blown that away with Pinochet."

"In other words," Harris said, "the Doctrine of
Sovereign Immunity, the idea that a former head of state
can't be held liable for crimes committed as an official act
while in office, has been invalidated by Britain's rulings in
the Pinochet case, with respect to allegations of torture
under this treaty."

"Yes, sir. Well stated. That's exactly right."

"You forgot I was a lawyer, Alex?"

"No, sir. But few of us are current on that treaty. Anyway, Mr. President, they have only two basic choices. Send
you to Lima for trial, or try you themselves in Italy. The
latter just won't happen, so there is a chance that you could
be extradited, and we doubt you'd get a fair trial in Peru
under the current regime."

"These are not good choices, fellows. Let me ask you
this. The captain of this aircraft happens to be a U.S. Air
Force reservist. If he should be so inclined, is there some
other nearby nation I should visit instead of Rome? I don't
want to run from this, but I'm not interested in being Miraflores's victim either."

John Harris could hear Rudy Baker clear his throat. "Ah,
well, we haven't had time to poll surrounding nations, but I
doubt, sir, that there is anywhere we could divert you to,
other than U.S. soil, that would be safe."

"And I couldn't get safe conduct to one of our embassies?"

"Not unless you could land in an embassy courtyard,
which would be a bit disastrous in a jetliner. Even then,
we'd be under incredible pressure to turn you over on the
theory that not even an embassy can be used as refuge
from this treaty."

"So, what would you suggest?" Harris asked. "Mr.
Rollins? Can you help me out here?"

More embarrassed sighs on the other end.

"Mr. President, this is Jack Rollins. We're going to keep

working on this and see what options we can develop
quickly. Maybe . . . maybe your pilot there could slow
down or hold in the Rome area and buy us some time, depending on your fuel, I guess."

"I'll look into that," Harris replied. "But to sum up the
options as they exist right now, I'm heading for an arrest
and possible extradition in Rome, and we have no reason
to believe it wouldn't be the same situation in Paris,
Geneva, Bonn, Madrid, or maybe even some off-the-wall
place like Malta?"

"All the ones you just mentioned are cosigners of the
treaty, sir," Baker replied. "Give us twenty minutes. We'll
poll virtually every country within range."

"Very well, gentlemen."

"And, Mr. President? President Cavanaugh is following
this and is very concerned. He's asked me to tell you that,
and to tell you we'll do everything within our constitutional power to . . . to help end this."

"Tell the President I deeply appreciate it."

"Call us back in fifteen minutes, sir."

"I'll do that."

"Mr. President, wait a second," Alex McLaughlin
added.

"Yes?"

"Ah, I . . . while we're working on this, I have to tell
you, sir, that it would be . . . ah . . ."

"Spit it out, Alex," John Harris said gently.

"Okay. You need your own lawyer, sir. Beyond a point,
we're going to be handicapped in helping you. You need a
really top name in international law who can assemble a
team very rapidly. I'm frankly not sure how far the Justice
Department can go to help you, but I can tell you we won't
be able to provide your primary counsel."

"Understood, Alex. Thanks for pointing that out. I have
one other question for you."

"Sir?"

"Who's representing Peru? Is it one of their own, or
have they hired someone on the Continent, as I suspect?"

"They have, sir. An Englishman who practices in Brussels and was very involved with the treaty."

"He's not English, really," Harris replied smoothly. "He's actually a Scot by birth. We *are* talking about Sir William Stuart Campbell, correct?"

"Yes, sir."

"I was afraid of that."

"You know him personally, Mr. President?"

There was a long pause before John Harris replied. "Thank you for the advice, Alex."

In Washington, Alex McLaughlin sat holding the dead receiver, acutely aware of the question President Harris hadn't answered.

When he had replaced the phone, John Harris sat a few seconds in thought before realizing that Sherry had been sitting in agonized silence, watching him and waiting for a summary.

"In brief, Sherry? I need to hire a lawyer, right now, from way out here." He filled her in on the rest of the call.

"Do you know anyone who fits that description, sir? Top international lawyer?"

He snorted, surprising her, and nodded his head. "I did. Once upon a time in a galaxy far, far away. The best legal mind I've ever encountered in the field of international law, but too big a heart."

"Sir?"

He shook his head and sighed. "Sorry. Old memories. I had him on a short list for my administration, but appointing him became impossible. Something he did."

"Would he be available now?" she asked.

John Harris looked at her for the longest time.

"That was his problem. He was too available."

"But, could you hire him now?"

"Only if I were certifiably crazy. At least, that's the advice I'd get if I asked Washington."

SIX

Leonardo Da Vinci International Airport, Rome, Italy—Monday—2:20 P.M.

A constellation of serious faces were orbiting around a small conference room in the offices of Rome's airport authority, each man picking at a basket of fruit and plucking bottles of water from the conference table.

A half dozen police officers were in conversation with two plainclothes officers of the Carabinieri, while three uniformed pilots stood by themselves in a far corner, watching the others. A few feet away, the manager of the airport stood with a mid-level representative of the Italian Foreign Ministry as Sir William Stuart Campbell gestured toward the airport ramp, where a passing rain shower had left a glistening film of water. A haze of cigarette smoke filled the room, and several ash trays were threatening to overflow. The hint of background music leaked in from the passenger areas, the songs too distant to be identifiable.

"Is there any further news from air traffic control?" Campbell asked the ranking police commander in Italian.

The commander shook his head. "Nothing, signore. The

aircraft has refused to confirm a hijacking and they are not sending the right signal for a hijacking on their transponder, but . . . we are treating it as a hijacking."

"I can assure you," Campbell said, "that there is no hijacking. The pilots concocted this fiction in order to leave Athens unopposed."

"Perhaps," the commander replied. "But we are ready." He stubbed out his cigarette as he pulled out a fresh pack and hesitated before offering one to Campbell, who politely refused.

"Thank you, no. I gave up those years ago. Cigars only now, I fear."

The commander smiled and lit up another for himself.

Campbell continued. "And what are your plans if the aircraft lands and taxis up to the gate?"

"Then my men will meet them at the door," the commander said.

"Gentlemen," Campbell added, turning to the airport manager and the Foreign Ministry's representative, "if the press and television reporters appear, you are prepared to control them?"

The airport manager's head bobbed up and down energetically. He wore a scowl and a rumpled gray suit that hung loosely on his razor thin, almost emaciated frame. He pulled his cigarette out of his angular face and blew a small plume of smoke to one side before answering.

"Yes," the manager confirmed. "We are ready for them, and they are coming."

"They are?" Campbell replied, strategically raising an eyebrow, thoroughly aware that the entire national and international press corps had been anonymously notified by his staff.

"Yes, sir. We do not know how, but four different television crews are en route to the airport at this moment."

"Pity," Campbell added, rapidly tiring of the smoke. "And the officers here know that they are to treat President Harris with dignity? No handcuffs or searches?"

"Yes. Absolutely."

The official from the Foreign Ministry inclined his head

toward the office window, beyond which the dome of St. Peter's could be seen.

"Mr. Campbell, Minister Anselmo has already specified these things. Provided there is no piracy going on and we get him off safely, President Harris will be housed at a very good hotel until tomorrow's hearing."

"What about the chartered aircrew over there?" Campbell asked.

"We have rooms for them near the airport," the Foreign Ministry official said. "They are fueled and ready to go, in case they are needed immediately."

Campbell nodded gravely. "Well, I think it is quite appropriate that we provide Mr. Harris with the option to waive extradition, and to minimize media exposure, I would suggest the pilots over there get back aboard their craft and be ready in case he elects that option. I will discuss it with him alone on arrival."

A burst of two-way radio noise filled the background, the voices exchanging routine information in Italian.

"In any event," the manager continued, "I am told they have enough fuel to make Lisbon, Portugal, where they'll transfer Mr. Harris to a transcontinental jet."

He stubbed out his cigarette at the two-thirds point and promptly pulled out a silver case to retrieve another one, the act quite unconscious.

"Very well, gentlemen," Campbell said. "I thank you. We have a little time, so I believe I'll step out for some air and meet you at the arrival gate."

Stuart Campbell left the office and descended the stairway at an unhurried pace, feeling thankful for the relatively fresh air of the terminal. He pushed through a door into the main terminal and pulled out his GSM cell phone, punching in an overseas number as he sidestepped a river of passengers streaming by from customs.

"Hello. Stuart Campbell here in Rome. Yes. We're on track. I wanted to let you know that Mr. Harris is due to arrive in a half hour, and I will call you back when we have served the warrant and the police have taken him into custody."

He listened closely, nodding occasionally.

"Well, I warned you to brace yourselves for an international firestorm of publicity and pressure. I trust you're ready?"

He stepped sideways to let a woman and three children race by.

"Excellent. I assume the President is monitoring this closely. Please give him my regards."

He finished the call and folded the cell phone before replacing it in his coat pocket and looking around for the nearest coffee bar. Moments like this, he thought, begged for an espresso. Caffeine on top of adrenaline. He would probably need it.

EuroAir Flight 42, Airborne, Southeast of the Italian Coast

Captain Craig Dayton rolled his seat back on the floor tracks, trying to sit as close to sideways as the diminutive 737 cockpit would allow.

Alastair's seat, by contrast, was in the proper position for flight, his seat belt securely fastened as he monitored the autoflight system and the instruments while listening to the urgent discussion among Craig and the two women standing in the cramped, narrow alcove just inside the cockpit door.

Jillian Walz had brought Sherry Lincoln forward with an urgent request: Could they slow or somehow delay the impending landing in Rome?

"We can go into what's called a holding pattern once we get there, but slowing out here won't buy us much time," Craig told her, speaking a bit louder than normal to overcome the background hiss of the stratosphere passing at seventy-four percent of the speed of sound. "We're over Italy and only thirty minutes out of Rome right now."

"But you could go into some sort of hold, you say?" Sherry asked.

Craig nodded, straining to see her eyes. "I can, and will."

"We do have fuel limitations," Alastair interjected from the right seat.

Craig looked forward at the fuel tank gauges and ran a quick mental calculation on the fuel remaining. "About two hours of cruise flight, which means we could hold no more than forty-five minutes if there's any chance we'll need to fly somewhere else."

"Excuse me," Alastair interjected. "Somewhere else? Where, perchance, did you fancy? Honolulu? Seattle, perhaps?"

"Cut the sarcasm, Alastair," Craig snapped.

"We don't know," Sherry replied, ignoring the sharp exchange. "There probably isn't anywhere else to go, but . . . there are people in Washington, D.C., frantically checking right now."

"Excuse me," Alastair added, ignoring the captain's hand raised in a stop gesture. "Everyone does realize, I hope, that if we fly anywhere else, *we* will be basically stealing this aircraft?"

"I realize that," Craig replied.

"Captain, we just need to buy some time," Sherry continued. "For all I know, they may just need time to get American Embassy people to the airport."

"If we're only going to Rome," Craig continued, "I can hold for over an hour, but they're going to be screaming at me to tell them why."

"Don't forget," Jillian added, "we've got one hundred some-odd paying passengers aboard who would like to land somewhere close to Rome sometime today."

"I know that," Craig said.

"That raises something else," Jillian said. "We have the snack service on board for the leg to Paris, and this wasn't a snack segment. Should we serve them now, if you're going to hold?"

Craig laughed and shook his head before nodding. "This is bizarre," he said under his breath.

"At long last, a rational statement!" Alastair snapped, anger barely disguised in his tone.

"Go ahead and do the snack service, Jillian," Craig told her over his shoulder. "I'll do a PA in a minute. Tell them about holding. I'll blame it on traffic. We'll also need to find out who may have tight connections."

"Okay."

"And, Ms. Lincoln . . . Sherry?"

"Yes?"

"As soon as you or the President or your Secret Service guy know anything that will help me plan what to do, please get up here immediately."

"Don't worry. I will."

"My first officer is being rude, but he's also quite right: I've put both of us in terrible jeopardy with respect to our airline. I think all we can do is delay the landing."

"I understand, Captain. So does President Harris, who is eternally grateful for what you've already done."

The two women started to leave and Craig Dayton reached out to stop Sherry.

"Wait . . . look . . ." He took a deep breath and exchanged glances with Alastair before looking back up at her. "Just tell me what you need, okay? I'll deal with any job consequences later. As far as Alastair, here, I may have to say I clubbed him and tied him up."

She smiled thinly. "Looks like he's bound and gagged to me."

"You may jolly well have to do just that!" Alastair said without humor. Sherry and Jillian left the cockpit as Alastair's eyes shifted to the window beside his captain, his face registering surprise. "Craig, you might want to have a look at this," he said, pointing.

Craig Dayton looked toward the left wing, startled by the presence of two jet fighters with Italian Air Force markings descending from above and ahead of them, a position only the occupants of the cockpit could see.

"Jeez!"

"Toronados," Alastair said. "Probably scrambled from Naples because we're supposed to be hijacked."

Craig was shaking his head. "And if I had some hysterical trigger-happy commando in the cockpit here with a gun to my head, that sight would really calm him down!"

A new voice came over their headsets speaking English,

the accent clearly Italian. "EuroAir Forty-Two, please come up frequency one twenty-five point three."

"Guess who?" Alastair muttered, dialing the frequency into the number two VHF radio.

"I'll get it," Craig said, punching the appropriate transmit selector. "This is Forty-Two. Is this the lead Toronado?"

"Affirmative, sir. Do you need assistance?"

"Negative."

"Are you squawking seventy-five hundred?" the fighter pilot asked, referring to the international hijack code.

"No, but I can't discuss it. Please back off, and stay out of sight of the cabin."

"Roger."

The two fighters rose in their windscreens and disappeared, but there was no doubt in either pilot's mind that they would be trailing the 737 the rest of the way.

John Harris was sitting in deep thought when Sherry slipped back into the seat beside him. He looked up suddenly as if she had materialized without warning.

"Oh!"

"Are you okay, sir?"

"Yes, of course."

She relayed the conversation in the cockpit.

"It will be time to phone Washington back in just a few minutes," Sherry told him.

Harris nodded absently, tapping his finger on the seat's armrest. "I've been thinking, Sherry, of all the good lawyers I know. Those who were in my administration. Those we considered for judgeships at all levels, those I looked at for Justice. And those whom I ran into from time to time in the Oval and elsewhere. The good, the bad, and the unspeakable."

"Yes, sir."

"But while you were up there I had to come to a rather frightening conclusion. The only lawyer I'm absolutely sure I can trust to help me with this is the last one I should be hiring."

"I don't understand, Mr. President," she said, surprised

by the sudden smile that crossed his face. He looked at her and slapped his hand gently on the armrest, as if bringing a gavel to rest on a decision.

"Sherry? How do I get hold of an information operator Stateside?"

"They used to call them directory assistance operators, sir, but I think they're extinct now. Ma Bell shot them all. You can only talk with computers. What do you need?"

"The main number of the University of Wyoming in Laramie."

"And for . . . who . . . ?"

"Don't ask, Sherry. Not yet."

✈ **SEVEN**

The assistant dean of students of the University of Wyoming pulled the blanket below eye level, verifying her suspicions: It was indeed morning. She pulled the covers down a bit farther, sampling the cold air in the room with her nose and opening one eye far enough to see a clock and other vaguely familiar surroundings before considering where she was—and with whom.

Jay! A warmth spread over her at the thought of him. His arm was characteristically draped over her in sleep, his hand still cupping her breast.

She pulled the covers up and went back to sleep.

There was the smell of bacon in the air when Dr. Linda Collins awoke again around 6:30. Stretching luxuriously, she could hear Jay in the kitchen turning an economy of noise into a gourmet breakfast. The soft sounds of something vaguely Celtic wafted through the bedroom door.

It's not fair! she thought, chuckling to herself and blowing a tendril of blonde hair from her face as she sat up. *He can eat anything and never gain an ounce.*

Eggs Benedict, a little Chablis, and a few pieces of crisp bacon on the side was his favorite morning meal, and it rankled her that he was a better cook than she.

There was a faint hint of sweet wood smoke in the air, probably from the fireplace in his small living room. They both loved crackling fires, especially those fueled by the fragrant piñon pine logs they'd brought back from Taos, New Mexico, during the winter.

Linda slipped from the bed into a green silk robe, tying it loosely around her waist. Jay didn't have a class to teach until late afternoon, and she was taking the day off. No reason they couldn't spend the next few hours in bed. After breakfast, of course. All it would take, she knew from experience, was a glimpse of her getting up from the table with the robe falling open and barely covering her breasts, and he'd scoop her up again and head for the bedroom. He was an incredible lover, totally focused on her pleasure, as if his enjoyment of sex depended entirely on the level of ecstasy he could coax her to achieve.

She smiled and nibbled on a fingernail, feeling sexy and decadent, and wondered if their torrid six-month affair was about to get more serious. At the ripe age of forty-two and weary of being divorced, she was ready.

But he was the question mark.

Linda rounded the corner of the kitchen and stopped, completely puzzled. "Jay?"

"Yep," he replied without looking at her.

"Why are you dressed, baby? There are still some springs we haven't broken." She came over to him, holding him from behind, her arms loosely encircling his waist.

He turned and smiled at her, the same sad, vulnerable smile that had attracted her so in the first place. "Let's eat, Linda," he said in his metered way of speaking, each word following the other at a comfortable, reasoned pace. "And then we should talk," he added.

"Talk about what?"

She circled around in front of him and reached up to pull his mouth to hers, but he resisted.

"No . . . let's eat first."

She studied his eyes, which he averted, and she felt a

small trickle of alarm. "I don't want to eat. I want to know what's wrong."

"Linda, let's just sit down, and . . ."

"No, dammit!" she snapped. "When a woman gets up from her lover's bed and finds him dressed and distant, the last thing on her mind is food. What do you mean, 'We need to talk'? Suddenly you don't want to kiss me, and you want to talk? What's wrong? Are you mad at me for something?"

"No! Of course not, no."

"Then what? Tell me," she said, an overwhelming sense of panic engulfing her.

"Now?" he said, hopeful she might change her mind.

"Now!" she replied firmly, suddenly not sure she wanted to know. She had seen that faraway look in his eyes before, when the ghosts of his past gathered in the room around them.

He nodded and turned down the flame under a pan of hollandaise sauce, wiped his hands, and put his arms around her, holding her, but not too close.

"Linda, I . . . this is very difficult, but I've got to leave Laramie."

"*What?* Why? Have you done something terrible I don't know about?"

"No."

"Jay! Get a grip, honey. They're about to offer you tenure, and I've got a very good position here I don't want to leave."

"I'm going to accept an offer to teach at a small college in Kansas."

She looked stunned. "You applied without *telling* me?"

"I wanted to tell you, Linda, but . . ."

"Is it a law school? Would you be a law professor?" she asked evenly, struggling to keep control.

He shook his head no. "Liberal arts. Business law."

She pulled away from him and backed up, her eyes flaring. "That's what you're teaching here! If you were . . . were going to get your law career back . . ."

"I'm still a lawyer in Texas. My suspension's up."

"But . . . why Kansas if it's not the law? I mean, I don't

want to move, Jay, I love it here . . ." she gasped as her hand went to her mouth in disbelief. "Oh my God, you're . . . you're *dumping* me, aren't you!" she said, staring hard at him.

"No, I'm . . . that's a terrible term, Linda. It's just that . . . we're getting too close."

"Oh?" she replied, her voice hardening. "Too close? And precisely how close would that be? Like a while ago? Physiologically, I'm not sure we can improve on that performance!"

He hung his head. "Linda, I care about you very deeply."

"Then . . . *why?*"

For a short eternity, he stared at the floor, his right hand gesturing silently, before looking up at her.

"Because when I'm holding you, I can't get her out of my mind. I doubt I'll ever be free of her, and you don't need that."

She ripped the robe off and threw it at him, marching naked into the bedroom to find her clothes, her voice angry and hurt as it raged back through the open door.

"Damn you, Jay! You don't have a clue what I need!" She disappeared around the corner, then burst out again carrying a bra and a small framed picture of a woman on a mountainside, her blonde hair blowing free in the wind, her eyes haunted by things unseen as she stared an unfathomable distance off camera.

"Here!" Linda snarled, pushing the picture frame into his chest. "I'm sorry as hell she's dead, Jay! I really am!" Tears were streaming down her face now and her teeth were gritted in anger. "But you know something? Believe it or not, you're still alive, and you've got a helluva lot to offer! DAMN!"

She turned and rushed back to the bedroom, her voice echoing around the corner. "You are *not* responsible for her death, Jay. You gave her everything you could. But you ARE responsible for your own life, and if you won't live it, no one can help you!"

He moved slowly to the bedroom door. "Linda, please . . ."

She turned. "Don't Linda me! Dammit, Jay!" She finished pulling on her panties and jeans and buttoning her blouse, sticking the bra in an overnight bag as she struggled with her shoes. "Look, if you ever decide you've something better to do with your life than camp on her grave and cry, give me a call. Maybe I'll still be around. Then again, maybe I won't."

"I just need some more time," he said.

"No! You need to make a commitment. To life. To one particular town and college. Maybe to some poor girl who's been throwing herself at you for months, warming your bed, and . . . and . . . loving you!" She tried to fight back a flurry of sobs, but it was useless.

"I'm so sorry, Linda."

"I am, too," she said at last, dabbing at her glistening face with a Kleenex.

He followed her to the door and held it after she yanked it open and turned back to him.

"I just might have been in love with you, Jay, but I can't live with a ghost, too. I should have fallen for a simple cowboy with an old pickup and an IQ of six. At least then I could expect to be dumped for the next rodeo."

She pulled the door from his hand and slammed it hard. He could hear the door of her Firebird open and close. The sound of squealing tires melded with the ring of a telephone as she burned out of the driveway and careened down the street.

Jay walked slowly back to the kitchen trying to ignore the phone and wishing he knew how to lose himself in a bottle when life got so painful. But he'd always hated getting drunk. It solved nothing. The pain was always still there in the morning, with the added agony of a headache.

He yanked the receiver up at last just to silence the bell.

"Yes!"

"Jay? Jay Reinhart?"

The voice sounded vaguely familiar. "Yes. Who's calling?"

"Your old senior partner and employer, Jay. John Harris."

A shuddering cascade of memories flooded Jay's mind. "Mister *President?* What . . . ? I mean . . ."

"I've been out of office a long time, Jay. Please call me John."

"Yes, sir . . . John. How are you?"

"That was going to be my question to you, Jay. Is Karen okay?"

Adrenaline squirted into Jay's bloodstream at the mention of his dead wife's name.

"Ah, no, John . . . she's not."

"What's wrong?"

He swallowed hard before answering. He should spare John Harris the shock of the answer, but there was a perverse satisfaction in telling the truth, like some form of miniature retaliation against the injustice of her loss, knowing the embarrassment it always caused on the other end of a phone.

"Karen's dead. She died last year."

"Oh, Jay, I'm so sorry. I didn't know. A sudden illness?"

He couldn't hold it back. He could feel the words gather like a shotgun blast at fate. "Actually, John, she killed herself."

"Oh, no!"

"She was in constant therapy, but in the end . . ."

"The years of abuse from the first husband," Harris offered.

"Yeah."

"Jay, I apologize for reopening the wound."

"You didn't know. It's just kind of a bad morning." He took a deep breath and forced his eyes to open. "Now, Mr. President, where are you?"

"In a bit of trouble," John Harris said, explaining the situation in brief and raising the immediate question of what to do about the warrant undoubtedly waiting in Rome. "So, I want to hire you as my lawyer, Jay, if you can take a few days off."

"You want to hire *me?*"

"That's right."

"The last time we talked, you were in the Oval Office

and I'd just been suspended from the Texas bar after they threw me off the bench."

"Doesn't matter now, does it? You're not licensed in Italy anyway. We can hire local talent to follow your orders, but I need your international legal expertise. You are familiar with the Pinochet situation?"

"Of course. I keep very current. I don't know why, since it's obvious I'll never get to . . ."

"You were going to say, 'practice again'?"

"Yeah," Jay replied.

"Well, here's your chance."

"This is really curious timing."

"How so?"

"I just received notice last month that my suspension is over and my law license is current again."

"Good."

"And if I never said it . . . John, I'm so very sorry I let you down when you were just starting your administration."

"You're forgiven, provided you help me out now."

Jay rubbed his forehead, feeling his mind still swimming with a cascade of emotions and thoughts and alarms. He had a class to teach, but he was quitting. He should chase Linda down, but he had to let her go. And the chance to practice again was illusory. No one in the legal profession respected a defrocked judge.

"Okay," he heard himself saying. "What can I do?"

"No, Jay, the question is, what can *I* do? This is a dynamic, unfolding situation, and the Justice Department has already informed me they will not provide my lead attorney."

"All right. Ah, first, I need to sit here and think and then jump on the computer and confirm something I remember about Italian criminal procedure."

"How long? Should I hold?"

"Yes. Five minutes. Maybe four. Don't go away!"

"I'm not about to, Jay. Keep in mind, though, we're less than fifteen minutes from arrival in the Rome area, although the pilot has promised to delay his landing for at least forty-five minutes."

"Hang on, John. Be right back."

Jay carefully placed the receiver on the tile counter as if he might break the connection by putting it down too hard. He stepped back, staring at the instrument, letting his mind organize itself around the problem. The essence of it! What was he always trying to teach the dullards in his class who wanted to conquer Wall Street but had no idea how the legal system worked? First, reduce the problem to its bare essence: We have a Pinochet warrant waiting for an ex-President. He quickly ran through the facts Harris had given him, coming to the same conclusion Sherry Lincoln had reached some five thousand miles distant: if the warrant was in Rome, it would be all over Europe. Only real estate under full U.S. control could forestall an arrest and give him time to start defensive maneuvers.

U.S. soil. U.S. control. U.S. bases.

Jay began to lunge for the phone, stopped himself, and raced instead to the bedroom to fire up his laptop. He struggled to plug the cable into the jack connecting him to the university's computer network and toggle on his Internet connection, loosing a flurry of keystrokes to enter the words "United States Military Bases and Detachments" into a search engine.

A list of possibilities came back and he paged through them, amazed at the fact that American military bases all seemed to have their own web sites. Ramstein Air Base in Germany, two in the U.K., none in France, a Navy base in Spain, and . . .

"Yes!" he said to himself, clicking the name he'd found.

A screen popped up and he ordered the computer to print the image, then switched to a map of the globe and zoomed in on the location, triggering a printed copy of that as well.

The printer disgorged both pages and he took them and fairly skidded back into the kitchen to scoop up the phone.

"John? Are you there?"

The line was dead. He replaced the receiver, realizing his hand was shaking, and yanked it up again the second it rang.

"Mr. Reinhart?"

"Yes?"

"This is Brian with MCI Worldcom, sir. How are you today?"

"Too busy for you!" Jay snarled, slamming the receiver back in its cradle.

He had no phone number for the President. How did one go about calling a foreign airliner in flight halfway around the world, especially one presumed hijacked?

This is intolerable! he muttered to himself. *What on earth do I do now?*

The phone remained silent. He checked his watch. If John Harris had been right, they were on descent into the Rome area right now. What if the pilot decided not to hold, but to land instead? That would be the wrong thing to do.

Maybe I could call through their air traffic control system, Jay thought. *No, I can't tie up the phone!*

He rushed back to the bedroom and leaned over the computer keyboard again to enter a search command for the main airport in Rome.

Information on Rome, Ohio, came back.

He tried again with "Italy" attached as the phone rang again.

He leapt from the chair, turning it over in the process of dashing toward the kitchen, before remembering the bedroom extension. He reversed course and answered the phone by the bed.

"Hello?"

"Jay? John Harris. Sorry. It dropped out on us."

"Thank heavens! Do not land in Rome!"

"Say again?"

"Do not land in Rome. Instead, I think we'd better get you to an airbase in Sicily called Sigonella. It's a U.S. Navy contract base not far from the city of Catania. There's another American base near Milan called Aviano, but it's too well known. I think Sigonella's a better choice."

"American soil, in other words?" John Harris asked.

"Not . . . entirely. Only embassies truly fit that description, but this will more than likely buy us time. Can the pilot do it?"

"I don't know. I'll have to ask him. This is a commercial flight and he's already gotten himself in trouble for helping me."

"If I lose you, John, how do I phone you back?" Jay asked.

"I doubt you can. I think I'd better call you, if you can keep that line open. Do you happen to have a second line into your home?"

"No, I don't."

Jay scratched his head frantically, trying to think how to make the calls he was going to need and keep the line open at the same time.

"You have a cellular phone?" John Harris asked.

Jay shook his head in disgust. "Of course! We can keep this one open, and I'll use the cell phone. Have you talked to anyone in Washington I need to talk to? I mean, do you have any telephone numbers into the White House or Justice?"

"Yes. Hold on. I'll put you on with my assistant, Sherry Lincoln, and she can brief you on the contacts at the State Department and Justice Department, as well as the direct White House numbers you'll need while I talk to the captain."

"All right. I'll need to book the fastest flight available to get over there."

"Whatever you need to do, Jay. I'm reasonably wealthy. I'll cover any expense necessary and you can name your fee."

Jay started to protest, but Sherry Lincoln was already saying hello. He took down the names and numbers she gave him and asked her to monitor the line while he pulled out the cellular phone, hoping the battery was fully charged. There would be at least a day of work to do in the next fifteen minutes.

✈ EIGHT

"What do you want to do, Craig? It's decision time," Alastair asked, his finger poised over the transmit button.

"Hold. We hold. Tell them we need some time to sort out a problem. Don't tell them what."

Alastair punched the button and made the requisite call as Craig lifted the PA microphone and blamed the arrival delay on Italian air traffic control.

The mixed nationalities of the 118 passengers aboard Flight 42 were typical of the melting pot that Europe was becoming in the first years of the twenty-first century. Scattered through the cabin were Turks, Italians, Greeks, British, Germans, Swiss, Dutch, Spaniards, French, and a single Dane, all in the company of forty-four Americans on a guided tour.

With the exception of two British passengers, only the Americans were aware that a former U.S. President was on board, a fact that had spread excitement through the group on the ground in Istanbul when John Harris was ushered into the otherwise empty first-class cabin by the EuroAir station manager.

Several members of the tour had come forward in flight to invade the first-class section and say hello, each of them graciously received by the President, who each time had waved down Jillian's attempts to chase them back to coach.

As the President finished talking to Jay Reinhart and handed the phone to Sherry Lincoln, the tour director herself came forward and knelt by his seat.

"Mr. President?"

"Yes?" he replied, forcing a warm smile to his face and offering his hand to the well-dressed woman, who appeared to be in her sixties.

"It's an honor to be aboard your plane, sir!" she gushed. "It feels like Air Force One."

He laughed easily. "Well, hardly that. Air Force One has a lot more room. I didn't get your name?"

"Annie Jane Ford, sir, from Denver. I'm the tour director for the group back there. All Americans."

He held her hand and squeezed slightly. "Annie, please don't tell anyone, but I'm working on a bit of a scheduling problem at the moment, and I need you to excuse me so I can go talk to the captain."

"Oh! Sure! I'm sorry!" She got to her feet and stood aside as he thanked her and moved forward. Jillian had seen him coming and opened the cockpit door.

John Harris moved inside the small alcove and put his left hand on the captain's shoulder as he nodded to Alastair Chadwick.

"Captain?"

"Yes, sir?"

"Where are we?"

"Descending through twelve thousand, Mr. President, and approaching a holding fix south of Rome. You can see the city up there about thirty miles." Craig Dayton pointed in the right direction and Harris followed his finger as Craig let a few seconds of silence elapse. "Do you have any word from Washington?"

"Captain, I have a very large favor to ask you," Harris began. "I know you already raised the issue, but I didn't know I was going to get the advice I just received." He explained his counsel's recommendation of Sigonella. "Are you familiar with the base?" Harris asked.

"Yes, sir," Craig replied.

"And . . . you have enough fuel?"

"That shouldn't be a problem," Craig answered, aware that Alastair had tensed in the right seat.

The President turned to the copilot. "Alastair Chadwick, isn't it?"

Alastair turned, surprised his name had been remembered. "Yes, it is."

"You're from the U.K., correct?"

"That's correct."

"And while Captain Dayton here, as a U.S. Air Force officer, feels an obligation to help an ex-president, you obviously have no such allegiance, and your job is very much at stake. Is that a correct analysis?"

"I'm very much afraid that it is, Mr. President," Alastair replied cautiously. "I'm sorry to be thinking of myself."

"Nonsense. That's responsible. However, I am in a jam here, and I would very much appreciate any help you could provide in getting me to Sigonella instead of Rome. I can tell you that the legal process waiting ahead is being misused, and while I'm rather prejudiced on the subject, I think you'd be doing international justice a substantial service by preventing what Peru is attempting. Other than that, I have no right to pressure you."

"I . . . understand," Alastair replied, turning back to the forward panel.

"Regardless of what you decide you can do, I want you to know I deeply appreciate the help you've already given me so selflessly. Thank you!" Harris patted Alastair's shoulder, saluted Craig, and left the cockpit, securing the door behind him.

"Entering holding," Craig announced, triggering a radio call from Alastair to Rome Approach Control.

They made the first outbound turn in silence, the race-track-shaped pathway showing on the horizontal situation indicator screen in front of them as generated by the flight management computers. They were cleared to fly south on a heading of 170 degrees for a minute and a half before reversing course and flying a heading of 350 degrees back to an artificial point in space ten thousand feet above the Italian countryside, then were to repeat the outbound and inbound legs until cleared to leave and make their approach.

A call chime rang softly through the cockpit and Craig toggled the interphone to answer.

"Captain? This is Ursula in the back. We have two men back here who will miss their connections to New York if we hold very long. They insisted I call the cockpit."

"Tell them we're doing the best we can."

"What does that mean, exactly? Jillian has briefed us why you're holding, but these men are quite upset."

"It means we'll know in a few minutes when we're going to land, Ursula. Don't tell them anything more."

"They're not the only ones grumbling, but I'll tell them. Elle is also being questioned."

He disconnected and studied the forward panel as they flew in silence for several minutes. Alastair's fingers were drumming an insistent, nervous tattoo on the control yoke, the muscles along the side of his jaw working overtime, his mind in furious thought.

"It's bloody professional suicide," Alastair said suddenly. "For both of us."

"I know it."

"We're as good as sacked right now!"

"I am, at least. I still say I can get them to believe I made you go along with it."

"Look," Alastair continued, "I know I wouldn't be doing anything but practicing law if you hadn't sat in that bar in Abu Dhabi and bullied me an entire night about flying commercially someday. Of course, come to think of it, I would never have had to listen to you in the first place if you and your juvenile delinquent wingman hadn't blown down my bleeding tent the week before with your F-15's."

"Yeah. That was fun. You RAF types were being too standoffish."

"It was funny, I'll grant you that. But, dammit Craig,

now that I've got this job, I rather like it! I love flying more than the law. I've told you that ad nauseam. That's why I took so long leaving the RAF, despite your harassing E-mails."

"Alastair, seriously, what if I ordered you to get out of the cockpit and go sit down in the back?"

"Herr Wurtschmidt, our esteemed chief pilot, would still cashier me for not breaking down the cockpit door and clubbing you into compliance."

"You're probably right," Craig said.

"But you are going to bloody well do this thing regardless, aren't you?"

"I don't know how I can do it without you, Alastair, and yet I don't know how I could possibly land and turn him over to Peru, for God's sake."

"It isn't Peru, you know. It's Italy. Peru will have to fight to get him. You heard that. And besides, Sigonella is Sicily, which is also Italian territory."

"Do I have any legal latitude?" Craig asked, turning to him. "As captain, I mean? Put on your lawyer hat and tell me."

Alastair Chadwick mulled over the question and turned to meet his friend's gaze. "Actually, I think you do. I believe I was wrong earlier."

"You mean, when you said we'd be stealing the aircraft?"

"That's right, I was wrong," Alastair said. "The international conventions, as well as German law, all give the captain of an aircraft in international flag service complete authority to do whatever he or she thinks necessary once the flight has begun. That's the key. We didn't make the decision until the flight had begun."

"Great!"

"But, Craig, that merely means they can't put us in jail. We'll still be sacked on sight by EuroAir, and I still don't want to do this. Neither of us is going to find as good an airline job anywhere."

Craig sighed. "I can't make you do this."

"No," Chadwick laughed ruefully, "you bloody well can't!"

"Which means," Craig continued, his words metered, "that this tremendously important and pivotal decision in the evolution of international law—the determination of whether this legal travesty happens or not—turns entirely on what *you* decide, as historians will undoubtedly note. They'll probably call it 'Chadwick's Decision.'"

"Oh, thank you so *very* much! You spread guilt quite effectively for a non-Catholic, you know."

"We've already started this show, Alastair. If we land in Rome, we pulled our little stunt in Athens for nothing."

"We? What is this 'we' business, Captain, sir? I seem to recall begging you not to take off."

"You said, and I quote, 'Don't leave without a clearance.' So we got a clearance."

"I'm beginning to see why King George let the bleeding colonies go."

"Wasn't his choice. We whipped Cornwallis."

"Yanks!"

"Brits!"

They fell silent for nearly a minute as the 737 turned once more on an outbound heading.

"Oh, bloody hell! All right! I'll plug in Sigonella if you'll give me some semi-intelligent reason to give Approach Control."

"Thank you, Alastair. But don't refile for Sigonella. Tell him we want to divert to Naples. We don't want them figuring this out just yet."

"And what's my reason?" Alastair asked.

"We can't tell them. And that's the truth. We can't."

✈ **NINE**

Laramie, Wyoming—Monday—6:50 A.M. Local

Jay Reinhart squeezed the cell phone between his left ear and shoulder as he waited for Assistant Attorney General Alex McLaughlin to return to the line. He picked up the house phone meanwhile and pressed it to his right ear.

"Still there?"

Sherry Lincoln's voice was a welcome sound. "Right here, Mr. Reinhart."

"Still working. Hang on," he told her, setting the receiver down again by the yellow legal pad, the first two pages of which were already filled with notes.

"Mr. Reinhart?" McLaughlin said from his Washington office.

"Yes. Right here." He readjusted the phone and almost dropped it, catching it with his left hand in time. "Go ahead."

"Well, we're all going to have to move very fast on this. I'm glad President Harris was able to retain you so rapidly."

"This *is* rather a shock," Jay replied, massaging his forehead.

"State assures me the arrest will be respectful, and there will be a first-class hotel waiting, but the problem comes tomorrow morning Rome time. Peru's counsel already has an extradition hearing scheduled for eight A.M. Now, we have no one in Rome from Justice, and even if we did, our role becomes essentially amicus curiae, friend of the court. All we need is the equivalent of a motion for continuance in civil law terms, but, as I say, Justice can only support your argument, we can't make the motion. Does your firm have someone in Rome who can enter an appearance and do the initial argument for delay?"

"I . . . don't have a firm, Mr. McLaughlin."

There was stunned silence from the Beltway. "You don't have a . . . you're not part of a firm?"

"No."

"You're a *sole practitioner?*" McLaughlin asked in amazement.

"Actually, right now I'm not even practicing. I teach at the University of Wyoming."

"I see. The law school?"

"No. The main university."

More silence, and the sounds of a man completely off balance clearing his throat. "Ah, I hate to ask this, Mr. Reinhart, but you are a lawyer, I hope?"

"Yes. I'm licensed in Texas."

"May I . . . may I ask your area of legal expertise?"

"Calm down, Mr. McLaughlin. I'm an international legal scholar, and a former practitioner. I am current, even though I've technically been on the sidelines for a while."

"I see."

"I do understand this, and I do know as much about what to do as anyone else would at this point."

"Mr. Reinhart, forgive me, but this isn't going to work. President Harris needs the immediate services of a substantial firm with offices all over Europe, where someone can get to him within the hour. I doubt very much even the U.S. Air Force could get you personally from Laramie to Rome in time."

"The motion for continuance is very simple under Italian law, Mr. McLaughlin," Jay replied evenly. "I can hire local counsel in Rome from here in half an hour."

"Well . . . that may be true, but what's needed is a network of long-time polished legal contacts and the ability to work with us from experience, and clerical, secretarial, and paralegal support."

"I know all that."

"Mr. Reinhart, I do not want to demean your expertise, sir, but this is not a job for a sole practitioner."

"The President hired me, Mr. McLaughlin. You are speaking to his lead counsel. Let's get to the substance of this matter so I can make the necessary calls."

"Are you familiar with our embassy staff in Rome?"

"No."

"You don't know the American ambassador?"

"No."

"Do you know our liaison to the World Court at The Hague, or the U.S. ambassador to the United Nations and his staff?"

"No."

"Then how in hell, Mr. Reinhart," McLaughlin said, his voice hardening and his volume increasing, "can you possibly hope to defend not only President Harris's right to remain a free man, but also the broader interests of the United States of America in a very critical and immediate matter from the MIDDLE OF FRIGGIN' WYOMING?"

"By phone, by fax, by logic, by training, and by virtue of the fact that I am his lawyer! How much time are we going to waste on this debate? The man's hovering over Rome as we speak, he's at the mercy of two commercial pilots, and I'll bet you your limousine privileges there's a Peruvian jet of some sort sitting at the next gate to their's at Da Vinci Airport as part of a quiet little plot to whisk him away on arrival while the local police look the other way. I seriously doubt that John Harris would ever make it to the hotel in Rome, let alone that hearing tomorrow. He'll be over the Atlantic on the way to a show trial in Lima."

"How did you know about that plane? Our intelligence sources just told me."

"Logic, Mr. Assistant Attorney General. That's how I'd do it if I were Sir William Stuart Campbell."

"You know him?"

"Yes. Do you?" Jay asked, permitting a little sarcasm into his tone.

"No. Only by reputation."

"Well, sir, I know him all too well. I'm handicapped by distance, but not by experience."

"Are you aware of some plot to, as you say, whisk President Harris away?"

"I'm telling you what they may try. I could be wrong, but I wouldn't count on it."

"That would be a form of kidnapping, not extradition. Italy would never permit that, and Peru could be held accountable!"

"You want to go argue that with Presidente Miraflores while President Harris is rotting in a Lima prison cell? I'd rather keep him out of their hands."

"Well, of course, so would we. Excuse me a second . . ."

Jay could hear the sound of voices in the background as McLaughlin conferred with someone. He heard the sound of paper being sorted or pages being turned, and a barely disguised grunt of amazement. When the Assistant Attorney General returned to the line, his voice had taken on a coldness Jay recognized immediately.

"Mr. Reinhart, you say you're from Texas?"

"That's right. And yes, I was, at one time, District Judge Jay Reinhart of Dallas County, and I'll make this easy for you. The suspension was up last month. Now, for God's sake, let's talk about substance and what we're going to do while I've still got an open line to the aircraft, because there's one major thing you don't know."

"And that would be?"

"He's not going to land in Rome, and we're going to have as much of a diplomatic fight ahead of us as a legal one."

"If not Rome, where, in fact, is he going to land? And how do you know?" McLaughlin asked, his tone sarcastic and exasperated.

"I can't tell you until he's safely on the ground. Attorney client privilege."

"I see."

"And, I'm talking to you on a nonsecure analog cell phone anyone could listen to."

"Oh," McLaughlin replied. "Well, at least that makes sense."

"I'm guessing he will land in about forty-five minutes. In the meantime, I need you to be ready to tell me exactly what, if anything, the U.S. military can do for President Harris. I'll call you back."

When Alex McLaughlin had agreed and disconnected, Jay folded the cell phone and sat down on his only kitchen stool, his hands shaking and his mouth cotton-dry.

God Almighty! I just beat up an Assistant Attorney General of the United States!

He sat for a few seconds, trying to think through the next moves, and the people he would need to talk with, if not command: the State Department, the White House, perhaps the Chief of Staff and the sitting President, the government of Italy, maybe officials of other nations as well, not to mention the entire infrastructure of the international and European legal community.

And here he sat in the middle of "friggin' " Wyoming, as McLaughlin had said, with a single line, a cell phone, and no staff.

Jay realized his stomach felt queasy. McLaughlin was right. *There's no way I can pull this off!*

He picked up the receiver to the house phone, wondering if the connection to the 737 was still good. "Ah, Ms. Lincoln? Are you still there?"

"This is John Harris, Jay. Where are we?"

"John, I'm sorry. I'm ethically bound to step aside. I can't do this."

✈ TEN

"EuroAir Forty-Two, your requested clearance is denied. Your destination must be Rome, sir."

Craig Dayton turned to Alastair Chadwick with his eyebrows raised.

"What the heck does that mean?"

Alastair was shaking his head. "I've never been refused a clearance before and told where to land. At least not in civilian flying."

Craig toggled the transmitter. "Rome Approach, do you understand that we are not asking, we're telling you we want a clearance to Naples?"

"Disapproved, Forty-Two. Those are my instructions. You will be cleared from holding to the approach at Da Vinci Airport as soon as you request it."

"And if we request clearance direct to Malta instead?"

"Ah . . . stand by, Forty-Two."

There was a brief pause before another voice—clearly a supervisor—came on the channel. "Forty-Two, the Italian Air Force central command is instructing you to land immediately at Da Vinci Airport. Are you ready for your approach?"

"Check our squawk, Rome!" Craig snapped. "Then see if you want to tell me what to do." He reached over the center console to the transponder control head and changed the numbers to 7500, the international code for hijacking.

"The alarms will be going off down there now for certain," Alastair said. "We haven't just crossed the Rubicon, we've burned the bridge behind us."

He could see Craig gritting his teeth in anger and shaking his head. "I can't believe their arrogance!"

The first controller's voice returned to their headsets, far more cautious than before.

"EuroAir Forty-Two, we have received your seventy-five hundred squawk. What is your request?"

"Direct Malta," Craig said, releasing the transmitter button and turning to Alastair. "That'll take us right over the top of Catania and Sigonella."

Alastair nodded as the controller replied.

"Roger, Forty-Two. You are cleared present position direct Malta. Climb and maintain flight level two eight zero."

"Departing holding and departing one zero thousand for flight level two eight zero," Craig replied. "Initial GPS heading is two one four degrees."

Leonardo Da Vinci International Airport, Rome, Italy

The apparent frenzy of activity at the arrival gate just ahead had caught Stuart Campbell's attention as he approached the departure lounge. An overabundance of grim-faced police officers were milling around and talking urgently into their two-way radios, occasionally glancing out at the empty spot on the ramp which should have held the Boeing 737 designated as EuroAir's Flight 42.

Campbell found the airport manager in a huddle with two members of the Carabinieri.

"Gentlemen? Is something happening I'm not aware of?"

"They were in a holding pattern," the airport manager began, "but now they are refusing to land."

"What, precisely, do you mean, 'refusing to land'?" Campbell asked.

One of the officers lowered his radio and spoke a few words directly into the manager's ear.

"What?" the manager replied, his eyes wide.

"Si," the officer responded.

"What is it?" Campbell asked.

The manager was shaking his head. "Now the captain is requesting to fly to Malta."

"You've got to be joking," Campbell said with a disbelieving smile. "That's not going to solve his problem!"

Stuart Campbell pulled out his GSM phone and punched in a number as he walked slowly toward the floor-to-ceiling window of the terminal lounge. Outside, at the adjacent gate, he could see the captain and first officer sitting in the cockpit of the Boeing 727 he'd chartered to fly John Harris to Portugal. He saw the captain suddenly reach for his ringing cell phone.

"Yes?"

"Captain Perez? Stuart Campbell, here. Have you been monitoring the frequency?"

"Yes, sir. Forty-Two is in holding and asking for a clearance to Malta. What do you want us to do?"

"Get airborne and, wherever he decides to go, you file for the same location. Understood?"

"Yes, sir. Will you be coming with us, Mr. Campbell?" the captain asked.

"Let me think about that. Stand by."

Stuart Campbell mentally reviewed the options. The Italian warrant based on the Interpol warrant would be good anywhere in Italy and could be faxed to the Maltese authorities. But what if EuroAir's captain decided once again to head somewhere else, such as Morocco or Spain? He'd have to scramble to get to wherever they went, and coordinating the capture would be even more difficult if he was sitting in the cabin of an airplane.

He was having to think three moves ahead, precisely like a game of chess. He smiled to himself and shook his head. *So my choices are, move the king's knight to king three, or leave the knight in place.*

And he was the knight to the Peruvian president's king.

He raised the phone back to his ear. "No, Captain, I'll stay here. Check in with me when you're on the ground, wherever that might be."

EuroAir 42, in Flight

President John Harris sat in silence for a second with the phone pressed to his ear as he revisited his decision and concluded he was right. Sighing, he straightened in the seat.

"Jay, I want you to listen to me very closely."

The disillusionment in the voice from Laramie was painfully obvious.

"Yes, sir. I'm listening."

"My best strength has always been my judgment of character and capability. I think my presidency was successful, and if so, the reason was that I appointed the best people."

"Thank God I wasn't on that list. I would have destroyed your record."

"No, Jay, you wouldn't have. Quite the contrary. You would have done a superlative job, and we both know the error in judgment that got you in such trouble was an affair of the heart, not some act of greed or ambition."

There was a short laugh on the other end. "Definitely not ambition."

"No, and if Karen's case hadn't come before your court before I announced my appointments, you would have been the President's lawyer, and perhaps later, attorney general."

"You're far too gracious, sir."

"No, as I say, I'm an extraordinary judge of character, and yours hasn't changed."

"Mr. President . . . John . . . it makes no difference now. I can't . . ."

"That's enough," Harris interrupted. "Now listen. We both understand that this is a very serious situation both for me personally, and for our country, and for every other ex-president who ever leaves home. Believe me, I do *not* want to fall into the hands of the Peruvians, or under the control of this warrant. I am *not* handing you this assignment with the expectation that you'll fail. But, I also have no illusions about the difficulty ahead of you, or the extreme mismatch between what kind of staff support you *don't* have, and what some of the major international firms could provide. So why do I insist you handle it? I have two things going for me on this decision, Jay. First, I will trust my life to the international legal abilities I saw in a young lawyer named Jay Reinhart, whom I hired many years ago; and second, my gut tells me the only way to beat Campbell and Miraflores at their game is to adhere to the doctrines of Sun Tsu."

"The . . . Chinese philosopher?"

"I'm not sure how much of a philosopher he was, except on the doctrine of warfare, but the man was millenniums ahead of his time when he asked why anyone would fight an enemy on the enemy's terms. To hire a major firm would be to do exactly what our friend Campbell expects. We'll do just the opposite."

"Sir . . ."

"You've fulfilled your ethical duty to warn me of the potential consequences of hiring you, Jay. For the record, I hereby accept that risk and waive that concern. Now, that's the last I'm going to hear about it. You get your tail in gear and get me the hell out of this mess. Understood?"

"Yes, sir."

"I'll call you back in thirty minutes for a progress report."

John Harris disconnected and smiled to himself, wishing he could see the expression on Stuart Campbell's face when he found out who the former leader of the free world had hired.

Sherry had slipped into the seat next to him as he finished the conversation. She sat studying her boss for a few seconds before pulling him out of his reverie with a question.

"Could I ask what that was all about?"

John Harris turned to her, still smiling. "I just hired my lawyer."

"Okay . . ."

"And he's sitting in Wyoming, wondering if I've lost my mind."

"I see. Have you?"

Harris laughed and shook his head. "Nope. He comes with baggage, Sherry, but he's the best, as I said earlier." He described the handicaps and the challenges Jay Reinhart would face, as well as his background, watching her expression darken.

"Why was he thrown off the bench in Texas?" she asked.

"He was a very good judge for four years. Being a judge was a radical departure from international law practice, but it was something he'd always wanted to do. And he was caring, fair, and tough. The very model of a jurist. But one day he got a murder case. A beautiful young woman, a battered wife who'd had the hell beaten out of her for a decade by a local monster with social standing and a successful business career. One evening she blew him away with a twelve-gauge just before the nightly beating and rape could commence. The district attorney, a wife abuser himself, ignored the realities of the case, charged her with aggravated first-degree murder and went after the death penalty."

"Good grief!" Sherry exclaimed, looking up as a man in his upper seventies stopped just behind their row of seats. The President followed her gaze, his eyes landing on Matt Ward, who had intercepted the visitor.

"Matt?"

"Mr. President, excuse me," Matt said, gesturing to the man behind him in the aisle. "This gentleman wanted to say hello."

Harris turned farther around and smiled at the man, noting how frail and gaunt he looked. He raised an index finger in a "wait" gesture and the man nodded.

John Harris turned back to Sherry. "Anyway, in a nutshell, the woman had no money—the husband had seen to that. She hired an incompetent hack as a defense attorney and Jay could tell on opening arguments she was, without question, headed for death row, and he simply couldn't stand it."

"But what can a judge do?"

"Nothing, legally," he said, aware of more movement behind him. Glancing back, the President saw a second man crowding in beside the first, a small American flag pin on his lapel.

"You want to talk to these fellows now, sir?" Sherry asked under her breath.

"Shortly," he said, turning around toward the two. "Gentlemen, give me just a minute here, okay?"

"Absolutely!" the first one replied, moving back slightly.

"Yes, sir," the other echoed, a bit loudly. Harris could see a large hearing aid in his left ear.

Jillian had spotted the small gathering and moved into the first-class cabin from the galley to shoo them away, but Harris waved her back with a smile and a small stop gesture of his hand before turning back toward Sherry. "So, Jay simply couldn't stand seeing this beautiful, battered young woman railroaded by circumstance. Remember, this is long before the acceptance of the concept that a battered spouse who murders her batterer may be acting in self-defense even if the killing *didn't* occur during the beating. Anyway, Jay released this emotionally damaged young woman on an exceptionally low bail, which he paid himself, anonymously. He also tried, anonymously, to hire a better lawyer for her, but that didn't work. Finally he started meeting with her surreptitiously to advise her and try to save her, and along the way he fell helplessly, hopelessly in love with her."

"What happened, then?" she asked.

"Judge Reinhart waited until the trial had essentially passed the point of double jeopardy, where she couldn't be retried, and then he sabotaged the case in a very clever way. The prosecutor and DA went nuts, discovered the ex parte contacts, told the media, and everything blew into a major public scandal. When the smoke cleared, he escaped criminal liability, but they removed him as a judge and suspended him as a lawyer, a difficult procedure in Texas. This, of course, all occurred about the time I was taking office."

"He stayed with her?"

"He married her," the President said, snapping his seat belt open, "and then did his best to rehabilitate her. The poor woman was under constant psychiatric care, but I'm sad to hear . . . he just told me . . . she killed herself last year." Harris moved forward in the seat and prepared to stand as Sherry reached out to touch his arm, her face a study in concern.

"Sir, are you sure that Reinhart is . . ." She stopped as he raised his hand to silence her.

"Am I sure I want Reinhart defending me given what Washington or the media might say? Yes, Sherry, I'm very sure." He got to his feet and turned to the men in the aisle, who had been joined by two more of roughly the same age. Extending his hand, President Harris smiled broadly at them.

✈ ELEVEN

"So what are we going to tell them?" Alastair Chadwick asked as the 737 climbed through fifteen thousand feet.

"Who?" Craig Dayton asked, his concentration elsewhere.

"The passengers. *Our* passengers. The ones who paid money of one sort or another to have their carcasses carted to the eternal city of Rome. Sicily is not an acceptable substitute, you know. They shan't be fooled."

Craig glanced at the copilot and shook his head. "I don't know. What do you think?"

"I realize," Alastair answered, "that in America the airline industry shrinks from this radical idea, but perhaps we should tell them the truth."

"That *is* a novel idea," Craig agreed.

"I thought so."

"You do it."

"Not bloody well likely, Captain," Chadwick said, grinning.

Craig Dayton took a deep breath and pulled the PA microphone from its holder.

In the first-class cabin President Harris stood in the aisle greeting the four male passengers who had been waiting to meet him. All American veterans of World War II, they told him proudly, and all on a tour of Europe that would end with the dedication of a new D-Day War Memorial. The first one, a retired Army colonel, had just begun a description of the tour when the click of the PA grabbed their attention.

> *Folks, this is your captain. I want you to listen very carefully to what I have to say. Now, first, there is nothing wrong with this aircraft ... there is no safety problem. There is, however, a problem with our trying to land in Rome. The problem is ... diplomatic and legal. We have aboard our aircraft, as some of you know, a former President of the United States, President John Harris. It is our responsibility as an airline, and mine as captain, to keep all of you safe, and that includes a former head of state. I have received credible information that there is a very serious threat to the personal safety of President Harris if we land at Rome, and therefore—despite the severe inconvenience to some of you who need to be in Rome on schedule—we are flying south to a safe location near Catania, Sicily, an air base called Sigonella. Now, when we get on the ground at Sigonella, we will be making arrangements to get you either back to Rome or to your ultimate destination. I am truly sorry for this necessity, but I have no choice.*

The retired colonel had been looking in the direction of the overhead speakers. His eyes now latched on the President. "Sir, what, may I ask, was the threat?"

The others crowded in to hear the answer over the repeat of the announcement in French and German.

•   •   •

In the cockpit, the call chime started ringing as Craig replaced the PA microphone in its holder.

"Captain? This is Ursula in the back. Can you come back here? There is much anger."

"What do you mean, anger?" he asked.

"Some passengers are very angry with you."

"Are they in the aisles?"

"No. They are sitting, but they are talking loudly and won't calm down."

"Okay. Thanks." Craig clicked off the interphone and pulled the PA microphone back to his face.

This is the captain again. I know many of you are very angry at me for this decision, but you must stay in your seats and accept my explanation for now. When we get on the ground, I'll come back there and talk to anyone who'd like to discuss the matter, but not now! Do NOT give my flight attendants a hard time. They didn't make the decision. I did.

Once again he translated the words as closely as possible before replacing the mike and turning to Alastair. "I may have to go back."

Alastair nodded, checking the aeronautical map against the flight computer readout.

"We've two hundred forty miles to go, Craig. About a half hour. Are we planning to chat up Sigonella in advance, by the way, or just drop in out of the blue and violate some more regulations?"

"Best to say nothing, I think, until we're almost overhead. I don't want some military commander having an opportunity to tell us we can't land."

"We'll declare an emergency then?" Alastair asked.

"What's to declare?" Craig replied, pushing his seat back and grinning. "We *are* an emergency."

Jillian opened the cockpit door at the same moment. "Craig, you'd better come on back. Ursula and Elle say it's getting ugly."

He swung his legs around the center console and pulled himself up. "How so?"

"Some people in the back are demanding to talk to you and are cursing at us."

"What nationality?" Craig asked.

"Does it matter?" Jillian replied, looking alarmed.

Craig stopped and cocked his head.

"If I'm going to speak to them, it would help if I knew what language."

"Oh. Of course. They're grumbling in two or three languages."

He shook his head as he followed her out of the cockpit.

Laramie, Wyoming

Three yellow legal pads were spread across the tile counter, the words and symbols on their pages an impressionist portrait-in-progress of the intense activity in their owner's mind.

Jay took a quick sip of orange juice and suppressed his desire to make more coffee as he concentrated on the first pad, labeled "logistics." The now-stale aroma of fried bacon and overheated hollandaise sauce still hung in the air, but he was oblivious to it.

The question "Where do I go?" was written carefully across the top, along with the names of London, Frankfurt, Geneva, and Stockholm. Paris had been written in and crossed out. So had Rome. The names of the airlines flying to the Continent from the Denver airport followed, along with the average flying times and several airline reservation numbers. There would also be the problem of getting to Denver. Driving normally took two hours, but with a late season snowstorm slicking the roads and the pass on U.S. 287 into Colorado, it could take much, much longer.

The second pad contained the evolving roadmap of the legal problem, beginning with an annotated plea to himself for research on the codes of civil procedures that guide Italian, French, Swiss, and Swedish courts. Most of what he needed could be downloaded from one of the legal reporting services, Lexus/Nexus or WestLaw, but time was the problem. A quickly extracted printout of the Treaty Against Torture downloaded from the United Nations web site was strewn across the counter just beyond the legal pads, the black and white pages sporting red ink from his underlining.

He picked up the phone and punched in one of the numbers he'd been given by Sherry Lincoln. The third pad was filled with names and numbers, including that of Rudolph Baker, Assistant Secretary of State, who had just come on the line, his tone conveying approximately the same level of caution normally reserved for communist leaders and Iraqi foreign ministers.

"Mr. Reinhart, I've just been briefed by Alex McLaughlin at the Justice Department, and I must say I'm flabbergasted at your attitude. Would you care to explain to me why you're refusing to tell the U.S. government the destination of President Harris's aircraft?"

"You have no need to know, sir," Jay replied, "until the President's aircraft has landed. There are no advance preparations necessary, and in fact, advance notice could be detrimental if the destination leaked. Do I need to remind you that people are chasing this man with an international warrant?"

"Hardly, but you're too late in any event. We already know he's headed to Malta. We're contacting Maltese authorities as we speak."

Jay chuckled out loud. "If you're convinced it's Malta, then by all means, go right ahead. Meanwhile, what I need to know is whether the Air Force has any long-range transport aircraft in the mid-Mediterranean area. Something that could drop in, get the President out, and make it nonstop back to the U.S. mainland?"

"What do you mean, 'If I'm convinced'?" Baker asked suddenly. "Is he going to Malta or not?"

"I'm not playing games, Secretary Baker, but you're going to have to trust me on this for about an hour, for his good as well as for your own plausible deniability."

"I see. That response essentially means that you *do* believe he's going somewhere else. Let me tell you something, Mr. Reinhart. You're way out of your league! You're going to mess around with this like some dilettante and get Harris in real jeopardy."

"That's the last thing I'm going to do."

"Well, if you've put him up to going to Morocco, you're making a huge mistake. Same thing with any attempt to get to Gibraltar, Spain, Portugal, Egypt, or just about anywhere else within range. The legal complications in any of those nations will make Italy seem like Vermont by contrast, and you have no idea what you're doing diplomatically."

"Relax, Mr. Baker. He's not going to any of those countries, and if I weren't aware that I'm an amateur at international diplomacy, I wouldn't have called you in the first place. I do need your help, but the immediate question is whether we can get the President evacuated by the Air Force or Navy when he lands."

"What do you mean, evacuated? How can I answer that if I don't know what sovereign state he's to be evacuated from?"

"All right, let's assume for the sake of argument that we've managed to get past whatever diplomatic problems might arise from landing him where he's going to land . . ."

A short, derisive laugh on the other end cut him off. "Find me a place on this planet, Mr. Reinhart . . . other than the U.S., that is . . . where the diplomatic aspects are *not* a problem. We're talking about an international warrant for his arrest and prosecution, for heaven's sake. Wherever he lands, someone's going to be waiting with a copy of that warrant and he will be arrested and detained. Give up the idea that you can protect him from being arrested. The real fight will be the extradition attempt, and that will require a galaxy of experienced attorneys and deep research and . . ."

"Sir, that's enough!" Jay snapped. "Like it or not, I'm his lawyer. For the record, though, I tried to turn him down and he wouldn't let me, so kindly drop the lectures. You can snarl at the President himself later for his employment indiscretion, but for now, would you please focus on the most important question we've got before us? We are not going to let him get arrested, because at that point we've truly lost control. Now. Can the Air Force or Navy pick him up or not?"

At last there was silence on the other end as Baker thought through the question. "I don't know. That's a question the Pentagon must answer first, and then we'd have to get to the diplomatic and political complications. It might well be that he'll end up in a country that won't permit such a rescue. I mean, we're talking about sovereign states. It could be considered an act of aggression for the Air Force to pop in and extricate a former president. I *will* find out about the military availability, however."

"Good."

"But what *you* need to understand, Mr. Reinhart, is that only President Cavanaugh can approve that sort of rescue."

"I realize that, but given the threat to any ex-president ever traveling abroad again and the clear consequences of not acting, how on earth could he refuse?"

There was no answer.

The White House—Washington, D.C.

The summoned members of the government had first been ushered into the Cabinet Room, but at the President's relayed request, they were escorted to the Oval Office by the Deputy Chief of Staff. Under the watchful eye of the President's secretary, Alex McLaughlin from Justice, Rudy Baker from State, the Deputy Director of the CIA, the National Security Advisor, and an Air Force lieutenant general had milled about for the previous ten minutes before the President swept into the room and pulled up a chair in front of his desk.

"Sit, everyone. Where are we on President Harris's dilemma?"

The Deputy Director of the CIA started to respond, but the President stopped him.

"First, I should tell you I know he's headed to Malta, and that somehow the commercial aircrew he's flying with has decided to be his protector, which is rather strange for a German airline."

"Not strange at all, sir," the general interjected. "We've got an Air Force reserve officer in the captain's seat of that airliner. He's not under our orders or anything, but he's definitely one of ours. An expatriate commercial pilot who lives in Frankfurt."

"Really?" the President responded. "That's fortunate."

"Mr. President," Rudy Baker interjected, "I have reason to believe Malta may not be the destination." He described his conversation with Jay Reinhart.

"When was that call, Rudy?" the President asked.

"Just before we left the Cabinet Room, sir. About twenty-five minutes ago."

The President nodded and raised his hand for silence. "Okay, and what the heck is this about some defrocked Texas judge playing attorney for Harris? What's up with that?"

Alex McLaughlin began relating Reinhart's history, but the President cut him off. "Okay, okay. I get the picture. For some unknowable reason, Harris has hired a maverick who's a walking liability, which means we have to pick up the slack. Right?"

"No, sir," McLaughlin said, detailing the reasons the Justice Department had to remain in the background.

Rudy Baker repeated Reinhart's request for Air Force or Navy assistance, while the CIA Deputy Director chimed in with an assessment of the places Harris could land, and the National Security Advisor briefed them on the possible consequences for U.S. foreign policy of a long battle to extradite Harris to Peru.

"All right," President Cavanaugh said at last. "We obviously can't solidify an option list until he lands somewhere."

They all nodded.

"Very well. General, you said he couldn't stay airborne more than two hours, so let's meet again in two hours." He looked at the Deputy Chief of Staff. "Can we do that?"

"Yes, sir. We'll move the schedule."

"And the press isn't onto this yet?"

"Not really, sir. The wires are reporting a possible hijacking, but no one's connected it with Harris as yet."

"Amazing. Usually *we* don't know about it until CNN's got live pictures and Peter Jennings is doing a special report from New York."

The group fanned out of the Oval Office, the Air Force general moving rapidly into an adjacent room to use a secure phone. He punched in the appropriate numbers and drummed his fingers on the table waiting for a voice on the other end.

"Joe? I'm going down to the Situation Room in a minute. Get the AMC command post at Scott on a secure line and get the duty controller to identify every available C-17, C-5, or C-141, or even one of the Andrews Gulfstreams, within five hundred miles of Italy that we could use for a mid-Med evacuation nonstop to the CONUS over the next few hours. ID the bird and the crew, in flight if possible, and stand by to order them in. We'll need inflight refueling, too, so they better scare up a few tankers in the plan."

He listened to the reply and nodded, his eyes on the door to make sure there were no other ears around.

"I want the jump on this, Joe. The way I see it, the President's only option is to snatch Harris out of there, but he also heard the word *Navy* on the list of possibilities a few minutes ago and we've got to make sure the swabbies don't steal this one. They'd just love to chopper him out to some carrier and fly in the media to interview him all the way to Norfolk."

The general listened for a bit, nodding at intervals.

"Just get the plan cocked and ready, okay? The second we find where Harris is, I want an Air Force bird turning on final to the same runway. I want to hand the President an easy solution already in place."

✈ TWELVE

The sight of contrails streaming behind a high-flying Airbus 340 fifty miles distant had begun to worry Alastair as he waited for Craig to return from the cabin. The plumes of crystallized water vapor—ephemeral epitaphs to the stratospheric passage of the giant machine—stood in stark relief against the clear azure sky to the southeast.

We're probably leaving our own contrail, Alastair thought. *Hardly the most effective manner of sneaking away.*

The contrail would last for many minutes after their passage, and any eye, airborne or on the ground, could follow it back to its source. The Italian air traffic controllers knew precisely who and where they were, of course, but the incongruity of such a visually heralded getaway left him amused and concerned at the same moment.

He checked the radar again to make sure the cumulus buildups directly ahead over Sicily weren't hiding thunderstorms. A few rain showers adorned the digital color radar screen as light green splotches located just beyond the city of Catania and Mount Etna, but otherwise the weather was cooperating. He checked the altitude again. Steady at flight level two eight zero, or twenty-eight thousand, the airspeed Mach .72, seventy-two percent of the speed of sound.

Just for a moment, Alastair let his stomach tighten at the thought of what lay ahead professionally, but he quickly squelched the process, returning his thoughts instead to the growing mental list he'd been making of why he should leave EuroAir anyway. It was hardly a matter of money. He had plenty saved, and access to his father's estate as well, but he'd never been dismissed from a job, and that small indulgence of pride was now threatened.

The cockpit door yielded to a key and Alastair looked around as Craig reentered and swung expertly into the left seat, rolling his eyes. There was no smile.

"I take it the natives are restless?" Alastair said.

"What? Oh. That would be British understatement, right?" Craig replied, the shadow of a grin crossing his face.

"You tell me," Alastair said.

Craig nodded. "We've got about a dozen or so back there who would probably come after me with the crash axe if they could get to it. Missed flights, missed appointments, a missed wedding, missed opportunities . . . I lost count."

"And you're surprised?"

"Not really. I'm just not much of a diplomat. Where are we?"

Alastair gave him a quick synopsis and voiced his concern over the contrail. "I don't know why it seems important."

"I do," Craig said, looking back over his left shoulder as his right hand found the heading select button on the autoflight panel. He began cranking the heading around to the left until the 737 entered a thirty-five-degree left bank.

"What are you looking for?" Alastair asked. "ATC will surely see this turn and ask what we're doing."

"Say nothing just yet."

The aircraft's heading was now more than forty-five degrees to the left of the course, and as he strained to see behind them, their contrail swam into view streaming back for many miles until it passed under another jetliner on the same course.

"Aha!"

"What, Craig?"

"We're being followed. I thought so."

"By whom?"

"It's probably that charter flight they cleared to Malta just after us."

"Aren't we being a bit paranoid? If he's going to Malta, there is a reasonably good possibility he *would* be behind us."

Craig shook his head. "If you're going to snatch someone back to Peru, wouldn't it be smart to have a plane waiting? I could be wrong, but I'll bet he's literally tailing us."

Craig reengaged the navigation link between the autoflight system and the flight computer and the 737 obediently rolled out of the left bank and into a right turn to resume course.

"So what do we do, if anything?" Alastair asked. "I rather doubt he's carrying missiles, but it's a bit difficult to hide a 737 streaming a fifty-mile contrail."

"Any cells in those buildups?" Craig asked, pointing to the towering cumulus looming less than ten miles ahead.

"No. A little rain is all I see."

"And right over our destination," Craig muttered to himself as he leaned over the radar display. "Good. Let's pull out the tower frequency for Sigonella."

"And what, pray tell, are you planning, oh captain, my captain?"

"Just a little F-15 maneuver."

"I see. You will keep in mind won't you, old boy," Alastair said, "that this little bird from Seattle doesn't maneuver quite as well as that overfed F-15 you used to fly?"

"Sure it does," Craig replied, his eyes boring into the clouds they were about to penetrate.

Rome Air Traffic Control Center, Italy

The controller in charge of EuroAir 42 forced himself to stub out his cigarette and concentrate. With several supervisors hovering over his shoulder, the uncomfortable task of watching the hijacked aircraft as its data block crawled southbound across his scope had become an agony of trying not to forget any procedures. The sudden left turn had been worrisome, but he'd resisted the temptation to ask the pilots what was going on. Who knew what was happening up there, and how the wrong word at the wrong moment might infuriate a hijacker holding a gun or a bomb? Fortunately, he noted, the aircraft was still in the sky, so hopefully there was no struggle going on in the cockpit. He remembered the videos of a Boeing 767 crashing into the water off the Seychelles years before amidst a monstrous struggle for control on the flight deck. Hopefully nothing so dramatic would occur today.

The data block for the Boeing 727 cleared to Malta had closed on EuroAir 42 by a half mile because of the sudden unexplained turn, but the spacing between the two jets was still legal.

EuroAir 42 was just crossing the shoreline of Sicily when the data block began to coast, the computer displaying the last readout of position and altitude in the absence of any updated information. The controller came forward slightly in his seat, watching for the aircraft's transponder to resume "talking" to the ATC computer. But nothing was happening, and the warning symbol that told him the data from the aircraft had been lost was now flashing.

"What's happening?" one of the supervisors asked with a self-importance that disgusted the controller.

"I've lost his transponder," the controller said simply.

"What does that mean?" a visiting ATC manager who had never been a controller asked.

"It means, sir, that we may have just temporarily lost the signal, he could have turned it off, or something catastrophic could have happened to stop its transmissions."

He toggled his transmitter. "EuroAir Forty-Two, Rome Control. We've lost your transponder, sir."

No reply.

He tried again.

"There! You've got a skin paint!" his supervisor said, the man's breath fetid and heavy over the controller's shoulder.

There was in fact a faint return, but it wasn't traveling in a straight line. It was off to the right of the original course, now disappearing, then returning as the controller changed the display's polarization control. Suddenly the area was blanked by the appearance of rain echos, and he switched back. The "skin paint" echo, if that's what it was, had all but reversed course now and seemed to be spiraling.

The controller realized he was holding his breath. Jetliners didn't just spiral out of altitude without a word, their data block suddenly going blank. But airliners that suddenly broke up in flight would look exactly like what he was seeing.

Oh my God, he thought to himself, imagining an explosion in the cockpit. *We've lost them.*

Sigonella Naval Air Station, Sicily, Italy

A sudden rain squall had approached from the southwest and blanketed the field for the past ten minutes, obscuring the usually magnificent vista of Mt. Etna to the north, and most of the east-west runway. The two U.S. Navy controllers manning the control tower had watched with amusement as some of their fellows went dashing across the ramp below to reach the military passenger terminal, their khakis completely soaked. A four-engine Navy P-3 Orion submarine hunter, the military version of the Lockheed Electra, sat on the ramp below the tower, its crew off somewhere enjoying local pleasures. Next to it a twin-engine E-2 Hawkeye had just arrived from the *Kennedy,* one of the carriers currently on patrol in the Mediterranean. The pilots had shut down just as the squall hit and were waiting it out. The controller working the tower frequency saw the door opening now that the rain was ending, then raised his field glasses for a routine sweep of the airport at the same moment a blaze of landing lights appeared over the eastern end of the runway.

"Who the hell is that?" the controller asked his partner as the radio speaker came alive.

"Sigonella Tower, EuroAir Forty-Two on short final to runway two seven for an emergency landing."

The controller yanked the microphone to his mouth, his mind embracing the regulations the approaching aircrew might have violated by not contacting him sooner, and discarding the thoughts just as quickly. The word "emergency" overrode all other considerations.

"Ah, EuroAir Forty-Two, you're cleared to land runway Two Seven, wind two four zero at seven, gusts to fifteen, altimeter two nine eight eight, rainstorm over the field and in progress. Runway is wet."

"Roger," was the only response. A British accent, the controller noted, wondering what on earth could have happened that would have sent them a commercial flight with no advance warning from Rome.

The controller turned to his partner again. "Did you have anything on him?"

"Hell, no. Nothing!"

"Call Rome Control and at least let them know he made it in."

The landing lights had coalesced to a Boeing 737, a late-model design, he could tell, with the larger CFM-56 engines with the oval openings in the front. Whoever was flying made a smooth touchdown and deployed his thrust reversers quickly, slowing the aircraft at midfield, where he made a sharp right turn off the runway, following the taxiway toward the tower.

"Ah, do you need any assistance, Forty-Two?" the tower controller asked.

"No," was the monosyllabic reply.

"Contact ground . . . no, stay with me. Where do you want to park?"

"Which ramp is under U.S. Navy control?"

The tower controller hesitated, wondering why anyone

would ask that question. The pilot of the 737 was making a beeline toward the parked P-3.

"Ah, sir, the whole base is U.S. Navy, and you're heading to the passenger ramp now. Do you have authorization?"

"We do now" was the response, this one a different voice, and one that sounded American.

The controller reached over to the crash phone and hesitated, then pulled up the handset and punched the button to alert the security police. The 737 taxied rapidly behind the P-3 and turned to pass between the Orion and the Navy terminal, coming to a stop with its right wingtip practically touching the building.

"Sigonella Tower, EuroAir Forty-Two. Please listen closely. No one is to approach this aircraft except the commander of this Navy installation. Do you understand?"

"Forty-Two, I will relay that request, but what is your circumstance, sir? If there's a problem, please . . . ah . . . tell me what. Do you need assistance of some sort?"

The other controller had been on hold on another line. Suddenly he lowered his receiver, his eyes wide. "Rome says this bird's hijacked, and they thought she'd exploded a few minutes ago in midair."

"Jesus!" the first controller said, his hand mashing the crash alarm button at the same moment to summon the entire base to alert.

✈ THIRTEEN

Rome, Italy—Monday—4:15 P.M.

When it became apparent that John Harris was not going to
land at Da Vinci International, Stuart Campbell returned to
his temporary hotel-based office in central Rome to wait
for word on EuroAir 42's ultimate destination. From the
back of his car in the middle of midday Roman traffic he
ordered his staff in Brussels into action, directing a quick
profile on Malta's legal structure, and making sure the
young lawyer he'd dispatched to the island as a remote
contingency was actually in the airport with the warrant.
Back in his suite and satisfied that all possible preparations
had been made, he ordered coffee and sat back, watching
the clock and wondering why he still felt vaguely unprepared.

The coffee arrived with the news that EuroAir 42 had
engineered a disappearing act and turned up on the ramp at
Sigonella.

"What?" Campbell barked, startling the airport manager, who had just found out and phoned. "Surely you're
joking!"

"No, signore. Sigonella is a U.S. Navy base in Sicily," the man offered.

"I know that," Campbell replied, trying and failing to suppress a chuckle.

Clever thinking, Harris! he thought. *Won't get you out of this, of course, but not a bad move under pressure. I wonder how you talked the commercial pilots into it?*

The bizarre thought that a former U.S. chief executive might have actually hijacked the commercial aircraft fluttered across his mind, bringing an even broader smile. Whatever had occurred, that certainly wasn't the explanation.

He thanked the manager and ended the call, then summoned his secretary.

"Isabel, have the car brought around to take me back to the airport, and have my pilots ready to go to this place in Sicily." He handed her a page of yellow legal paper with the information. "Call Minister Anselmo and tell him I will wait if he or one of his people wants to come along. Ask him to prepare the local Carabinieri commander in Sicily to meet me at Sigonella, and to please arrange diplomatic clearance or whatever's necessary to get my aircraft onto that airport. Also, they need to clear that charter aircraft to the base as well. If the pilot of that charter calls . . . a Captain Perez . . . patch him through to the car or my GSM immediately."

She finished the shorthand transcription of his orders almost as soon as he finished speaking. "Anything else, sir?"

Campbell hauled himself effortlessly to his feet and smiled at her. "That's all for now. Tell the driver I'll be down in five minutes. Oh, first, get the American Embassy here in Rome on the line, and ask for the Naval attaché."

His GSM phone rang and he flipped it open as she turned to make the embassy call.

"Mr. Campbell, this is Captain Perez."

"Yes, Captain. Where are you, and I trust you're going to say Sigonella."

"No, sir," the charter captain replied, relating the fact

that for nearly ten minutes he and Rome Control had lost track of EuroAir.

"So where are you?"

"In holding near Sigonella. They are refusing to let me land."

"Stand by, Captain. That clearance will come in about ten minutes. Land and park wherever they tell you and just wait. I'm on my way. I'll be arriving within an hour and a half in a Learjet thirty-five and will park beside you."

He folded the GSM phone as the secretary reappeared at his side to report the attaché was unavailable.

"Relay the call to the car if you can get the attaché before I take off, Isabel," Campbell said. He scooped up his briefcase and headed for the door, stopping in the hallway to concentrate on the dilemma rapidly evolving in his mind. The equation, he thought, might well be more complicated than he'd initially estimated. Sigonella was Italian soil, but now he was going to have to navigate through legal difficulties and diplomatic complications raised because he was a British lawyer representing a South American nation trying to assert Italian jurisdiction over a leased American military installation in order to arrest a former U.S. President under an international warrant!

His esteem for his adversary went up a notch.

U.S. Air Force C-17 70042, Call Sign "REACH 70042," in Flight

The aircraft commander of Reach 70042, like all pilots for the Air Force's Air Mobility Command, had been thoroughly trained on how to handle an unexpected message suddenly received in flight ordering them to divert somewhere other than the original destination. There was always the chance that the message could be bogus, even if the radio link it came in on was satellite-based or otherwise secure. Whoever was sending the diversion order had to stand by to be challenged by the aircrew from an ever-changing code table. If the ground station answered with the right coded response, the aircrew would obey and change course.

The call from the main AMC command post at Scott Air Force Base in Illinois had come as a complete surprise to the crew of Reach 70042. Cruising at flight level four one zero in a brand-new Boeing/Douglas C-17 Globemaster III on a routine nonstop flight from Spain to Daharan, Saudi Arabia, Aircraft Commander Ginny Thompson had taken an embarrassingly long time to dig the "secrets" out of her flight suit ankle pocket, and even more time to find the right table and extract the right codes. They were passing south of the southeastern edge of Italy by the time she made the appropriate transmission and received the answering authentication.

"They match," she announced. "It's real."

"And that would mean?" the male first lieutenant in the copilot's seat asked.

"Punch in the identifier for Sigonella NAS and get us a revised clearance. The orders are to proceed immediately at best speed, and I think we're only about a hundred miles out."

"Close. We're ninety-eight miles," the copilot said, finishing the task of reprogramming the flight management computer.

When Rome Control had cleared them to reverse course and descend, Major Thompson molded her right hand to the control stick and disconnected the autopilot, smoothly bringing the huge transport around in a left bank as she started the descent and pulled the power back on all four engines.

"Bill, go back and brief the loadmasters," she told the copilot. "Make sure they're awake."

"Did I hear that right?" the lieutenant asked. "Did he say a former DV code 1 pickup?"

"That's what I thought I heard, but that couldn't be right."

"That would be a former President of the United States, right? A 'DV 1'?"

"Yes," she said. "Although I don't think I've ever heard the word former used with a distinguished visitor code before. Anyway, we're supposed to be ready to go instantly. Be sure they understand that."

"Roger."

"We'll be there in twenty minutes," she added, wondering what the nature of the emergency might be. If there was a former chief executive at Sigonella, was it a medical problem? Were they supposed to fly him out as a medevac? If so, they should have been told. It took time for the loadmasters to set up the cabin. No, she thought, that wouldn't make sense. More than likely someone other than a former President needed a fast, free ride home.

They obviously got the DV code wrong.

Laramie, Wyoming

The wait was becoming excruciating by the time John Harris phoned to confirm they were on the ramp in Sicily.

"Great," Jay replied.

"Now what?" the President asked gently.

"Well, now I talk to the White House. Is anyone trying to leave or come aboard?"

"No," Harris said, his voice deep and concerned. "The doors are closed, and we have a lot of very unhappy commercial passengers aboard, but right now the engines are still running and we're just sitting here. No one's approaching as far as I can see."

"John, whatever you do, do not get off that aircraft until I tell you, okay?"

"Very well. I think I understand."

"I'm gambling a bit, but while the Italians might be inclined to come into a leased military installation, they will be very slow to actually invade a foreign flag carrier to remove anyone. Stand by, now. Let me call the White House on the cell phone. If the line goes dead, phone me back at five-minute intervals."

Jay put the receiver of the house phone back on the counter and picked up the cell phone, punching in the number he'd been given to the White House Situation Room.

"This is Jay Reinhart," he announced when a male voice answered. "I need to speak to . . ."

"Stand by, sir."

There were a few electronic clicks before another male voice filled the earpiece.

"Mr. Reinhart?"

"Yes."

"This is Lieutenant General Bill Davidsen. I'm Deputy Chief of Staff of the Air Force. I asked that you be put through to me if you called."

"Thanks, General. I want to let you know that President Harris has landed at Sigonella Naval Air Station in Sicily and is currently sitting in the commercial aircraft on the Navy ramp."

"Yes, we know, Mr. Reinhart. We got the information just ten minutes ago from Italian Air Traffic Control."

"General, you need to know that I have President Harris holding on another line," Jay said. "I've advised him to stay on the airplane. I think I need to coordinate with the commander of that Navy facility."

"Mr. Reinhart, we're already in motion. We had a C-17 passing less than a hundred miles away and we've turned him toward Sigonella. Now, we still need approval from President Cavanaugh, but the plan is to get that C-17 on the ground in about twenty minutes, transfer President Harris from that civilian craft to the C-17, and then get him the hell out of there and fly him nonstop back to the States."

"Thank God, General!" Jay exclaimed, sighing in relief. "That's wonderful news."

"I'd better talk to President Harris directly at this point, Mr. Reinhart. Can you tie the lines together?"

"Uh, no, I don't have the equipment. I could have him call you on that number, though."

"Good. As fast as possible."

"But, General, as his lawyer, I have to keep everybody focused on the fact that there's an international arrest warrant out there and some powerful people who will be trying to serve it. I must stay in the loop and on the line. Can you conference me in at the same time if I break the connection and have him call?"

"Yes, Mr. Reinhart. As soon as he calls, we'll patch you back in."

Jay passed his home number, relayed the plan to John Harris on the home phone, and disconnected both calls. He sat staring at his home phone, mentally calculating how long it would take to establish the three-way connection and trying to envision what was happening at that moment in Sigonella. He could imagine the big C-17 barreling toward the Navy base at four hundred fifty knots, and he could imagine that Stuart Campbell would be closing in on Sigonella as well with a certified copy of the warrant, an Italian arrest version, and a carefully planned formation of Italian authorities ready to make the arrest. But if the President could make the transfer to the C-17 before Campbell found an Italian official brave enough to authorize an intrusion onto leased American military real estate, he would be safe. There was no way they would try to stop an Air Force aircraft from departing in such a confused diplomatic situation.

He checked his watch again. Twenty minutes, the general had said, before the Air Force transport arrived, and maybe another five minutes to taxi to the ramp and open a door. He could feel his heart pounding and wished there was some sort of television camera on the ramp broadcasting on the World Wide Web. Waiting was an agony.

This may all be over in forty-five minutes! he told himself.

For the first time in over an hour, he got to his feet and opened the refrigerator for more orange juice, thinking how nice it would be to build up the fire and sit there for hours with a cigar, something he seldom let himself do anymore.

Escapist thinking!

He closed the refrigerator and looked to the left, catching a glimpse of the open bedroom door. Linda's angry departure flooded back on a tide of guilt. Had it really been necessary to hurt her? It seemed like days ago, but once the President was safely airborne, maybe he should chase her down, go to her house, somehow try to explain what he meant.

Thank God we're going to get him out of there! I can't imagine what would have happened otherwise.

Images of a frantic flight to Europe, an endless string of twenty-four-hour days, voluminous research, and high-stakes poker with Harris's adversaries unreeled like the blueprint of an unfathomable nightmare, now that he didn't have to pretend to himself that he could handle it. The reality that it wasn't quite over yet was better suppressed.

He sat on the kitchen stool and stared at the phone, which remained silent.

✈ FOURTEEN

Interrupting the President when he was immersed in a serious meeting was contrary to White House policy, and Chief of Staff Jack Rollins was the man who'd set the policy in the first place.

Yet, there had to be exceptions.

Rollins hesitated outside the door to the Cabinet Room, aware of the voices filtering through from the intense discussion on the other side. They had one last chance to arm-twist the budget through the House, and the President was the only one with the charisma and political IOU's to do it. He'd been working his magic on twelve angry swing-vote congressmen for the last thirty minutes, but the Harris situation was becoming critical and it was time to act.

Jack Rollins opened the door and moved quietly to Cavanaugh's side.

"Excuse me, folks," the President told the group when he saw Rollins enter and come over to stand by his side. Rollins whispered in his ear, "The situation with Harris is ripening. We'll be to a major decision point within twenty minutes."

"Give me a few seconds," the President said to the group as he stood and moved to the door with a hand on Rollins's shoulder.

"You need me right this minute?" the President asked.

"I think we do, sir. The Air Force has already set a rescue in motion, but it needs your sign-off."

"Why don't I just authorize it from here?" the President asked.

"I wouldn't do that, Mr. President," Jack Rollins counseled. "There are some volatile aspects still unfolding."

Cavanaugh nodded. "Okay. Ten minutes."

"Should I send someone in to get you?"

"No, Jack. I need to finish this. I'll be there as quickly as I can."

Rollins slipped out as the President turned back to the assembled group.

Once again the Oval Office was filling with worried advisors watching the clock. General Davidsen flanked Jack Rollins beside the President's desk with a phone to his ear. Press Secretary Diane Beecher and National Security Advisor Roger Villems occupied one of the couches facing the Deputy Attorney General and Assistant Secretary of State on the other, all of them holding coffee cups and balancing notebooks and briefing papers.

At the opposite end of the Oval—as staffers referred to the world's most photographed office—the newest member of the administration stood in deep thought by the fireplace. Michael Goldboro, the Assistant to the President for National Security affairs, otherwise known as the National Security Advisor, had scanned the briefing papers and reread the Treaty Against Torture before coming over from the Executive Office Building by specific request of the President. A quiet man with darting, suspicious eyes, his years as a tenured professor at Georgetown, plus a long list of honored books and papers on the history and future of statecraft, had made him a favorite of President Cavanaugh's—though the Ivy Leaguers in the Cavanaugh administration and the Democratic Party considered him a poor successor to an office once held by Henry Kissinger. Goldboro was well aware of his nonacceptance, and as a result, he chose his battles with great care.

General Davidsen pulled the receiver away and motioned to Jack Rollins.

"We're getting critical on timing here, Jack."

"Tell me."

"The C-17 is on the ramp and waiting, but the commander of the base, a Navy captain, tells me he's got a delegation from Catania at the gate, including a magistrate, a bunch of police officers, and someone from the Carabinieri national police. He also says he was bullied into letting both a private jet and an empty chartered airliner land, both of them from Rome."

Rollins nodded. "Are they ready to make the transfer?"

"President Harris is ready. I was just talking to him. Our crew is ready to crank and go as soon as he's aboard. They've positioned Navy security police around both airplanes, but no one's trying to force their way . . . hold on."

The general put the phone back to his ear, listening and responding for a minute before turning to Rollins again.

"Now they're making demands, Jack. There's a representative of the Italian Foreign Ministry aboard that private jet, and there is a demand being relayed, presumably from him, that the base commander essentially step aside and surrender the 737 and all the passengers, including the President, to Italian authority."

"Who's the Navy skipper on that base?"

"Captain Swanson."

"Is he asking for instructions?"

"Not yet. He's informed them that the base is under the jurisdiction of the U.S. Navy, and any unauthorized attempt to enter will meet with armed resistance."

"Strong words." He turned toward the sitting area, where Assistant Secretary of State Rudy Baker was in animated conversation.

"Rudy? May I ask for your help?" Rollins said. Baker got up and moved to stand beside them, listening intently as General Davidsen briefed him.

"That base commander does not have the right to refuse access to Italian law enforcement officers," Baker said, noting that Alex McLaughlin, the Assistant Attorney General, had followed him over from the couch and was listening intently.

"What do you mean he doesn't have the authority to refuse?" the general asked.

Baker nodded, his brow deeply furrowed. "That isn't United States soil, gentlemen. It's Italian."

"It's a leased base, Mr. Baker," the general said.

"Leased, yes, but not immune to Italian legal authority. Let me talk to him," Baker said, stepping closer and taking the phone from the general to introduce himself.

"Captain Swanson, you can't keep them out if they insist on entering the base."

He listened carefully, shaking his head. "No, Captain, listen to me. You do not have the legal right to protect that real estate as if it were American territory, and if your orders are otherwise, they're wrong. You'll create a substantial diplomatic mess with the Italians if you keep this up."

Baker looked at Jack Rollins and rolled his eyes before interrupting the Navy commander. "I . . . I . . . *excuse* me, Captain, can I get an edge in word wise? Thank you. I *know* I'm not in your direct chain of command, okay? But I'm trying to advise you on the reality of the situation. They didn't cede that land—they merely rented it to us. You above all people should understand the Status of Forces Agreement with Italy, since you're charged with upholding it. By the time you're through, you may just get us kicked out of there and the base closed. This has to be handled delicately."

Rudy Baker listened to the reply, nodding his head. "All right. We'll see to it that your commander is briefed. But in the meantime, please realize that you're walking on razor blades."

He handed the phone back to the general. "He says he's going to let them on NAS-One, which is the main, nonflying portion of the base about four miles from the flight line. But he says he's going to keep them away from NAS-Two at this point, which is the ramp and the aircraft. He said they have agreed that they won't enter NAS-Two without his approval." He lifted the phone. "Captain, please stand by." He handed the receiver back to the general and turned to Jack Rollins and Alex McLaughlin. "If we're going to snag him out of there, we'd better do it right now. Otherwise this will deteriorate into an impossible standoff. Right now, letting President Harris get on our Air Force jet and leave is simply an 'Oops, we're sorry we didn't stop to ask your approval' situation. In ten or twenty minutes, however, any rescue will become a direct challenge to the sovereign authority of Italy, and I'll bet my desk we'll lose the lease on the base."

"We need the President's approval," Jack Rollins said. "Anybody disagree?"

"We also need someone, if not the President," Baker continued, "to brief the Chief of Naval Operations quickly so they can get this cowboy under control."

"Excuse me, Mr. Assistant Secretary," General Davidsen said, his voice acidic and his hand still over the mouthpiece, "but I believe Captain Swanson is quite under control and admirably handling a difficult situation."

Rudy Baker sighed and raised a hand. "Sorry, General. Bad choice of words."

The general brought the phone back to his ear as an aide to the Press Secretary entered and whispered in her boss's ear. Diane Beecher got to her feet immediately and moved to the television console to the left of the President's desk to pull out the remote and click it on. The image of a CNN anchor filled the screen.

"Excuse me, everyone. The story's broken." Diane said.

Various file photos of President John Harris and old footage from his administration were showing in a box on the screen as the anchor related the reported hijacking, the previous uncertainty of the situation, and new information from a source in Rome that President Harris was about to be arrested on criminal charges that he'd personally ordered the CIA-driven torture and murder of Peruvian civilians during his time in office.

*We are going to bring you a live picture, now, by
satellite, being broadcast by Italian television . . .
the shot is apparently of the EuroAir Boeing 737
carrying former President John Harris. That airliner, which was earlier reported to be hijacked, is
now sitting on the ramp at an American Navy Base
in Sicily called Sigonella.*

The Air Mobility Command C-17 could be seen clearly
sitting to one side of a P-3 Orion, with the 737 visible on
the other side.

"Oh, wonderful!" Jack Rollins muttered under his
breath. "Our quick and easy little covert operation in living
color." He turned and motioned to his secretary, who'd
been hovering at a discrete distance. She moved rapidly to
his side.

"Tell the President I need him in here immediately. Tell
him things are critical and we're at the decision point."

Aboard EuroAir Flight 42—on the Ground, Sigonella Naval Air Station, Sicily

A set of portable stairs had been brought to the forward entrance of the 737 before Craig had given approval to open
the door, but with the Navy commander asking to come
aboard, it was time.

The Navy captain and the airline captain conferred
briefly at the front door before Captain Swanson was
shown into first class and introduced to President Harris,
who was still holding a telephone receiver connected to the
White House Situation Room.

John Harris handed the receiver to Sherry as he stood to
shake Swanson's hand and listen to his assessment of the
situation.

"Are they going to try to stop me from getting on that
C-17?" the President asked evenly.

Captain Swanson shook his head no. "We have two
groups. One is from Catania and they are taking their orders by phone from Rome. The other is a small group that

flew in on a Learjet from Rome. One person on the Lear is, I think, the deputy to the Italian foreign minister. The other is a tall guy, a civilian lawyer representing Peru, or so I'm told."

"That would be Stuart Campbell."

"That's the name. I've left them in my office on the other part of the base we call NAS-One, essentially under guard."

"Other part of the base?"

"About four miles away through flocks of sheep and Sicilian countryside. Campbell and the Foreign Ministry representative are in a deep disagreement over their jurisdiction. Campbell believes they have the right to just charge out here and pull you off the plane, and the Italians believe they're prohibited during the duration of the lease from entering any area we've designated as secure, which is primarily the flight line. I personally don't think they have the right to enter *either* base unless I approve it, which I did under pressure from the White House. Finally, sir, the Italian representative is arguing that even if Campbell is right and they could enter the ramp, they have no right to enter a foreign flag airliner."

"They *do* have that right, actually," the ex-President said. "Foreign registration of the aircraft is legally irrelevant when it's on foreign soil. But the Italian government may be purposefully dragging their feet to give me time to get out of here."

"That thought crossed my mind, Mr. President. And if that's true, that's all the more reason to make you disappear."

"Indeed. With all due respect, Captain, I'd rather see your base some other time. So what do we do?"

"Well, sir, all we're waiting for is the formal sign-off from the White House. No one's going to stop your C-17 crew from leaving once you're aboard. They'll be off the ground in an instant. I could escort you over to the C-17 right now, but I had a rather rancorous talk about that with several people in the White House a minute ago, so now I think we'd better sit tight for a few more minutes just to make sure they've got all the i's dotted and all the t's crossed."

"All they're waiting for is President Cavanaugh's approval," Sherry interjected, the phone still pressed to her ear. "Any minute now. He's headed back to the Oval Office to give the green light."

"They're supposed to call me back, too." Swanson held up a GSM cell phone. "It's just pro forma from here."

A small two-way radio crackled to life and the Captain pulled it from a belt clip.

"This is Swanson. Go ahead."

"Sir," an excited voice began, "we have a line of vehicles at the front gate of NAS-Two demanding to get in and saying they're under Italian authority."

"What kind of vehicles, Yeoman?"

"Ah . . . sir, two are military jeeps, there's a Suburban-type vehicle, and two of what appear to be APC's, armored personnel carriers."

"Who's making the request?"

"Mr. Campbell in your office, and the front gate guard is relaying the same thing."

The captain stood in thought for a second, remembering the words of the Assistant Secretary of State. He lifted the radio.

"Okay, listen up. Have a Security Police Humvee join up with them at the front gate and escort them over to NAS-One and to the same parking lot by my office. They are to go nowhere else. First, however, inspect for weapons, including any troops in the APC's. Any weapons they're carrying must be unloaded."

"Aye, aye, sir."

He lowered the radio and stepped onto the top of the air stairs, motioning to a lieutenant who bounded up the stairs.

"Jerry, how tall are you?"

"Five nine, sir."

"Good. Stay put."

He hurried back to the President's seat. "Sir? How tall are you?"

"Five ten, Captain. Why?"

"I want to run a quick test. I need to borrow your suit coat."

"Do I want to know?"

"Not yet."

"What's happening out there with those vehicles?" President Harris asked.

"I'm not sure, sir," Swanson replied. "But this may be more than a casual show of force, and that's what I've got to find out."

✈ FIFTEEN

Stuart Campbell stood in the corner of Captain Swanson's office looking out the window toward the flight line several miles away as he talked on his GSM phone to the managing director of EuroAir Airlines in Frankfurt.

"No, Herr Niemann, I am not attempting to tell you how to run your airline, but you have a distinct problem. You need to order your pilots to empty that aircraft right now and warn them against protecting a man who, as of this moment, has become a fugitive from justice, largely because of the actions of your crew."

The call to Frankfurt was a long shot, but any pressure would be helpful. Obviously the EuroAir crew had elected themselves John Harris's guardians.

"There isn't time, Herr Niemann. You need to order them to comply by phone right now from Frankfurt. Coming here will be too little, too late."

This is getting nowhere, he decided, ending the conversation as amicably as possible and turning toward the office door as a Carabinieri officer came inside.

"Signore Campbell?" the officer said in Italian.

"*Si.* Stuart Campbell," he responded, noting the absence of Giuseppe Anselmo's deputy.

"My instructions are to assist you, sir," the man said, quickly running down the list of men and equipment that were waiting at the gate of the airfield. "My men are being told they must come over here, rather than go to the airfield side."

"Major, I need for you to instruct your vehicles that they are to move slowly and steadily into NAS-Two, regardless of Navy protests, and go to the flight line. Just ignore any Naval resistance. They will not actually fire on you, I can assure you of that. If you have to roll through a fence, go ahead."

"Very well."

"There will be some sort of gate at the flight line itself. Do not go in, but line up there and stay ready, and . . ." He handed the major a second cell phone from his briefcase. "Please answer this if it rings. It will be me with further instructions."

The major nodded and left as a grim-faced man in a well-tailored pin-striped suit reentered the room.

"What was that, Mr. Campbell?" Giuseppe Anselmo's first deputy asked.

"Why, Mr. Sigerelli, I have asked the Carabinieri personnel to force the issue, refuse the Navy's request that they come over to this side of the base, and position themselves instead next to the flight line, not to enter."

"Mr. Campbell, are you aware that I'm talking in another office with my government?"

"Yes, sir, I'm aware of that. I had Giuseppe in my office this morning. I know he's calling the shots from Rome."

"Do you also know that the determination that the flight line of this base is inviolable comes from Mr. Anselmo and the highest levels of our government?"

"I do, and I have no intention of violating that interpretation until I can convince all of you that your reading of

the lease with the United States is entirely incorrect. You
own this base, and the flight line."

"That is not the current position of the Italian government, Mr. Campbell. Please give no other orders to Italian
units without my approval."

"As you wish. But if you don't mind, I think I should
speak to Giuseppe myself at this point."

"Please!" Sigerelli said, pointing to the hallway. "By all
means."

Laramie, Wyoming

Just as the temptation to call the Situation Room had become almost irresistible, the phone rang. Jay yanked it up,
relieved to hear Sherry Lincoln on the other end.

"Mr. Reinhart, I'm on with Sergeant Jones from the Situation Room. General Davidsen was summoned to the
Oval Office and we're just waiting. Sergeant Jones will
keep the line open and I'll stand by if you'll keep your line
open there."

Fifteen minutes had crawled by with only the news of
the Navy commander's arrival at the aircraft and a news
helicopter's arrival in the Sigonella area to break the tension.

Jay reached over to a small TV on the counter and
flipped it to CNN, startled to see the Sigonella flight line
on the screen.

There were voices in the background noise of the
phone.

"What's happening there, Sherry?" Jay asked.

"The President is still talking with the commander of
the base, and they're moving the aircraft that was between
us and the C-17. They're towing him out of the way."

Jay glanced back at the television monitor, feeling
slightly disoriented to see the P-3 Orion begin moving as
Sherry Lincoln had described.

"I'm watching it on television," he said, leaning forward. "Sherry, I'm seeing something else. The cameraman
is zooming in on a line of . . . vehicles of some sort wait-

ing just to one side of the flight line. They're not on the flight line, but it appears . . . they're at a gate."

"What kind of vehicles?" she replied. "I'm looking out the window here, but I can't see them."

"They're off toward the, ah, one o'clock position from your pilots' perspective. Armored personnel carriers, jeeps, and several others. Has anyone been trying to convince the President to leave the plane and go to the visiting officers' quarters or anywhere else?"

"No."

"I can't read their markings, but I'm sure they're not there to help get him on that C-17."

"I still don't see them."

The cameraman aboard the news chopper zoomed to a tighter shot, and Jay could see several soldiers working with what appeared to be the lock to the gate separating them from the 737, the C-17, and the President.

"Okay, Sherry, this is getting very serious. I'd recommend getting him aboard that C-17 right now, before they move onto the flight line."

"Stand by," she said. He could hear the receiver being placed on her lap or against a cloth surface. She returned just as quickly.

"The Navy commander wants to wait for confirmation from the White House. He says his men are guarding the perimeter of the flight line."

"Sherry, if anyone is guarding that flight line, they're invisible in the TV shot. No one's interfering with that group at the gate. What I'm looking at may well be preparations for an assault, and if that happens, they could either storm aboard and pull him off or surround the plane and make it impossible for John to get to the C-17. But if he's already aboard the C-17, they won't interfere. Please! Get him moving!"

"Understood."

"Sergeant Jones, are you still with us?" Jay asked.

"Yes, sir," the voice came back crisp and immediate.

"Can you get General Davidsen back?"

"He's in the Oval Office, sir. Stand by."

Nearly a minute ticked by before the general's voice returned.

"Yes?"

"It's Jay Reinhart, General. We've got a problem." He quickly related what he'd seen along the fence. "Can't you authorize moving President Harris into the C-17 right now?"

"Just a second, Mr. Reinhart," the general said. There was a muted discussion in the background with an occasional word filtering through.

"Okay," Davidsen said at last. "Here's where we are. President Cavanaugh is on his way to the Oval to approve this, and we have to wait a few more seconds for him to get here."

"We may not have a few more seconds, General. Are you, by chance, watching this CNN coverage?"

"Yes, we have it on, and I've seen the same shot, Mr. Reinhart, but they're not through the gate yet. Just hang on."

Aboard EuroAir Flight 42—on the Ground, Sigonella Naval Air Station, Sicily

As promised, Craig Dayton had gone back to coach again to try to defuse some of the fury that was threatening to spill into first class and interfere with the impending transfer of the President. Secret Service Agent Matt Ward had moved to the rear of first class for just that reason, increasingly concerned that three of the most aggravated passengers, all European males, would decide to rush him at the very moment he needed to be escorting the President across the ramp to the C-17. He watched the captain moving slowly down the aisle, making promises and trying to explain what was happening, without giving all the details. The strategy, however, was not working.

Exasperated, Craig pushed through six or seven men who were out of their seats and charged back to the front of the cabin to a small PA microphone the airline had added at the forward bulkhead.

Ladies and gentlemen, this is Captain Dayton. Please look forward. I'm here at the front of the cabin. Now I want you to listen to me. For the next twenty or thirty minutes, we are going to be in the middle of a major diplomatic confrontation between the governments of Italy and the United States. You may have noticed the news helicopters hovering in the distance. You are on TV right now, I've been told, and the whole world is watching. In a few minutes, President Harris will be transferred to that large Air Force jet you see next to us. At that point, I will let all of you off the airplane and we will deal with the question of when we can fly you back to Rome, or get you directly out of here to whatever other destinations you have. But no one is going to leave this cabin until the President has left. For those passengers who are upset and angry, let me tell you that yelling at me or at the flight attendants or at other passengers will not get you where you want to go any faster. For those of you who have been patient and understanding, my heartfelt thanks. We'll have this resolved as quickly as possible.

Craig replaced the microphone and watched with relief as most of those standing began to sit down. Judging that things were under control for the moment, he turned and walked back to first class and was startled to see President Harris disappearing into the cockpit and Alastair standing just outside.

"Someone was ringing him on our cockpit satellite phone," Alastair explained when Craig reached the entry area. "Someone named Campbell."

John Harris eased into the proffered copilot's seat and picked up the receiver.

"Well, Stuart, you've been a busy man," Harris said.

"And you, Mr. President, have been an exceptionally clever one in the last few hours."

"Why are you calling me? It's rather customary for an attorney to limit his contact to the other party's attorney, as you well know."

"I wasn't aware that you'd had time to retain counsel. Of course I'll contact your lawyer and his firm, but only as a courtesy, you understand. This is, after all, a criminal matter, Mr. President, and I merely represent the complainant, which is Peru. I think you should know, by the way, that I have the smoking gun. That's why I rang you. Just to let you know personally that this is no frivolous matter."

"What are you talking about, Stuart?"

"We have the evidence. I thought you ought to know that in advance. We know you were in the Oval Office when the order for that raid was given, and we know it was after the initial CIA finding. We also know there was a deliberate effort to make it appear that no one from Langley was anywhere near the White House that day, but in fact, one very important CIA operative was there, and you relayed the order through him."

"I gave no orders, directly or indirectly, to conduct that raid," John Harris snapped, "and I'm not about to engage in a debate with you on this meritless nonsense. In fact, there is no point to this conversation."

"Oh, I think there is. I know you to be a statesman, John, and running from this action is beneath your dignity. Since you no longer have a Chief of Staff to remind you of this, then I might as well be the one to do so."

Harris chuckled. "So now you expect to *shame* me into surrendering to Peruvian jurisdiction? Stuart, please, you know better than that. You're asking me to voluntarily agree to face bogus charges in a monkey trial run by a dictator in Lima who has sworn to execute me? Don't hold your breath."

"We're in Italy, Mr. President. I expect you to submit yourself to Italian jurisdiction and let the Italian courts decide if and when you should go to Lima, and I can assure you that despite your scandalous characterization of the Peruvian president and the Peruvian courts, they are a civilized nation in full compliance with international law and with this treaty, which is more than I can say for the United States. The John Harris the world knows . . . the moralist and statesman . . . would do the right thing and stop this little escape attempt, which is clearly beneath the dignity

of perhaps the only American President to ever refuse
guaranteed reelection. By the way, I've always thought
your devotion to the concept of a single six-year term was
exceptional and historic."

"I see no purpose in continuing this exchange, Sir
William, and your backhanded compliments are of no interest to me. You're far too good a lawyer to be rolling dice
with the Italian courts. You had this all set up, but you
didn't expect me to slip out of your grasp."

"You haven't escaped in any event, have you? You're
still here, just a short distance away from where I'm standing."

"Don't create a diplomatic confrontation, Stuart. You
can't win it. It didn't work for you fifteen years ago, and it
won't work now."

"That was then; this is now. You've certainly assumed a
cocky attitude for a Republican asking a Democratic President to rescue him. Your faith in President Cavanaugh is
misplaced. Surely you know that."

"Sitting American Presidents, as a rule, are disinclined
to see former American Presidents mistreated, arrested, or
subjected to show trials. Good day, Stuart. Contact Mr. Jay
Reinhart, my attorney, for any further discussion." He
passed the number in Wyoming and disconnected before
getting out of the copilot's seat and returning to his seat,
visibly angry.

"What was that about?" Sherry asked, but he waved her
off, his mind increasingly consumed with remembering
everything he could about the events leading to the disastrous Peruvian raid.

"It's just a matter of minutes now, sir," Sherry was saying.

He sighed and rubbed his eyes. "It'd better be, Sherry. I
really want out of here."

✈ **SIXTEEN**

The White House—Monday—12 Noon Local

President Jake Cavanaugh burst through the east door of the Oval Office and moved immediately to the front of his desk, motioning to the Press Secretary to turn down the volume on the television.

"Okay, everyone, what do I need to know before we get Harris out of there?"

Jack Rollins had been standing beside the desk when the President entered. He caught the President's eye and pointed to the screen.

"Take a look, sir. We've got it in living color, playing for a worldwide audience."

The President turned and moved toward the TV, his arms folded. "What am I looking at? CNN?"

"Unfortunately, yes." Rollins briefed him on the line of soldiers and vehicles waiting just behind a now-open gate to the Sigonella Naval Air Station flight line, and the fact that the Navy commander was ready to escort President Harris to the Air Force craft.

The President turned to survey the room, counting noses one by one.

"Where's Langley?"

"The Director is on his way here from New York, and I didn't press Langley to send the Deputy Director," Rollins answered.

"We need them in on this as soon as possible." He looked at Jack Rollins and shook his head as he gestured to the television. "Obviously, with CNN providing the pictures we don't need the National Reconnaissance Office."

"Different world, isn't it?" Rollins agreed.

"What are the Italians saying?" the President asked, turning to single out Assistant Secretary of State Rudy Baker, who was by the couch folding a cell phone.

"Sir, they've sent a formal request to our ambassador asking for our permission to let the Italian Carabinieri gain access to that flight line for the purpose of serving the warrant and making their arrest. Interestingly enough, the Italian government is pretending that they do not have the legal right under the lease to enter the flight line. They have to know better, so they're buying us time. They obviously don't want this party in their backyard."

"Some party," the President growled. "So we're not going to screw up relations with Rome by plucking Harris out of there?" he asked.

"No, sir. Not substantively."

"Is the Secretary of State up to speed?"

"Yes, sir," Baker replied. "He's airborne over some godforsaken corner of Australia right now, but I briefed him fully and he concurs that they're purposefully giving us a window to get Harris out of Italy. That doesn't mean Rome won't scream and cry and rattle our cage in public for a while, but it will have no impact on keeping the base."

"That would worry me if the Status of Forces Agreement for that base were in trouble," the President said.

"We do not want to lose that base, Mr. President," General Davidsen confirmed. "I'm relaying that for the Joint Chiefs, sir."

The President nodded as Diane Beecher sounded an

alarm from behind his desk where she'd been watching the TV screen. "Someone's moving a vehicle through that gate!"

The President turned to the screen as he gave a "wait" gesture to the general. "That looks like a single car. A staff car, maybe?"

"Could be, sir," Beecher said. "The other vehicles in that line are still sitting there."

"What are my options, Jack?" The President asked the Chief of Staff.

"One, you give the word, and we pull him out right here, right now. Two, we stall while we arm-twist the Italians to ignore their treaty obligations and let him leave on some chartered aircraft, since there's no civilian airline service there. Three, we do absolutely nothing right now, leave him to be arrested without apparent American intervention, and then use Justice and State to try our best to help quash that warrant and get him released through the normal legal process under the treaty. Four, we do nothing at all now or later and let it take whatever legal course it will."

"Option four is nonsense, Jack."

"You asked for all options, and we've had this discussion before, sir."

"Is there anything to accomplish by stalling and talking?" the President asked, turning to the group. "Anyone?"

Rudy Baker sighed and shook his head. "No, Mr. President."

"That leaves me with two options. To rescue or not to rescue." President Cavanaugh stood in silence for a moment, his eyes wandering to the far wall before looking at Jack Rollins again. "How do I do this?"

"What do you mean, sir? Get him out?"

"Yes. If I'm ready, and I think I am, what do I do?"

"Just tell me it's a 'go,' Mr. President," General Davidsen said quickly, gesturing with the phone. "I've got Captain Swanson on the line, and the C-17 aircraft commander holding, sir. The second you tell me, we'll move. President Harris is waiting at the door of the 737 as we speak."

"Okay," the President said, turning to the others, "I think we should do it. Let's get him out of there."

The President turned toward General Davidsen as a voice rang out from the other side of the room.

"Just a minute, Mr. President."

The National Security Advisor, Michael Goldboro, stood suddenly from where he'd been sitting near the fireplace. The President turned, puzzled, before seeing Goldboro, who moved forward slightly, his head cocked. The general turned as well, alarm showing on his face. "We're out of time, sir," the general said.

Once again the President's right hand went up in a "wait" gesture to the general as his eyes fixed on Michael Goldboro.

"What is it, Mike?"

"This would be a mistake, Mr. President," Goldboro said in a calm tone of voice. There had been a few other murmurs of conversation in the room, but they all ceased as everyone's attention turned to Goldboro.

"Explain, please," the chief executive said.

"Consider what message we'll be sending to the world if we whisk President Harris out of harm's way in a United States Air Force military aircraft. We're saying that the Treaty Against Torture should be used against an Augusto Pinochet, or perhaps a Saddam Hussein, but it doesn't apply to American leaders."

"That's ridiculous!" General Davidsen began, but the President cut him off with a quick look.

"This *warrant* is ridiculous, Mike," the President replied. "We're saving an American President from a bogus warrant and a trap."

"Does the rest of the world know that, sir? Has the legal process under that treaty we signed run its course and made the determination that there is no legal merit to that warrant? I know that's a rhetorical question, but it's a vital one."

"That legal process, Mike," the President replied, his hands migrating to his hips, "is what's flawed here. The fact that Peru could get some alleged Peruvian judge to sign an alleged legal instrument they loosely call a warrant, a thinly disguised death warrant, in fact, which President Miraflores probably wrote himself . . . none of that justifies using a legal structure designed to protect the world against real torturers and murderers."

"Mr. President," Goldboro continued, his voice steady and subdued, his eyes locked on the President, "to the rest of the world, especially the Third World nations, we are, at times, an arrogant bully, and that perception has caused us untold trouble for decades in every matter from economics and trade to our attempts to advance human rights. Most of that misperception comes from being the most powerful and economically dynamic nation on earth. But some of it has been deserved, from the necessary arrogance of the Monroe Doctrine to the unnecessary arrogance of too many CIA adventures in decades past."

"Mr. President, we really don't have time for this debate," General Davidsen said.

The President turned sharply to the general. "Bill, that's enough! I'll tell you when I'm ready to end the debate, as you call it."

Davidsen frowned but nodded immediately. "Yes, sir."

The President turned back to the group. "I want to hear every bit of what any of you has to say about this. I realize this has important overtones, even though I'll tell you I'm still convinced we've got to do it. But continue, Mike."

"Very well, sir. Look, I want President Harris out of there, too. I have great regard for the man. But if you give General Davidsen over there the green light for this rescue, you'll be feeding the lurking suspicion in the world that the United States has not changed its ways from the days when we actually did plot the overthrow of governments and the occasional assassination of dangerous foreign leaders, and tried to dictate economics and morality to everyone. I don't believe we can afford to feed that perception, regardless of whether it's right or egregiously wrong. Mr. President, you must focus here on the appearance of arrogance as much as the legality of the thing. That appearance, if fed by this rescue, will set us back in more ways than I could tell you in a year of briefing papers. The world needs our leadership, but to the extent we appear to be a self-serving bully to whom international laws apply only at our convenience, we seriously diminish our capacity to lead. There is a legal process here that we endorsed, and that process alone must determine whether this warrant has merit, not the fact that we can call in a C-17 and rescue whomever we want."

"That process is clearly flawed," Assistant Attorney General Alex McLaughlin said, "which no one realized at the time of ratification."

Michael Goldboro shook his head. "The reality is that using legalistic interpretations to justify what we're considering is arrogance. If we're to be the champion of international law, it's our responsibility to conform to its principles. In our domestic legal system, what do we tell ourselves? If a law is bad, a procedure flawed, work to change the law or procedure, not ignore or disobey it. We must honor international law with the same dedication."

"Mr. President," Jack Rollins said, "there's additional activity around that gate. I really do think it's probably now or never."

The President turned to General Davidsen. "What's the status, Bill?"

"That staff car is in position to intercept President Harris, sir, and the rest of them may move on the ramp at any moment. Jack's right."

The President turned back to Michael Goldboro. "Mike, what changes would fix this, and how would that process be served by leaving Harris to twist in the wind? Quick answer. We don't have time for a panel discussion."

"Modify the treaty with a specific procedure, requiring a preliminary hearing on any warrant to determine quickly and fairly whether it sets up valid charges. Each nation can hold such a hearing in accordance with its own legal system as long as it's fair. If the evidence is insufficient, the warrant is quashed then and there and the former head of state or whoever is free to leave in a few weeks."

"There's a helicopter with Italian military markings landing in front of the 737," Diane Beecher said.

President Cavanaugh nodded. "All right. Then let's get him out of there, tell the world why, and then put on a full court press to make the case for an addition to the treaty."

"From what position of moral authority, Mr. President?" Goldboro shot back. "The moment that C-17 lifts him off Italian soil, we have no moral authority on this issue, and we will not be able to change the treaty. Once again it'll be the might of the United States of America making right."

"Excuse me, Mr. President, may I add something?" General Davidsen said.

The President nodded, his eyes still fixed on his National Security Advisor.

"Sir," Davidsen began, "we have an assumed imperfection in a treaty. He's suggesting we essentially sacrifice a former Commander in Chief in order to be able to raise the issue that a new procedure is needed. Sir, excuse me, but that's bullshit!"

"Okay, Bill," the President said.

"No, sir. With all due respect, let me finish. If the Italians want this problem off their shores, and they most obviously do, then they'll find a way to send him to Lima if we leave him there, and then we're into a monstrous propaganda problem and maybe even the spectacle of a U.S. President facing a firing squad or climbing a gallows. It's absurd to knuckle under to the possibility that some Third World nations will take this as an example of arrogance."

"Alex?" the President said, looking at McLaughlin, then turning to Baker, "and Rudy . . . do you two think we can put enough diplomatic pressure on Italy to keep them from shipping John Harris out of the country before we can get full judicial process on the merits of the warrant?"

"I don't understand the question, sir," Alex McLaughlin replied.

"Nor do I," Rudy Baker said.

"Okay, quickly. The main danger here is that Harris gets whisked away to Lima. I agree that must not happen."

Alex McLaughlin was shaking his head. "It's very unlikely the Italians will foster that, but they can't control their judiciary any more than we control ours."

"From State's point of view," Baker added, "the Italians are trying to help us right now. God only knows what kind of political pressures they may face in the next few hours, days, or weeks. You want certainty? Getting Harris on that

C-17 right now is the closest version of it you're going to get."

The President turned and paced to one end of his desk in absolute silence as General Davidsen held the telephone receiver and watched him for the slightest sign of a "go" gesture. Taking a deep breath, Jake Cavanaugh turned toward his Chief of Staff and shrugged.

"The hell of this office is dealing with the reality that so often doing the right thing will yield the wrong result, while doing the wrong thing is even worse."

"Sir?" Jack Rollins prompted.

"Mike's wrong to discount the role of perceived power and occasional arrogance in keeping us strong. It's still a vital tool of American foreign policy in a dangerous world. But he's right about our responsibilities. The way to tame a dangerous world is through respectable leadership." He shook his head. "I can't do this."

"Sir?" General Davidsen said, his mouth dropping open.

The President took another deep breath and turned toward the general.

"Get that C-17 off the ground immediately. Without President Harris. Rudy? Have our ambassador relay this decision to the Italians with my personal request for rapid negotiation on how we may cooperate to protect both due process and our former chief executive. I'll want to talk to them within the hour, and I'd like the Italian ambassador here as fast as possible. Diane? Stay a few minutes along with Jack so we can figure out what to say when this hits the media. Who has the connection to President Harris? I'll tell him personally."

"Line four, sir," Jack Rollins prompted.

"Mr. President," General Davidsen began, "are you sure? I mean, before we let that C-17 go . . ."

President Cavanaugh turned to look him in the eye as he placed his hand on the general's shoulder.

"Yes, Bill. I'm sure."

✈ SEVENTEEN

The frustration of not being able to access the same live broadcast of the Sigonella flight line that half the world could see had driven Stuart Campbell to keep his staff in Brussels on the phone line from their conference room, where the projected TV image filled a wall. One of his partners narrated the scene as it unfolded, describing everyone moving on or around the ramp area in the picture.

"If a mosquito moves down there, I want to know," Campbell had demanded, listening carefully as his partner described the movements of people around the Boeing.

Without warning the C-17 had started engines and tax-ied away, leaving Stuart Campbell in a sudden quandary over whether John Harris might have somehow slipped aboard.

"Did you see anyone walk from one to the other?"

"Well, yes, as I said. Two mechanics, and several uni-formed officers, and one or two others. But always as many came out as went in the C-17."

"Were you taping it?"

"Yes."

"Play it back, and look very closely. See if Harris could have changed clothes with one of them and slipped out that way."

Several minutes passed.

"Ah, Stuart, I hate to tell you this, but looking at the tape? There's a man walking between two Navy officers and trying to stay invisible, but I can see him in the shot."

"Does it look like Harris?"

"He's about the same height, and he's wearing a suit coat, although the pants look like Navy uniform."

"Good Lord!" Stuart Campbell said.

"They walked directly from the 737 to the Air Force jet, but . . . only the two uniforms left. I'm afraid that's him."

"But it might not be."

"Maybe not, but whoever I'm looking at, at least no one dressed like that left the C-17, and the others were trying to conceal him."

"Damn him!" Campbell said, letting his mind race over the problem as his eyes fell across the note pad he'd been using. "I honestly thought that kind of escape was beneath him."

The name of one Jay Reinhart was inscribed on it with a number in the States. "All right, thank you. I'll ring you back shortly." He toggled the phone and dialed through the local system to a direct U.S. long-distance operator and passed the number. The response from the other end was immediate.

"Hello?"

"Is this Mr. Reinhart?"

"Yes. Who is this?"

"I don't believe we've met, sir, but I understand you're counsel for ex-President Harris."

"That's correct" was the caution-tinged answer. "And you are . . . ?"

"Stuart Campbell, counsel for the Peruvian Government, Mr. Reinhart. I need to speak directly to President Harris in that 737. I rang him a while ago not realizing he had hired an attorney . . . I called on their satellite phone . . . and I need to reestablish the connection, with you on the line, of course. I believe I may have a quick and easy solution that does not involve immediate extradition to Lima."

"Getting on the phone at this point is not possible, Mr. Campbell."

"And why would that be? It was possible fifteen minutes ago. I suppose I could request to go talk to him in person, but . . ."

"Did you see that C-17 depart, sir?"

"Yes," Campbell answered, suddenly off balance.

"Well, since I don't have a phone number for that aircraft, I can't help you."

"Are you implying, Mr. Reinhart, that President Harris is aboard the C-17? No one saw him leave the Boeing."

"And you're surprised, Mr. Campbell? This is a former U.S. President under the protection of the Secret Service. Now, when that C-17 reaches the U.S., perhaps we can arrange the conference you're seeking, but even if it were possible at this moment, it would serve no purpose."

"I see."

"In case I need to reach you, Mr. Campbell, may I have your phone numbers, please?"

Stuart Campbell passed the numbers by rote, his thoughts centered on the upsetting task ahead of informing Lima he had failed. He rang off and replaced the phone, then walked absently to the window as he explored the options.

There were none.

With Harris gone and under the protection of the U.S. Air Force, all that remained would be the task of presenting the warrant to a U.S. court, which would be akin to punching a giant marshmallow. It could take years of long, exhausting, and ultimately useless effort only to prove in the end that no American President was touchable by the treaty as long as American military might remained.

Well, old boy, you've been well and truly snookered, I should think.

He turned as the Deputy Foreign Minister walked in.

"Mr. Sigerelli, I believe that about concludes our business.

I assume you will want the Carabinieri to withdraw, and to that I have no objections."

Laramie, Wyoming

Jay cautioned himself to calm down. The phone would ring again, and this time with John Harris on the other end. Without a number he could call in Sicily, it would be up to the President to reestablish the connection.

There's no way this is going to work! he told himself. Yet Campbell had given him a totally unexpected opportunity and the words had formed without conscious thought, careful words that neither confirmed nor denied that the President was aboard the C-17.

Hearing Campbell's voice on the other end had been a true shock. The big man's deep, resonant tones were indelibly etched in his memory from a long time ago. He smiled at the fact that Campbell hadn't even recognized his name. Or was that a purposeful slight? No, he concluded. Too many years, too many miles to remember some faceless little lawyer back in the States. He wondered if even John Harris remembered that Campbell and Reinhart had met once on the legal battlefield. Probably not, and it wasn't worth mentioning at this point.

He got up from the kitchen stool and looked at the clock, wondering if he dared to block either inbound line long enough to cancel his three o'clock class. He would have to get to Europe now as fast as possible, but when and how were still unresolved issues, especially with events unfolding so rapidly.

Aboard EuroAir Flight 42, on the Ground, Sigonella Naval Air Station, Sicily

When President Cavanaugh had ended the conversation with an apology and a promise, ex-President John Harris had slowly lowered the telephone receiver, keeping his face a mask of impassivity.

"What is it, sir?" Sherry Lincoln asked, noticing that Captain Swanson had suddenly moved out of sight toward the front of the aircraft, his cell phone pressed to his ear. She knew the connection had been with the Oval Office.

John Harris took a deep breath and turned, smiling thinly. "I knew it was too easy," he said.

"Sir?"

He relayed the decision, shaking his head to neutralize the anger and shock showing on her face. "It's a tough call, Sherry, and he had to make it on a broader basis than just helping me."

"This is stupid!"

"It's done." He handed the receiver to her. "The conference call was through the White House. I'll have to call Jay back."

The sound of engines winding up had reached their ears through the open door of the 737. Through the left windows Sherry could see a puff of smoke billowing from the rear of the C-17's right outboard engine, making her feel like an unseen survivor watching the last chance for deliverance sail over the horizon. Her name would not be found on the warrant. Her passport would take her home at any time. But empathy and loyalty were incarcerating her emotions as effectively as if she were the target. There was a black hole out there labeled "Lima," and they were being sucked toward it like a leaf in a whirlpool.

Craig Dayton appeared in first class.

"Mr. President, I just heard."

He nodded. "They're leaving without me, Captain."

"What . . . would you like me to do, sir?" Craig asked in confusion.

John Harris shook his head. "I wish I knew."

"I . . . was expecting to let my passengers off when you left," Craig said as he looked toward the coach cabin.

The Navy base commander reappeared beside Craig Dayton, relaying the same news and asking the same question.

"Mr. President, I have no specific orders from Washington or my commander at the moment. I'm trying to figure out what to do."

"Are they closing in on us?" Harris asked.

Captain Swanson shook his head. "They're still respecting the flight line. That one car that came through is mine. I wanted it standing by."

"I was worried about that," Sherry said.

"Sir," the Navy commander said, "the way I see it, right now we have a standoff. Unless the Italians change their minds, they're going to leave this ramp alone, and this fellow Campbell . . ."

"William Stuart Campbell, Captain. World-class international lawyer from the U.K., a Knight of the British Empire, and a very substantial adversary."

"Understood. Unless the Italians cave, he'll be held at bay as long as you're out here."

"In this airplane, you mean?"

"Yes, sir."

"But this is a civilian airliner, and Captain Dayton here needs to get these passengers back to Rome. Is there a place I could safely stay on base?"

The Navy Captain shook his head, looking cornered. "No . . . sir. I mean, I'd put you up in admiral's quarters in a second, but the accommodations are not on the flight line, and worse, they're at the other base, NAS-One. To get you there we'd have to transport you through civilian Italian landscape where we have zero jurisdiction. The only place I can protect you is the flight line. The ramp. Here."

"Captain Dayton," Harris said, turning to Craig, "what if I personally paid for transportation for all these passengers wherever they want to go, and chartered this aircraft from EuroAir?"

"*Chartered* . . ." Craig asked, his mind flashing through the probability of Frankfurt agreeing to such a plan.

"Yes. Chartered. At premium rates, so we have a place to stay for at least a few hours. Captain Swanson? If I could charter this bird and the crew, can I leave with them?"

"I . . . hadn't thought about it, Mr. President. I guess the question is whether the Italian authorities would try to stop you the moment you taxied out of here."

"What's your best guess?"

"I wouldn't have one, sir, at this point. Not one I'd want you to stake your freedom on."

Craig turned toward the front of the plane lost in thought. He moved rapidly back to the cockpit, where Alastair was watching the C-17 disappear around the corner of the terminal.

"Get Frankfurt on the satellite phone for me."

"What? Are we throwing ourselves on the mercy of the chief pilot then?"

"No. We're going to charter ourselves."

"I beg your pardon?"

"Just . . . make the call and hand it to me."

Laramie, Wyoming

The live coverage from Sigonella had included a spectacular shot of the C-17 lifting off and banking immediately toward the west, literally disappearing into a beautiful sunset. The media knew that John Harris had been aboard the 737, and they knew that only a few mechanics and Navy personnel had entered or left the Boeing, but despite the absence of any video of John Harris leaving the EuroAir jet, the anchor in Atlanta was actively mentioning the possibility that John Harris had just departed, escaping whatever threatened arrest had been in the offing.

Jay looked at the phone again, a plan forming suddenly in his mind. He opened the cell phone and punched in the number for the White House Situation Room. They would be formulating a public response, and he might have only seconds.

✈ EIGHTEEN

The telephone some six thousand miles distant was answered on the first ring.

"Mr. Reinhart? Jay? This is Sherry Lincoln."

"Thank heavens, Sherry. There's a lot to tell you and I'm holding with the White House right now on another line. Where is the President?"

"Sitting next to me. Why?"

"In first class?"

"Yes."

"Who on that base knows he's still there?"

"I . . . what do you mean?"

"Who knows? Who's seen him? He hasn't stepped out the front door, has he, where anyone could spot him?"

"No. I suppose . . . uh, let's see. Other than those of us on the aircraft, the Navy commander, Captain Swanson and several of his aides, that's about it."

"Is Swanson still there?"

"Yes. He's talking on his phone."

"Please ask him not to talk to anyone about the President's presence on the aircraft. And keep him hidden."

"Who? The President? I don't understand."

"Yes. Keep the President hidden. Do the passengers know he's aboard?"

"They all did, but . . . I don't know."

"Listen very closely, please. Since the C-17 started engines, have any of the passengers seen him in your airplane?"

"He's been in his seat the whole time, and the curtain to coach is closed, and there are no other passengers in first class. Why?"

"Please, take the President to the . . . I don't know, maybe the forward galley. That's a 737?"

"Yes."

"Then get him in the forward galley without the coach passengers seeing him, and pull the curtain, if they have one, then ask the captain to get the rest of the passengers off the airplane, if he will. Also, do you have a cell phone I could reach there while you're on the ground?"

"Ah . . . yes, as a matter of fact. I forgot. Let me turn it on." She passed the number to him while she pulled it from her purse and hit the "on" button.

"Okay, Jay, I'm still not sure what you're planning."

"Please, just do what I'm asking, and get the Navy commander on this phone . . . and make sure the flight crew doesn't tell anyone he's still there."

Sherry took a deep breath and lowered the receiver as she took in John Harris's puzzled expression and made the decision to act before explaining. She put the phone on the seat and jumped up to find Captain Swanson in the entryway.

"Why?" Swanson asked her when she relayed the requests.

"I don't know yet, but this comes from his attorney. Wait a sec." The cockpit door was ajar and she opened it to see Alastair Chadwick handing a telephone handset to the captain, who turned and stopped as she entered.

"Sherry?"

She raised a finger to her lips and pointed to the phone,

and Craig covered the transmitter with his hand. "What's up?"

"The President's lawyer is asking that you please reveal to no one that he's still aboard. You haven't, have you?"

"No," Craig replied, looking at Alastair, who shook his head as well.

"Please don't. I'll be right back."

"What is he thinking?" Craig asked.

"I don't know," Sherry said as she turned.

Craig pulled at her sleeve as she turned to go. "Wait! I was just getting ready to try to charter this aircraft as President Harris asked."

"Hold off. Please!" Sherry said, turning to leave again and pulling the cockpit door closed behind her.

Craig sighed and shook his head as he raised the handset and promised the director of flight operations he'd call back in a few minutes.

"Bang on!" Alastair said suddenly when the connection had been broken. His face brightened into a broad smile.

"I beg your pardon?"

"Bang on, I said."

"I know *what* you said. It's what you *meant* that has me baffled. More Britspeak?"

"It means how bloody clever! They couldn't get the President on that C-17, but if they pretend they did, the men with the warrant go away."

"Pretend . . ."

"Yes. Pretend! He's not here, eh what? He sneaked out in plain view. We could probably fly back to Rome, discharge everyone, and go happily on our way and no one would pay the slightest attention to his presence. Of course, they'll be there to shoot *us,* but that's another story."

"But the passengers . . ."

"Probably haven't seen a thing since Fat Albert left."

"Fat *Albert?*"

"The C-17."

"No, no, Alastair. We called the C-5 Fat Albert. I don't know what strange names they have for the seventeen."

"Whatever. He's gone. That's our story and we're sticking to it, as the country-and-western song says. Bloody brilliant."

Laramie, Wyoming

"Mr. Rollins? Jay Reinhart here. Have you said anything to the media yet about President Harris not leaving Sigonella?"

There was momentary silence on the White House end of the call.

"No, but we're in the process of planning a release, and an explanation. Why?"

"I . . . suppose I can understand why President Cavanaugh decided not to pull President Harris out of there . . ."

"His reasons are sound, Mr. Reinhart, although I must tell you, completely off the record, that I was disappointed, too . . . that it didn't work out."

"It still can."

"No, the decision's made and the aircraft has . . ."

"I know that," Jay interjected. "But we still get most of the benefits if, for a few hours, at least, we let the other side of the equation *believe* he's on that C-17."

Jack Rollins repositioned the phone receiver and sat down behind his desk. "Go on."

"I talked to Peru's lawyer. He called me immediately after the C-17 left, and he was assuming that President Harris was aboard. I fed that assumption without actually saying so, and the upshot is, the lawyer, Campbell, and the Italian forces that were there to make the arrest are probably leaving. As long as they think President Harris is gone, I have a chance to engineer a civilian escape." He explained the idea of chartering the 737 and was gratified at Rollins's immediate response.

"The main reason the President canceled the operation, Mr. Reinhart, was the damaging message it could have sent. I doubt a little temporary charade would be a problem for him, as long as we clear it up at the other end."

"Thank you. What will you say?"

"Don't know, but I'd better get off this line and stop any releases. They're headed for the press room as we speak."

Aboard EuroAir Flight 42

Sherry Lincoln returned to her seat and sat down heavily, her head swimming with a mélange of hope and worry. She picked up the receiver to ask Jay Reinhart to wait while she briefed the President, but there was no answer—although she could hear Jay talking in the background against the slight hiss of the satellite connection. The bill for all the calls would be in the thousands, she figured, but Harris could afford it, and the thought of trying to deal with this nightmare without instant communication was a nightmare in itself.

She turned to John Harris and explained Jay Reinhart's idea and what they were doing to support it.

"You are kidding?" he asked at last with a skeptical expression.

"Not in the least. Why?"

He smiled as he stroked his chin and looked away. "I suppose it could buy us some time, Sherry, but I'm still in the crosshairs of that warrant. And there's the not so insignificant matter of the other passengers."

"The passengers are going to be off-loaded here in a minute as soon as we have you stashed in the forward galley."

"Why don't I just duck into the cockpit?"

"Italian journalists have telephoto lenses, too, and even through a cockpit window your face is familiar."

"Good point." He looked around carefully over his left shoulder before turning back to her. "Now? Should I go up there now?"

Sherry rose up to see over the seatbacks behind them. She nodded. "Go, sir. Keep your back to the curtain when you're in there, in case anyone tries to peek."

"I'll brief Matt and have him stand guard."

The President got to his feet quickly and moved toward

the galley, motioning to Matt Ward to follow as he slipped past.

Jillian had remained in the rear cabin with the other two flight attendants trying to keep tempers under control. Craig briefed her by interphone, then quickly left the cockpit to talk to Captain Swanson.

"I need to get these folks off the plane, sir. We've hidden the President in the galley."

"We have a military terminal right next to the ramp, you know," Swanson replied. "We can keep them in there for at least a few hours until you tell me what your company wants to do."

"Can some of your guys get their baggage off?"

"Sure. I can make that happen."

"How soon can I off-load the people, then?"

"Right now, if you like."

"In five minutes, then."

"You got it," Swanson said.

"Thanks, Captain," Craig said, starting to turn away as the senior Navy officer placed a hand on his shoulder.

"Look. The objective here is to protect the President. Unless I'm ordered to do something else, I'll support you any way I can, but I've got to warn you . . . and I know you're former Air Force . . ."

"Current Air Force, sir. I'm a major and a pilot in the active reserves. That's . . . kind of why I got myself into this to begin with this morning. Protecting the President. I've essentially lost my job for doing all this."

"I'm sorry to hear that, but I respect your sense of duty, Major. I just wanted you to understand that I could be ordered by my commander to change course and do anything from impound this airplane to God knows what. If it's legal, I'll have to obey."

"Understood, sir."

Craig moved quickly back to Sherry Lincoln's seat and knelt down. "Are you ready for us to off-load them?" he asked.

She nodded. "But one other favor, please. We want to charter the aircraft, but instead of the President being the client, it would be his staff doing the chartering. Tell your company we'll either wire money to them or use an American Express."

"I'll make the call, but that's a lot of money, Sherry. We could be talking thirty, forty, fifty thousand dollars, depending on how long and where."

"Not a problem. Just . . . don't say anything to diminish the idea that he's hanging over the Atlantic on the way home."

"Don't worry, I won't. But I've still got to figure out what to do about the passengers after they're off the airplane."

"I don't know. Can you charter another aircraft to take them back to Rome? We'll pay for that, too."

Craig sighed and inclined his head. "Maybe. Let me talk to the company once everyone's off."

He got to his feet and stopped, turning back to her. "What's the plan now, Sherry? I mean, where else can he go?"

"I don't know."

"I thought he'd be safe if we landed here because it's a U.S. base, you know? You are aware, by the way, that we can't make it back Stateside in this aircraft?"

"I'm aware of that."

"I mean, we could hop to Iceland, then to Canada I suppose, and maybe even make it safely from Iceland to the old Loring Air Force Base in Maine, but Iceland is a foreign country and if anyone gets wind of the President being on board, we may be back to square one."

She shook her head. "I don't know what the next step will be. His lawyer is literally making it up minute by minute and we're all trying to figure out what's next. I don't even know if they'll let us leave here."

Craig smiled and arched a thumb in the direction of the forward door. "Captain Swanson told me that the Carabinieri have left the base, and Campbell is on his way back to his Learjet. I'm not sure how, but they took the bait."

Craig returned to the cockpit, stopping at the forward galley to check on the President. Matt Ward intercepted him as he touched the curtain. The Secret Service agent moved back as soon as he recognized the captain.

"Is he ready?" Craig asked.

"Yes."

"Jillian's coming forward to help guard the curtain and the galley."

"Good," Ward replied. "I'll be just inside."

Craig stepped into the cockpit and slid into his seat to brief Alastair before pulling the PA microphone out of its cradle.

> *Ladies and gentlemen, this is the captain. I promised that as soon as that C-17 left and we had this problem resolved, we would let you get off the airplane. We're ready now. Please bring all your personal belongings and deplane through the forward left door, the same one you came in. I will be in the passenger lounge in a few minutes to answer questions and tell you how we're going to get you to your destinations.*

Craig did the same announcement in French and German before turning around to lock the cockpit door.

"Get the company back on the line, Alastair, if you would please. We're going back to the let's-charter-ourselves chapter."

✈ NINETEEN

Sigonella Naval Air Station Flight-Line Ramp—
Monday—6:40 P.M.

For a man with a six-foot-four-inch frame, climbing into the compact cabin of a Learjet Model 35 was always a minor challenge. But Stuart Campbell eased himself into one of the leather seats of his Lear with practiced ease and unfolded a wall-mounted table. In his peripheral vision he saw the Navy car that had brought him from the NAS-One part of the base to his aircraft pull away to a respectable distance and park.

He reached for the onboard satellite phone and stopped, his hand hovering just short of picking it up.

You're moving too fast, your tubship! he thought to himself, specifically using the derogatory pet name a former lover had given him when he purchased an estate in Northumberland, which came with the amusing title, "lordship of the manor."

"Tubship, I should think," his lady decided.

He'd been a few pounds heavier then, as well as thoroughly unfamiliar with the institution of regular exercise,

but the intervening years of workouts had shed the once-
developing pot belly, along with the young woman who'd
declared it unlovable. Only the epithet remained, and for
some reason it still amused him.

Campbell leaned forward, intertwining his fingers on
the small desk as he concentrated on the flaw in his thinking. The shock of apparently losing Harris to an American
rescue had obscured the fact that he had no real confirmation yet that the rescue had actually occurred.

Could that sly old bastard still be on that 737? he wondered. Probably not, but he should put off the call to Lima
until he was certain.

The captain of the Learjet came in the door as his employer hauled himself out of the seat and back onto the
ramp.

"You and Gina stay here, Jean-Paul," he said, smiling at
the female copilot, who was also Jean-Paul's wife. "I'll be
back."

As his feet touched the concrete, the Navy staff car
lurched into gear and headed back toward the Lear. The
driver's mission, Campbell was sure, being to keep him
under tight control.

Aboard EuroAir Flight 42, on the Ground, Sigonella Naval Air Station, Sicily

One hundred eighteen passengers trundled down the
airstairs and across the leased Sicilian ramp as the last ves-
tiges of twilight faded around Sigonella, casting an un-
earthly glow about the summit of Mt. Etna to the northeast.
All the helicopters had departed, the two from competing
Italian television outlets leaving the moment their assignment editors had learned that the American mission was
complete and the former American President was on his
way back to the United States—a myth propelled and per-
petuated by several key interviews given by an unnamed
source at the White House. John Harris's presence on the
Air Force jet had not been confirmed by the source, but the
fact that an official reception was being planned for the C-

17's arrival in D.C. had been happily relayed and was entirely true. There was, of course, the small, unmentioned detail that the assigned reception committee consisted of a low-ranking White House aide and a steward, both of whom were expecting to "receive" only a tired aircrew on arrival at Andrews AFB. The resulting misunderstanding by the media had flashed around the globe: *"Arrest of American Ex-President Foiled by Air Force Rescue!"* The headlines instantly lowered the news value of Flight 42's displaced passengers.

In the cockpit of EuroAir Flight 42, Captain Craig Dayton watched the exodus of his passengers as he waited for EuroAir's director of operations to answer the satellite line. It was not a call he'd been looking forward to.

"They want to do *what*?" the director of operations, Helmut Walters, asked from Frankfurt.

"Two things, sir. First, charter this aircraft for at least two days. Second, pay for whatever charter you can get together to take the passengers out of here and bring them back to Rome. They also want to pay for any additional expenses this diversion has cost."

"Captain Dayton, you call that a diversion? None of us yet knows what you were doing! Were you hijacked?"

"No." Craig sighed as he rubbed his forehead and tried to choose the right words.

"At one time Rome Control thought you'd crashed. *We* thought you'd crashed! Wait . . . I'm putting you on speakerphone. The chief pilot is here, too. We all want to know what you were doing."

"All right, here's the deal," Craig began. "I had a situation in Athens where I thought we were about to be either hijacked or attacked. I wasn't sure whether we were facing the outfall from a Greek coup d'état or a direct assault because of the presence of the former U.S. President."

He could hear consternation on the other end.

"Captain, operations said they told you to hold at the gate, and yet you started and blew over all sorts of things backing out," the operations director said.

"And you may have hurt the engines with foreign object

damage, Dayton," the chief pilot added, "not to mention the fact that backing out violated all our procedures."

"Gentlemen," Craig countered, "if I'd stayed there and been the victim of some bloodbath and lost our passengers and the airplane, would you feel the same? Keep in mind that I had no way of knowing whether someone was holding a gun to the head of the operations agent or not."

"But that was not the situation, eh, Captain Dayton?" the director of operations said.

"No, but it's all too easy for you to declare that now, in hindsight, Herr Walters, and to thump me on the head with the news that there was no real threat. But I perceived a threat! I perceived a major, immediate threat. And I was the one in command, right there, right then, who had to make a decision, and I'm always going to err on the side of safety. Would you want me to act otherwise? Certainly our passengers wouldn't."

There was sudden silence from the other end, and Craig could tell they'd been momentarily halted by the logic of his argument.

"Very well, Captain, but why did you then fail to land in Rome, fly to Sicily, keep your passengers cooped up, and make Rome Control think you were crashing?"

"Same reason, sir. Whatever or whoever was after us at Athens appeared to be lying in wait in Rome for reasons I absolutely cannot discuss on a nonsecure telephone connection."

Craig could see Alastair stifling a laugh in the right seat as he continued.

"I was completely convinced that everyone aboard was at risk, and I chose Sigonella because it was an American base, I had an American ex-President aboard being chased by God knows who, and I felt my passengers—who included an American tour group of forty-four, by the way—would be far safer here than anywhere else. I don't know the Italian military bases. I do know this one. And, okay, why the sudden descent without the transponder into here? Because, if you didn't know it, we were being literally followed by another aircraft and several fighters, and I wanted to lose them. I wasn't interested in being shot down on final approach when

I'm most vulnerable and have no countermeasures or missiles on board."

At the mention of missiles, Alastair lost it, laughing quietly in the right seat as he covered his mouth and shook his head. Craig looked at him and almost lost control as well, holding his voice barely in check as he listened to the increasingly befuddled response from Frankfurt.

"That's . . . what do you mean, shot down, Captain Dayton? Why would you think, for heaven's sake, that anyone would be trying to shoot you down?" the operations manager sputtered as the chief pilot weighed in.

"Dayton," the chief pilot snarled, "that is without a doubt the most delusional nonsense I've ever heard from an airline captain!"

"When you gentlemen hired me, you knowingly hired an experienced pilot with thousands of hours in top-of-the-line military fighter jets. In fact, Herr Wurtschmidt, I recall you yourself saying that was a very valuable commodity to this airline. As a veteran fighter pilot, I'm very sensitive to airborne threats that you may not even know exist, and if I overreacted here, then please explain to me who was chasing us and why."

"Well . . . we do not know that yet . . . it's still early . . ."

"Look," Craig said, "you can fire me or give me an award for bravery later. Right now, let's just get to the heart of what we need to do while we've got the crew duty time left to do it. Do we let these folks charter this aircraft or not? And before you answer, I've got a number for you to call in Washington, D.C."

"What number?"

He passed the name and telephone number. "That's the Chief of Staff of the White House. The call will be confidential. The United States Government is formally requesting our assistance."

"But . . . but I thought you said this would be paid for by credit card or a wire transfer? Now the American government is trying to charter us?"

"No. President Harris's staff is trying to charter us. Herr

Walters, have you ever had experience in the world of intelligence operations or security matters?"

"No."

"Then just trust me. There are reasons for paying for certain things by personal credit card or check or wire that are sometimes necessary for political and security reasons. Again, I can't explain over a nonsecure line."

More silence on the other end, and in the cockpit, except for the sound of the air-conditioning and the muffled chuckling from Alastair, which increased with the phrase "nonsecure line."

"Well," Walters said at last, "do you have any idea where they want to go?"

"Not yet. They may just want to stay here. Give them a price that covers everything."

"Very well. We will call you back. This is very irregular."

"Please, gentlemen. Call the White House first."

"We will. Thank you, Captain. And . . . you're correct. We want you to exercise your judgment for safety. We did not mean to imply we don't. We will need to discuss this at length when you return, but . . . very well. We accept your explanation."

"Thank you, sir," Craig said, as deferentially as he could manage.

He disconnected the call and turned to the copilot with his eyebrows raised in feigned innocence as Alastair audibly exploded in laughter.

"That . . ." Alastair said, pointing to his captain, "was by far the funniest . . . dishing of basic bull I've . . . ever heard!"

"I beg your pardon?" Craig managed, a huge, involuntary smile on his face as he tried in vain to look offended. "What do you mean, 'bull'?"

"A nonsecure line! HAH!" He wagged an index finger at Craig again. "*Missiles?* Blinking MISSILES, for Chrissakes? Good Lord, you're a bloody bullshit champion, Dayton!"

"I'm a fighter pilot. The terms are synonymous."

Laramie, Wyoming

If President Harris couldn't fly to the United States, Jay Reinhart had concluded, his lawyer would have to fly to him.

And fast.

No other plan made sense. There was only so much he could do by telephone from Wyoming and whatever battles lay ahead would have to be fought in person on the other side of the Atlantic. That meant another nauseating, close encounter with his least favorite activity: plummeting through the sky at insane speeds in an overcrowded aluminum tube otherwise known as a "jetliner."

Okay, he told himself, *I have to fly there. I'll be okay. I have no choice.*

Fear of flying was a phobia he'd tried to hide and conquer all his adult life with only limited success. He'd taken courses, used hypnosis, patches, pills, and platitudes, but ultimately it always came down to the same simple, barely controllable fear of engaging in the unnatural act of being supported by nothing but air.

I will fly to Europe. Or London. Or Paris. I won't enjoy it, but I'll do it.

Jay sighed, realizing he'd been drumming an increasingly frantic beat on the kitchen counter with the tip of his pen.

First things first! he cautioned himself. The prime problem was picking a place to send the President, if he could be extricated from Sigonella at all. Italy was not the best place to fight the battle. He didn't speak Italian and the system was based on Napoleonic Civil Law: significantly different from British and American Common Law, enough to leave the average American lawyer or British solicitor feeling like a fish out of water in most of the Continent's courtrooms. There were exceptions, of course. There were some British, Irish, Scottish, and even some American lawyers specifically schooled in civil law and admitted to practice in one or more of the European courts. And there were a few superstars of international practice such as Sir William Stuart Campbell. For the rest—even

someone as expert in international legal matters as he—
not being a member of the local bar meant having to hire
the right local firm or local lawyer and possibly struggling
to make sense of what he or she was doing.

He understood the law and the myriad variations of European practice, but he had never taken the time to attempt
admission. Even in the U.K. he would need a local solicitor and barrister, though he wouldn't be allowed to speak
in open court.

I've got the priorities wrong, he decided. *I've got to figure out how to get myself over there first.*

In the few breaks between the vital transatlantic calls
he'd been fielding, Jay had tried to find which nonstop
flights left from Denver to European destinations. It had
been a disjointed effort represented by wildly scribbled
notes in the margins of the third legal pad as he raced back
and forth to his computer to make the inquiries.

There was only one, a new daily United nonstop to
London. All the others made at least one stop somewhere
on the East Coast.

"Regardless of where you end up, John, I can get airline
connections from London," he had told the President during the last call, "but I'll be partially out of contact for up
to ten hours."

"Book only first class for yourself, Jay," the President
had directed, "and only on an airline that has satellite
phone service."

"But . . . that's thousands of dollars more," Jay had
replied, looking for excuses to stay in coach, which was
considerably closer to the tail than any first class cabin.
His stomach churned at the prospect of being in the very
front of an airplane. Despite the impassioned pleas of an
airline pilot friend that he was holding onto a groundless
myth, Jay refused to believe a passenger wasn't safer in the
back.

"I'm perfectly okay flying coach."

"I won't hear of it," John Harris had replied. "It's the
cost of doing business. Think about it, Jay. I need you
working and communicating all the way across the Atlantic. Only first class."

"If you insist," Jay said as he fought the conclusion that he'd just been sentenced to die in a plane crash.

"Okay, let's talk about what we're going to do. What's your strategy?" John Harris asked.

"I wish I had one!" Jay replied. "Right now, I'm still trying to guess how long this little charade about where you are is going to work. I mean, we probably have at least as long as it takes the C-17 to get to Andrews, but what then? That 737 you're on can't carry enough fuel to fly nonstop across the Atlantic, so even if we can charter that aircraft and crew and get you out of there, we have to face the prospect of landing you somewhere else outside of U.S. control, and that means we've got to expect Campbell will be there, wherever that is, with the warrant and local authorities."

"Suppose we don't tell anyone where we're going to land? Could Campbell move that fast?"

"The pilots have to file a flight plan, John. I promise you Campbell will be informed of the destination as soon as its filed."

"But, Jay, if they believe that just my staff is on board and I'm gone, who'll know?"

"The media. They'll be waiting at Andrews Air Force Base when the aircraft arrives and they won't see you get off. That's when the cat will depart the bag at high speed."

"But . . . let's suppose they arrange to taxi the aircraft right into one of the Air Force One hangars and out of sight. I mean, I've been there, Jay, as President. Those hangars are huge!"

"You're overlooking something really basic," Jay said, shifting the phone to his other ear. "Cavanaugh decided he couldn't pull you out of there because the U.S. couldn't be seen as an international hypocrite when it comes to enforcing a major treaty."

"I know. He explained his reasons to me. I can't fault him."

"Well, he's agreed to smokescreen the media for a little while to help us, but that's probably as much as he can do, since this ruse to fuzz up where you are carries a lot of political risk."

John Harris sighed. "I know. I was trying to ignore that. He really does need to tell the world he didn't stiff-arm the warrant."

"I've been flipping through the channels, John. The negative publicity and second-guessing has already started, and Cavanaugh's likely to get a double backlash. I doubt we can rely on the White House for anything else until this actually lands in a courtroom. I mean, it's true that many Americans are going to be outraged that he left you there, but when the media finds the White House pulled a half-truth deception, they'll howl that the President personally orchestrated it specifically to help you escape international justice. And, his opposition will scream that he didn't have the guts to do the job right by using the Air Force. Either way he loses whatever value he might have gained by leaving you there. And just watch. As soon as everyone knows you're still in Sigonella or anywhere else in Europe, Campbell will race there with the warrant. I'm sure he's got every country covered."

"I'm sure you're right, Jay," Harris replied, falling silent for a while. "You know," the President began, his voice betraying fatigue, "I wonder if the right thing to do . . . the best thing . . . wouldn't be to just pick the best place and surrender. After all, this is a borderless process, and I do support the basic idea of the treaty."

"Well . . ."

"When Campbell called here in the plane, he said to me that the act of running from this warrant is beneath my dignity. Jay, he may well be right."

"I don't know, John. If I could be sure . . ."

"Maybe we'd be best off figuring out which country would never accelerate the extradition process, and just accept the arrest there. I am scared of this thing, Jay. It scares me because there's always an outside chance some judge will go temporarily insane and grant Campbell's request, and you know if they ever get me to Lima, I won't get out for a long, long time, if ever."

Jay closed his eyes and tried to think it through. "John, surrendering is too big a risk. And you're not being a hypocrite to avoid an illicit warrant. We do know it's illicit, right? I mean, I hate to ask . . ."

"Of course," Harris replied quietly. "Of course it is."

"Well, then you know Campbell. Hell, John, he *wrote* that treaty, and I'll give you even money he's already constructed a detailed plan on how to accelerate the extradition process in a half dozen countries, if not all of them. The man is famous for thinking way ahead of the game. That's what frightens me the most. You could end up trapped somewhere for a year, and *still* be sent to Lima!"

"Only if a judge ruled the warrant valid, and I don't think that would ever happen in a properly constituted common law system. Think about it, Jay. Think about whether I should just surrender or not. Get yourself on a plane moving in this direction, but think about it, because . . . I'm not sure trying to run from this is the right thing."

"I will."

"And consider the U.K. Maybe I should go there and surrender. They were careful with Pinochet, even if they were only temporarily ready to pack him off to Spain a year later. After all, the English system is the mother of our system—absent the sanctimonious wigs, of course."

"I always liked those wigs, John. They lend dignity to a process that's often anything but dignified."

There was another long sigh from Sigonella. "Well, that's the operative word, isn't it?"

"Sir?"

"Dignity. I do not want to do something undignified, Jay, no matter how frightened I might be. Even out of office, an American President carries the dignity of the office with him, and I'm trying hard not to forget that."

✈ TWENTY

Sigonella Naval Air Station, Sicily, AMC Passenger Terminal—Monday—7:45 P.M.

For the past hour, Edwin Glueck had been quietly moving among the milling passengers in the Air Mobility Command passenger lounge, talking quietly one by one to the male members of his tour group.

Twenty years had gone by since he'd retired as a U.S. Army brigadier general, but his mind and his instincts were still sharp—even at the age of seventy-nine.

His wife of twenty-six years, Joanie, was in a far corner of the terminal talking to the tour director to keep her distracted. Ed glanced in her direction, pleased at her image. She was still attractive and even shapely at sixty-nine, and the sight of her now momentarily ignited other desires, threatening to divert him from the mission.

Joanie saw him looking and smiled back, nodding just enough to let him know she had things under control. She was exceptionally aware of what was going on around her, he thought. Before they'd left the aircraft, no one else had noticed as he strolled the aisle and momentarily glanced through the curtains separating coach and first class. No one but Joanie, that is. She'd known instantly that something was up.

"I shouldn't ask what you're up to, should I?" she'd said in a whisper after the captain announced the delay was over and they'd be leaving the 737.

"No," he'd replied. "But I'll tell you anyway. President Harris didn't leave. He's still on this aircraft."

She knew that tone of certainty and respected it. He wasn't always right, of course, but when he focused on a problem, the General—as his grandchildren called him— could be trusted to be on target the majority of the time.

"Did you see him?"

"No."

"Then how can you be sure?" she countered.

"Trust me."

"Always."

When they were filing out, the General had pretended to stumble as he passed the forward galley, his foot deftly flipping up the bottom of the galley curtain as he bent over and braced himself against the forward bulkhead for a second before straightening up. The fleeting view beneath the curtain had revealed what he expected: two pair of men's shoes in a crew section of an aircraft carrying three female flight attendants.

Two men hiding in the galley. If it's not the pilots . . .

He stepped onto the top platform of the airstairs and reached down to adjust his pant leg in order to glance back toward the cockpit.

Both pilots were inside, clearly identifiable by their uniform shirts.

None of those who walked to the C-17 looked like him, so he's still here, and he's hiding, which means he's still in serious danger.

The general said nothing as he descended the airstairs and walked toward the terminal, a plan already forming in his mind.

• • •

Captain Swanson had just arrived at the passenger terminal when the information came that Peru's lawyer wasn't leaving immediately after all.

The reappearance of Stuart Campbell on the ramp and the call from the security officer driving the staff car that had immediately collected him startled the commander of Sigonella NAS.

"You've got to be kidding. I'll be there in five minutes to deal with this personally," he told the driver, chiding himself for failing to check with the control tower earlier to make sure Campbell's Learjet had departed with Campbell in it.

Obviously it hadn't.

Swanson jumped in his staff car and hesitated, thinking the situation through. He lifted the GSM phone connected only to his base's cellular network and dialed the driver's number, making sure his ear was pressed tightly to the receiver before issuing a specific set of orders.

"I'd like to go get aboard that EuroAir jet, Captain," Campbell told him when Swanson had emerged from the staff car.

"Why, Mr. Campbell?" Captain Swanson asked. "I thought your business with us here was concluded. I let you in before because you were with the Italian delegation, and the right of entry they were asserting was based on a treaty. Do you have some official claim to enter my base now?"

"None, whatsoever," Campbell replied pleasantly. "If President Harris left on that Air Force craft, officially, I have no reason to be here."

"What do you mean, 'If'?"

"This is merely a request for your courtesy and cooperation, Captain."

"I understand it's a request. But why are you making it?"

"You're a smart man, Captain, or you wouldn't be wearing those small eagles on your shoulders. You know we're dealing with very high-level international legal matters here, and you must know that I have to be certain of every step, and every occurrence."

"What are you talking about, sir? I'm also a very busy man right now."

"I need to make certain, Captain, by personal inspection, that Harris is no longer aboard that 737. Plain and simple."

Swanson worked hard to keep his expression virtually unchanged, but a small muscle was twitching in his cheek. He could feel it, but he couldn't stop it. "I see," he said, as evenly as possible.

"Is there a problem with that request, Captain?" Campbell asked in an overly solicitous tone of voice.

"Yes, sir. There is a problem. My superiors are not happy about my granting you and the Italians immediate access to this base to begin with, and I'm going to have to relay your request through channels."

"I know your theater commander personally, Captain. Would you like me to call him?"

"I'm quite capable of working through my own chain of command, Mr. Campbell," Swanson snapped, regretting the sharp response instantly. "Look, get in and we'll go back to my office and you can remain there while I make a call. Provided the aircraft is still here by the time I get approval, I'll be happy to take you out there personally."

Stuart Campbell smiled and cocked his head. "Captain, delay tactics raise suspicion. Especially my suspicion. If the President is truly gone, just let me get aboard and see for myself. Then I'll leave you alone."

"Sir, I told you . . ."

"Captain Swanson," Campbell interrupted, "you and I both know you have full authority to make that decision by yourself, which means you could say 'Yes' or 'No,' just like that. You've parked my aircraft and that chartered airliner as far down the ramp as you could to keep us under tight control, and that's fine. But now, the fact that you're willing to play an 'I've-got-to-get-approval' game means that you don't want to make the decision yourself, which, in turn, means that there's much more at stake here than just being criticized for making the wrong call. So what could be so serious that you need to stall? The fact that you and Washington have been pretending that President Harris is gone, when, in fact, he's still here. Otherwise, you'd just take me out there."

"That's absurd, Mr. Campbell. That kind of convoluted pseudo-reasoning leads to ridiculous conclusions."

"Captain, there is no legitimate need to get official approval from anyone, and that tells me that I probably need to call the Italian Foreign Ministry back out here."

"Very well, let's stop talking about this and go, Mr. Campbell," Swanson said suddenly, turning toward his car.

Campbell looked surprised, letting a broad smile slowly dominate his face. "Excellent! To the aircraft, then?"

"NO, sir!" Swanson replied in exasperation, turning back to him. "As I said, we're going to my office at NAS-One."

Stuart Campbell maneuvered himself around to look the naval officer in the eye. "Captain, on your honor as an American field grade officer, is President Harris on that C-17 or not?"

"I can't . . ."

"NO!" Campbell barked, causing Swanson to flinch. "You're making a representation by your actions. I'm asking for a straightforward statement from you, on your honor, on behalf of the Department of the Navy, on behalf of the American Government, and on the record. Is he on that C-17, or is he still somewhere on this base? If you tell me he's gone, I'll leave, based on the honor of your word alone."

"Sir . . ." Swanson began, hesitating just long enough to register the fleeting internal conflict Campbell was waiting for, "President Harris's status is classified military information. I am not at liberty to divulge that to you or anyone else."

Stuart Campbell nodded slowly, his eyes carefully noting Swanson's slightly accelerated breathing.

"Very well, Captain. I understand thoroughly. John Harris is still here."

"I didn't say that!"

"Oh, but you did. Very clearly."

Swanson shook his head as he leveled an index finger at the lawyer, his eyes angry slits. "Get in the car, Mr. Campbell. Now! Against my better judgment I'm going to violate my orders and take you down to the aircraft. And then, sir, you're going to get your sanctimonious ass off my base. Understood?"

"As you wish, Captain," Campbell said, noting that Swanson's radio was in plain view on the dashboard, cancelling any hopes the commander might have of making an emergency warning call to the EuroAir pilots.

Sigonella Naval Air Station Passenger Terminal

There was a young Navy policeman guarding the door to the ramp and the Boeing 737 beyond. He was just a boy in a sharp sailor suit, and little more than nineteen or twenty years old, General Ed Glueck thought. He'd watched the boy carefully for several minutes, trying to discern his level of sophistication, watching as he occasionally looked up to smile at the music on the PA system when it switched to something upbeat.

The general approached him quietly.

"Son?"

"Yes, sir?" the young sailor said, somewhat taken aback to be approached by one of the passengers.

"I want you to take a look at the rank on this ID card," the general said, handing over his gray U.S. Department of Defense credential card that identified him as a retired brigadier general.

The young man's eyes grew a bit wider. "Yes, sir, General. What . . . can I do for you?"

The general gently reclaimed the ID card and slipped it back in his wallet as he turned and looked at the milling passengers, speaking conspiratorially out of the side of his mouth.

"I need to get back out to that aircraft."

The Navy guard inhaled sharply and stiffened as conflicting duties swirled in his mind against the background of orders and limited experience.

This was a *general officer*! But this was a *retired* general officer.

"Sir, I . . . I can't do that . . ."

The general turned and leaned close to the boy's ear. "This is a matter of national security, son, and neither of us has time to seek formal authority. If your captain was here, I'd talk to him. But I need to slip out there right this minute. This is one of those times you were trained to expect where you have to be brave enough to do what you know is right even without formal authority."

"But, sir . . ."

"I'm unarmed, and my wife, Joanie, is standing right over there. Obviously I'm not going anywhere without her, and I can't be up to no good."

"Yes, sir, but my orders . . ."

"Are superseded by mine. I'm giving you the authority. You do realize that a general officer is never off active duty, by the way?" he fibbed, knowing full well that only five-star generals were never retired, and with the death of General Omar Bradley decades before, there were no more living five-stars.

"Really, sir?"

"Just open the door. I'll be back in ten minutes. All I need to do is confer with the captain of that airliner. If your captain gets upset, I'll explain everything. I outrank him anyway, don't I?"

"I suppose."

"Didn't they teach you that? A star beats an eagle?"

The young man nodded and swallowed as he surveyed the room and quietly turned the knob on the door behind him, letting Edwin Glueck slip into the cool and humid night air.

The distance to the aircraft was minimal, and he was in sufficiently good shape to jog to the airstairs. The forward door to the Boeing was closed but not sealed, and he knocked gently.

The man he'd suspected was a Secret Service agent peeked around the edge of the door and he slipped his ID card through. There were voices in the entryway before the door swung open and the man handed the card back.

"What do you need, General Glueck?" the man asked.

"Access to the captain."

"Why?"

"Because I know the President is still here and I've got a terminal full of U.S. military veterans ready to help protect him."

✈ TWENTY-ONE

Laramie, Wyoming—Monday—11:45 A.M. Local

The last direct flight of the day to Europe from Denver International was scheduled to leave in less than three hours, and Jay Reinhart was still at his kitchen counter in Laramie, a hundred fifty road miles from the airport.

"There's got to be another way," he said to the travel agent whose help he'd enlisted on his cell phone.

"No, and I doubt you'd make it anyway. That snowstorm has U.S. two eighty-seven closed over the pass, and I hear there's a real mess on the interstate south of Cheyenne."

"How about Chicago? Could I fly through there? Or . . . or Atlanta?"

"Sure, but any transatlantic connections will probably leave tomorrow morning, getting you in late tomorrow evening."

"Dallas?"

"Same story. I can't even get you on a commuter to Denver in time. But, look, may I make a suggestion?"

"Are you kidding? I'm desperate."

"Charter an airplane to take you to Denver International. Even a Cessna can make it in an hour."

"Charter . . ."

"An airplane. Yes, sir. It's expensive, but if you really want to get on that last flight tonight, it's the only way."

The thought of fighting panic for eleven hours in a jumbo jet had been bad enough. Suddenly he found himself battling images of crashing to his death in a small jet, and a small wave of nausea pulsed through him.

"Mr. Reinhart?"

"What?"

"Did you hear me?"

"Ah . . ." He swallowed hard. "Yeah. Yeah, I . . . I'm sorry. That's the only way, huh?"

He thanked the agent and yanked the phone book out of the desk to flip to air charters, trying to keep his mind on anything but the fact that he was trying to pay money to get himself inserted into a small aircraft that would undoubtedly plunge to earth at the first opportunity.

Straighten up! People do this every day!

There were three charter operators listed, but none could help.

"I'm sorry, sir. All our birds are out for the day, including our Citation."

"Your what?"

"It's a jet."

"Oh. Could you recommend someone in Denver who could come get me?"

"We tried that an hour ago for another customer, Mr. Reinhart. There might be somebody available, but we couldn't find anyone. There's some big function going on in Aspen for the rich and shameless, and it's sucked all the charter aircraft out of the area."

"I'll pay double," he heard himself saying, feeling almost giddy at the thought of paying for his own demise.

"Sorry."

Jay replaced the phone with his mind racing. There had to be another way. No time to drive, no charters, no commuters, but . . .

The thought of a conversation with one of his students

during the fall semester flashed in his head. David somebody. He was a private pilot and had his own plane and they were arguing in good-natured fashion over whether humans should fly, with his vote firmly in the negative. Was there any remote chance, Jay wondered, that he might be available for hire? He would eat the requisite crow as long as he could get to Denver in time.

Dammit! What was the name? David . . . David . . . Carmichael! That's it!

He punched in the number of the University's registrar and begged for David Carmichael's number using the first excuse that came to mind.

"Good enough for me, Professor," the lady on the other end said, reading him two numbers.

The first didn't answer. The second one caught the graduate student between classes on his cell phone. Jay explained the situation and his desperation.

"Ah, I don't know, Professor Reinhart, the weather's kind of gamey today."

"It's too bad to fly?"

"Well . . . probably not, but I've also got a class."

"How about if I get you out of it? I can't tell you how important this is, David. This literally involves the life of a U.S. President."

"You said that. Wow. Well, uh, as long as the forecast isn't too bad . . ."

"You do still own your own plane?"

"Yes, I do. And it's instrument equipped, and I'm an instrument pilot, but you still want to be careful, y'know?"

"Absolutely. Look, I hate to push, but I have no other way to get to Denver fast enough. So can you do it for me?"

"I think I'm legal for passengers . . . I haven't flown for a few weeks, but I can probably be ready in about an hour."

"How about forty minutes? I'll pay you whatever you ask."

"I can't accept money, sir, except to pay for gas. I'm only a private pilot, not a commercial pilot."

"All right. But is forty minutes okay?"

"You want to go to Denver International?"

"Yes."

"I'd better get moving, then. I have to check the weather and file a flight plan. Where can I call you back, Professor?"

"Let's just meet out there, David."

There was a hesitation. "Oh. Okay." Carmichael passed directions on how to find the so-called fixed-base operator, or "FBO," at the airport where his plane would be waiting.

"I'll . . . see you there, Professor."

The thought of diving into a business suit without benefit of showering or shaving was anathema, but there was no time for anything else. The airspace in his bedroom was momentarily filled with socks and underwear and shirts as he tossed the minimum requisites into a suitcase and compressed his morning routine into ten minutes before racing out the door to the garage and into his car.

The image of his cell phone on the counter popped into his mind and he ran back to retrieve it, along with an extra battery and the charger, then returned to the car and opened the garage door on an overcast, gray sky—a reality he was trying hard to ignore.

David Carmichael had been a good student. He'd earned an A. Surely he was as good a pilot as he was a student. Surely he could find Denver in an overcast sky. Maybe they could fly low and follow the roads.

Carmichael was waiting for him at the door of the private terminal, a green headset in one hand and a small flight bag in the other. Jay forced himself to ignore the worried look on the young man's face.

"They're warming up the engine right now with a heat cart," he announced.

"I don't know what that means," Jay said. "Is that a problem?"

"No," Carmichael said. "But my plane's been cold-soaked for the last week, so that'll help get the engine started."

"Okay. This is a jet?"

David Carmichael's eyebrows shot up in surprise. "A *jet?* I wish!"

"What then?"

"It's a Cessna 172, Professor. A single-engine propeller driven four-seater. What'd you think?"

"I . . . don't know much about private planes," Jay managed, his stomach contracting to the size of a pea.

"Professor," Carmichael began carefully, recognizing the panicked look on Jay Reinhart's face as he placed a hand on his professor's shoulder, "this is a great, stable airplane. In fact, the Cessna 172 is the only aircraft in history to ever successfully penetrate Soviet air defenses."

"I'm sorry, what?" Jay managed.

Carmichael smiled slightly and shook his head. "Back in the eighties, some loon of a guy from Germany flew a 172 into Russia and landed in Red Square, and the entire Soviet Air Force couldn't shoot him down."

"Oh. Yeah. I think I remember," Jay said, his eyes falling on the tiny high-wing aircraft he'd spotted just out front on the ramp. He suddenly realized it was the very one David Carmichael was referring to. It didn't look big enough to carry a passenger, he thought. In fact, it didn't look big enough to carry a pilot!

"Weather okay?" Jay managed.

"Well . . ." David Carmichael began. "We'll have to go on an instrument flight plan. We'll be in the clouds all the way, but I think we'll be okay. No real icing predicted below twelve thousand, so, ah . . . as long as we don't encounter any, the turbulence shouldn't be too bad."

"What do you mean, icing?"

"I can't fly in known icing conditions. I don't have any deicing boots."

"Boots?"

"Rubberized devices on the leading edge—the front edge—of the wings that inflate to break off ice."

"Oh."

"I'll shoot an ILS to Denver."

The acronym meant nothing but Jay nodded. "Okay."

"It should take us about an hour."

Jay checked his watch, anxious for something to do other than think of the flight ahead. "We'd better get moving."

David Carmichael reached out and caught his arm. "Professor, this is really vital, right? There's no time to drive and no alternate flight you could take?"

Jay shook his head. There was a warning tone in Carmichael's voice, but Jay forced himself to ignore it, fearful he might change his mind. The image of Stuart Campbell closing in on John Harris loomed larger than his fear of flight. Surely David Carmichael was just reacting to the pasty look on his face. A pilot wouldn't fly unless it was safe.

David Carmichael sighed and glanced toward the airplane, then back at his passenger. "Professor, you might want to make a quick bathroom stop first."

Jay looked at him suspiciously, trying to form a coherent question as wild images flashed in his head.

"Why?" he managed.

"Because," Carmichael began carefully, "there's no bathroom aboard."

"Oh."

"The plane's too small."

"Of course," Jay heard himself say. "I'll . . . be right back."

"It's over there, sir," Carmichael prompted, pointing to the men's room.

Aboard EuroAir Flight 42, on the Ground, Sigonella Naval Air Station, Sicily

The call on the satellite phone had come as a complete surprise, and for a second, Craig wasn't sure how to react.

"What was that?" Alastair asked as Craig replaced the receiver.

"One of the Navy security guys telling me Captain Swanson is on his way back here with that lawyer, Campbell."

"To our *airplane?*"

"That's . . . the impression I got."

"Oh, jeez! I'll tell them," Alastair said, scrambling out

of the right seat and opening the door as Matt Ward was bringing General Glueck through the forward entry door.

"Agent Ward, we've got a problem," he said, inclining his head toward the older gentleman with a questioning look.

Ward glanced at the general and back to Alastair Chadwick, quickly introducing the retired flag officer and the fact that he wanted to help. "What's the problem?" Ward asked.

Alastair relayed the phone call, watching Ward's eyes get large as he turned and bolted to the first-class cabin, leaving the general in the entryway. He was back in a few seconds.

"Okay, we have to assume Swanson's being forced to bring Campbell aboard to see if the President is here."

"If that's true," Alastair said, "he'll want to check the entire plane and the rest rooms."

"Any place to hide a man on board?" Ward asked, already aware of the answer.

"Yes. No. Not on board up here, but . . . if we could do it without anyone seeing, and if the President could scrunch up, we could get him in the electronics compartment aft of the nosewheel."

"How big is it?"

Craig had left the cockpit and joined them, listening to the intense exchange.

"Cramped, but he could do it," Alastair said. "We'll have to move fast, though. He'll be very visible climbing in there, but once the hatch is closed, no one will find him."

"General? Stay here, please," Matt Ward directed as he moved back toward the President, giving Craig a rapid introduction to Glueck.

John Harris listened to the plan and shook his head. "No. I'm not going to do that."

"What? Sir, look," Matt Ward protested. "I'm here to protect you, but you've got to cooperate."

"Haven't we had this discussion a few times, Matt?"

"Yes, Mr. President, we have. But seconds are ticking away and that lawyer is on his way here."

"And I am not going to be seen scurrying like a rat into a hole in the belly of this aircraft," Harris said, his voice firm and determined.

"Sir," Sherry began, but he held up a hand to stop her. "No! If Campbell comes aboard, I'll meet him head on. Does he have the Italian authorities with him?"

"We don't know, Mr. President," Ward answered. "Look, will you at least go stand in one of the aft rest rooms or something? Please don't make it easy for him."

John Harris thought it over. "I'm going to the rear galley to make a cup of coffee, Matt. If the man wants to inspect the airplane, I'll greet him back there. I'm not going to hide and cower."

"No one's calling it cowering, sir. This is false vanity."

"Matt! That's entirely enough!" the President snapped. "It's your job to provide the opportunity for my protection, but my job to make the decisions on what to accept. Mine alone. Clear?"

"Yes, sir."

"Excuse me, Mr. President," a voice said from behind. Ward, Dayton and Chadwick turned to see the aging general who had been listening to the rapid debate. He extended his hand and the President took it.

"Yes?"

General Glueck introduced himself quickly. "I've got twenty-three fellow American veterans of World War Two out there in that terminal, sir, who are ready to block this bastard you're talking about. I've already got them organized. If someone will order the young guard to open that terminal door, I guarantee you no one will be removing you from this airplane."

"That's all of your tour group, General?"

"Not all of us, sir. We're traveling with wives, lovers, sons, and daughters, too. But I've got my men organized and ready to stay with you wherever you decide to go. I figured this was coming."

"Thank you, General."

"No thanks needed, sir. Protection of the President is

our duty, and in my view, once you've held the office, your security is still our responsibility."

"Well, I appreciate it."

Matt Ward turned and hurried toward the door with General Glueck behind as the President got to his feet and moved toward the rear of the 737.

✈ TWENTY-TWO

Word that EuroAir was agreeing to charter the Boeing 737
to John Harris's staff came by cell phone as Jay Reinhart
left the men's room at the Laramie airport, his mind and
stomach still rebelling at the idea of flying in David
Carmichael's small plane. He made the requisite call to
transfer forty thousand dollars from the President's account to EuroAir as Sherry had directed, then called
Sherry's cell phone.

"They've also chartered another jet to take the other
passengers back to Rome," he reported when she answered, "and they're charging fifteen thousand for that."

"How soon?"

"The plane is already at Sigonella, they told me, so they
can make the transfer almost immediately."

"Good. And what's your status, Jay?"

Several acerbic phrases about the inevitability of death
by airplane flickered through Jay's mind, but he didn't feel
humorous enough to use them.

"I'm just getting ready to take off for Denver, and I'll connect with a direct United flight to London. Now listen, Sherry. I've been thinking as fast as I can. I think I want you to head for London, but wait until I get to Denver and on the international flight. I'll decide by then and call you."

"Why London?" she asked.

"The President will understand. We'll surrender him there and fight it out in the British system."

"Are you sure that's the best method?" she asked.

"No," Jay replied. "I'm not at all sure. That's why I want to think hard about it for a couple of hours. I just don't see much of an alternative, and it won't be long before the world knows he's still in Sicily."

Jay glanced out the windows of the reception area at the Cessna, another thought interposing itself. "Sherry, if you don't hear from me in three hours, try calling. If still no response, assume I've crashed or something and get on the way to London."

"That's not funny, Jay," she said.

"That wasn't meant to be funny," he replied.

He ended the call and moved rapidly through the glass door to join David Carmichael in the small Cessna, climbing carefully through the right-hand door into the copilot's seat.

"It's a standard seat belt, Professor. Just get it snug around you," Carmichael instructed from the left seat.

The panel in front of him was as mysterious as a treatise in Sanskrit. Dials and switches and gauges displaying arcane information not understandable to the uninitiated were spread before them, and Jay was momentarily puzzled when David handed him a second green headset.

"What's this?"

"Put it on, please, and adjust the microphone in front of your mouth. I've got an intercom and we can talk over this thing."

"Okay."

David began reading down a plastic laminated list of things to do, flipping switches and adjusting dials before starting the engine.

The shock of the engine and propeller roaring to life and the sudden shaking of the little aircraft confirmed Jay's worst fears: neither man nor Cessna was meant to fly. How could something that shook so violently at idle on the ground possibly last in the air? It was less a spoken question in his mind than a general feeling of inevitability, and he closed his eyes, remembering the last time he'd let himself be talked onto a high-tech roller coaster. From the moment it began, he'd felt completely out of control, the forces on his body so startling and strong that he found himself simply along for the ride, neither frightened nor convinced he would survive and completely stripped of control.

Karen had been the Pied Piper who'd lured him onto the thing. He was convinced now that her death wish was already showing by that time, but he hadn't seen it that way at the time.

He thought of Karen now, the image triggering the same familiar flood of grief and guilt that quickly filled the space where raw fear had resided seconds before.

"Ready, sir?" David asked, jolting him from his daydream. The question was straightforward, but there was a hesitation in the pilot's voice, and once again the prospect that any hesitation might lead Carmichael to cancel the flight forced the answer. Jay nodded as forcefully as he could, well aware he was fooling no one, least of all himself.

Sigonella Naval Air Station, Sicily

Captain Swanson had driven Campbell on a circuitous route through NAS-Two to the terminal. He brought his staff car to a halt in front of the passenger terminal at last and pointed Campbell's attention to the door.

"We'll go through there. I try not to drive on the operations ramp any more than necessary, for safety reasons."

Campbell said nothing as he unfolded his six-foot-four frame and followed the uniformed commander into the terminal and through the mixture of curious and upset passengers to the ramp-side door. He caught himself casually scanning the crowd for the familiar form of the ex-President before concluding that Harris would never try to slip out in such a manner. He could hear buses pulling up behind the staff car as an announcement was made for the passengers to get ready to board.

"Are they headed to the charter aircraft?" Campbell asked, remembering a brief, open exchange Swanson had just had on the radio as they drove toward the flight line. Apparently EuroAir had chartered the same 727 he'd just released a half hour before.

Just as well, Campbell thought. *If Harris is here, the fewer passengers in the way, the better.*

The Captain spoke to one of his enlisted security men, who opened the door to the ramp and let them pass.

The Boeing sat a hundred feet away, still pointed west, as Campbell followed the Navy officer around its nose and up the airstairs. The forward entry door was partially closed, and Swanson spoke a few words to someone inside before the door opened, and first one, then several older men stepped onto the top of the platform, one of them having difficulty walking, the weight of his years forcing him to hold on tightly to the top of the railing.

"What do you want, Captain?" one of them asked.

"I need to get this man aboard to inspect the aircraft," Captain Swanson said evenly, taking in the presence of the men without comment.

"And who is he?" the first man asked, pointing to the lawyer.

"Excuse me," Stuart Campbell said firmly, "who are *you*?"

"Brigadier General Edwin Glueck, United States Army, retired, sir. And, again, who might you be?"

Stuart Campbell hesitated as he thought through the possibilities without finding a clear answer to what was going on. He held out his hand, but the self-identified general refused to take it.

Campbell identified himself anyway.

"We've chartered this airplane, Mr. Campbell," General

Glueck said. "We're on a tour that's been interrupted and we'd like to get on with it."

"You've . . . chartered . . ."

"Yes, sir. We called EuroAir and chartered this aircraft, since no one else is using it now. The other passengers are going back to Rome on another aircraft. This one is ours."

"I see. Well, I'd simply like to take a look aboard."

"Why?"

Campbell smiled and looked at his shoes, the picture coalescing. "Why? Well, sir, if you're truly a retired general, then you jolly well know why. I need to be assured that one John Harris, former President of the United States, is not aboard this airplane."

"By what authority, Mr. Campbell?" General Glueck asked. "I'll admit I'm not a lawyer . . ."

"I am," a frail man at his side said in a surprisingly firm voice.

"And you would be another general, I suppose," Campbell said with a slight sneer.

"No, sir. I would be, and am, a retired Air Force colonel from the Judge Advocate Corps, and unless you have some exotic jurisdictional claim I've never encountered, you have no official status here and no right to come aboard."

Campbell laughed as derisively as he could manage. "Very well, gentlemen. The geriatric army, eh what? You're all on some misguided quest to let your ex-President hide behind your skirts, so I'll just go get the authorities and the proper arrest warrant and we'll plow through whoever wants to stand in the way and arrest him anyway."

"No you won't, Campbell," Captain Swanson snapped.

"Excuse me?"

"The situation hasn't changed. This ramp is off-limits to the Italian authorities, and regardless of who is or isn't aboard, without my authority no one is arresting anyone in this aircraft."

"Oh, give it a rest, Captain!" Stuart Campbell said, real irritation melding with fatigue.

"Get away from our aircraft," General Glueck added.

Stuart Campbell began to turn away, then faced Glueck

again. "Very well, General. Your over-the-hill gang can keep your President for now, but . . ."

"That's quite enough abuse from you, Stuart!" A firm voice reached the lawyer from behind the assembled veterans, and John Harris stepped onto the top of the airstairs and gently pushed through them to face Campbell. "These are brave, honorable men trying to protect the office, not the man. Don't you dare sneer at them or abuse them!"

"Well, well, John. You're looking exceptionally present for a man in a C-17 a thousand miles from here."

"Cute, Stuart. If you concluded I was gone, that was your mistake."

"Oh, of course. Well, now that I know for certain you're here, we'll simply get this circus started again."

"No, you won't. You're going to get your tail back in that jet of yours and go to London. I'll meet you there, and we'll hash out this inane warrant in the British courts."

Stuart Campbell looked stunned for just a moment, then recovered.

"I see. Well . . ."

"You *are* still a British citizen, aren't you, Stuart?"

"Of course."

"An expatriate Scot, of course, and a loyal, obedient servant of the Queen."

"Ancient insults, John?"

"This is a dirty quest you're on, Stuart. You're going to damage the very treaty you're trying to uphold."

Stuart Campbell looked at the ashen faces of the old men arrayed around them and decided to mute his reply.

"Well, Mr. President, we shall see. I do not accept your London offer. I will reassemble the Italian authorities and we'll accept your surrender right here. We're going to extradite you from Italy to Peru, and the sooner you accept that fact, the better for everyone . . . including the office."

"Over our dead bodies," General Glueck muttered, the other veterans echoing agreement.

"Mr. Campbell," Swanson interjected, "this visit has ended. I'll escort you off my ramp." Swanson took his elbow, but Campbell yanked his arm free and turned back to John Harris, looking him in the eye for a few seconds before regaining control of himself and deciding to say nothing. He turned away and descended the airstairs, walking rapidly, his broad shoulders hunched forward in determination as Swanson hurried to keep up.

Campbell climbed back in his Learjet in a state of agitation, barely acknowledging his pilots as he plopped down in one of the plush captain's chairs, consulted a small notebook, and yanked the satellite phone from its cradle. He punched a flurry of numbers into the instrument and waited, drumming his fingers on the fold-out desk.

"Giuseppe? Stuart Campbell. Please listen closely, old friend. Harris, it turns out, is still on the ground in Sigonella, and I have a proposition for you."

✈ **TWENTY-THREE**

**Laramie Airport, Wyoming—Monday—
12:45 P.M. Local**

David Carmichael scanned the air traffic control clearance
he'd jotted down and pressed the transmit button on the
Cessna's small control yoke.

"Roger, ah, ATC clears Cessna Two-Two-Five Juliet
November to the Denver airport via the Laramie VOR,
then Victor Five Seventy-Five to the Ramms Three Arrival
to Denver International. On departure, climb to twelve
thousand, departure frequency one two five point nine,
squawk two six six nine."

"What is all that?" Jay asked, hearing Carmichael's
words in the headset against the background noise of the
engine and propeller as they sat by the end of the runway.

David raised a finger in a "wait" gesture for a follow-up
exchange with the controller.

He turned to Jay as he changed frequencies. "It's our instrument clearance to Denver," David explained.

"That's the control tower?"

"No. There's no tower here. That's Denver Center. We take off on our own, then talk to them."

Jay checked the tightness of his seat belt for the fifth time and forced his mind onto the more practical question of catching his transatlantic commercial flight in Denver. If it took an hour to get there, as David had said, he would have less than ninety minutes to get from the private terminal to the huge commercial terminal, buy his ticket, navigate the mysterious barriers the commercial industry always erected in the path of its customers, and board his flight.

"Laramie area traffic, Cessna Two-Two-Five Juliet November taking runway one two for departure to the south, Laramie."

The sound of the engine revving to maximum power yanked Jay's attention back to the present as the small Cessna leapt forward and began accelerating down the runway, bounding and swerving slightly on its spindly landing gear before David pulled on the control yoke and powered them into the air, leaving the concrete to drop away beneath them with sickening finality.

David banked the airplane to the southeast and leveled the wings as they climbed into the overcast sky and the world outside the windscreen became gray. Jay watched with growing alarm as the last images of pastures and ranch land and a westbound Union Pacific freight train disappeared below. His hands gripped the sides of his seat as he watched the pilot shift his concentration to the glowing instruments on the forward panel, adjusting the controls and throttle in accordance with the obscure and arcane things the instruments were telling him.

"This is some sort of black art, flying in weather!" Jay managed to say, his voice strained.

"Sorry?" David asked.

"I said . . . I don't see how you're doing this . . . flying blind, I mean."

David reached up to change the radio frequency. "Denver Center, Cessna Two-Two-Five Juliet November, airborne Laramie, climbing one-two thousand."

The movements of the small Cessna, the up-and-down

and side-to-side bouncing and lurching became an ac-
cusatory voice in Jay's ears screaming that he shouldn't
have pushed this young man to fly to Denver, regardless of
the need to help John Harris.

"We are . . . right side up, right?"

"Yeah." David chuckled.

"I can't tell. I can't read those instruments."

Jay realized he had only one thing to hold onto: the reality that David didn't seem to be panicked.

"It's not that hard," David said, his eyes boring into an instrument just in front of him. He turned and glanced at Jay and
took his right hand off the throttle long enough to point to the
round dial in the center of the panel.

"See this?"

"Yes, but are you sure you should let go of that?"

"Don't worry. It's okay. Now, that instrument is called an
'ADI,' Attitude Deviation Indicator. In the old days they
called these 'Artificial Horizons.' What I'm doing is called
attitude flying. See that little bar that looks like an airplane?"

"Yes."

"Well, I keep the wings of that little artificial airplane
level against that line that represents the horizon—my attitude, in other words—and it's almost like flying on a clear
day by visually looking at the real horizon."

Jay tried to loosen his grip on the seat long enough to
lean over and interpret what David had just said. He could
see the horizontal bar within the circular instrument, and
the little artificial airplane, but figuring out which way to
push or pull the control wheel to keep the display in correct alignment was still a mystery.

"Then I watch my altitude, my heading, and my airspeed, and it all works," David said.

The Cessna bounced through some sort of air current,
and Jay felt himself being shoved upward as he heard the
sound of the propeller change for a second, an alteration
that caused what was left of his stomach to finish contracting into a singularity.

David refocused his attention on the so-called ADI, and
Jay decided that distracting him with any more questions
was a bad idea. He forced himself to focus on the legal bat-

tle ahead, and the question of where to send the President, if he could escape Italy.

"Denver Center, Cessna Two-Two-Five Juliet November, airborne Laramie, climbing one-two thousand," David called again.

Still no answer, Jay noted, his concentration broken. "You doing okay?" Jay said, instantly angry with himself for saying another word.

"Yeah," David Carmichael replied, hoping his passenger couldn't see how nervous he really was. "We're probably just not hitting their transmitters yet."

David adjusted the throttle again and checked his altitude as he continued climbing through ten thousand. He looked out at the wing on the left side as casually as he could, checking for ice and relieved to see none. The outside air temperatures were probably too cold for icing, but there was a question in the Denver area.

David took a deep breath and realized his mouth was cotton-dry. They had ninety miles to go, and he had to do an instrument approach in a tiny airplane to one of the largest airports in the world, flying down to probably two or three hundred feet above the surface before seeing anything. He was also acutely aware of his inexperience as a newly minted instrument pilot with only six hundred hours of total flight time—and he hadn't flown in nearly two months.

Carmichael, this was a stupid idea! he thought to himself, as he tried yet again to make radio contact with the controller.

"Denver Center, Cessna Two-Two-Five Juliet November, how do you read?"

What was it his instructor had said? The most important element of piloting an airplane was judgment, and he'd just exercised precious little of it by jumping at the chance to please a professor without really thinking through the risks.

This is an important mission! he argued to himself. *It's worth pushing the envelope.*

But pushing the envelope was what killed people in aviation, especially pilots who flew beyond their experience or their capabilities.

He forced himself to take a deep breath and calm down, but his hand was shaking slightly on the control yoke, and the thought that he might be forgetting something was eating at him.

Oh my God, did I bring the approach plates for Denver?

Making an instrument landing required having the right pages aboard from a book full of such procedures. The "plates," as the five-by-seven-inch pages were called, were packed solid with information about frequencies and minimum altitudes and headings and all the additional information a pilot needed to approach an airport safely without seeing the ground outside the windscreen until the last few hundred feet.

David felt his heart in his throat as he turned around. With no autopilot aboard the 172, he had to maintain control every second, but the brown leather, loose-leaf manual he needed—containing his Jeppesen instrument charts— sat where he'd placed it on the back seat. He reached around to grab it, pulling it back to his lap in time to realize he'd let the Cessna roll into a steep right bank.

He righted the airplane and held it steady while he flipped through the book with his right hand to find the ILS approach he needed for Denver International.

"Can I help you with that?" he heard Jay ask.

"I'm fine," he lied.

Another unexpected gust shoved the Cessna to one side slightly, enough to cause a flutter in his stomach. He could imagine what Professor Reinhart was feeling.

There was high terrain ahead, he knew. The minimum safe altitude through this area was eleven thousand three hundred feet, and they were just climbing through ten thousand five hundred very slowly. The engine was at maximum power, and the cumulo-granite ahead—as pilots sometimes called mountains—reached ten thousand feet.

Once again he called for Denver Center, hearing nothing but static in return.

"I don't understand this. It was working on the ground," he said in frustration, immediately sorry he'd spoken his concern.

"We, ah . . . have a problem?" Jay Reinhart asked, his voice tense.

"No . . . not really. I just . . . it would be better if we could talk to them."

There was a small electronic chirping suddenly in the cockpit, heard over both headsets. The warning noise was totally unfamiliar, and David began looking for the source of the warning, checking his airspeed and instruments.

That's . . . what IS that? That's not a stall warning? Engine's okay. What the hell?

He noticed movement to his right and looked around to see his passenger pull a small cell phone from his pocket and point to it before placing it to his ear.

David brought his eyes back to the ADI and felt his heart leap. The artificial horizon line was nearly vertical when it should have been horizontal.

"*Jeez!*" He rolled the control yoke to the left, instantly realizing he'd gone the wrong way. They had rolled almost ninety degrees left and the nose was dropping, the altitude beginning to unwind as he rotated the yoke to the right and righted the horizon, bringing the nose back to level flight.

Ten thousand one hundred! Climb! Dammit, dammit, dammit! Control yourself!

He'd lost five hundred feet to a momentary spatial disorientation, but Professor Reinhart had been busy talking on his phone and hadn't seemed to notice.

Thank God, David thought. The professor was nervous enough as it was.

Lord! Do NOT do that again! David told himself. *Eyes remain on the ADI. Don't forget that's exactly what killed JFK Junior!*

David checked the mileage from Laramie on one of the instruments. They were twenty-two nautical miles from the field and approaching the mountain ridge crossed by U.S. 287. He checked the altitude again. Ten thousand three hundred, climbing very slowly. His heart was pounding but he kept a poker face as he scanned the instruments and began wondering whether they should turn back.

No, I can't turn back on instruments. I'm cleared to Denver. If I can't talk to the controllers, there's no way I

*can get cleared for an approach back to Laramie. I'd bet-
ter go on. Besides, Denver International has a lot more fa-
cilities than Laramie.*

Having to peel his hand away from the edge of his seat to
grab the cell phone had been a small agony for Jay Reinhart, but the moment Sherry's voice came on the line, his
entire concentration shifted to what she was saying.

"Yes, Sherry. I'm . . . in flight . . . heading for Denver.
It's pretty rough. What's happening there?"

She quickly brought him up to date on the approval of
the charter, Campbell's visit, and her suspicions that he
was regrouping for another try.

"Shouldn't we get out of here now?" she asked. "The
captain says he can leave at any time."

"Not yet, Sherry. I don't know where to send you."

"I thought you said Britain."

"I did, and that's probably right, but I've got some research to do, and I can't do it in this small plane. Is there
any reason to think the Italians are changing their minds
about not invading that ramp?"

There was a burst of static on the line and a muffled
voice where Sherry had been.

"Sherry? Hello?"

More static, then a click, and a series of squeaks and
squawks before the line went dead.

"Damn cell phones."

David's eyes remained welded to the forward panel, but
Jay could see him nod. "They're not supposed to be used
in the air, and we're probably in a marginal area anyway."

"Still no contact with Denver?" Jay asked.

David shook his head, gesturing to the panel. "I tried
switching to my second radio, but I totally forgot it's been
intermittent. I meant to have a radio shop look at it last
month. But they know we're here. See that little blinking
light on the transponder?"

"The what?"

David pointed to it. "That little panel. When the air traffic control radar beams sweep past us, they trigger that little transmitter, and it sends the controller our altitude and

position. The blinking light means they're tracking us, even though I can't talk to them."

"That's a relief," Jay said. "I think."

David checked the mileage from the Laramie VOR, the radio navigation beacon he was using to navigate down the center of the invisible air lane called V-575.

Forty-three miles. We're past the highest terrain.

He felt himself relax slightly for the first time.

The White House

The Chief of Staff was back in his favorite perch on the forward edge of his desk while his secretary and three other staff members stood, leaned, or sat in various positions in the cramped office.

"So they know already?" Jack Rollins asked.

Richard Hailey, the Deputy Communications Director, glanced at Press Secretary Diane Beecher before replying. She diverted her eyes, leaving Hailey to speak.

"The Italian Foreign Ministry was informed about ten minutes ago by Peru's lawyer that President Harris was still aboard."

"That's Stuart Campbell who did the informing, you can be sure," another staff member added, checking the name on a notebook.

"Right," Hailey agreed. "And we expect he'll be informing the media almost immediately to try to portray Harris, and us, as purposefully deceptive."

"So," Rollins said, "Diane? We'd better talk to them."

She nodded. "I've got a tentative briefing scheduled in fifteen minutes."

He nodded. "Same script we all agreed on?"

"Yes," she confirmed. "We're really concerned that some members of the media may have misunderstood our previous briefing that the reception at Andrews was for President Harris, when in fact we're simply saying thank you to the flight crew for their rapid response. The President was not on board because President Cavanaugh determined that it would be inappropriate, yada, yada, yada."

"Will it wash?" Rollins asked, already shaking his head.

"That's a rhetorical question, right?" Beecher replied. "At least it'll be on the record."

National Security Advisor Michael Goldboro had come in quietly.

"Jack," he said, getting Rollins's nodded acknowledgment. "Campbell apparently had a plan B on the shelf. His people have snagged an Italian justice from the Court of Cassation, their equivalent of a supreme court for criminal matters. The judge is at home, and they're trying to convince him to issue an order that would essentially require the police to forcibly enter the flight-line ramp at Sigonella and arrest Harris."

"How?" Rollins asked. "I mean, that affects a treaty, right?"

Goldboro shook his head. "The Foreign Ministry's been fudging that interpretation for us. They know, and the judges know, that the lease on that base—more accurately called the Status of Forces Agreement—does not preclude Italian jurisdiction. The flight-line thing is a red herring. If that order is issued, the police, or the army in Sicily, can blow past the Navy guards in an instant, and we can't, and shouldn't, try to stop them."

"In other words, the judiciary may take over the issue."

"That's right. The second an order is issued, the Foreign Ministry is out of it."

"Does Harris know?"

Goldboro glanced at Diane Beecher, who was already on her feet. "Well, that's all for me, fellows," she said, exiting Rollins's office before any more could be said that she would not officially want to know.

"Michael?" Rollins prompted when she was gone.

"That's what we need to talk about, Jack. Is it our responsibility to tell President Harris he needs to get the hell out of there if he can? Or does that constitute the very interference that President Cavanaugh agreed we have to avoid?"

"And your recommendation, of course, would be silence?"

"You know how I feel, Jack," Goldboro said quietly.

✈ TWENTY-FOUR

The electronic data block for Cessna 225JN was steady on the scope, but the numbers were disturbing. The air traffic controller working the low altitude Fort Collins sector glanced at the data strip again, double-checking that the altitude clearance was eleven thousand.

It was.

Yet the Cessna's transponder was reporting ten thousand one hundred and descending.

The controller triggered his transmitter again, trying once more to raise the pilot.

"Still having problems with that guy?" a voice said over his shoulder. The controller glanced around at his supervisor and nodded. "He can't hear a thing from me, but I've heard every call he's made."

"Partial radio failure, then," the supervisor grumbled.

"He's on the proper course, and he's past the highest mountains, but he's started descending without clearance."

"Transponder's not on seventy-seven hundred, either,"

the supervisor said, referring to the emergency transponder code. "He should squawk the radio failure code, at least."

"Yeah, but he hasn't yet," the controller said

"You tried calling him over the VOR frequency?"

"Yep. No luck."

The controller checked the clearance again on the hand-written paper strip to his side. If he couldn't regain contact, he could expect the pilot to bore on in toward Denver's International Airport using the very specific published procedure known as the Rammes 3 arrival, and probably try to fly an ILS to one of the runways. He would have to notify a Denver approach controller in a minute or so, and a sky full of commercial traffic would have to be routed around the little Cessna to keep everyone safe.

"Better let Denver Approach know," the supervisor said.

The controller nodded, cringing inwardly at the disruption the private pilot was about to cause. 747's, DC-10's, 737's, and a myriad of other large airliners would be wasting untold gallons of jet fuel all because a solitary pilot hadn't made sure his radios were working before departure.

He looked back at the glowing data block next to the target that represented the Cessna's position on his computerized radar display.

Now he's down to nine thousand eight hundred. Why? What's going on up there?

Aboard Cessna 225JN, in Flight, Sixty Miles Southeast of Laramie, Wyoming

"What's happening, David?" Jay asked, his fears reaching new heights as he watched David Carmichael glance repeatedly at the left wing and the engine cowling and windscreen in front of them, which had frosted up.

Jay saw him check the throttle, pushing it as far in as it would go.

"Just . . . a second . . ." David managed, as he looked again to the left.

Jay followed his gaze to the left side brace that came up from the lower fuselage to the bottom of the wing on the left side, holding the wing in a rigid position. The brace was intact, but there was something on the leading edge of its metal surface.

Ice, Jay thought to himself. Even as he watched, the crust of ice thickened. Mostly clear, there were flecks of white, as if they were picking up sleet or snow as well.

"I ah . . ." David began, his eyes still outside.

"What?"

David turned to look at Jay. "I wasn't expecting this. We're picking up ice. I've got to get us out of here."

"Where?" Jay asked as he felt a wave of cold rush through his body. "Turn around?"

David shook his head. "Too late. We're over the pass, and . . . the ground below us is probably about six thousand feet. We're sinking slowly at full power."

"What . . . what do you mean, 'sinking'?" Jay stammered.

"I can't hold this altitude with the added weight of ice," David said quietly.

The sound of the engine had been a steady, cacophonous drone, but it changed suddenly, sputtering and surging and sputtering again.

David's hand snaked out to pull a knob on the forward panel and the sputtering was replaced again by the steady drone of gasoline-powered pistons.

"What was that?" Jay asked, his words coming too fast.

"Carburetor ice. I needed . . . carb heat."

"Is it . . . going to keep running?"

David nodded. "Oh, yeah. Just . . . routine problem."

Even I *know that's a lie!* Jay thought as his cell phone rang again. He fumbled for it and flipped it open.

"Yes?"

"Jay? Sherry Lincoln."

"Yeah . . . hold on, Sherry. We've, ah, got a problem up here."

"What is it?" he heard her say as he pulled the phone from his ear and held it in his lap, his mind whirling with conflicting emotions and thoughts. They were sinking, David had said. Did that mean they were going to crash?

"David . . . what are you going to do?"

The pilot's right hand came up in a "wait" gesture, but Jay could see it shaking, and only shards of a sentence came out of David's mouth.

"I . . . ah, we're going . . . wait . . . wait a minute . . ."

Jay forced himself to disconnect from the nightmare and focus on the cell phone and Sherry Lincoln and Sigonella.

"Yes, Sherry," he said.

"What's happening there?" she asked.

"Not important," Jay replied. "We'll be in Denver shortly. What's going on there?"

Jay could see David pushing on the throttle again, even though they both knew it was at full power.

"When I lost you a while ago," Sherry was saying, "you'd just asked if we had any reason to think the Italians might change their mind about letting us stay on the ground here undisturbed. We're worried, Jay, that we need to get in the air and aim for someplace else. Campbell was pretty mad when he left the airplane and I'm not sure what else he can pull. Do you know?"

There was a momentary shrill sound, an electrical buzzer or horn of some sort, and he saw David shove the control yoke forward slightly in response.

Jay shook his head, reminding himself suddenly that she couldn't see the gesture. He forced himself to ignore the needles of the instrument David had identified as the altimeter, even though he could see them slowly unwinding in his peripheral vision.

"I don't know for certain, Sherry, but his only real option is to find a high court judge there in Italy, probably in Rome, and try to get a ruling that Italian jurisdiction covers that flight-line ramp as well."

"How long would that take?"

"The Italians don't react like our judges, but then, Campbell is well known and respected. It's not impossible that some jurist would let himself be disturbed at home."

A hand appeared in front of him as David changed a radio frequency and adjusted several knobs, calling once again in vain for Denver Center.

"What should we do, Jay?" Sherry asked. "Plain and simple. It's decision time."

He swallowed hard, trying to weigh the options with a mind badly divided between considering the situation in Sicily and considering the possibility of his own imminent demise.

"All right, Sherry. I . . . need to make a few more calls to verify that nothing's changed in the British approach to the torture treaty and extradition. Have the pilot file a flight plan for London, but stand by and don't leave for an hour. Call me back in an hour. If I'm . . . not available . . . take off, go to London, and have the President surrender to any properly constituted authority trying to serve the warrant. But, if they aren't waiting, refuel and get as far toward the U.S. as possible. Canada would be okay."

"What do you mean, if you're not available?" Sherry asked, aware of his frightened tone.

"Just . . . don't worry. Call me in an hour."

Jay ended the call as David once again twirled radio frequency dials, his hand pausing suddenly over one of the knobs. Jay saw him grab the outer ring of the dual plastic knob and turn it back and forth.

"Oh, DAMN!"

"What?"

"Denver Center, Cessna Two-Two-Five Juliet November, how do you hear me now? I think I've fixed my radio problem."

A male voice boomed into their headsets, the tones as welcome a deliverance as suddenly flying into clear skies would have been.

"Cessna Two-Two-Five Juliet November, Denver Center. Can you hear me, sir?"

"YES! Thank heavens!" David managed to say. "I've got you five by, Denver."

"I've been hearing all your transmissions, Juliet November, but you apparently weren't hearing me on any transmitter."

"I . . . somehow the volume control slipped, sir. I apologize."

"Observe your altitude to be nine thousand three hundred and descending, Juliet November. You were cleared to eleven thousand."

"I can't control it, Denver! I've picked up ice. That wasn't an intentional descent."

"Understand, sir. Are you declaring an emergency at this time?"

"Yes! I've got full power and I can't stay level . . . and I got a stall warning a minute ago." David's voice was several levels higher than normal, the extreme stress showing in the pace and timbre of his words, and the controller had obviously picked up on it.

"Okay, stay calm, Two-Five Juliet November, we'll get you home. Are you still picking up ice?"

"Yes! I need to get away from the front range."

"Understood, sir. Come left this time to a vector heading of one-zero-zero degrees. I'm going to clear out everyone ahead of you and bring you into Denver for an ILS to runway nine left. Weather at Denver is indefinite ceiling, visibility one-half mile, runway visual range on nine left is three thousand feet, temperature twenty-nine, dew point seven, altimeter two nine seven four, winds calm."

"Roger. I'm descending through nine thousand feet!"

"Okay, sir, you've got twenty-six miles to go, ground speed shows to be one hundred twenty knots, and I show you descending at about two hundred feet per minute. You should be fine."

"Denver, we're still picking up ice!"

Jay felt a sudden shuddering of the aircraft.

David shoved the control column forward, partially lifting them from their seats as the nose came down. Again he let the speed build back and slowly raised the nose.

"What . . . was that?" Jay asked in a voice barely above a squeak.

"Stall. We stalled. I've got to keep the speed up faster than normal because we're carrying a heavy load of ice and it's redesigning the wing."

"Oh, wonderful."

David was breathing hard, his eyes all over the instrument panel as the voice of the Denver controller returned.

"Okay, Juliet November. I see you suddenly lost several hundred feet there. You okay?"

"I . . . almost stalled, Denver."

"Call me Bill, okay?" The controller said. "And your name?"

"Uh . . . Dave . . . David," he swallowed hard.

"Okay, David, we're gonna get you in. I'm a pilot, too. Just keep that speed at least five knots above wherever she wanted to stall. What's your descent rate?"

David leaned forward, peering at another round dial before answering.

"Ah . . . three hundred feet per minute . . . about."

"Still should work. Now, David, don't try to look up anything, I'm going to read you the frequencies and all you'll need to do is the ILS. You are, of course, instrument rated?"

"Yeah. Yeah, don't worry. I'm IFR rated."

"Good. I was sure you were, but we have to check. Okay, I want you to carefully dial in the ILS frequency one one two point four and visually check to make sure it's in your navigation radio and not your communication radio."

"Got it," David replied, after quickly rotating the knobs.

"Altitude, David?"

"Ah, eight thousand four hundred. Still three hundred feet per minute down, speed one twenty-five."

"Very well. You're twenty-two miles out, and we need to make a decision here. I can try to land you at Centennial Airport, which is south of you about five miles, or we can continue on to Denver International. You could make Centennial just fine, but the ILS is out, and while they're reporting a three-hundred-foot ceiling, it's an automated ASOS report. Fact is, sometimes the ASOS can't detect rapidly changing conditions. It could be much worse there."

"Okay." David glanced at his passenger, calculating the reason for the flight to begin with and the danger of descending closer to the front range of the Rockies to find a fog-shrouded Centennial.

"Ah . . . International. Denver International," he said.

"Okay. Are you out of the icing?"

David looked to the left at the wing and then through the windscreen at the cowling before answering.

"Yeah . . . I think we're out of it. But it's not melting."

"Nineteen miles out, David, and your altitude is still good."

"Okay."

"Now, put your course selector on the ILS inbound heading of zero nine zero degrees."

"Okay. Done. Am I going to change to Denver Approach?"

"No, David, I'll stay with you the whole way. Denver Approach is keeping everyone else away."

"I'm sorry!"

"Don't worry about it. You're approaching the localizer."

"What's a localizer?" Jay heard himself ask.

"It's . . . this needle . . ." David answered, pointing to the Horizontal Situation Indicator on the forward panel. "When it slides over to the center, it means I'm on course to the runway."

"Okay."

David triggered the transmitter. "Intercepting localizer, Denver. I'm turning on course."

"Roger. Sixteen miles to the runway."

Shuddering coursed through the aircraft again and once more David shoved the nose over, waiting for the airspeed to come up before shallowing the rate of descent.

"What's your altitude, David?"

"I had to lose some to avoid stalling. Seventy four hundred."

"Okay, you're fourteen miles out, doing two miles per minute, we've got to keep you airborne for seven minutes more, the field is at five thousand three hundred feet above sea level, which means you can't descend at more than three hundred feet per minute maximum. As a fellow Cessna driver, let me advise you not to use flaps. Don't do anything to increase your drag."

"Understood," David replied, his heart in his throat as he did the math in his head and watched the rate of climb indicator holding just under three hundred feet per minute rate of descent.

Denver Air Route Traffic Control Center, Denver, Colorado

"He's not going to make it, Bill," the supervisor said.

The controller nodded reluctantly, his blood running cold at the thought that he might have steered the panicked pilot wrong. Only plowed fields surrounded Denver International, though. If he couldn't make the runway, perhaps he could put it down safely in a field.

The controller swallowed hard and looked over at his supervisor. "Alert DIA to get the fire trucks ready to look for touchdown short of runway nine left."

"Okay."

"He might still make it."

The supervisor picked up the tie-line handset without comment and punched the appropriate buttons.

✈ TWENTY-FIVE

Sigonella Naval Air Station, Sicily—Monday—9:10 P.M.

Captain Swanson took the unexpected call from the foreign minister of Italy at his desk, where he'd been sitting in thought, rubbing his eyes and wondering if there was anything else he should be doing to defuse the situation on his ramp.

"Yes, sir?"

"Commander Swanson?"

"Captain, actually."

"Very well. This is Giuseppe Anselmo, and this call has never happened."

"Ah, you mean this is completely off the record?"

"If that's the correct phrase."

"Very well, sir. Go ahead."

"I will be brief. I am aware that you know all the appropriate names. Mr. Campbell's representatives have been at the home of one of our highest judges asking that our interpretation of the lease on your base be changed to include immediate Italian jurisdiction over the flight line."

"Yes?" Swanson said with a sinking feeling.

"The judge is considering his request. We have no control over that, any more than you control your courts in the United States."

"Yes, sir. I understand. If the captain of that aircraft wants to leave Italy, will you protest?"

"That's a diplomatic question, Captain," Anselmo replied with a chuckle. "A military officer should not be so astute. Let me answer in this manner. As of this moment, no request for an air traffic clearance for that aircraft would be handled in any other manner than normal and routine. In other words, the government of Italy has no interest in blocking or interfering with air traffic at Sigonella at this moment."

"But . . . if the judge rules otherwise . . ."

"Then we shall behave in accordance with the law, and even though our government may appeal any court order or decision, we may still have to honor it in the meantime."

"How long, sir? When is the judge likely to rule?"

"Not until noon on the day after tomorrow. He has refused to make a decision until then, and has set this for a hearing. Nothing changes until then. After that, who knows?"

"Understood. Thank you."

Aboard Cessna 225JN, in Flight, Sixty Miles Southeast of Laramie, Wyoming

David Carmichael looked closely at the temperature gauge on the end of the vent above the dash panel and shook his head.

"What?" Jay asked.

"I was hoping it'd warm up and we could shed the ice, but there's a temperature inversion, and it's getting colder as we descend."

"Five miles to go, David," the controller was saying.

David looked at the altimeter, now reading five thousand six hundred fifty feet, the rate of descent steady at two hundred ninety. If he tried to stretch his flight path a bit farther by pulling more back pressure, he ran the risk of stalling again, and a stall so close to the ground would undoubtedly be fatal. But all he needed was to stay in the air a short distance more.

"What can I do?" Jay asked.

"Pray," was the response.

"Four miles," the controller told him. "You might pick up a small tailwind that will help you. Just a couple of knots."

"Good."

David forced his eyes around the panel as he fought through the wall of panic obscuring the other thing he knew he was forgetting. Was there anything else he could do to make the airplane fly more efficiently?

Wait a minute! He glanced at the mixture control. He had set it just after takeoff and it was partially lean, but nowhere close to maximum performance!

He reached over and pulled the knob carefully, watching the cylinder temperature gauge as he felt the power increase slightly.

"Only two miles to go, David," the controller said, his voice utterly calm and reassuring.

The engine power suddenly diminished and David backed off on the mixture control, pushing it in slightly, his heart almost stopping before the power revved again. He pulled his hand away and returned his eyes to the gauges as the stall warning sounded momentarily, then stopped.

One hundred twenty indicated and I can't slow! I must be carrying a ton of ice!

"One mile now, David. I show you right on centerline."

"Roger."

"It's a huge runway, and it should come swimming into view in just twenty seconds or so."

There was nothing but gray in front of the windscreen.

"Can't I do anything?" Jay asked.

"Yeah," David replied. "Look hard. It'll show up just ahead of us."

"I see fuzzy lights!" Jay replied. "They just appeared."

Splotches of red and white and something flashing furiously swam into view just ahead of the aircraft, and visions of setting the Cessna down in a tangle of steel approach light towers sent yet another shudder through David as he worked to resist the tendency to pull back on the yoke, a move that would instantly stall the airplane and kill them for certain.

"Half a mile to go," the controller said.

David couldn't force himself to push the transmit button to answer. All his concentration was focused on keeping the airspeed precisely the same, the airplane aligned, and praying they'd stay clear of the metal approach light structures that were reaching up to grab his airplane, closer and closer with every second. All he could see ahead were the approach lights, the sequential strobes leading him forward, the galaxy of lights steadily flattening.

We're not going to make it! he felt himself think, rejecting the idea in the same microsecond.

The last approach light tower was just ahead, coming up at him, the lights bright and threatening, the metal structure unyielding and unforgiving to the thin skin of a Cessna. If the landing gear snagged those . . .

And just as suddenly they were past the structure with concrete coming up at them and the runway visible ahead of them, the main wheels of the 172 passing just two feet over the lip of the runway's threshold before David yanked the yoke back to break the descent. The aircraft shuddered, the wings losing the battle to stay airborne with the wheels less than six inches off the pavement.

And suddenly they were rolling down the runway after a bone-jarring touchdown.

David found the top of the rudder pedals with his toes and pressed forward to apply the brakes, wondering why the pedals were shaking before realizing his feet were doing the vibrating, propelled by a bloodstream full of adrenaline.

There was a turnoff just ahead and he guided the little Cessna toward it, remembering at the same moment the Denver controller who was probably not breathing.

"Denver . . . ah . . . we're down okay. We're on the runway."

The transmitter came on without a voice, but he and Jay

could hear cheering in the background at Denver Center and a long sigh on the controller's headset microphone.

"Understood, David. Great job," he said simply.

"You, too," David managed. "Thank you, sir."

"No problem. Turn off when you can. Call Denver ground now on one one nine point two, and we'll give them back their airport."

Aboard EuroAir Flight 42, on the Ground, Sigonella Naval Air Station, Sicily

Sherry Lincoln punched off the GSM cell phone and looked up at the starfield above Sigonella as she stood on the small platform topping the portable airstairs. She'd stepped out into the night for better reception, but the air had cooled considerably and she was shivering now in the light breeze.

Most of the clouds overhead were gone, leaving the stark blackness of the sky as an inky canvas for the stellar work of art above, the spiral arm of the earth's own Milky Way galaxy spread above in spectacular profusion, diminished only mildly by the filtered glow of the sodium vapor lights bathing the ramp.

Sherry took a deep breath and exhaled, her mind still whirling from the intensity of the past few hours. There was a window of opportunity now to take control of the situation and, depending on Britain's attitudes, perhaps quash the warrant within a few days. Thanks to the Italian leaders, they could safely wait until tomorrow before leaving, with no concern that the enemy was going to reappear.

She thought about the C-17 out there somewhere in the darkness thousands of miles distant as it hung in the sky over the Atlantic, moving ever closer to American shores—an utterly wasted flight without John Harris aboard. She wondered what the crew was thinking. Military men and women felt the ache of an unsuccessful mission far more than civilians could ever understand, their entire purpose for being called into question by any political override of a military operation.

The Vietnam syndrome never leaves us, she thought, suppressing a flash of anger.

The warning the President had given her just twenty minutes ago replayed in her head: his could be a long stay in Britain, and she should be thinking about other career plans. "Nonsense," she'd told him. "I'm sticking with you, regardless of where you are, and I'll be there for you as long as you need me."

"Need you? Are you kidding?" John Harris had replied. "I certainly can't imagine handling things without you, Sherry."

She smiled at the memory and the fact of being needed, the smile quickly fading with the reality that he was about to surrender to an uncertain fate and become a gold-plated pawn in an international tug-of-war.

Sherry remembered the mission of the call she'd just received from Jay Reinhart and turned to hurry back into the 737 to brief the President.

"Jay was just boarding his commercial flight in Denver," she explained. "He said he had about two hours of research to do before giving us the green light for London. He'll call from the plane."

"Okay." John Harris nodded.

"His voice sounded strange. I got the impression something happened on the flight to Denver, but he wouldn't tell me what. He sounded really spooked."

"Jay hates flying. He'd take Amtrak to London if they served the market."

"I got that impression."

"Where are General Glueck and his folks?"

"Inside, sir. Captain Swanson's having a dinner catered for them in the terminal, and sending food out to us, too."

"Did you see what those fellows did, Sherry?"

She nodded. "I did. I didn't hear everything that went on . . ."

"I mean, you talk about something to make you humble, that level of . . . of . . ."

"Honor?"

"Just love of country, Sherry. General Glueck talked all of them into turning down that charter back to Rome."

"Sir, they're having fun with this in a manner of speaking. I imagine it's been a long time since some of them have felt really needed."

He nodded slowly. "Good insight. That's something I have to consider. I was concerned about their wanting to come with us."

Sherry looked startled. "Wait a minute. They're coming with *us*?"

"Their next stop was Rome, but, according to Glueck, the whole group . . . including their tour director, Annie Ford . . . want to stay with us. They even had their baggage put back on the plane when the others left. You . . . have a problem with that?"

She smiled. "Your call, sir, but I would rethink that. Once we leave here, I really don't think they can help."

"Well, as far as I'm concerned, I'm honored to have them along if they want to go, and if it makes sense. Yeah, I'll reconsider. What I do have a problem with is why we need to wait here until tomorrow afternoon."

"Jay Reinhart's insisting he needs to get to London ahead of us and make arrangements."

"But what arrangements?" the President asked. "Campbell will have already presented the warrant to a judge somewhere in London. There's almost no question they'll be waiting wherever we touch down."

She shook her head. "He just wants to get there first, and that's eleven hours from now."

"How long for us to fly to London?" he asked.

"An hour and a half, about," she replied. "He said he expects we should take off about four P.M. tomorrow. That will give him most of the day to get things arranged."

"To surrender to the British authorities?"

"That's . . . what he's thinking."

"It's always possible," John Harris began, tapping his fingers on the side of his face, "that the British Foreign Office may decide to find a way to slow Stuart down just long enough for us to gas up and go."

"Yes, sir, but where *do* we go?" Sherry asked, easing into the seat next to him. "Captain Dayton tells me we can make Iceland or maybe Canada, but we can't make it all the way home from London without refueling, because this model seven thirty-seven doesn't have long-range fuel tanks. Campbell would surely know that. One of his henchmen will be waiting in Iceland too, and London's probably a far better place to battle this."

"Words of wisdom, Sherry," he said, falling silent for a few moments. "Unless Jay has some fantastic brainstorm to pluck us out of here, London it is."

"The British PM would never send you to Lima, right?"

"I knew Maggie Thatcher, John Major, and even Tony Blair. I don't know the current occupant. So I can't be sure. All we can depend on is that the fight would take at least as long as Pinochet's battle, which was more than a year. Hell, I'll probably turn as senile as Pinochet before they get to that point."

Denver International Airport, Denver, Colorado

David Carmichael stood in the doorway of the Signature Flight Service private terminal and watched a United Airlines 777 begin its takeoff roll on runway 17R. It accelerated slowly, pulled by two giant engines straining against the considerable weight of a planeload of passengers and baggage and a fuel load sufficient to power them through the 4,700 nautical miles separating Denver and London.

He glanced at his little Cessna 172, safely chocked in front of the private terminal, the ice now gone from its wings and windshield. He thought of the incredible difference in weight between the two metallic birds. The one approaching liftoff would leave the ground at a hundred fifty knots, weighing nearly three-quarters of a million pounds. The 172 could barely hit a hundred fifty knots in cruise flight or lift more than twelve hundred pounds.

The triple seven's nose rose majestically, the bulk of the aircraft lifting effortlessly into the air and almost immediately disappearing into the fog as the muted sound of the engines rolled over him.

He knew it was Professor Reinhart's flight. He'd checked and monitored the tower's takeoff clearance on his portable aviation scanner once his rubber legs had stopped shaking long enough to walk.

David turned and reentered the lounge.

I need another few minutes to wind down, he told himself. Then he'd ask for a ride to the nearby hotel he'd called and get a much needed night of sleep. Tomorrow he'd rent a car to get back to Laramie, unless the sky was crystal clear.

He looked back at his bird, feeling a strong determination to ferret out all he'd done wrong and make certain it never happened again.

And he would undoubtedly hear from the FAA, if they weren't already on their way to talk to him.

Aboard United Flight 958

Jay Reinhart turned off his computer and ended the modem connection with the seat phone.

Thank God for modern communications and computers and databases, he thought. A little more than two hours of paging through the Pinochet decisions in Britain and studying British civil procedure, and the Treaty on Torture itself had led to a quick and dirty conclusion: Britain was the right venue.

Jay took a deep breath and leaned back in his seat, feeling relaxed at having made that decision. He glanced out the window to his right and suddenly the fact they were in flight and he wasn't afraid in the least became a jolting realization.

The departure from Denver had triggered a beginning of the usual gut-wrenching fears as they taxied to the end of the runway, but amazingly enough, his apprehension had evaporated on the takeoff roll. The contrasts between the gentle motions of the flying living room he was occupying and what had occurred a short while before in David Carmichael's tiny Cessna had tamed the terror, reducing it to a numbed acceptance, a psychological acquiescence and knowledge that nothing about being airborne could ever scare him quite as profoundly again, especially in the benign environment of a luxury jetliner.

Amazing! he thought. *All these years all I needed to cure my fear of flying was a near-death experience in a single-engine kite.*

He looked around the plush first-class cabin of the Boeing 777, taking in the alluring feminine form of a young flight attendant handing a drink to an aging British rock star he'd recognized two rows ahead.

But he had work to do and calls to make. He tore his concentration away from an instantaneous daydream involving the raven-haired flight attendant and focused instead on the first call he was about to make.

I say it here and it happens there! he thought to himself, any feeling of power overwhelmed by the sense of urgency and responsibility and risk of getting it wrong. He was, after all, up against perhaps the smartest international lawyer on the planet, a man who'd lived and breathed little else besides international law and treaty law for the past thirty years.

Stuart Campbell's confident, smiling face swam into his mind's eye, sending a jolt of adrenaline through his bloodstream. The close encounter with the fog-shrouded surface of northeastern Colorado had numbed his fears somewhat, but the thought of Campbell honed the sharp edge of his apprehension once again. Was London a naive choice? Worse, was it a stupid choice, playing right into Campbell's plans?

Jay closed his eyes and shook the thought from his mind as best he could. He couldn't be making decisions based on fear instead of logic. Campbell was, after all, just a lawyer, as was he. It was a matter of reading the law and the procedures of each country and deciding where John Harris would be most protected while he built his case against the warrant.

Jay picked up the phone and ran his credit card again before dialing Sherry Lincoln's GSM phone. She answered on the second ring.

"Go to London, Sherry. Please tell the President. On second thought, let me brief him directly, okay?"

There was a brief delay as she passed the word to John Harris and handed him the phone. His warm and friendly voice betrayed none of the tension or the peril he was in.

"John, I have to warn you of something," Jay said.

"Go ahead."

"It's not likely, but . . . the current government and the current prime minister have not been tested on this issue, and they seem to think quite differently from their predecessors."

"Meaning?"

"Well, it's not impossible that their stance toward rapid compliance with the warrant could dramatically change from that of the Pinochet situation."

"You mean, uphold sovereign immunity as a bar to the warrant?"

"No, John. I mean they could decide that they have a duty to hear the extradition case immediately with no interference from the Law Lords."

"But you don't think so?"

"Highly unlikely, but that's why I need to get there first."

"And if not Britain, Jay?"

"I don't know," Jay said at the very moment a new possibility flashed across his mind. "I don't know, but I'm working on alternatives. Don't leave until I call you from London in about nine hours."

"I heard you hesitate," Harris said. "What are you thinking?"

Jay snorted on the other end. "Something . . . an idea . . . completely off the wall and not worthy of discussion right now."

"In my experience, Jay, those usually turn out to be the best of all."

✈ TWENTY-SIX

Jay Reinhart awoke with a start in his first-class seat, instantly upset at himself for having slept for the last three hours when he needed to be working. The flight attendants were already moving about the cabin with a fragrant breakfast, their efforts spotlighted occasionally by bright sunlight streaming in the windows and the welcoming smell of rich coffee.

He glanced at the small color TV screen at his seat displaying a map of their progress over the Atlantic and read the time remaining: one hour, ten minutes.

Jay sat up and rubbed his eyes, feeling exceedingly grubby. He got to his feet and headed for the lavatory, surprised at how wobbly his legs felt but determined to at least sponge his way back to social acceptability—an imperfect process that took less than ten minutes as he leaned heavily on a selection of colognes and amenities the airline provided in a small survival kit. He returned to the seat and gratefully accepted a cup of coffee and a sweet roll before pulling out his legal pads and trying to focus on planning the high-speed sequence of events he needed to orchestrate in London. It was a task he kicked himself for not completing hours ago, before the effect of time zones, loss of sleep, and dry cabin air began to muddle his thinking.

The first order of business would be to hire the right solicitor—the right British lawyer—to represent John Harris under Jay's control.

But which one? He needed a lawyer who could quickly help him determine which magistrate court Campbell's people had taken the warrant to, what rulings might have already been issued, and specifically what the extradition procedures were in Britain. He also needed to know whether or not Campbell was already in town. And he needed a best guess from an up-to-speed local practitioner on even the most far-out stunt Campbell might try to short-circuit the process and convince the appropriate branches of the British Government to turn Harris over to Peru when the courts had finished with the matter. So he would probably need an international firm.

No, wait. The first order of priority is to call them in Sigonella, he reminded himself, checking his watch. It was 8 A.M. in Italy, 7 A.M. in the U.K. He needed to call before heading for central London, just to make sure nothing had changed.

Next, I need to talk to the government. I've got to know how they're going to react to a request to seize and extradite a former U.S. President.

Another flash of apprehension and doubt rang a warning buzzer in his head, much as the stall warning in the little Cessna had cut through the heart of his confidence on that incredible flight.

Was it only a few hours ago?

Jay forced his mind away from that scene and back to the issue. The fact that Campbell was a highly placed Brit—a Knight of the British Empire and a senior barrister known as a QC, or Queen's Counsel—meant Jay was at a tremendous disadvantage. Campbell knew everyone. He knew no one. How could he possibly equalize such odds in time to discover what he had to know?

This is all about law, though. Not politics. The courts should be blind to Campbell's position.

But he knew better. Ultimately the British Secretary of State and the policies of Her Majesty's government would determine whether or not to extradite.

Indelibly etched images of Parliament, the interior of the House of Commons, and long-dormant memories of past contacts with British officialdom came to mind, as did the reality that he no longer had even one active contact in Her Majesty's Government.

Whom do I call? How on earth do I penetrate that maze?

He'd tried searching the Internet for names of knowledgeable lawyers among the solicitors listed with London offices, but the search had yielded only three possible names, and since London was in the early hours of morning, there had been no open offices to call.

The thought of John Harris sitting in the aircraft in Sigonella interposed itself. Had something happened during the night? He knew it was partially to divert his mind from the Herculean problems ahead, but he couldn't resist yanking up the phone. He swiped his American Express card and punched in the number of Sherry Lincoln's GSM cell phone, the sound of her voice like music on the other end when she answered. She reassured him that nothing had changed. Jay promised to make regular progress calls from London and rang off, then opened his laptop and connected it to the satellite phone again, establishing the link with the Internet just as the Boeing 777 began descent over Ireland for the landing in London. Jay was still on-line and searching frantically for legal contacts as the big jet steadied onto final approach over the English countryside. One of the flight attendants appeared at his side, standing in mock disgust with her hands on her hips to order the laptop turned off.

"Otherwise we'll explode immediately," she said, "and it will all be your fault, and I'll never speak to you again."

"Really? I mean, the explode part?"

"No, that's just a wind up, as the British call a good leg pulling. But that's the kind of nonsense this industry teaches us flight attendants, since all of us are supposed to be bubble brains. Actually, the only way that laptop of yours could be dangerous is if you physically bashed one of the pilots with it, which is probably a bad idea, by the way. They get very testy when attacked with computers."

"I'll keep that in mind," Jay said, pushing a smile through his fatigue.

"But, you've really got to turn it off now, sir, or I'll have to kill you."

"Done. Are you sure you don't work for Southwest? You've got a Southwest Airlines sense of humor."

"I would, but I'm allergic to peanuts."

Jay hardly noticed the landing and wondered absently if the close encounter near Denver could have permanently scared him out of his fear of flying—an oxymoronic concept to say the least.

Probably not. I'm just too numb and too tired to care.

The trip through British immigration and customs in Heathrow's Terminal 3 was a rapid blur and within fifteen minutes he was in the baggage claim atrium resisting the urge to head immediately for central London. There was little point, since he had no specific place to go as yet.

Cash! Jay reminded himself. He located a cash machine a few steps away and waited in a brief line before swiping his main cash card and punching in his PIN number.

"The card you have used is not supported by this service," the screen announced.

Jay fumbled through his wallet for another credit card and pulled out a little-used VISA.

"Incorrect PIN. Reenter the correct PIN," the machine proclaimed in bold type.

He tried again, trying to remember the number he thought he'd memorized.

Again the machine refused.

He pulled out his American Express card.

"Your account is not set up for this service."

Jay opened his wallet and counted the remaining American bills: $50. Hardly enough for a taxi, let alone all he needed to do.

He looked at his watch, reading just after 9 A.M. and

feeling the time already slipping away. There was a money exchange window nearby and he converted the $50 to pounds, taking some in change, which he used to feed a pay phone to call the three solicitors he'd researched in flight.

"I'm terribly sorry, sir, Mr. Thompkins does not accept international cases."

"So sorry, Mr. Reinhart, but international law isn't my specialty. Frankly, I don't have a recommendation for you."

"Mr. Blighstone is out of the country this week."

Jay opened a London phone book and riffled through the yellow pages for solicitors, writing down the numbers of several other firms before calling them one by one and finding only one firm with any promising experience.

"But Mr. Smythe won't be in until ten this morning."

"That's okay," Jay replied. "Give me your address and I'll be there at ten. I'm going to need to use someone's office and phone as well."

Jay wrote the address down and headed for the exit, stopping at a GSM cellular phone concession he'd spotted in the terminal. He filled out the paperwork quickly and used one of his credit cards to rent a phone, then headed to a ticket booth for the new high-speed Heathrow Express train, relieved to see familiar credit card logos adorning the counter.

Thank God! Jay thought. *American Express!*

He bought a round-trip ticket and arrived less than 20 minutes later in Paddington Station where he transferred to the underground, emerging at Holborne into a light, cold rain. Jay buttoned his topcoat and began walking resolutely toward where the solicitor's office was supposed to be.

The address, he'd been told, was less than two blocks from the Old Bailey, as the central criminal courts of London were called. But after dashing back and forth several times and wasting a half hour, he finally stopped a policeman for directions. Jay's dark hair was matted with rain and his pants legs soaked as he unfolded the piece of paper once more to show the officer the address he was struggling to find.

"Oh, there's the problem, sir," the police officer said with irritating cheerfulness. "Around the back of that street on the left. Just go down here, make a left again at the Viaduct Pub, and you can't miss it."

"That's the one by the small restaurant that's making me ravenous with all the good smells?" Jay asked.

"The very same. They pipe it out over the doorstep for that purpose, you know."

A shiny brass plaque on the masonry exterior proclaimed the name of the firm, and the office was on the second floor. The building had been old when Queen Victoria reigned, but the interior reflected the sort of modern affluence he'd hoped to locate, one that bespoke connections and capabilities he could draw on rapidly.

Jay glanced at his watch as the receptionist called the appropriate secretary. It was almost exactly 10 A.M.

"He's not in yet, Mr. Reinhart, but we have an office space you may use until Mr. Smythe arrives." A conservatively attired young woman with an indulgent smile appeared and escorted him to a small cubicle by the firm's library.

"These are all local calls, I trust?" she asked.

"Yes, but I'll compensate any expense."

"Of course, Mr. Reinhart, but you understand, I'm sure, that we would need Mr. Smythe's approval before . . ."

"Before you consider me a client? Yes. I'm an American lawyer. I understand the protocols."

"Very well, sir."

"Mr. Smythe does have contacts in the government associated with foreign affairs and treaty compliance and such?"

"Yes. Certainly. He used to be an MP."

"Good."

"Member of Parliament," she explained.

"I understand. That's excellent. Oh, one thing I forgot to ask," Jay said. "I need to be certain there's no conflict of interest. Your firm doesn't in any way have a correspondent relationship with Sir William Stuart Campbell of Brussels, does it?"

The woman's expression changed from a pleasant, conservative smile to a broad grin.

"Is this a test, then?" she questioned.

"I beg your pardon?" Jay asked, thoroughly alarmed.

Her smile diminished. "Mr. Reinhart, we handle all of Sir William's business interests in London. In fact, he owns this building."

"I . . . thought he had his own firm."

"Indeed, he does. That's why we handle the commercial affairs for his business interests. Is this a problem?"

The rain had intensified slightly when Jay regained the street, intent on finding a London taxi to get him to the firm Smythe's office had given him as a referral to a Geoffrey Wallace. The address was halfway across the center of London, and he stopped in a dry doorway to call them on the GSM phone, a process that ate up another fifteen minutes before Wallace came on the line and listened to his abbreviated plea after promising he had no connections with Stuart Campbell.

"Fascinating, Mr. Reinhart. And it was shaping up to be a boring day."

"Can you help?"

"I don't see why not. I haven't had an American President as a client for at least the last few decades that I can recall."

"Great. Here's what I need you to do before I even get there."

Jay passed along string of questions, including the problem of finding someone in government.

"Can't help you greatly there," the solicitor said. "But I do know a chap in the foreign office who might be a start. You could see him while I work on these other items."

"How do I get there?"

"It's just by St. James Park on St. George's Street," he said. "Just by Parliament. Take a taxi, mind you. The driver will know how to find it."

Jay passed the number of his rented GSM phone and

rang off with a promise that the man in the foreign office would be called to pave the way.

As he disconnected, Jay realized he'd been leaning against an ATM machine. He pulled a scrap of paper from the recesses of his coat pocket and rechecked the PIN number he'd suddenly remembered on the train from Heathrow. He inserted his MasterCard and keyed in the numbers and required choices, relieved to hear the sound of £20 notes being counted out by the machine.

The ride to a nondescript government building took nearly thirty minutes through the metallic molasses of London traffic. Jay entered the massive government structure acutely aware of his less than stellar appearance. A labyrinth of halls and corridors, stairways and doors unfolded ahead of him as he tried to carry his belongings with the unperturbed air of one who always arrives at professional meetings with his suitcase. There were wheels on the bottom of the bag, but he refused to let himself use them. Carrying the damn thing was bad enough, he thought, but rolling it would utterly violate what Linda had dubbed "the guy code."

He followed a shapely secretary into an inner office, her image sparking memories of how sexy Linda always looked when she walked.

Jay shook his head to expunge the thought, forcing himself to focus on the task at hand.

"Geoffrey Wallace told me you were coming," the deputy minister who handled treaty affairs told Jay when he'd introduced himself and sat down. "But I'm afraid I can't help you directly. We are aware of the Pinochet matter, of course, but I am personally not connected with the Secretary of State's Office, the Law Lords, or any official position regarding the hypothetical question you're raising."

"Who is?"

"May I offer you some tea or coffee, by the way?"

"That's okay, I'm fine," Jay lied, suppressing a growing desperation for coffee. "If not yourself, who would be able to help me?"

The deputy minister smiled, cocking his head as he

folded his hands over his not inconsiderable belly and leaned back in his chair. "I suppose I could send you scurrying all over the government asking the same question, Mr. Reinhart . . ."

Jay leaned forward, supporting himself on the edge of the man's desk.

"Look, this problem is about to fly into your airspace, and it will be a very large political problem with major foreign policy and legal and treaty ramifications, and it will run the risk of deeply affecting U.S.-British relations. I need your help in finding the person or persons who can tell me, point blank, what the British government will do when presented with this warrant."

The man nodded slowly. "Well, Mr. Reinhart, you just effectively and eloquently enunciated most of the reasons why your questions are so far above my level as to be effectively unanswerable." He hauled himself up and walked around the desk with his hand outstretched. "Sorry I can't help you, old man. I always admired President Harris, by the way. The gentleman has true style."

"Who, then? Whom do I see?"

The man sighed. "Very well. Let me write down four names. You will most likely be wasting your time, of course."

"I'll take that chance."

The deputy minister pulled a pad of paper across the desk and uncapped a Montblanc pen, inscribing the names and office locations, then tore it off and handed it over.

Jay thanked him and left, going in succession to the first three offices and finding the same distant and indeterminate response from each.

Back in another corridor he looked at the fourth name and decided he'd had enough. He ducked into an office at random and asked to see the government phone directory, copying down a particular number before begging the use of a phone.

What he was contemplating probably *would* be a complete waste of time. Pure desperation. Maybe even a small act of defiance.

But he was determined to try.

Jay dialed the number and waited.

"Office of the Prime Minister," a cultured female voice said.

"Please listen carefully," Jay began. "I'm Jay Reinhart, attorney for Mr. John Harris, former President of the United States of America. I have a matter of urgent national security affecting both the United States and Great Britain, and I need to personally come over and discuss this with the Prime Minister or one of his immediate deputies as soon as possible."

There would be a long pause or a dial tone on the other end, he figured, but the woman answered him cheerfully. "We've been expecting your call, Mr. Reinhart."

"I'm sorry?"

"Won't you please hold?"

Jay stood in abject confusion holding the phone. Within a minute an aide to the Deputy Prime Minister came on the line and confirmed an immediate appointment.

"I was told you were expecting me," Jay asked, thoroughly confused. "Might I ask, how, and by whom?"

"I'd rather discuss that in person when you get here, Mr. Reinhart. I don't particularly trust open telephone lines."

"Ah, certainly. I understand. How do I find you?" Jay asked after passing his location.

"A car will be out in front of the building to collect you, Mr. Reinhart, in five minutes. The driver's name is Alfred. He's in a black Daimler."

"Thank you very much," Jay replied, hanging up and taking a deep breath, his mind spinning with unanswered questions.

✈ TWENTY-SEVEN

Stuart Campbell knelt in the aisle just behind the two pilot seats of his Lear 35, a scowl on his face as he looked at the red splotches covering the radar scope on the forward panel. "I don't have time for this, Jean-Paul!" he said to the captain.

"I'm sorry, Sir William," the pilot replied, "but a storm cell is moving directly toward the Luton airport and an approach simply isn't wise. Stansted is also in a rainstorm, but we can hold for Luton and wait until the storm passes, if you like."

"I don't have time!" Campbell snapped again. "I need to be in the Covent Garden area almost immediately. At the speed that storm's moving, we'll be on the ramp and in our cars before it gets close."

"You forget the gust front that precedes a thunderstorm. Such gust fronts can hide windshear."

"Well, blast it, let's divert to Heathrow then."

"We don't have a slot for going into Heathrow."

"So we're stuck with waiting for Luton?"

"I'm afraid so."

"Jean-Paul, for heaven's sake, we're five miles from the runway! At least be so good as to *try* an approach, will you?"

"Take the airplane, Gina," Jean-Paul Charat said quietly in French to his wife in the copilot's seat.

"Oui," she replied. "Remain in holding?"

"Oui."

Jean-Paul slid his seat back and snapped off his seat belt as he looked around at his employer. "Sir William, may I speak to you in the cabin?"

"Why? You can say anything you'd like right here," Stuart Campbell grumbled, backing up when he realized the captain wasn't taking no for an answer. Jean-Paul swung his body out of the command seat, and Campbell retreated to the cabin ahead of him and sat down, aware that his pilot was angry.

"Permit me to apologize, Jean-Paul," Campbell began, but the pilot was shaking his head and his jaw was set as he settled onto the compact couch opposite Campbell's seat and faced him, his hands clasped in front of him.

"This is a very serious occurrence, Sir William. When you employed Gina and me, you made us a solemn promise that you would never attempt to put pressure on us to override our better judgment as pilots, and that is exactly what you have just attempted to do."

"I said I'm sorry, old boy. It shan't happen again."

"I will require a blood oath from you, Sir William, or as soon as we park this aircraft, we will leave your employ."

Stuart Campbell shook his head and held his hand up. "I *humbly* apologize, Jean-Paul! You are correct. I made you that very promise, and I let my own scheduling anxieties get the best of me."

"I must have your renewed promise," the pilot said, his eyes boring into Stuart Campbell's.

"You have it," Campbell replied, extending his hand. "You have my word this will not happen again." He started to get out of the seat. "I'll go up and apologize to Gina as well."

Jean-Paul stopped him from standing as he shook Campbell's hand with formality. "No. I shall reassure Gina. But you do have a choice to make, Sir William. We have another hour and ten minutes of holding fuel, and if the storm clears the airport we might be able to land then, or we can proceed immediately to Gatwick and have a car or a helicopter waiting for you."

"Let's go to Gatwick," Campbell said without hesitation.

"Very well. And a helicopter, perhaps?"

"No. A car will be fine."

Jean-Paul nodded and got up as Stuart Campbell lightly touched his arm.

"Jean-Paul? I really do value your professionalism and your conservative thinking. Thank you for keeping us safe."

"You're welcome, Sir William," Jean-Paul said evenly, studying his employer's face and hesitating. "This situation . . . with the American President . . . it has you agitated, no?"

"It does," Campbell agreed with a sigh. "It's a very serious, precedent-setting action, this. Very important to the development of international law."

"And, I think to you, personally, it is important," the captain offered.

"You mean, is there some old score to settle? There will be that criticism, but the truth is plain and simple, Jean-Paul. He's guilty . . . although I'm not even sure John Harris knows it."

Stuart Campbell waited until Jean-Paul returned to the cockpit before pulling the phone out of its cradle. He punched in a string of numbers and waited for a male voice to answer.

"What's our status, Henri?" he asked.

"We have the judge for four o'clock in the Bow Street Magistrate Court. That's the court that by law will eventually have to rule on extradition."

"The committal hearing, as we call it for some obscure reason?" Campbell added.

"Absolutely."

"Henri, please double-check my memory of the extradition procedure. First we're essentially asking the municipal police to take the Interpol warrant to the magistrate and apply for a British arrest warrant."

"That's correct, Sir William. When we get the warrant, the police make the arrest, and then Peru has to send a formal request to the Secretary of State for extradition . . ."

"Already been done," Campbell said, stopping the other man.

"Really?"

"Yes. Last week. Go on."

"Very well. Once the arrest has been made, the Secretary will decide whether to sign the so-called Authority to Proceed."

"He will."

"And . . . then we deal with the committal hearing, which could drag on for several days. With Pinochet, it tied up the Bow Street Court for a week."

"True, but Amnesty International was there, as was Spain, all represented by a gaggle of QC's."

"Well, once that's over and it goes against Harris, his counsel may ask the Divisional Court for a habeas corpus writ."

"Which he will not get."

"Sir William, with Harris still on the ground at Sigonella, is there any chance the Italians will change their minds?"

Stuart laughed. "None. Anselmo is praying that Harris escapes as quickly as possible. He has no reason to guess that I'm hoping the same thing."

"No flight plan has been filed as yet. You're certain they'll come to London?"

"It was John Harris's own idea," Stuart chuckled, "although he's obviously misread the political climate."

"Rather badly, I would say. Any chance he'll discover that in time?"

"I would think not. Now, in the meantime, I want you to proceed with the plan I gave you this morning."

"Right now?"

"Yes, Henri. Right now. The sooner we flush them out

of there, the less time they'll have to think it over. Make the call."

Residence of the Prime Minister, London, England

Being chauffeured to #10 Downing Street was a baffling turn of events, Jay Reinhart thought, as he got out of the government car and followed a grim-faced man in a gray suit into a compact conference room to wait for the Deputy PM. Why they would have been expecting his call was even more of a mystery, although it was probably a result of White House efforts to help.

Hopefully that's it, Jay thought. *Hopefully the British want John Harris out of this, too.*

Perhaps he could arrange a quiet little deal to give the chartered 737 time to refuel at some British airport and be on its way before the courts could get involved. That might work, he thought, provided Stuart Campbell hadn't already taken the warrant to a British magistrate. He couldn't expect the government of Great Britain to defy its own courts.

The fact that the aircraft couldn't make it back to the United States without another refueling stop in Iceland or Greenland was still a significant problem. He wondered if they could charter another, longer-range aircraft, or even shift the President to a regular commercial flight at Heathrow.

If not, perhaps they could make Canada in one hop, although the reaction of the Canadian government couldn't be taken for granted either. They, too, had ratified the treaty.

Deputy Prime Minister Anthony Sheffield entered suddenly with two aides and shook Jay's hand warmly before sitting in a chair across the table.

"Let me get right to the point, Mr. Reinhart. Her Majesty's government is aware of your mission to defend Mr. Harris from the international arrest warrant issued by Peru. We're aware he's at this moment in Sicily, and the circumstances of that presence. We understand the Italian government's stance, and we're aware that you've been making inquiries about our official attitude toward the Peruvian warrant if Mr. Harris should arrive on these shores."

Jay nodded. "That's all quite correct."

"Very well. While we will need several hours to give you a formal answer, as a lawyer I'm sure you understand fully that, whatever our point of view, it is in no way controlling. I know you're aware that our courts are independent, as are yours in the States. This matter will be decided by judges."

"Well, sir, unless something has changed drastically in the last few weeks, the Secretary of State still has final authority."

"Yes, but only after the judiciary."

"Has the warrant already been presented to a magistrate court, Mr. Sheffield?"

"I really don't know," Sheffield replied. "But I should think we would be wise to expect that step at any moment."

"I do believe that the government's attitude, and your degree of interest, will very likely weigh in the thinking of any judges who get this case."

"Again, I firmly doubt that," Sheffield replied. "Let me ask, is your plan to fly President Harris here this afternoon?"

"Yes," Jay said cautiously, "provided . . ."

"Provided our position is not interpreted by you as a threat?"

"Yes."

"I can guarantee nothing, you understand, and I cannot even give you an idea until the PM has had time to consider the situation. We have been in touch with the White House, of course."

"I thought you might."

"And we are, as you might guess, very distressed to hear a legal process under a treaty to which we are a party, and to which we have unavoidable obligations, has been initiated against an American ex-President."

Jay studied Sheffield's eyes, looking for the deeper meaning behind his chillingly phrased words.

"As you can imagine, President Harris was equally distressed," Jay replied. "Mr. Sheffield, let me emphasize that this . . . this *warrant* is a ridiculous and fraudulent instrument in essence, and one that will ultimately be quashed for lack of credible charges. But . . . in the meantime, we need to ask that there be no government support for any short-circuiting or speedup of the extradition process. That *is* your governmental province, and the Secretary of State is certainly a member of your government."

"I understand."

"May I tell the President he can count on that?"

"No, Mr. Reinhart, you may not. Only the PM can decide what, if anything, we can do from this level, and what, if anything, should be communicated to the Secretary, whose obligation is primarily legal, and not political. Now, how may I contact you later this afternoon?"

Jay hesitated a few seconds, slowly accepting the reality that nothing more of substance was going to be said. He was already alarmed by the distance Sheffield had placed between John Harris and the British leadership.

"I have a rented cell phone," Jay said at last.

"Splendid," the Deputy PM said, motioning to one of his aides to write down the number Jay repeated.

"Where are you staying, Mr. Reinhart?"

"I . . . don't have a hotel yet. I came straight from the airport."

"Well, I shall be happy to arrange one for you, and transportation to the hotel as well." Sheffield got to his feet. "I'll ring you in a few hours." He began to turn.

"Excuse me, Mr. Sheffield."

"Yes?" Sheffield turned back, balancing himself with one hand on the table as he waited for the verbal postscript.

"You . . . indicated you would answer my question when I got here . . . how did the PM's office know to expect my call?"

Sheffield laughed. "Oh, that! Well, Mr. Reinhart, let's just say that we had some advance information that President Harris had retained you, we knew you arrived this morning at Heathrow, and no lawyer in your position would fail to contact Her Majesty's government. So . . ."

Jay met the man's gaze, feeling a small chill run up his back at the obvious sidestep.

"Who told you, sir?"

There was a telling hesitation and a frozen smile.

"I'm not really at liberty to say, Mr. Reinhart. But it really doesn't matter in the grand scheme of things, now does it? Good day, Mr. Reinhart."

He turned and left before Jay could reply.

Aboard EuroAir, Sigonella Naval Air Station, Sicily

"Mr. President?"

John Harris stirred in the first-class seat and opened his right eye, focusing instantly on Sherry Lincoln's face hovering over him.

"Yes, Sherry?"

"I hate to wake you."

He sat up and stretched. "I'm not sure I was really asleep. What time is it?"

She sat down next to him. "After three P.M. I just spoke with Jay Reinhart, and he's waiting for the British Prime Minister's office to ring him. In a nutshell, he says that based on what the Italian foreign minister told Captain Swanson, we're safe here until tomorrow, and he's worried about what the British may decide to do. So he wants us to wait until morning before flying to London."

"Oh wonderful! Another night at the Boeing Arms Hotel."

She laughed and rolled her eyes. "I know it! And I can't find a working shower on the entire plane."

"Swanson is okay with this?"

"That's another reason to wake you, sir," she replied. "Captain Swanson is coming across the ramp as we speak. He called ten minutes ago and told us to wake the pilots and stand by. He wouldn't say why."

Craig Dayton met Captain Swanson at the top of the airstairs and escorted him to the President immediately.

"We've got to get you out of here, sir," Swanson announced. "Apparently, Mr. Campbell has convinced a judge to declare this ramp under exclusive Italian control. There's nothing to stop them now."

"There wasn't supposed to be a ruling until tomorrow! Why did the judge issue the order early?"

"I don't know, Mr. President, but I was told the judge has probably already signed the order, or whatever they do here in Italy. When my commander and the Pentagon get the word, I fully expect I'll be ordered to stand aside and let them come aboard and arrest you."

"Captain," the President said, "who relayed all this to you?"

"An assistant to the Italian foreign minister. I'm afraid I've forgotten the name, but it's back in my office."

"That's okay," Harris said, rubbing his chin in thought, then looking squarely at Glen Swanson. "You feel the call was authentic?"

"Yes, sir. He seemed to know everything I would expect him to know in that position. He knew about my earlier call from Mr. Anselmo."

"All right."

"And I know he was calling from Rome because of the operator."

"How long do we have?" Harris asked.

"I don't know, but I would expect them to move rapidly. Having to leave empty-handed yesterday was an affront to the local Carabinieri commander."

Craig Dayton had been standing behind Swanson and taking in every word.

"We can go, then?" Craig asked, turning and gesturing to the President. "If you're ready, that is, sir."

"You can depart anytime," Swanson said. "We did fuel the airplane, right?"

Craig nodded. "Yes. Late last night. But, Captain, I need to know whether I'm going to have problems getting an air traffic control clearance to London. I mean, the clearance will come from Euro Control, which is in Brussels, but Rome Control could ask them to block us."

"I doubt that will happen," Swanson said, "but I wouldn't advise you to wait and test Rome's resolve. And there's another reason I think you need to go immediately.

This is Sicily, and . . . quite frankly, Rome is only marginally in control here. When the Carabinieri are thwarted at something, the results can be unpredictable."

"I don't understand," the President said.

"Remember, sir, that we're still subject to their jurisdiction. I'd just rather get you out of here as soon as possible."

Craig looked at John Harris, Sherry Lincoln, and Matt Ward, then back at the President.

"Mr. President?" he asked, waiting for the response.

John Harris sat deeply in thought, his chin resting on his hands. After a few moments he took a deep breath and looked up at Craig. "Okay, I'm ready. Even if Jay's concerns are right about London, I'd rather take a chance on them than stay in Italy. The one loose end is getting another plane chartered to take the veterans and their families back to Rome."

"I'll handle that, sir," Swanson said.

The President turned to Swanson. "Captain, if you think it's safe to do so, I want to walk into the terminal and talk to General Glueck and his group."

"I'll make sure we seal the doors, sir. It will be safe." He raised his handheld radio and gave the appropriate orders before escorting the President into the terminal and placing the PA microphone in his hand.

Folks, may I have your attention?

John Harris's voice carried through the large passenger lounge as he stood by one of the doors to the ramp and held the microphone. Most of the forty-four members of the group had been picking through a buffet table set up at the far end of the terminal. They turned now and moved toward the President as he waited for them to gather.

I wanted to come in personally and talk to you. I have decided to head for London and battle this fraudulent Peruvian legal action from there. I know you all volunteered to come with me, but that's not necessary now, thanks to what you've already accomplished. We're arranging another charter flight

*to get you to Rome this evening, but I want to tell you
again how deeply I appreciate your loyalty to the office I once held, to your country, and by association,
to me personally. Your decision to forgo that flight
back to Rome and stand with me here has made a
critical difference, and I'm more than humbled that
you would massively impact this marvelous once-in-
a-lifetime tour of yours to stand with me in an hour
of need.*

There was an immediate murmur of approval followed
by applause, which John Harris waved down gently.

*Please . . . let me finish. I know that . . . there was
considerable concern that the White House was
abandoning me, but that's not so. President Cavanaugh had a difficult decision to make, and he
made it for the good of our nation, and I applaud
him for that. It would have been easier to fly off with
that C-17, but he felt that both the United States, and
this particular former President, would be viewed as
cynically evading an international process we, ourselves, helped to create. He's right.*

Harris spotted General Glueck and nodded to him.

*Before I leave here, I want to shake the hand of each
and every one of you, and I especially want to thank
General Glueck for leading this heartwarming show
of support. I want you to know that this is not just me
personally you've been defending, but the ability of
every former president to travel the world without
fear of arrest on trumped-up charges. And . . . being
a veteran myself from a slightly younger generation,
I want you to know how much I honor your service
and sacrifices, and that goes equally for all you
twenty-two men and our one female Marine veteran,
Virginia MacCabe, over there, plus the spouses and
lovers who've stood by you, and the three children
and one grandchild who've come along on this trip.*

He replaced the microphone to applause as General Glueck approached. "You're certain you don't need us to come along, sir? I've polled everyone. We're ready."

John Harris put a hand on the general's shoulder. "No, I'll be fine from here."

"Go home, Mr. President, as fast as possible. Please."

Harris nodded. "I want to, believe me." He shook Glueck's hand and turned to the others, greeting each in turn and hugging several of the older vets before turning to the Navy commander who escorted him through the door and onto the ramp.

"Thank you so very much, Captain," John Harris said, shaking his hand. "I'd better get moving."

"Yes, sir, but I think we've got things under control. It could be a premonition, but for some reason I predict we're going to have a little maintenance problem with the outside phone lines into the base. Too bad, too, because we just won't be able to receive any phone calls from Rome until it's fixed."

"Why, that could take hours," Harris said, smiling.

"Yes, sir, it sure could," Swanson replied.

"Thank you, Captain," John Harris said. The naval officer turned and started up the aisle before stopping and turning around.

"Ah, Mr. President. A personal note?"

"Yes?"

"When you left office like you did . . . honoring your dedication to the idea of a six-year term . . . it made me feel ashamed, because . . ."

"I'm truly sorry to have disappointed you, Captain," Harris replied, interrupting him.

Swanson's eyebrows shot up in alarm as he raised his hand in a stop gesture. "No, no! Not ashamed of *you*, sir. I was ashamed of *me* . . . because I didn't vote for you. Your refusal to run again was the most inspiring thing I ever saw a President do."

✈ TWENTY-EIGHT

London, England—Tuesday—2:45 P.M.

In normal circumstances, the plush surroundings of the multi-room hotel suite provided by the Deputy Prime Minister's office would have riveted Jay Reinhart's attention for at least an hour. His love of antiques and fine furniture usually dictated a happy search for the pedigree of each piece in a well-furnished room. Instead, fatigue and the surreal nature of the mission had already numbed him to the luxurious surroundings.

Jay dropped his roll-on bag in the entryway and went to the bedroom to plop down on the king-size bed in deep thought.

So now what, Kemosabe?

Sherry Lincoln had called him when he was in the car on the way to the hotel to report their imminent departure.

"I'm nervous," he'd told her, "about bringing the President to London until I'm sure what this government is thinking, but I agree you'd better get out of there."

"We're starting engines now," Sherry said, falling silent for a few seconds as the whine of jet engines rose in the background. "Can you tell me exactly what you're afraid of, Jay?"

"Well . . ." he began, gauging how much of the swirling doubt to share with her. "I'm not afraid that London would send him to Lima as fast as Italy might have done, but . . . there's a lot of discretion in the British extradition process and it scares me. If this government for some reason decided they wanted or needed to extradite him, they might just succeed. I just don't know their attitude, and I can't risk guessing."

"You sound tired, Jay," she said suddenly. "Are you okay?"

"I'm . . . ah . . ." he started to reply.

"I know it's presumptuous of me to ask," she continued, "since we've never met." Her voice was exceptionally soothing, and he found himself almost forgetting that she'd just asked a question.

"What? Oh, no, Sherry. That's not presumptuous at all. I mean, I appreciate your asking."

"So, what *is* the answer?" she prompted.

"Ah, the answer is 'no,' I can't be tired, because I've only been up about twenty-eight hours now. I'm just marginally incoherent," he insisted.

"Well, you can collapse in a minute," she said, "but right now I need to give you the number for this plane's satellite phone, since the GSM phones we've been using won't work in the air. This is the one the cockpit crew will answer."

Jay grabbed a notepad from the bed behind him and took the number down. "I can reach you in flight on this?" he asked.

"Yes," Sherry replied. "By the way, our estimated arrival time at Heathrow is five-thirty P.M. your time. It's an hour later here in Italy. Are you going to meet us there? Or what do you suggest we do on arrival?"

"I'll call you in flight with instructions."

"And what if we don't hear from you?"

"Then . . . tell the President it's his choice, but if no one stops you, refuel immediately and go on to Iceland, refuel there, and head as fast as possible for Maine. But, Sherry, you can depend on my being there."

"I was hoping you'd say that. I'll be looking forward to meeting you in person."

"Me, too. You, I mean." He replaced the receiver and sat quietly for a moment, balancing the need to hear from the Deputy Prime Minister's office with the need to call the solicitor he'd hired, Geoffrey Wallace, to find out what he'd discovered. Wallace had yet to phone him back.

Jay punched in the number to Wallace's office.

"He's out at the moment," Wallace's secretary said. "But I'm sure he'll be calling you, Mr. Reinhart."

He thanked her and disconnected just as the room phone rang.

"Mr. Reinhart? Would you hold please for Ambassador Jamison?"

"I'm sorry, who?"

"Ambassador Richard Jamison, sir. American Ambassador to Great Britain."

"Oh. Of course," Jay replied, trying to pull up a mental image of Jamison, whose picture he'd seen quite often on television over the years.

Why is he calling me? Jay wondered as a small shadow of guilt crept into the periphery of his thoughts. *Should I have called him as John Harris's attorney?*

"Mr. Reinhart. We haven't met, but I wanted to thank you personally for what you've been doing for President Harris."

"Certainly, Mr. Ambassador. I'm his lawyer, after all."

"I understand. Can you tell me when he'll be arriving in London? I've been briefed by Washington to expect him sometime this evening."

"Actually," Jay began, caution slowing his response, "I'm not certain yet. Is . . . that why you're calling?"

"Well, there are two main reasons," the ambassador said, his voice crisp and tinged by a hint of New England.

"First, we need to compare notes on what you intend to do, and second, I need to let you know that the team from Washington should be here in about two hours."

"What team?"

"The Secretary of State, several representatives of the Justice Department, and a handful of others. President Cavanaugh dispatched them a while ago to help you prepare President Harris's defense when he lands here. I assumed you knew?"

"No, sir, I didn't. I mean, I welcome their assistance more than you know, but I knew nothing about it. Did you say two hours?"

"Less than that now, actually. They're coming into Heathrow, to the private facility there. If you'd like, I'll swing by in an embassy car and pick you up."

"That would be appreciated."

"About the British. I'm aware of your trip to see Tony Sheffield this afternoon."

"How do you know that, sir, if I may ask?"

"I'm your friendly local ambassador. When an American lawyer comes calling on the British government regarding the fate of an American President on British soil, the Foreign Office feels somewhat constrained to bring me into the loop."

The shadow of guilt Jay had felt became a cloud. This was, after all, a matter affecting two great nations, and he'd treated it as a private problem.

"I apologize for not calling you, Mr. Ambassador."

"Not a problem. May I call you Jay?"

"Yes, sir."

"Good. And I go by Richard. Now, look. Neither Sheffield nor the PM is going to call me first. They'll call you, if that's what they promised. So, if you'll take down my personal number, I'd appreciate a call as soon as you learn anything of substance."

He passed the number and Jay quickly wrote it down.

"In your opinion, Mr. Ambass . . . Richard, what can we expect the British to do about this?" Jay asked.

"Frankly, I don't know, Jay. I *can* tell you this government has been critical of the way the Pinochet case was handled by the Home Office."

"In other words, they think the Blair government should have supported Pinochet's assertion that he couldn't be arrested or extradited because of sovereign immunity?"

"No. The opposite. Some members of this PM's administration seem to think Pinochet should have been shipped to Spain within twenty-four hours of his arrest, though that's not really legally possible."

Jay felt momentarily disoriented. "They . . . *support* rapid extradition?"

"I wouldn't say they support it as a matter of general policy, or that they're prepared to bypass normal legal process, Jay. But I would warn you that there are voices in this PM's ear telling him that Britain doesn't have the right to delay extradition as a matter of political decision. In other words, one of the reasons President Cavanaugh scrambled our Secretary of State over here is to try to convince the PM that Britain must not interfere with their courts in any direction."

"I'm slightly stunned," Jay said. "Surely they can't feel the Pinochet case is directly similar to President Harris's? I mean, with Pinochet the whole world knew very clearly the charges of official torture were valid. These nonsense charges against John Harris are anything but. They're absolutely groundless."

"Well, that's a good distinction, counselor, but you have another problem. With Pinochet, it was Spain, a third-party country, trying to get their hands on him. Even the Blair government would have supported shipping the general back home to Chile if anyone had thought Chile would really put him on trial. But there was a bad taste in everyone's mouth about Spain making the complaint. Here was Spain demanding that England ship a Chilean to Spain to be tried in Spain for killing mostly Chileans in Chile. It was a real stretch."

The ambassador continued. "Now, with John Harris, the problem is that the nation that considers its citizens to have been victims of official torture is the very same nation signing this warrant and demanding Harris's extradition. In other words, Peru wants him in Peru to answer to charges of ordering the torture and killing of Peruvians. That's a different ball game."

"My problem is, sir, that I need time to show in court that the charges are bogus. Obviously the Peruvians want to try him in Peru, where the charges will automatically be considered valid whether they are or not."

"It's a real dilemma, I'll grant you, and I can't guess whether or not the British PM is going to think it's sufficiently different from the Pinochet case to justify helping us. I just don't know, which is why I'll be waiting with bated breath to hear what they tell you."

The ambassador ended the call and Jay toggled the phone to try Geoffrey Wallace's office again. Wallace was still out, he was told, and Jay left a terse message before replacing the receiver and jumping to his feet to pace and think.

An entire delegation of heavyweights was inbound from Washington. Why had no one bothered to tell the President's lawyer? A small administrative oversight, or a pointed one? He couldn't decide, and the positive prospect of acquiring bigger guns for the fight ahead was being diminished by the prospect of losing control to the servants of a sitting President who had already made the decision to distance himself from John Harris's dilemma.

Jay checked his watch, envisioning the EuroAir 737 already in the air and headed toward London. Should he phone them? Should he even consider turning them around or sending them to some other capital?

Jay moved to the largest room of the suite, where he'd spread out his three legal pads on an elegant mahogany dining table. The track of his thinking so many hours ago in Laramie and over the Atlantic was clearly visible on one of the pads, the various candidate capitals crossed out one by one until only London remained.

Am I wrong about this? Good Lord, the stakes are too high to be wrong!

Jay moved into the kitchenette and loaded the coffee maker with his mind a half continent away. If the Prime Minister decided to throw the weight of government in the direction of rapid extradition, could he essentially override the legal process? And if so, to what degree?

I've got to know the status of the warrant, Jay thought.

There was nothing he could do to stop that process, of course, but once the President had been arrested, Geoffrey

Wallace could move instantly to challenge the legality of the arrest, the legality of the warrant, and the legality of any decisions made.

Calm down! There is no way the British PM would send John Harris off in chains to Peru without months of hearings and appeals.

He was sure of that. He was *almost* sure of that.

The phone rang and Jay moved to sweep up the receiver, relieved to hear the prodigal solicitor on the other end.

"Terribly sorry, Mr. Reinhart. But it's been a bit of a cock-up getting this figured out, and now that I have, you'd better get yourself down here."

"Where is 'here,' and what are you talking about? I've been trying to reach you for hours."

"Indeed. I'm at the Bow Street Magistrate Court near Covent Garden. I'll give you the address. Campbell has already arrived, but the matter isn't slated for a half hour. You have time to get here."

"This hearing is to perfect the Interpol warrant?"

"Righto. I'm ashamed to say that it took me a while to discover that only the Bow Street Magistrate Court handles extraditions. Then, when I checked the Bow Street docket, I was wrongly informed the matter wasn't set yet. But it was, you see. In fact, it was set this morning for a hearing at three-thirty this afternoon, which is thirty minutes from now. Could have been an administrative error, I suppose, but the earlier misinformation smells like a favor to a crony." Wallace passed the address quickly, adding, "You realize there may be little we can do to oppose this first step?"

"Yes, I understand."

"I rang up someone who knows this magistrate, and I'm told he's unlikely to do anything but quickly issue the arrest warrant. The extradition warrant will take a later hearing."

"May I speak at all in court?"

"It's rather informal, so I doubt if the magistrate would toss you in the Tower of London for interjecting a few words. Whatever you might be able to say, however, will most likely have no legal significance at this stage. This is merely a formality to translate the Peruvian Interpol warrant into a provisional British arrest warrant. You can oppose it if the judge allows, but on a very narrow basis. You know, did Peru *really* send it? That sort of thing."

Jay rang off and raced to the elevator with his briefcase. He punched the button repeatedly, then gave up and ran to the stairway, descending the six flights to the lobby, where the doorman whistled up a taxi. The ride to the court took less than fifteen minutes, and Geoffrey Wallace was waiting for him at the curb as he climbed out of the cab.

"Mr. Reinhart?"

"Yes. How'd you know?" Jay asked.

"You look appropriately stressed," Wallace said, introducing himself and ushering Jay through security into the small and somewhat scruffy lobby and off to one side. The solicitor was probably sixty and just under six feet tall. Jay memorized his cheerful features, round face and a full head of sandy hair that almost looked like a rug.

"Let me introduce you to our QC," Geoffrey Wallace said, as a spectacled man approached. "Nigel White, this is Jay Reinhart, the American attorney representing President Harris, who is your client."

Jay and White shook hands as Wallace raised his finger and gestured toward the far side of the hall. "That's Campbell over there," he said, inclining his head toward Stuart Campbell, now huddled with several other men in dark suits.

"It's been a long time, but I recognize him," Jay said.

"Really? So you know the old bugger?" Wallace said, surprised.

Nigel White had begun consulting his notes and was paying no attention as Jay nodded. "How much time do we have before the matter's called?" he asked White.

"Perhaps ten minutes," the senior barrister replied without looking up.

"Wait here, please, gentlemen," Jay said, squaring his shoulders and moving toward Campbell, mindful of the small flutter in his stomach.

Sir William Stuart Campbell, QC, was the adversary,

but he was also a legend in international law, and it would almost be an honor to lose to such a man.

Almost.

The thought left him momentarily amused, even with a squadron of butterflies now performing airshows in his stomach. He had no intention of losing John Harris to Stuart Campbell.

"Gentlemen, excuse me," Jay said in a metered tone as he reached the group. The three men talking with Campbell turned and parted slightly when they saw Jay's eyes locked on the big Scot.

"Yes, hello?" Stuart said pleasantly, his eyebrows arched slightly in an unspoken question.

Jay offered his hand and Stuart took it firmly, saying at the same time, "I'm sorry, I failed to catch your name." He leaned over slightly as if needing to bring his ear down to a lower flight level to accommodate Jay's shorter stature.

"Why, Sir William, you don't remember me?"

The broad smile that had mesmerized and conned innumerable jurors and witnesses flashed across Campbell's face, masking his deepening confusion, as he let go of Jay's hand.

"I'm terribly sorry, but I'm very much afraid I don't."

"Really? Let me refresh your memory. The year was nineteen seventy nine, and you were representing British Airways and trying to keep an upstart little airline from Texas named Braniff from flying to Gatwick. Ultimately, you lost."

"Oh, yes! Mrs. Thatcher ran roughshod past the law on that one. I recall the case, but . . ."

"Do you, perhaps, recall the young American attorney from a Washington firm who came over to assist the primary counsel?"

"Yes, but you couldn't be that same young man," he said. "That chap later became a judge somewhere in the States and was thrown off the bench and disbarred, as I recall."

"One and the same, Sir William, although I was never disbarred. Merely suspended. The license is reinstated now."

"Really? And your name is . . ."

"Reinhart. Jay Reinhart."

Campbell's eyebrows arched again as he recognized the name. "Of course. Well, Mr. Reinhart, what brings you here to this humble court?"

"We talked yesterday, if you recall," Jay said evenly, enjoying the progression of emotions playing across Campbell's normally placid face as he sized up his opponent.

Campbell smiled then and glanced away before returning his gaze to Jay. "Certainly you're not attempting to tell me you're the lawyer representing President John Harris?"

"I am, indeed. John used to be my senior partner, if you recall."

"Yes. Now I do. Are you still associated with that firm?"

"No. I'm a sole practitioner, and I've retained local counsel, of course." He gestured to Geoffrey Wallace and Nigel White, and Campbell nodded in their direction with perfunctory courtesy.

"Surprised to see me here, are you, Sir William?"

"There is little that surprises me at my age, Mr. Reinhart. I must say, though, I *am* surprised that John Harris's attorney would waste his time here. All we're doing today is perfecting the Interpol warrant as a provisional arrest warrant, as I'm certain you know. The London Municipal Police are actually the applying party, and considering the validity of the warrant, it's hardly an adversarial process."

"Of course. And yet I'm here to make it an adversarial process."

Stuart Campbell gave Jay a condescending look, his head at an angle as if not believing the stupidity of the statement he'd just heard. Jay saw him shake his head as he leaned closer, his eyes on a far wall, his voice very low and meant just for Jay's ear.

"I should help you out a bit here, old boy, to save you embarrassment. You see, this is a magistrate court, and this is really not the forum for opposition in this sort of matter, despite the circuslike atmosphere they created here in the Pinochet case. Pity that Mr. Wallace hasn't briefed you on this, but as an American lawyer, you are not entitled to speak in open court for your client. I'm sure you wouldn't want to be reprimanded by the likes of a mere municipal magistrate."

"I've been reprimanded by the best of them, Sir William. What's the difference if one of them's wearing a wig and dispensing petty justice in a legal backwater?"

Campbell straightened up, his voice resuming a normal volume.

"Really? Well, please don't tell our esteemed magistrate in there of your innate contempt for his little court. Oh, and by the way, we don't wear wigs in the magistrate courts."

"That's not contempt—it's reality. This is a very basic level of the judiciary for England. In centuries past, if I recall, this would have been the court of common pleas, and we'd be jostled by men holding geese and fighting over disputed chickens."

"Not really. The courts of common pleas were a bit more common than this. But, very well, Mr. Reinhart. This should be entertaining. I shall enjoy jousting with you before the bar."

"Until then," Jay replied, turning with a barely contained smile to return to Geoffrey Wallace.

✈ TWENTY-NINE

Aboard EuroAir 1010, Sigonella Naval Air Station, Sicily—Tuesday—4:50 P.M.

Craig Dayton looked at his watch and exhaled in frustration. They were sitting with both engines running on the taxiway by the end of the runway, waiting.

"I think we're into the quagmire, Alastair," he said, his eyes on the tower in the distance. "Someone's holding up our clearance purposefully."

The copilot raised an eyebrow and glanced knowingly at his partner. "And, if I may get this straight, oh captain, my captain, we are surprised, are we?"

Craig glanced at him and smiled. "I guess I'd let myself hope this was all arranged. Ask him again."

"Your wish is my futile gesture, sire," Alastair said, pressing the transmit button to question the ground controller for the third time.

"Ah, roger, EuroAir," the young American controller responded. "Rome control says they're still coordinating. Please stand by."

"EuroAir Forty-Two . . . er, Ten-Ten, thank you," Alastair responded, remembering their radio call sign had now changed from a flight number to a charter call sign, EuroAir 1010. He glanced over at Craig, aware that the captain had punched the flight attendant call button on the overhead panel.

Jillian opened the cockpit door within thirty seconds, and Craig relayed a request for Sherry Lincoln to come forward.

"You wanted to see me?" Sherry asked as she stuck her head in the cockpit.

"Our clearance is being held up, Sherry, and I'm thinking I ought to phone Captain Swanson."

She thought for a few seconds and shook her head. "If it's being held up, Rome is responsible. Stand by. I'll be back in a few minutes. If the clearance comes through in the meantime, take it and go."

Sherry returned to John Harris's side and explained the situation as she looked for the name and number Captain Swanson had given her. She punched the long string of digits into the GSM and waited. A male voice answered.

"Yes?"

"Ah, this is Sherry Lincoln, aide to President John Harris. I would like to speak to Foreign Minister Anselmo if possible."

"Please wait, signorina," the voice said evenly.

There was silence on the other end, but no sound of communications being switched or extensions being rung.

"You asked to speak with Minister Anselmo, yes?" the man asked suddenly, causing her to jump slightly.

"Yes, I did. Is he available?"

"Apparently he is, Ms. Lincoln, since I am he. You are speaking to Giuseppe Anselmo."

She apologized quickly and relayed her suspicions. "I must ask you, sir, if the Italian government intends to prevent our departure?"

There was a pause on the other end before Anselmo answered.

"I will make that inquiry, Ms. Lincoln," he said with a careful side step. "Where may I reach you?"

She passed the number and thanked him before disconnecting.

"And?" John Harris asked when she'd replaced the
phone.

"Strange," Sherry replied. "He sounded startled, which
means someone else may be calling the shots."

Airborne, U.S. Air Force Special Airlift Mission (SAM52), 620 miles from London

Six men and one woman had settled into the plush conference alcove of the Air Force Boeing 757 executive jet from
Andrew's 89th Airlift Squadron's Presidential Fleet, all of
them watching U.S. Secretary of State Joseph Byer, who
was just hanging up one of the satellite phones.

"Okay, folks," Byer said. "They're just starting that
hearing in London. It's pro forma. They'll come out of
there with the English version of the warrant and then simply wait for Harris to step out of his chartered jet."

"That aircraft is still on the ground at Sigonella, sir,"
one of the men said, "but we're expecting departure for
London anytime."

The Secretary nodded. "Count on it. I don't know what
the delay is, but as long as they can fly, Rome will let them
out of there."

"You talked to Minister Anselmo's people?" Assistant
Attorney General Alex McLaughlin asked.

"I talked to Giuseppe Anselmo himself. They're over-
joyed." He looked around the table. "Okay, first order of
battle is to get this defrocked little Texas judge safely contained and out of the way. Harris doesn't need a maverick
lawyer, and I don't want any fallen cowboys riding into
Buckingham Palace and asking the blinking Queen for a
favor and screwing this up further."

"He's screwed it up already?" McLaughlin asked with
surprise. "I mean, I know he sounds like a bit of a carica-
ture, but I have talked with him, and I checked out his
background in international law before his close encounter

with judicial ethics, and he's no dummy. He practiced with John Harris for years."

The Secretary stared momentarily at McLaughlin. "Really?"

"Yes. And, by the way, the thing that wrecked his judgeship was falling in lust with a female defendant, whom, I might add, he later married."

"Well, your oversexed and knowledgeable international legal scholar just blasted into Number Ten Downing a few hours back and essentially put the British Government in a corner, demanding to know what they were prepared to do."

"That, I take it, was not the right approach?" McLaughlin asked.

"Are you kidding?" the Secretary asked with a smile.

"I'm a lawyer, Mr. Secretary, not a diplomat. I'm sure Mr. Reinhart and I share a propensity for finding the shortest distance between two points. Not to defend him, of course."

"Of course." The Secretary of State rolled his eyes and glanced around at the others again. "Defend Mr. Reinhart if you must, but just get him the hell out of my way. Understood? Send him on a tour, take him to din-din, buy him a cookie, get him drunk . . . whatever. Just get him out of my hair. This is a 'No Amateurs' zone."

Everyone nodded without comment.

"Good," Byer said. "We're on a mission from God in the Oval, and that mission is to contain this situation until the Peruvians give up and die of old age. No extradition, no release, just a long, laborious, boring, and essentially useful submersion of this into triviality."

"And what if the PM and the British Secretary of State won't go along with that?" McLaughlin asked.

The American Secretary of State looked him in the eye. "You're just a barrel of fun tonight, aren't you, Mr. Assistant Attorney General?"

"Just wondering, Mr. Secretary, what we're planning to do if the British judiciary claps the cuffs on our ex-Pres and has him carted off to a waiting Peruvian plane with the blessing of the PM?"

"Never happen."

"You're sure? What about the rule of law? Britain understands that concept. Heck, we got it from them in the first place."

"Never happen, Alex. First of all, you yourself briefed me about the extradition procedure. It takes time. And I know this Prime Minister is a bit of a rogue, but the Court of St. James is still far too interested in American cooperation diplomatically and militarily to buck us on something like this. Extradition isn't a worry. This Reinhart character is."

Office of the Foreign Minister, Rome, Italy

Giuseppe Anselmo replaced the receiver and held it in place for less than ten seconds before turning to his secretary and bellowing in Italian.

"Get the head of Rome Air Traffic Control on the line. Quickly, please!"

There was a flurry of activity in the outer office and several lighted trunk lines glowing on his desk phone before the intercom line rang.

"He's on three, sir." She passed the name and the title of the man and Anselmo stabbed at the button with a pudgy index finger, identifying himself with the subtlety of a gunshot.

"Why are your people holding up the clearance of that EuroAir flight in Sigonella?"

There was a confused response on the other end and a request to hold.

"Ah . . . I thought, Minister Anselmo, that we were not supposed to release him. That is why the clearance has been . . . delayed."

"*Who* thought that?" Anselmo demanded.

"I . . . ah, Minister, your staff told me your office did not want us to let him go."

"*My* staff? *Who* on my staff?"

"Rufolo Rossini, your deputy. He didn't tell me to do

this, but from what he said, I assumed that you would want us to act, since it made sense."

"You *assumed*? Has Air Traffic Control now taken on foreign and domestic policy decisions as well?"

"No, Minister, I . . ."

"Release that flight at once. Get him out of Italian airspace as fast as you can. Rossini had no authority to give you that order."

"But, Minister, Italy was trying to arrest the occupant of that aircraft, no?"

"Since you're intent on making national policy, let me tell you what the President, and I, want. We want that EuroAir flight and the former American President on it out of Italy as fast as possible! The last thing in the world Italy needs is a worldwide media circus focusing on whether we're doing the right thing with respect to President Harris. If we hold him, we lose. If we extradite him, we lose. If we try him, we lose. But if he flies away on his own to escape the warrant, we at least come out diplomatically intact. Where does he want to go?"

"London."

"Wonderful. Let the English battle this one. Get him out of here!"

"I'm very sorry, sir. If you'll let me go, now, we'll release the clearance."

"See to it! And don't you ever dare make an assumption like that on your own again."

The man rang off and Anselmo slammed the receiver back into place with enough force to startle his secretary, who peered around the corner of the office to make sure he was all right.

"Sir?"

"Find Rossini and get him in here immediately! I must find out who else he's been manipulating behind my back."

Bow Street Magistrate Court, London, England

Nigel White had briefed both Geoffrey Wallace and Jay Reinhart about the probable futility of any attempt to quash the Interpol warrant in the setting of a magistrate court.

"Basically, all we can do is listen and grumble a bit, unless you've got evidence that the warrant is truly bogus," White advised.

Sir William Stuart Campbell's presentation of the Peruvian warrant was predictable, but the image of Nigel White suddenly rising to his feet was not.

"Judge, may it please the court," Nigel said, watching carefully as the magistrate peered over the half-glasses he was wearing.

"Mr. White? What say *you* in this matter?"

Stuart Campbell turned in slight surprise.

"On behalf of Mr. John Harris, former President of the United States of America, I pray the court consent to hear important evidence that the offered warrant, while authentic in its issuance by Peru, states its cause fraudulently, not only under British law, but under Peruvian law as well."

The magistrate frowned and leaned forward. "Mr. White, in the court's view, this is not the forum for contesting the validity of those charges. In addition, I might add that you yourself just testified to the validity of the warrant's origin, which is all I'm concerned with at the moment."

"What better forum exists, sir? Should we wait for the injustice of an actual arrest of a former head of state of the most powerful nation on earth before discovering that this warrant is essentially a lie, alleging a crime that in no way could have been committed by Mr. Harris? This does not constitute the application of justice."

"Perhaps not, Mr. White, but it constitutes the application of the laws of Great Britain in the matter of arrest and extradition, in the order in which they are to be applied. Now sit down please."

"No, sir, I will not sit. I stand to beg you to permit Mr. Harris's American attorney, Mr. Jayson Reinhart, to speak to this matter."

The magistrate shook his head in mild disgust and pointed his gavel at Stuart Campbell, who had been standing at his respective table with a bemused expression.

"Mr. White, unless you can convince Sir William Campbell here to permit such a useless debate, and one which in no way will affect my ruling, I require you to SIT DOWN, sir!"

Stuart Campbell turned to the judge and raised a finger. "Sir, if you please."

"Sir William? Surely you're not prepared to say such argument is acceptable to your client?"

"On the contrary. However, the government of Peru also has no wish to engage in even the appearance of intransigence when it comes to presenting a full and complete evidentiary record. Regardless of the legal immateriality of it, I would be pleased to listen to Mr. Reinhart of America, if this court would consent to hear him."

The magistrate sat back as if struck. "Indeed. And just when I was prepared to expect you gentlemen to adhere to those boring procedures prescribed by law. But why should we stand on legality, eh? What do we think this is, a court? Very well, Sir William, I shall grant Mr. Reinhart an audience of five minutes, and that is that. Mr. Reinhart?"

Jay got to his feet feeling entirely off-balance and unprepared. "Yes, your honor . . . ah, I mean, Your Lordship."

"I'm not addressed as 'Your Lordship,' Mr. Reinhart, and you needn't be concerned with the courtesies of our court," the magistrate said, leaning forward and gesturing with his gavel, "since you are not a member of this bar and are not required to follow them. Not a whit of what you have to say will legally amount to a tinker's damn anyway, but as a courtesy to your client, and to yourself, you may address the court for five minutes."

"Thank you, sir," Jay said.

The judge sat back with an expression of mild amazement, his right hand cupping his face.

"May it please this court," Jay began, "I appreciate the opportunity to speak to this matter. I shall be very brief.

And I should tell you that I am very experienced in international practice and fully understand the mandates of the Treaty Against Torture under which this Interpol warrant is presented. We are not arguing that President Harris is protected by the Doctrine of Sovereign Immunity. That doctrine does not apply to such crimes as charged, as was properly established in the Pinochet case. What this court should consider, however, is that the charges in this warrant are patently false and do not state a sufficient criminal allegation to be afforded the full faith and credit of a British warrant. Peru alleges that President Harris personally ordered the para-military raid against a suspected Peruvian illegal drug factory that led to the admitted torture and murder of eighty-four men, women, and children. It was a horrible act, to be sure. Yet Peru has failed utterly to offer any proof whatsoever in this forum, or any other, that connects the order to commence this raid with any knowledge President Harris could possibly have possessed that torture and murder were to be used by the hired mercenaries who carried out this action. President Harris issued a blanket order to the Central Intelligence Agency . . . called a 'finding' under American procedure . . . that called for the CIA to search out and destroy the drug-making capability of the subject factory. That order is a matter of record in American archives. There is virtually nothing in that order, or anything else that Peru has presented, which indicates that President Harris knew, or could have known, that the CIA agent in charge in Peru was going to hire a gang of cutthroats and instruct them to do what they did. Sir, in the utter absence of any evidence to support this warrant, and under the common law and the rules of criminal procedure of Great Britain, Peru has a required burden to present a case that has some connection with the crime, and they have failed that burden. In the absence of such threshold offering of proof, this court should deny the warrant."

"Is that your statement, Mr. Reinhart?" the magistrate said, still sitting back, his chin on his hand.

"Yes, sir," Jay said, feeling completely ineffective.

"Thank you." The magistrate sat up. "Now, if you gentlemen don't mind terribly, I will proceed to issue my ruling and get on to the press of daily chores before this court."

Stuart Campbell had sat down as Jay spoke. He stood suddenly.

"Sir?"

The magistrate's face registered complete surprise. "Sir William? Whatever more can be said, sir?"

"I should appreciate the opportunity to answer, for the record, of course, the good Mr. Reinhart's challenge to the evidentiary basis of this warrant."

"Must you, Sir William?"

"Yes, sir, indeed I must."

"I shall warn you again that this bears in no way on my ruling. You don't need to answer his statement. What he said is immaterial to this case at this juncture. Need I remind you that this merely concerns the arrest warrant, not extradition?"

"I understand, sir, but this is a very serious case involving international legal precedent, and one which the world will be watching with great interest. It behooves us, I think, to make the record complete."

"Oh, very well. Proceed," the judge replied, sitting back and laying his gavel on the bench before him.

"Thank you," Campbell began, turning to look at Jay as he picked up a thick sheaf of papers. "I shall provide a copy of this brief for the court, and for Mr. Reinhart, but let me summarize. Mr. Reinhart alleges that there is no connection between President Harris's general orders to the CIA and the ultimate infliction of torture and death on the occupants of a rural building which, although serving as an illegal drug lab, also contained the wives and children of many of the workers . . . all of whom were tortured. In fact, in the torturous interrogation that proceeded over two days, some of the men, women, and even children were beheaded, many of the women and girls raped and brutalized, and ultimately all of them who were still living were then locked in the structure and burned to death. Only one person, a young girl, escaped to tell the tale. She was fifteen. She had been raped and maimed and left for dead with the others."

Nigel White was on his feet. "Sir, I must object to this shameless recitation of horror stories in place of legal substance!"

"Sustained, indeed!" the magistrate snapped. "Sir William? No more of that."

"Yes, sir. My point is this. The government of Peru has uncovered proof that on the nineteenth of November of that year, fourteen days before the raid began, President John Harris was briefed in the Oval Office of the White House by a CIA covert operations chief named Barry Reynolds, that there was a group of former 'Shining Path' guerrilla mercenaries who had agreed to conduct the raid and the destruction of the drug factory for the price of one million dollars, U.S. Mr. Reynolds left the Oval Office thirty minutes after he entered with the verbal approval of the President of the United States to conduct the raid and to pay for it from secret CIA funds. In that briefing, Mr. Reynolds had provided ample warning that the only force available to carry out such a raid were professional thugs, and that a high risk existed that they would be brutal and bloodthirsty in their work, and might well disregard their instructions and maim and torture the occupants of the factory before killing everyone. President Harris, having been informed of this and advised by Mr. Reynolds to disapprove the raid, nevertheless ordered the raid carried out because he was convinced that stopping the heavy supply of processed cocaine and heroin from that district was far more important than the lives of those involved. Of course, the President undoubtedly did not expect women and children to be involved, but he did expect human beings to be the victims of the raid he was authorizing. We have copies of the presidential appointment logs showing a gap of thirty minutes in his schedule that day. While there is no mention of Mr. Reynolds's visit in those logs, Peru's investigation has uncovered irrefutable evidence of that visit and has verified the details of what transpired, and it is this proof that forms the unshakable foundation of this warrant."

Nigel White began to rise but Jay put a hand on his shoulder and stood instead.

"Judge, may I ask a question?"

"I can't see why not, Mr. Reinhart," the magistrate said sarcastically, "since we're apparently making up a new criminal procedure here as we go along. By all means, proceed."

"Sir William, what is the nature of this so-called irrefutable evidence?" Jay asked.

With a supremely confident expression that sent cold chills down Jay's back, Stuart Campbell turned and faced him in silence for a few seconds.

"I'm very much afraid, Mr. Reinhart, that we have that information from the source himself. You see, Mr. Reynolds was sickened by what happened. He has had a long and distinguished career with Central Intelligence and is a man of conscience who was directed by his superiors to bring this onerous option to President Harris. He did so reluctantly, thinking that a President of the United States would never approve the use of thugs and the dangers such an act entailed. After the raid he was in an agony of conscience and felt personally responsible. The record will show that he resigned his CIA position and subsequently contacted the President of Peru personally to inform him of his own involvement and provide proof that the raid had been ordered from the Oval Office."

Jay took a deep breath and tried to look unperturbed. "That's simply a 'he said, she said' case, Sir William. You can't base such a warrant on one man's uncorroborated allegation, especially since we know nothing of this man Reynolds's credibility."

"Mr. Reinhart, I'm sorry you have had inadequate time to research this. Mr. Reynolds knew the orders he would receive from the President would be covered up and that the official line would be that the meeting never took place, and he knew his position was very perilous should anything go wrong. So he took a singular, if illegal and risky, precaution to preserve the record if he should be later accused of acting without authorization: he used a state-of-the-art electronic device to secretly videotape his meeting with the President. In other words, sir, we have the proof, and it's in our possession and ready for the committal hearing."

Jay sat down in confusion, trying not to look as stunned as he was. If there was a videotape, even one inadmissible in a U.S. court, the entire equation had changed.

But the John Harris he knew was incapable of approving such a thing! And even a videotape could be misinterpreted.

"Gentlemen, with your permission," the judge began, "I should like to reclaim my humble court and issue my ruling now, which is as it was to begin with. I find this Interpol warrant to have met all the requirements necessary for granting it full faith and credit, and I am thus going to sign the provisional arrest warrant for the apprehension of one John B. Harris, formerly known as President of the United States, for the charge of multiple specified violations of the international Treaty Against Torture. The arrest may be effected at the earliest opportunity when Mr. Harris is found within the territorial jurisdiction of the United Kingdom. And I shall now call a ten-minute recess and try to recall why I took this magistrate appointment to begin with."

The magistrate got to his feet as the assemblage stood and waited for him to disappear into his chambers. When he was gone, Stuart Campbell turned and laid a copy of his brief in front of Jay.

"I need a copy of that videotape," Jay said, managing a reasonably normal voice.

"Well, that will take some time, of course, if we're willing to release it at all at this stage. I shall make that determination and let you know. Where are you staying? If we release it, I'll see it's delivered to you."

"I need the tape today."

Stuart Campbell turned to one of the solicitors who had accompanied him. "Can we even physically provide the tape today, James, should we decide to?"

"Maybe," the man answered.

Campbell turned back to Jay. "Provided I agree you should have it, and I make no guarantees about that, I shall honestly do my best to get it to you rapidly, Mr. Reinhart."

"You realize it's probably inadmissible as evidence?"

"A major point for us to argue, eh?" Campbell replied. "That depends entirely on where Harris is tried, doesn't it?"

"This isn't over," Jay said.

"Indeed, it is not," Campbell said, shaking his head without smiling. He sighed and continued. "Please understand, Mr. Reinhart, I do admire your client, but even titans must answer to the law. We began moving in the direction of that little tradition nine hundred years ago with the Magna Carta and the legal restraints it placed on the original King John, if you recall. Eliminating sovereign immunity under this treaty is a great fulfillment of the rule of law, and I have no intention of breaking nine hundred years of progress by making an exception for *your* King John."

✈ THIRTY

Alastair finished the read-back of the air traffic control clearance and turned to Craig with a smile as he made a zooming gesture with his left hand and punched his transmitter button.

"Sigonella tower, Ten-Ten would like immediate take-off clearance."

"Damn right!" Craig echoed. "Let's get the flock out of here."

"Roger, Ten-Ten," the young Navy controller in the tower replied. "You're cleared immediate takeoff . . . ah, stand by, sir."

Alastair turned his eyes toward the tower. "Say again, tower?"

Craig had begun rolling forward, but he braked now, stopping the jet short of the white "hold line," which stood as a visual barrier to the runway beyond.

"What's going on?" Craig asked.

"I don't know . . ." Alastair began, following Craig's

gaze to the right. There were lights moving over the runway surface at the far end, more than five thousand feet distant.

"Cars?" Alastair asked.

Craig nodded. "I guess."

The tower operator's voice boomed in their ears, betraying surprise. "Ten-Ten, we, ah, have unauthorized vehicles entering the runway. Hold your position."

Craig's left index finger found the transmit button on his control yoke. "What do you mean, tower? What vehicles?"

"We're unsure, Ten-Ten. They came through a back gate or something. Stand by."

Headlights were aligning themselves with the reciprocal runway heading and racing toward their position. Two, three, and four more cars fell into formation behind and both pilots could now see red and blue rotating beacons flashing urgently on the top of each car.

"Craig, in the vernacular, 'Oh shit!' "

"Roger on the 'Oh shit,' " Craig replied, glancing at Alastair. "Get him to give us a blanket takeoff clearance."

Alastair nodded and punched the transmit button simultaneously. "We'll take the responsibility, tower, but give us a clearance to take off when we can do so safely."

There was silence for twenty seconds before the tower operator's voice returned with a defiant tone. "Roger, Ten-Ten, you're cleared to takeoff at pilot's discretion and at your own risk. Caution for men and equipment on the runway, and none of them is under the control of the tower.

"Get Captain Swanson on the phone!" Craig ordered, turning to Alastair. "You have the number?"

"Yes." Alastair yanked a piece of paper from his pocket with one hand while pulling the satellite phone from its cradle with the other. He punched in the digits and waited as they watched the official cars stop one by one in the middle of the runway at two-thousand-foot intervals, effectively making a takeoff attempt suicidal.

Seconds ticked by like minutes as Alastair waited for the Navy commander to answer his GSM phone.

"Captain Swanson? Alastair Chadwick. We've got a

problem out here." He quickly explained the dilemma, then turned to Craig.

"He says he just found out. It's the Carabinieri. They just came barreling onto the field. He says they smashed through a back gate."

Alastair turned back to the phone. "Yes, sir?" He listened, nodding at intervals. "I understand. We'll hold on."

"What?" Craig asked.

"He's trying to call Rome and find out what's happening. He says his orders haven't changed."

The car closest to the 737 began moving toward them again, accelerating toward the head of the runway, where it turned off and stopped, the headlights pointed at the cockpit. Craig could see the doors of the police car open and several men get out, each of them carrying what appeared to be automatic weapons.

Office of the Foreign Minister, Rome, Italy

Deputy Foreign Minister Rufolo Rossini had been on his way home when summoned. He raced to his boss's office to be confronted by the white-hot anger of a blindsided bureaucrat.

"He misunderstood, Giuseppe!"

Giuseppe Anselmo's secretary physically leaned around the corner and flagged his attention.

"Sir, I think you should talk to Captain Swanson at Sigonella."

Anselmo turned with a finger in the air to rebuke her for the interruption, then thought better of it.

"Why?"

"The Carabinieri are overrunning his base."

"The . . . *what?*"

She motioned to the phone and Anselmo launched himself at the instrument as he pointed Rossini to a chair. "Is this your work, too?"

Rossini had turned chalky-white and was having trouble getting a complete sentence out. "I . . . ah . . . don't know how . . ."

Anselmo motioned him into a chair disgustedly as he yanked up the receiver and listened to Swanson's complaint.

"I want you to stand by on this line, Captain. This is not being done on our orders. In fact, I just ordered Air Traffic Control to let them depart."

He replaced the receiver and bellowed around the corner for his secretary to get a connection with the Carabinieri commander nearest to the leased Navy base, then turned his full fury on Rossini.

"What, *exactly*, did you say to them?"

"You mean the . . ."

"You know exactly what I mean! Why are they overrunning an American base?"

"All I said was that we . . . appreciated their help, and were still trying to find a way to detain Mr. Harris and his plane."

"Wonderful! You said this to a Sicilian commander?"

"Yes."

"A Sicilian commander who was left red-faced yesterday when told to leave that base? Are you insane?"

The phone rang and Anselmo scooped up the receiver with his right hand in a rapid, fluid arc that ended at his face.

"Is this the commandant? Good. This is the foreign minister of Italy. Listen very, very closely!"

Aboard EuroAir 1010, Sigonella Naval Air Station, Sicily

Four armed men wearing uniforms of some sort had arrayed themselves in front of EuroAir 1010, one of them making a lateral gesture across his throat and pointing to each wing.

"He wants us to shut down," Alastair translated.

"Like hell I'll shut down!" Craig replied.

"Right. He's waving an Uzi."

"Let him wave it. I'm not shutting down."

Alastair pressed the satellite phone to his ear, waiting

for some sign that Captain Swanson had returned to the line.

"Alastair, check the runway diagram. Taxiway Bravo, the next one down. How much runway available from there?"

"Enough," Alastair answered.

Craig's left hand hauled the nosewheel steering tiller to the right immediately as he goosed the throttles and sent the four men ahead scrambling backwards. The 737 turned sharply right and reversed course as he guided the nosewheel back to neutral and then left to head back down the taxiway as if they were returning to the ramp. Craig glanced over his left shoulder, straining to see the reaction.

"No shooting, then?" Alastair asked evenly.

"No . . . no, they're standing there looking stunned."

"Craig, they still have three cars on the runway."

"You've heard of the good old American game of 'chicken' haven't you?"

"Dear me, you're not serious?"

"Am I serious?"

"Never mind!" Alastair said quickly. "Stupid question."

Craig let the 737 accelerate to thirty knots before braking and turning sharply left onto the second runway entrance. He barreled to the middle of the runway and turned right, aligning the nose of the jetliner with the runway heading. The roof lights of three police cars flashed defiantly in their faces at intervals down the concrete ribbon.

Craig advanced the throttles while holding the brakes, bringing the engines up to full power, the 737 straining and lurching against the locked friction of the tires barely holding the runway surface.

"Flash the landing lights three times, then tell the tower we're rolling."

Alastair complied as Craig released the brakes smoothly, feeling the craft leap forward.

In the landing lights, he could see the first car several thousand feet ahead as it sat in the middle of the tarmac pointing toward the moving jet. There were no doors open.

"They're still there," Alastair said. "Thirty knots."

"They'll move."

"Fifty, sixty . . . a thousand feet away from him."

"I know it."

Suddenly the car ahead jumped into motion and careened off to the right side of the runway, safely clearing the concrete before they rolled over the spot he had occupied.

"Eighty knots, Craig. Two cars to go."

"Roger."

The jet's acceleration began to slow slightly as aerodynamic drag began working against the smooth passage of the aircraft, but the lights of the next car were steady in the middle of the runway surface two thousand feet ahead, and the onrushing Boeing was covering the distance at a far greater rate.

"Move, damn you!" Alastair said under his breath, as that squad car lurched into gear and moved sharply off the surface to the left.

"The last one's going as well!" Alastair said, his voice almost gleeful. "Vee one, and rotate!"

Craig nursed the control yoke back, lifting the angle of attack of the wings until the lift exceeded the weight, and the powerful aircraft lifted clear of the runway surface heading west.

"Positive rate, gear up," Craig ordered.

"Right you are, positive rate, and the bloody gear is coming up. Well done, mate! But how did you know they'd get out of our way?"

"This is Italy. If one of those guys let's his car get smashed, he'd have to pay for it out of his own pocket. No way would they have left one on the runway."

Bow Street Magistrate Court, London, England

Jay Reinhart left the courtroom dazed and struggling to hide it. A dull ache in his middle was protesting his failure to eat or drink anything for hours. He tuned out the discomfort and turned on the rented GSM phone.

It rang almost immediately, with Sherry Lincoln on the other end.

"We just lifted off from Sigonella," she told him, relating the ninety-minute takeoff delay and her call to the Italian foreign minister that had apparently shaken the air traffic clearance from Rome Control.

"I thought you might already be on approach to Heathrow," Jay said, holding a finger in his other ear against the noise around him and mouthing the word *wait* to Nigel White and Geoffrey Wallace, who nodded and moved off to confer while he talked.

"No," she replied, "it'll be about an hour and forty-five, I'm told. What's *your* situation?"

He relayed the result of the hearing, but omitted any mention of Stuart Campbell's chilling revelation that a clandestine videotape existed that might implicate the President.

"So they issued the British warrant?" Sherry asked.

"Yes, and we can expect them to be at the plane with it when you get here."

"And now it begins?"

He sighed. "I still see no reasonable alternative, Sherry, but . . . I think I should speak with the President."

"Hold on. He's sitting next to me."

John Harris's voice came on the line quickly, and Jay repeated the basics.

"Sir, there's something I have to ask you."

"Go ahead, Jay."

"Does the name Barry Reynolds ring a bell?"

There was a very brief hesitation, and Jay imagined he heard a snort of disgust. "Of course. Reynolds was the CIA covert-operations man who set up the massacre in Peru that's at the root of this problem. Why? Did his name come up in that courtroom today?"

This is an open line, Jay reminded himself. *It could be monitored.*

"Yes, it did, John. Stuart Campbell claims he has a clandestine videotape of Reynolds talking with you for thirty minutes in the Oval Office. . . . I can't get to my notes right now, but the meeting allegedly took place around two weeks before the attack."

"A *what*?"

"A tape. A videotape. Supposedly, he was wearing a small camera."

"In the *Oval Office*?" John Harris almost roared the question into the phone.

"Yes."

"My Lord in heaven, Jay!"

"Look, John . . ." Jay interjected quickly. "I think we'd better save this until I see you in person. I don't know how secure these phones are."

"You're being bluffed, Jay! I can tell you that."

"Then no such meeting ever took place?"

"I'm . . . we'll talk on the ground. You're right to be cautious about this line. I heard Sherry say under two hours. Right, Sherry? She says 'Yes.' "

"Okay, Mr. President. I'll be waiting for you. And so will they."

"Damn!" Harris snarled on the other end, responding, Jay thought, to the imminent arrest.

But it was the Reynolds allegation that had prompted Harris's response: "I can't believe Campbell would stoop so low," the President said, correcting himself instantly. "Strike that. I guess I *can* believe it, and I suppose I should tell you the reason why." John Harris's voice sounded strained, his breathing heavy and audible over the pocket-sized phone even through the din of the Bow Street Court foyer surrounding Jay. "There wasn't time before now," Harris added.

"I beg your pardon?" Jay asked, looking at the floor and concentrating on the phone.

"Stuart and I have a bit of a history, Jay, that not even you know about."

"A history?"

"Something I interfered with that he was trying to accomplish. It goes way back before you joined the firm."

"I see."

"I think he's trying to even the score."

Two men in animated conversation brushed past, almost knocking the phone from Jay's hand. One mumbled a "Terribly sorry!" and rushed on, as Jay forced himself to focus on the conversation. "This would be a pretty excessive counterstrike just to get back at you for beating him in a lawsuit!" Jay said.

"It wasn't a lawsuit," the President added.

A commotion had broken out toward the main entryway and Jay glanced up to see several well-dressed men sweep in and fan out, questioning bystanders about something. He turned away, trying to concentrate on Harris's reaction.

"You have my word, Jay," John Harris said on his end. "This is not as it may appear. Don't jump to any conclusions."

"This man Reynolds. Is he a black hat?" Jay asked.

"You mean a bad guy? No."

"Campbell said Reynolds had a long and distinguished career at Langley."

"He did, Jay, which is why I made the mistake of trusting him."

Jay related the news that the Secretary of State and a delegation sent by President Cavanaugh were on the way.

"Good. I more or less expected that," the President said.

"But I'm worried, John, that they're planning on taking over the show, and that would be perfectly all right if I could be sure they're serving only your interests."

"But you doubt it, as you should."

"Yes."

"Don't worry, Jay. *You* are my lawyer, and their help is entirely subject to your discretion."

"Yes, but *should* it be? I mean, one error here and you could be on your way to Lima in handcuffs," Jay said, letting the enormity of the risk settle over him once more. "I'm still very concerned about the intentions of the British Government. I haven't heard back from the Prime Minister's office."

"Mr. Reinhart?" A male voice broke through his concentration, and he looked up to see one of the newcomers standing in front of him. He covered the mouthpiece of the GSM phone. "Just . . . just a moment."

"Okay," the man replied, his accent clearly American.

"John? I'd better go," Jay said into the tiny handset. "I'm headed . . . back to the hotel for now. No, wait . . .

I'm going straight to Heathrow on second thought. Do you know where at Heathrow the aircraft is going to be?"

"The general aviation facility by Terminal 4. Metro Business Aviation, I think," Harris said, passing the address as relayed by Craig Dayton. Jay scribbled it down before ringing off and turning to the man who'd called his name.

"Sorry about that," Jay said.

"No problem, Mr. Reinhart. The Secretary of State has arrived and would like to speak with you at his hotel. We have a car waiting."

"I'll be with you in a moment," Jay said, motioning Nigel White and Geoffrey Wallace over to thank them and arrange a meeting later in the evening.

"You realize," Geoffrey said, "that if they arrest him today, Campbell will try, and probably succeed, in setting the committal hearing for sometime tomorrow. That's assuming the home secretary signs the appropriate instruments and Peru has sent the formal request."

"That would be back here?"

"Yes. Committal hearings are only handled at Bow Street."

"But we simply file for habeas corpus with the . . . ah . . ."

"Divisional Court. Yes, but they might expedite that, as well."

"Have you ever heard of a contested extradition happening within, say, a couple of months?"

Geoffrey shook his head no. "But keep this in mind, Jay. It all depends on the government. If they want to grease the skids, so to speak, and if the Divisional Court refuses to assign the matter for review by the House of Lords, it could happen very fast."

"There's still a last appeal, though."

"You don't want to get into that territory. Look, probably we'll have a minimum of months, but I'm simply answering the question you asked earlier today. Could it be pushed? Yes, it could."

"This process is beginning to sound more risky than I envisioned," Jay said quietly.

"It is," Nigel White replied, "especially if Her Majesty's government makes the decision to get involved forcefully. Now, your man is no bloody Pinochet, so it's unlikely they would, yet . . ."

"Yet, you're not sure?"

"I've heard disturbing things about this Prime Minister's fury over the way Pinochet was afforded such kid glove care in Britain."

"Do you think I ought to keep him out of the country?"

Wallace shook his head. "I'm not saying that. I just need to warn you that even if the underlying charges are hogwash, getting this warrant off his back is not a . . . what do you call it in the States? A 'slam duck'?"

"What?" Jay said, shifting his eyes from Nigel White to Geoffrey Wallace. "Oh. No, that's 'slam *dunk*,' as in basketball. Not duck."

"Of course," Geoffrey replied.

"Well, *dead* duck would be correct if they hand your client over to Peru," Nigel joked, chuckling for a second before realizing the humor had fallen very flat. He cleared his throat and continued. "I will keep my calendar clear for you tomorrow."

Jay looked in the direction of the door, where the men were waiting for him, then back at Nigel and Geoffrey. "Okay. I'll call you later this evening after I've heard from the Prime Minister's office."

It took fifteen minutes of silence to reach the Secretary's hotel. The other men in the car were obviously functionaries, Jay realized, after climbing in the car and trying to squeeze even the most rudimentary information from them.

The driver stopped at a side entrance, where a hotel security officer was waiting to usher Jay up a flight of stairs to a service elevator, and then to the fifteenth-floor suite where the delegation was waiting.

Jay introduced himself to the Secretary of State and the Assistant Attorney General he'd sparred with by phone from Laramie, then joined them at an ornate conference table.

An aide to the Secretary ran through a quick briefing: the British Government would not want to ruffle American feathers; ex parte contact with the Prime Minister's office by anyone not a professional diplomat was highly inadvisable; and arrangements were already being made to rent a plush private residence for John Harris's extended stay under house arrest.

"Mr. Secretary," Jay replied, "I was promised a call from Deputy Prime Minister Sheffield. I still want to take that call."

Secretary of State Joseph Byer nodded and raised his hand, palm up. "Mr. Reinhart . . . or may I call you Jay?"

"Certainly," Jay replied.

"Very well, Jay, we've already indicated to Deputy Prime Minister Sheffield that we're here to serve as the diplomatic conduit now, so I wouldn't worry about not hearing from him. In fact, that's why I wanted to meet with you, to put you personally in the hands of Mr. McLaughlin here . . ."

"I want to receive that promised call, Mr. Secretary."

Byer smiled. "I know you do, Jay. Any good attorney would want to keep a death grip on this thing, but the current President of the United States did not ask me to come over here to stand on the sidelines. He knows, as does President Harris, how important it is to have direct government-to-government diplomatic understandings about these things, and having you in the loop actually muddies the waters."

"Meaning?"

"Well, Jay, meaning that Sheffield will tell you one thing in diplomatic doublespeak and will tell me—or more properly the PM himself will tell me—something entirely different. He'll tell me the truth as Britain's closest ally. This is statecraft, Jay. I know you're an experienced international lawyer, but this arena is very, very different from what you're trained to navigate."

"What do you propose, Mr. Secretary? President Harris is on his way inbound as we speak and will undoubtedly be met at Heathrow in an hour by police officers with the warrant."

"We expect that."

Jay warned himself to cap the rising anger in his gut at the paternalistic treatment. *I need their help, even if this guy's a sanctimonious windbag!*

"Okay, but what about tomorrow, when we know Stuart Campbell will try to get what's known as a committal hearing so he can press for rapid extradition? I'll be there to fight that request and appeal it immediately if it goes against us, but I need desperately to know the mind of the PM. Have *you* any confirmed word from them?"

Byer glanced at two of his people as if trying to restrain himself from a sarcastic remark, then looked back at Jay. "We know this government's mind already, Jay. They'll give good and proper lip service to the need to follow international law and procedure, they'll let the courts rule that President Harris should be extradited, and they'll make it quietly known to the court that they expect Harris to be given leave to appeal, knowing that the appeal hearing will be set for a month of Sundays from now. After that, the British will do what the British did in the Pinochet case: delay, delay, and delay some more while they write careful, learned opinions and massage the diplomatic problems behind the scenes, and release pontificating statements about law and treaty responsibilities. In other words, this is the start of a long, long process, which will eventually end with President Harris being allowed to return to the United States. There's really no cause for any of us to get too exercised."

"Have you the word of the Prime Minister of England on that sequence, Mr. Secretary?"

"Now, look, in diplomatic affairs . . ."

"No, dammit!" Jay cut him off. "As President Harris's attorney, I'm asking you a direct question with very grave legal import. With all due respect, Mr. Secretary, do you have the direct personal assurance of the Prime Minister of England that the scenario you've outlined is lock-down valid?"

Byer sat back and sighed disgustedly. "That's not the way it's done, Jay."

"Then we have a major problem."

"We have no problem at all, as far as I can see."

"First of all, Mr. Secretary, you and the rest of the folks in this room are not going to shove me aside here, statecraft or no statecraft. I'll certainly bow to and utilize your superior office and skills and support on understanding the equation, but I have a major decision to help John Harris make right now, and that's whether to continue to a landing in the U.K., or go somewhere else."

"That would be foolish . . ." Byer began.

"What would be foolish? Going somewhere else, or landing here?"

"Going anywhere else except the U.S., which that aircraft can't reach. This is the friendliest forum Harris could possibly find, Jay. And for the record, we're not trying to, as you put it, shove you aside. We simply have a better cross-section of talent to help you, and you should be guided by that. No, as Alex McLaughlin told you, we can't be Harris's primary counsel, but we can essentially handle this from the sidelines."

"*I* will handle this with your help. You will not handle this for me or for the President."

"Poor choice of words on my part, Jay," the Secretary said, trying to soften his stance. "Of *course* you're the President's lawyer. We respect that."

"Nevertheless you've made the decision without consulting me or him that the President should come here?"

"Well, Jay, it appears you already made that decision before we arrived. We're just advising you to stick with it."

Jay rose from the table. "Excuse me a minute, gentlemen." He walked to a far corner of the room and took out the piece of paper with the EuroAir cockpit satellite phone number and punched it into the GSM phone.

It took several minutes to get the President to the cockpit, and Jay could feel the contempt radiating from the conference table behind like a wave of infrared heat, felt but not seen.

Harris came on the line and Jay quickly explained what was happening.

"Very well, Jay," the President said. "Hand the phone to Joe Byer, will you please? Then come back on the line."

"Yes, sir." Jay walked back across the room and explained the President's request, handing the GSM phone to the Secretary of State, who put it to his ear and tried unsuccessfully to get a complete sentence out.

"Hello, Mr. Pres . . . yes, I . . . we're . . . President Cavanaugh is very concerned about . . . yes. I realize that. Yes, sir, I'm fully aware of that." Byer's face was turning beet-red as he shifted the phone to his other ear and nodded. "Mr. President, you're talking to the Secretary of State of . . . yes, sir. I understand. Yes."

Byer cast an angry glance at one of his aides before looking back at the table.

"Yes, sir. I will." He handed the phone back to Jay.

"Jay? You there?" President Harris asked.

"Yes, sir."

"Your ear is the only one near this phone?"

"Yes, sir."

"Good. I just read Byer the riot and sedition act and verbally spanked him. He's mad and he's embarrassed, so treat him like overheated nitroglycerine. Don't provoke. He's been told that you are lead counsel and that whatever you say is the law regarding my defense. And he's been told to tell Mr. Sheffield to call you immediately."

"Very well, Mr. President."

"We're forty minutes out, Jay. You'd better head for the airport."

Jay folded the phone and returned to the table, standing across from Joe Byer.

"Mr. Secretary, I've got a difficult task ahead of me, and I'm grateful for the support of everyone here. But I need to head for Heathrow now, and I need . . ."

"To hear from Sheffield. I know!" Byer interrupted, shifting his expression to one of resigned friendliness as he got to his feet. "Give me five minutes to reach him, Jay, and I'll join you in the car."

Jay hesitated, watching his eyes, which remained steady and engaged. The thought of leaving someone as crafty and arrogant as Byer to speak with the Deputy Prime Minister in private rang alarms in his head, but a Secretary of State could only be pushed so far.

And for that matter, the same limits applied to Sheffield.

Whatever else he might know, Jay thought, *he's nuts if he thinks he can dictate anything to the British.*

✈ THIRTY-ONE

The call from Anthony Sheffield came as they pulled away from the hotel.

"I apologize for being slow to call you, Mr. Reinhart. I had been given to understand that the delegation from Washington was speaking for you."

"No, sir. Working with me, most definitely, but I am the President's counsel."

"Very well. I spoke with the PM at length, and I can tell you that we feel strongly that our responsibilities under the Treaty Against Torture are clear and inescapable. The PM believes that we acted with reckless disregard in handling our treaty obligations in the Pinochet case when we refrained from taking an affirmative stand on the question of sovereign immunity and extradition."

Jay felt a small shudder of relief. "You mean that Prime Minister Blair should have been more forceful in opposing the extradition request and should have supported the concept that Pinochet had sovereign immunity from prosecution in England?"

"Heavens, no. Quite the contrary. The Blair government should have worked very hard to convince our courts to immediately extradite Pinochet to Spain. The extradition request and the warrant were valid, and there was obviously no sovereign immunity. To allow a former president to hide behind the concept of sovereign immunity would destroy the treaty, because who else but a head of state would be in a position to order state torture? If we permit such nonsense, we might as well scrap the treaty. After all, criminal scum like Milosevic or Saddam Hussein would claim sovereign immunity as well, and that would be absurd!"

Jay came forward in the seat, his face suddenly flushed.

"Mr. Sheffield, wait a minute. Do you understand that we're not in any way raising sovereign immunity as a defense?"

"Ah, but you would eventually, would you not, Mr. Reinhart?"

"I don't know. That's premature. He's not even in the country yet! And our main argument is that the warrant alleges crimes wholly unconnected with President Harris."

"But that's the essence of what a trial is for, isn't it? The sufficiency of the evidence is to be determined by a court of competent jurisdiction. I, too, am a lawyer by trade, Mr. Reinhart."

Jay could see Joe Byer leaning forward in his seat, straining to fill in the blanks and alarmed at Jay's alarm.

"Mr. Sheffield, I beg you to understand that in Lima there will be no court of competent jurisdiction, just a monkey trial orchestrated by a bloodthirsty dictator named Miraflores who is determined to put John Harris on the gallows."

"Mr. Reinhart," Sheffield replied with a condescending chuckle. "Please! You're talking about a sovereign nation who, by the way, ratified the Treaty Against Torture years before the United States did. Peru is not a renegade state, and I should tell you that one of the reasons we find your argument disingenuous is because the PM has just had personal assurances from Mr. Miraflores on behalf of the Peruvian government that Mr. Harris will be handled in strict accordance with established judicial procedures, and that they will open their doors to international monitoring and oversight of the process. Therefore, your concerns are misguided."

"The PM talked to Miraflores?"

"Yes, of course. That's what governments do."

Jay thanked him perfunctorily and ended the call, turning to the Secretary with a quick briefing on Sheffield's words.

"I'm a little shocked, Jay, but this is what happens when you put someone like Sheffield and his boss in a corner."

"You don't truly believe those assurances?" Jay fired back, a bitter edge underlying his words as his mind spun between the reality of the approaching 737 and the diminishing time remaining.

"Of course they don't mean it," Byer agreed.

"Why the contact with Peru? Are you going to tell me that's pro forma to make such a call?"

"It's . . . a bit unusual, and we know Miraflores can't be trusted."

Jay closed his eyes and pushed everything else away from his thinking but the key question: should they land or not?

"Stop the car, please," he said suddenly.

The driver turned from the right front seat. "Beg pardon, sir?"

"Stop the car, please. I need to get out for a moment."

Byer caught the driver's eye and nodded. "Do it."

The car glided to the shoulder of the motorway and Jay pulled the handle.

"Please wait for me. I need five minutes."

The din of traffic along the M-4 motorway to Heathrow was deafening. Jay stood behind the car, punched a number into the phone, and waited.

"EuroAir, ah, Ten-Ten," a British voice said on the other end.

"This is Jay Reinhart. Where are you guys?"

"Over the English channel, Mr. Reinhart. This is the first officer. We're on descent."

"How far out?"

"We just crossed the French shoreline."

"I need to speak with the President, and then with the captain."

"President Harris is still up here on the jump seat with us. Hold on."

"Yes, Jay?" Harris asked.

"I may only have seconds to explain, John, but you can't land in England."

"What? I thought . . ."

"It's all changed, sir. Trust me on this. It comes straight from the PM's office. They think they've got a Neville Chamberlain–style peace-in-our-time agreement with Miraflores to treat you fairly, and they're determined to accelerate the extradition process."

"But Jay, the courts won't let them."

"I can't take that chance, John! I've studied the procedure, and there are holes in there the Peruvians could pull you through."

There was silence from the other end, and Jay had to stick his finger even deeper in his free ear as he jammed the phone against the other.

"Are you still there, John?"

"Yes . . . I'm trying to make sense of this. Where else can we go?"

"I . . . I have an idea, but first we've got to get you clear of England."

There was a short laugh from the cockpit of the 737.

"Jay, we can't just hover out here."

"I know it! Look, John, give me your agreement, and let me talk to the captain."

He could almost make out John Harris sighing.

"In some ways," the President said, "I'm so tired of this, I'd like to just get it over with, Jay."

"John! Sir! We can't take the chance they could really get you to Lima. I know what will happen there. I did some research on Miraflores in the air coming here. He wants to hang you, John. And Britain's being ridiculous placing their trust in him. And . . . and . . ."

"And because of Campbell's invoking the name of

Barry Reynolds, you're suddenly not so sure you can win on the merits, right, Jay?"

The statement was a slap in the face, but John Harris had stabbed the source of Jay's panic with one rapier thrust, and there was no time to finesse the reply. He caught himself nodding, then reminded himself to speak.

"Yes."

More silence on the other end. An eternity of silence amidst the cacophonous traffic noise all around him and the clock ticking in his head and the presence of no less a personage than the United States Secretary of State waiting in the car behind him, all colluded with the forces of fatigue and hunger and circadian disorientation to make the crucible he was in seem like a scenario personally designed by Dante.

Finally, Harris spoke. "I'm handing the phone to the captain, Jay. I agree. Do what you think best."

There was a pause before the businesslike voice of Craig Dayton filled the line.

"Yes, Mr. Reinhart?"

"Captain, in a nutshell, here's the situation. If you land here, they'll not only arrest him at planeside, there's a very good chance they'll have him on the way to Lima within a few days or weeks. I was wrong to trust the Brits on this. I misread the whole thing."

"So, what do you want us to do, Mr. Reinhart?" Dayton asked evenly.

"Go somewhere else. You can't land in London."

"You realize how hard it was to get an arrival slot for Heathrow on short notice?"

"Can't be helped," Jay replied.

"Would it be begging the question to ask where you want us to go?" Dayton replied, instantly adding, "And I'm not trying to be facetious. We're almost into British airspace and we're under positive IFR control."

"I . . . don't know the terms, Captain. But can't you change the type of flight plan you're using and just fly wherever you want?"

"Not without the whole world knowing exactly where we are. We're too big a plane to just disappear . . . and we're running out of time. I mean, I can divert to probably any airport in the U.K., or go to Holland or Denmark, but I don't have enough fuel to make Iceland or Greenland, if that's what you're thinking."

"Forget the Continent. That would be an entirely new set of legal horror stories."

"Okay."

Jay could hear an exchange of radio messages in the background.

"What was that?"

"They were just clearing us on down to ten thousand feet with radar vectors for London."

"Could you fly up to Scotland?"

"Yes, but Scotland is in the United Kingdom, and I'm sure whoever's waiting for us at Heathrow will find a charter jet and get there almost as fast as we can."

Jay licked his lips and closed his eyes, thinking as fast as he could. The Irish Republic was a possibility he'd thought of earlier and had been loath to mention because there had been no time to research Ireland's feelings concerning the Treaty Against Torture. But he couldn't risk just having John Harris pop up in Dublin without knowing whether or not doing so would constitute jumping from the proverbial frying pan of the U.K. into a legal fire in Ireland.

What do we do?

"Mr. Reinhart, I may have an idea, but it's kind of risky," Dayton said, interrupting his thoughts.

"Tell me!" Jay replied, wondering what "risky" meant.

But there was no answer on the other end, and Jay realized the connection had been dropped.

"Damn!" He punched the number in again, but it rang uselessly.

✈ THIRTY-TWO

London, England—Tuesday—5:50 P.M.

Jay returned to the backseat of the car and closed the door.

"On to the airport, sir?" the driver asked.

The Secretary of State nodded and the driver pulled smoothly into traffic.

"Is there anything in your call we should know about?" Secretary Byer asked.

"Yes, sir. But this isn't the moment to discuss it."

Byer sighed and nodded. "Very well." He sat back in silence and focused his attention outside in thought until they pulled up to the executive jet facility ten minutes later.

"If you gentlemen will wait for me, I've a couple of calls to make," Jay said, slipping out as quickly as possible and entering the plush but diminutive terminal. There were glassed-in waiting lounges on both sides of the hall, each liberally equipped with phones, and Jay inserted himself in one to dial Geoffrey Wallace's number.

The sound of a phone receiver being fumbled from its

cradle and bumped across furniture reached his ears, along with a hoarse greeting.

"Yes? Wallace here."

"Geoffrey, Jay Reinhart. Where does Ireland stand on this issue?"

"I beg your pardon? You mean, where do they stand on President Harris and the warrant?"

"Where *would* they stand if he came to town with this warrant in hot pursuit?"

There was a short laugh on the other end. "Well, you know the Irish."

"No, actualiy I don't. I should. My grandmother was an Irish immigrant from Galway, but I've never been there."

"Well, they're a great people, but basically rebellious as hell, even to their own institutions at times. It's very hard to predict what they'll do at any given moment."

"But they're a nation of laws and a party to the treaty, right?"

"Oh, yes. Of course. They have our basic legal system, as you know. But in typical fashion, they signed the treaty over a decade ago and didn't ratify it until just last year."

"They ratified? I thought they hadn't."

"Only took them twelve years to get around to it. But yes, they're fully aboard now."

A flurry of activity in the largest waiting salon down the hall caught Jay's peripheral vision and he glanced over in time to see Secretary Byer in animated discussion with his aide, as the other officials milled around.

Jay turned his attention back to the phone. "Do you know any practitioners in Ireland?" he asked.

"I may know someone, but I'll have to look for his number and call you back."

"Let me hold, Geoffrey. While you get the number."

"Oh. Well . . . very well." Jay could hear the rustle of what sounded like bedcovers being moved in the background and an unhappy female voice.

"I'm sorry if I caught you at a bad moment," Jay offered, slightly amused.

Geoffrey was still holding the phone to his ear and chuckled. "Oh, it was anything but a bad moment, I can assure you! I just hated to end it. I'd thought you were through with me for the day. Hang on. I'll be right back." Wallace put the phone down, returning three minutes later.

"All right, Jay. There was a seminar in Edinburgh several years ago on international subjects that I attended, and the chap whose name I've got here spoke very eloquently on this very treaty. I recall talking with him afterwards. Smart, funny fellow, though I don't know how good he might be."

"Irish solicitor?"

"A barrister."

"So he's in Dublin?"

"Yes. Interesting, too. He apparently doesn't drink. Not even Guinness, or so he claimed. I offered him a pint, but . . ."

"Geoffrey," Jay interjected, "I'm sorry, but I'm in a rush."

"Of course. So am I . . . let's see." He passed the numbers in Dublin. "What else can I do for you, Jay? Would you . . . like me to call him for you?"

"No. I'll call from here."

"Good. That first one is a home number, I'm fairly certain."

"Geoffrey, ah, if you hear anything in the next few hours regarding President Harris, do not necessarily believe it, okay?"

"I love a good mystery, Jay. Can't you let me in on it?"

"I can't even tell you there's anything to let you in on."

"Oh, right. Got it."

Jay ended the call and dialed the barrister's home number in Dublin. He looked around at the salon at the end of the hall while waiting for the phone to ring, startled at the sudden burst of activity among the group of American officials. Secretary Byer was barking an order to an aide and pulling out a portable phone as another group entered, headed by Stuart Campbell.

"Michael Garrity here," a male voice answered, bringing Jay's attention back to the line.

"Mr. Garrity, you're a barrister, correct?"

"There have been scandalous allegations to that effect,

but few around Dublin pay them any mind. And who might you be, sir?"

Jay introduced himself and quickly explained the situation as he kept an eye on the increasing intensity of conversations in the lobby. Byer's people were watching Campbell's team without making contact.

"So, an American lawyer representing an American ex-President. This sounds intriguing from the beginning. How may I help you, Mr. Reinhart?"

Jay smiled in spite of himself at the cultured Irish accent riding a warm baritone wave of sound echoing with overtones of friendliness.

"I need some very quick advice," Jay said, "and then I may need to retain you. In the meantime, can we proceed under attorney-client privilege?"

"Well," Garrity said, clipping the word just a bit, "technically you'll need to hire me through a solicitor before I can take instructions from you here in Ireland, but that can be arranged later. There's nothing wrong with my advising you straightaway by phone. As far as the protection of client privilege? Done! Ask away."

Jay glanced around in search of Secretary of State Byer, who was now sitting on a lavishly upholstered couch, then turned back to the task of outlining the situation for Garrity, including the British position and the need to take the President to or through a country that wasn't hell-for-leather determined to send him to Peru. "Would I be smart or crazy to bring him to Dublin, Mr. Garrity?"

"Well now, that all depends. I could say that no High Court judge in Dublin would send an American President off to Peru in irons, but I'd be giving you a glib and unsupported opinion. You may not know that we just got around to ratifying the damn thing last year, so we're bound by the treaty now, and by the European protocols on the same subject. But, having said all that, the chances are very good, I would think, that while the Interpol warrant would be validated and an Irish warrant issued locally, and while your President might be arrested by some very confused Garda . . ."

"I'm sorry?"

"Garda . . . that's our police force. They're guardians of public safety. They hate to be called police, even when they're dashing about acting out an Irish version of *NYPD Blue*. Anyway, I think any attempt at extradition would take a very long time and would give you more than ample opportunity to appeal. It's really a torturous legal process. Frankly, without doing some fast research, I'm not even sure we have an extradition arrangement with Peru."

"Does that matter?"

"Probably not in the least. If Mr. Harris is extraditable under the charges you mentioned, he'd be extraditable under the Treaty Against Torture even if there isn't a regular agreement with Peru."

"How about government attitude?"

"Essentially that doesn't matter a great deal. Oh, with some of the jurists it may scratch at the back of their heads, but most of our judiciary are very independent thinkers and our Taoiseach, as we call our Prime Minister, would probably be very careful about stating a position."

"Can we control which judge we get?" Jay asked.

"Can one control the wind? No, not in Ireland, you can't. You just have to roll the dice. We have quite a gallery of judges. The good, the bad, the statutorily senile, and one or two who can't seem to sleep in their own bedrooms."

"Just like home."

"Indeed?"

"I'm a former judge. It's a long story."

"This becomes even more fascinating by the moment, Mr. Reinhart. Are you of German ancestry, with that name?"

"Way back on my Dad's side. Texas German."

"My God, what a combination!"

"Isn't it."

"Like Walter Cronkite," Garrity said.

"I . . . yes. But my maternal grandmother was from Galway. Look, Mr. Garrity, one other key question. Does the President actually have to be on Irish soil for Peru to perfect their warrant in Ireland?"

"No. All they need do is tell the judge they expect Mr. Harris to show up someday, and they'll get their warrant."

"Could you think hard about this, sir? Research it as far as you need to right now, and let me call you in a few hours."

"Provided you never again in this life call me 'sir,' Mr. Reinhart. I'm not a bloody English knight, y'know."

"Okay. Deal. We're on the clock as far as fees go, and if you'll find a solicitor for me who knows this area and hire him for me, I'd deeply appreciate it."

Garrity chuckled. "You have no idea how much I would love to do just that. Our solicitors always hire *us*, so that would be a brilliant turnabout, but . . . I'm also afraid it would strain my ethics. I can make you a recommendation and even put someone on hold for you, but the actual retaining has to be done by you, I'm sorry to say."

Jay listened to the names of two solicitors adept at international practice and picked the first.

"Ah, a fine choice, that," Garrity said, as if Jay had chosen a premium wine. "Good man." Garrity passed the solicitor's phone number after agreeing to call and alert him to the case.

"Mr. Garrity, will you need a retainer fee immediately?" Jay asked.

"That's an issue we always leave to our instructing solicitors."

"Okay. It's just that I'll need to transfer funds."

"Won't be possible until Thursday, then, because tomorrow's St. Patrick's Day. But that's all right. The solicitors will find a way to separate you from the appropriate amount of money, and I'm at your service in the meantime, I assure you."

Jay disconnected and left the smaller waiting room, feeling unsettled by the discussion of fees. He walked over to the Secretary's group, where urgent conversations were flying back and forth.

"Excuse me. What's going on?" Jay asked.

Secretary Byer turned and took Jay's arm, walking him toward an empty corner.

"The President's plane disappeared from radar just off

the coast over the English Channel. The pilot apparently indicated he was trying to work out some problem and canceled his flight plan."

Jay looked at him in total confusion.

"What?"

"The Air Traffic Control people are telling us he was in a sort of tailspin before they lost contact. Rescue forces are on their way to have a look."

"They think . . . he crashed?"

"They don't know, but it was very curious, I'm told," Byer said, studying Jay's eyes. "Should we think anything else, Jay?"

"I really don't know. I talked to them back there on the side of the road, and I was cut off . . . but I've had no contact since then."

The conversation ran back and forth through his mind, both ends and the middle all at once, yielding the captain's words of caution: ". . . but it's kind of risky." He felt a cold chill.

"I suspected you were calling the President," Byer was saying. "You said you'd tell me the details of the call later. This is a pretty good time."

Jay tried to swallow, his mouth suddenly dry as cotton. "I . . . ah, told him, Mr. Secretary, that they shouldn't land in London."

The statement hung in midair between them as the Secretary stared at him in silence, then nodded. "I understand. Let's pray things are not as they appear out there."

"Amen," Jay said, slowly fighting back from the sudden doubt that they were still airborne. Maybe something *had* happened, but maybe not. What had Dayton meant? "What are you planning to do, Mr. Secretary?" Jay asked.

"Well, go back to the hotel and wait for word. I see nothing to be gained by staying out here. May I give you a lift back?"

Jay nodded, thinking of his roll-on bag in the Savoy. "I'd appreciate that, but I'd better not leave just yet. I have some urgent phone calls to make back to the States."

Jay could see the questioning look return to Byer's face.

"The President's family," Jay added.

Byer nodded. "Oh, of course." He shook Jay's hand and turned toward the door.

Jay walked over to a refreshment tray and poured himself a cup of coffee, aware that his hand was shaking, and acutely aware that Stuart Campbell and his entourage were working somewhere in the building. He waited until Byer's car pulled away before walking outside into the night, conscious of the cool temperature, but needing to think. They were still airborne, of course. He refused to consider any alternative. He had to focus on what had to be done.

THIRTY-THREE

EuroAir 1010, in Flight—Tuesday—5:50 P.M.

When the connection with Jay Reinhart's GSM phone was lost, Craig Dayton turned to Alastair and studied his face for a few seconds.

"What?" Alastair asked.

"Ready to risk a crash?"

"I beg your pardon?"

Craig took a deep breath. "For God and country, Alastair."

"I don't want to bloody well know what you're talking about, do I?"

"Stand by to turn off the transponder."

"Talk to me, Craig. I do want to know."

Craig quickly explained the plan: drop to the surface, stay under radar, and fly north up the English Channel to the North Sea and then to an airport in Scotland. "Probably Inverness."

"Oh. The old tried and true Grinder maneuver. Very well. I'll go along . . . with one proviso," Alastair said.

"What's that?"

"We cancel our instrument flight clearance so that any conclusions they make about our fate are their responsibility. Otherwise, our licenses will never survive the ruse."

"You got it."

Craig notified everyone in back to buckle up for some unusual maneuvers, then disconnected the autopilot and rolled the 737 into a tight left descending turn as Alastair triggered the transmitter.

"London, EuroAir Ten-Ten, please cancel our IFR flight clearance and our Heathrow arrival slot at this time. We're descending now in visual conditions to work out a problem."

The controller's voice betrayed surprise. "Ah, EuroAir Ten-Ten, roger, IFR cancelled. May we be of assistance, sir?"

The altimeter showed they were halfway between thirteen and fourteen thousand feet over the English Channel, and the Global Positioning Satellite equipment had the small symbol representing their aircraft less than ten miles from shore in the deepening twilight.

Craig hit the transmit button on his yoke, adopting a tense, strained tone of voice.

"Ah . . . London . . . Ten-Ten,   EuroAir . . . we're . . . we're going . . ." He released the transmitter, waiting for the inevitable reply as he tightened his left turn and let the descent rate increase to four thousand feet per minute.

"Say again, please, EuroAir Ten-Ten."

They had already turned ninety degrees to the original course as he pulled the thrust levers back.

"Don't answer him, Alastair! And call out my altitude in thousand-foot increments."

"Roger. Ten thousand, down five thousand feet per minute," Alastair reported, his voice calm and steady, but the size of his eyes betraying concern.

Craig glanced at him and grinned, then glanced back at an ashen-faced John Harris.

"Hang on."

"Nine thousand, down six thousand per minute. Don't increase that descent rate!" Alastair warned.

"I won't," Craig replied, carefully watching the instruments as he came through the first three-hundred-sixty-degree point.

"EuroAir Ten-Ten, London, observe your turn and altitude loss, sir! Are you in distress?"

"Descending through eight thousand, Craig."

"Any oil platforms or other structures out here in the channel, Alastair?" Craig asked.

"I doubt it, but I wouldn't bet our lives on my memory, or the idea that we'll be safe under five hundred feet."

"We'll need lower than that."

"Seven thousand, down six thousand per minute."

"Roger."

"EuroAir Ten-Ten, London. Are you in distress, sir?"

"Don't touch that button, Alastair. I know you're tempted."

Alastair nodded and swallowed hard. "Six thousand, Craig. Of course I'm tempted! The poor bloke's heart is in his throat."

"Altitude?"

"Coming through five thousand three hundred."

"Stand by to cut the transponder and all our external lights on my command."

"Don't . . . overdo it, fellows," John Harris managed to say, his eyes huge as well.

The voice of the London air traffic controller took on a more urgent tone as he continued to call.

"I hate to do this to him!" Craig said. "He's watching our data block plunging out of control."

"Okay, Craig, we're through three thousand, still descending at six thousand a minute. Better shallow the descent."

"Speed?"

"Two hundred eighty."

"Good. Plenty of energy. I'll take it to one thousand before shallowing."

"That's awfully low, Craig! Give yourself enough room to level off or we could fly into the water."

"Altitude?"

"Coming through two thousand, Craig! It's getting too dark to see the water clearly."

"Call me at one thousand."

"Very well . . . fifteen hundred . . . thirteen hundred . . . twelve . . . eleven . . . ONE THOUSAND!"

Craig began pulling on the control column, far too slowly in Alastair's view. The Boeing responded sluggishly as the vertical velocity began backing off the peg.

"Craig! Pull!"

"I am. Kill the transponder and the lights."

"Done!" Alastair said, his fingers flipping switches he had already identified. "You're too low, Craig! Dear God . . ."

Metro Business Aviation Terminal, Heathrow Airport, London, England

Stuart Campbell had taken temporary refuge in one of the smaller waiting lounges provided for the well-heeled users of private jets. Two of his associates had cell phones plastered to their ears just outside in the hallway, as Campbell sat back and focused his thoughts.

"Stuart?" one of the men said as he leaned in the door, breaking Campbell's concentration.

"Yes?" Campbell sat forward, pulling himself back to the moment. "Come in."

Henri Renoux took a chair opposite Campbell's, his voice urgent: "They've got helicopters on the scene right now."

"There is, in fact, a 'scene'?" Campbell asked, looking startled.

Henri shook his head. "I'm sorry. Poor choice of words. They are in the area where the aircraft is presumed to have gone down about fifteen kilometers off Dover. Several boats are in the vicinity as well. They've found nothing so far."

Campbell nodded. "Well, something as large as that airplane wouldn't hit the water without leaving quite a bit of evidence."

"It will take some time, especially since it's dark out there."

Stuart shook his head. "There's nothing to be found, Henri. They're wasting their time. Clever ploy, that, cancelling his instrument clearance first. He'll feign radio failure and they can't get his license."

Renoux cocked his head slightly as he tried to decipher his senior partner's meaning. "I . . . thought you just said . . ."

Stuart got to his feet and paced to the far end of the room, then turned.

"It's a ruse, and a very effective one at that."

"A ruse?"

"Too convenient, Henri. First an alleged hijacking yesterday that was anything but. Then a dress rehearsal for this trick when they panicked Rome Control going into that Sicilian Navy base. We obtained the warrant, and Mr. Reinhart suddenly discovers that his President may not actually be as pure as the driven snow, and now, suddenly, the aircraft carrying President Harris to a certain arrest seems to be falling into the water with perfectly timed convenience just before reaching British jurisdiction."

"But . . . they were seen in an uncontrolled left spiral . . ."

"We don't know that it was uncontrolled. Whatever it was, it was cleverly crafted by a very innovative airline captain to fool London Center, which is precisely what he's done. This is a very smart adversary we're dealing with in that cockpit. A good partner for Harris, I should think."

"Forgive me, Stuart, but aren't we ignoring the fact that the airplane hasn't shown up anywhere?"

Campbell chuckled and turned to look out the window to the hallway. "No, I'm not ignoring that fact, Henri, and the reason is because John Harris and his chartered jet *will* show up at an airport somewhere." He pointed to the map. "Let's get some pilots in here with maps of the U.K. and Europe and figure out where he could be going."

"Good heavens, Stuart, there are hundreds of airports in the radius of a few hundred miles from here."

"But, not all of them can take a Boeing seven thirty-seven, can they? And the chap certainly hasn't enough fuel in that model to make the States, or probably even Ke-flavík."

Henri was already on his feet and moving toward the door.

"Oh," Stuart added, "and get a direct line to London Center, Henri. Suggest the same scenario, and see if there were any shadowy radar traces moving away from the supposed crash site."

"Okay."

"And . . . we'll need another team of people with phones, and rapidly so. We'll need to call every usable airport in the U.K. and expand the calls outward to match the amount of time they would have been in the air."

"You need Jean-Paul and Gina to be standing by with the Lear?"

Stuart nodded aggressively. "Yes. We might have to fly in any direction." Campbell smiled at Renoux. "Don't worry, Henri, we'll find Harris and win this little chess game. This is simply an unexpected gambit by the opposing king. Just when I think I have the little bugger in check, he scoots out of reach of my queen." He laughed openly. "An apt analogy, that, even if I do proclaim it so."

"I don't understand," Henri said, still hesitating in the doorway with a slightly worried look.

"It's a chess analogy, Henri. It's amazing how often I find them useful in law."

A shapely young woman in a tight-fitting little black dress appeared in the hallway, her jet-black hair bouncing luxuriantly and her face brightening at the sight of Stuart Campbell. She hurried in the office door.

"Sir William? There's an urgent call for you in operations, just down the hall."

"How very kind of you to come find me, my dear. Thank you," Stuart said, turning on his brightest smile and watching her blush slightly under his penetrating gaze as she turned to leave. "Deirdre, wasn't it?" he asked.

She looked back over her shoulder and smiled. "Yes, it is. Thanks for remembering."

"How could I forget the lovely name of such a lovely lady," Stuart said, crossing to the desk and watching in admiration as she flowed like a feminine wave around the corner.

He raised the receiver. "Stuart Campbell here."

The voice on the other end was instantly recognizable.

"Mr. Prime Minister! I appreciate your calling back. We need to talk most urgently."

✈ THIRTY-FOUR

The hard pull up required to level the 737 just above the surface of the English Channel had profoundly frightened Alastair.

"Good Lord, Craig!"

"There's one hundred! I'm level. Easy, Alastair! I'm trained to do this."

"Yes, in a blinking fighter! Not a seven thirty-seven! I thought we were dead."

"Altitude?"

"Back to a hundred."

"Heading?"

"Ah . . . zero six zero degrees."

"Okay . . . look at the GPS display and give me headings that will keep us moving just about up the center of the channel and way clear of the coast, then north up the North Sea. We'll round the shoulder of Scotland and come in from seaside to Inverness. Keep your eyes on the radar altimeter. Not an inch under a hundred feet, and, unless we get into fog, keep an eye out for any ships that might be sporting a mast over that height."

"Oh, too right! I can do all that! Do you have any idea what you're planning? That's hundreds of miles trying to evade radar!"

"What? I'm stressing you out, old buddy?"

The copilot sighed and shook his head, his expression deadly serious.

"You *are* bloody crazy, Dayton!"

"Maybe, but while I'm losing it, we need to get Reinhart on the phone," Craig Dayton said as he took his right hand off the throttles long enough to rub his right eye. The task of holding the Boeing precisely one hundred feet above the water—a distance less than the wingspan of the jet—had already become tedious, making him seriously consider climbing back up a few hundred feet even if they did risk being seen by air traffic radar.

"This is very dangerous, Craig!" Alastair reminded him.

"When we're another ten miles or so, we can come up a bit."

"There are ships with superstructures taller than this, you know."

"But we've got a cloud ceiling far enough above us to see ahead, Alastair. We spotted that other boat."

"Still steady at one hundred," Alastair said, his hand firmly on his copilot's control yoke, shadowing Craig's every movement.

"You think we've fooled them?" Craig asked.

"Probably. For a while. Until they find no wreckage. You know this is liable to reach our respective families with devastating results?"

"I know it. I figure you should call home as soon as we get on the ground," Craig said.

"I'll wager even at one hundred feet we're being tracked by at least one military radar."

"As long as Air Traffic Control can't see us and we're not streaking toward a British city . . ." Craig said.

". . . we should be all right." Alastair finished. "I ran a quick fuel calculation, and we're okay at this fuel consumption rate to Inverness. We'll land with an hour's fuel remaining."

Lights loomed in the distance directly ahead, seeming to close on them rapidly in the gloom.

"What's that?" Craig asked, his eyes moving constantly from the attitude display to the radar altimeter to the vertical velocity indicator and back to the ADI with an occasional glance out of the windscreen ahead.

"Probably a ship."

"I see a lot of lights," President Harris chimed in, startling Alastair, who'd almost forgotten they had a guest on the cockpit jumpseat. "It's tall, fellows, whatever it is."

"Craig, let's climb."

"Just a second," he replied.

"*No,* dammit! Not just a second, I mean now!" Alastair barked.

"Look . . ."

"Craig, you're going too far! You're into reckless flying and I'll have no more of it!"

"I know what I'm doing," Craig snapped.

"No, you bloody well don't! You're tunneling in on a single objective. That trait kills even testosterone-soaked fighter pilots like you! This is foolhardy."

Craig studied Alastair with a quick glance and began easing the yoke back to start a shallow climb.

"Five hundred okay?"

"For now, yes."

"All right," Craig said quietly.

"All right," Alastair echoed, watching the radar altitude increase until Craig leveled at five hundred.

"Sorry," Craig said as the lights of the ship ahead swam safely beneath their nose.

Craig looked at Alastair, noting the alarm still in his eyes.

"You still with me, man?" Craig asked.

"Barely," was the reply.

Heathrow Airport, London, England

Jay found a small bench just outside the door of the private terminal before punching in the first of several numbers. The reassuring voice of Michael Garrity answered on the third ring.

"This is Jay Reinhart again."

"Hello! A bit early to have answers for you, Mr. Reinhart, but . . ." Garrity said.

"I need just one," Jay said, interrupting. "If I bring the President's plane into Dublin tonight, and if the opposition arrives with their warrant, how quickly could they have the warrant perfected and arrest him?"

"Tomorrow's St. Patrick's Day here in the Republic of Ireland, and no one will be working at the Four Courts. Mind you, we don't get as carried away as you Americans do celebrating, but St. Patrick's Day is a grand excuse for an official holiday. So, unless your President commits an act heinous enough to attract the Garda's attention, I'd say he's a free man until the following day, Thursday. Certainly no one in the judiciary's going to pay any attention until then."

"Really?"

"It's the district court that would handle such an Interpol warrant, Mr. Reinhart, and Scotland Yard couldn't ferret out one of our district judges on a national holiday. Especially not St. Paddy's Day. They go in hiding, I'm all but convinced."

"So . . . we could safely get the President a hotel room?"

"I don't see why not. But wouldn't he prefer to stay at your American Ambassador's residence here? It's really quite large, and I know they have quarters fit for a U.S. president."

"No," Jay said. "Better to have no official involvement, I think. Besides, that could be misinterpreted as an attempt at asylum and create a diplomatic mess."

"Very well, a hotel it shall be. Do you have a credit card number I can use?"

"Ah . . . yes." Jay struggled to pull out his American Express and read the number and expiration date.

"Very good, Mr. Reinhart. I'll see what I can do."

"I'll call you back, then," Jay said. "I'm going to change the plan."

He rang off and dialed the 737's satellite phone, relieved to get a rapid answer. "Captain Dayton? Good job! Whatever you did out there fooled everyone. Campbell and Byer think you've crashed."

"This is the copilot, Mr. Reinhart . . . and as the old saw goes, rumors of our demise have been greatly exaggerated."

"They certainly have," Jay said. "This buys us time, but I've got a different plan."

Jay could hear deep concern and tension on the other end. "Go ahead."

"First, where are you?"

"Heading up the North Sea at barely five hundred feet in an insane attempt to sneak into Scotland."

"We need to change the destination."

Alastair looked over at Craig, then back over his shoulder at John Harris, and repeated Jay's words, adding: "And where would you like us to go now, Mr. Reinhart?"

"Dublin, Ireland. Can you make it?"

"Certainly we can, but *how* we get there is the question."

Craig turned to Alastair, mouthing the word, "Where?"

"Now he wants us in Dublin," Alastair replied, turning back to the receiver. "Look, Mr. Reinhart, Dublin's a big, controlled airport. We can't sneak in there. A little airport like Inverness, Scotland, doesn't have a control tower to worry with us, but Dublin's impossible. We'd be as subtle as a battleship in a bathtub."

"I don't really care how you do it, as long as you're safe," Jay said. "The fiction that you've crashed was to give you time to get to Scotland and refuel to go on to Iceland or Canada before they could show up with the arrest warrant. But that's no good now. We can't have President Harris land anywhere in Great Britain."

"And no one's going to come after the President in Ireland?" Alastair asked.

"Not for a few days. Let me speak with the President, please, while you fellows figure out how to do this."

Alastair handed the phone over his shoulder.

"Yes, Jay?"

"I've hired a legal team in Dublin, John. Ireland has ratified the treaty, but tomorrow's a holiday, so there won't be any judges around to sign a warrant. Besides, Ireland is a good friend of the U.S., as you know, and they, unlike the British, have no special axe to grind regarding Pinochet, so in my judgment we're far better off there."

"I'm in your hands, Jay."

"I'm doing my best, but I'm more or less having to turn on a dime here as I find out new things."

"Understood."

"We'll get you a hotel room near the Dublin airport so you can rest up. Our barrister thinks it will be the day after tomorrow before Campbell can hope to get the warrant converted. And I'm thinking, John, that we might be able to just buy you a ticket and get you on a direct commercial flight back to New York."

"I like that idea, Jay. About the hotel . . . we also need rooms for our two pilots and three flight attendants, plus Sherry, me, and my secret service agent." There was a long pause. "You really think I could just get on Aer Lingus or someone else and fly home?"

"It's possible, but if not, maybe we can refuel your bird, extend the charter, and make it to Maine. I haven't talked to the pilots about that, yet. All I know is I can't bring you down anywhere in the U.K. now."

"Hold on," the President said, cradling the phone as he leaned forward. "Craig? Alastair? Can we do this, and if so, how?"

Craig nodded. "I think we'll keep going the way we started and just skirt around the northern coastline of Scotland, then turn southwest and contact Dublin Center for a clearance into the airport when we're fifty miles out. We've already caused a massive, unnecessary search. If we try to go back into positive control now, we're liable to draw the RAF out with orders to force us to land."

John Harris looked at the copilot, who was nodding assent.

"What time do you expect to arrive?" Jay asked.

Harris leaned forward again. "How long to Dublin?"

"Around two hours and twenty minutes flying like this," Alastair said, and the President repeated the estimate.

"When you land," Jay said, "if I'm not there, call a Mr. Michael Garrity. He's our barrister." Jay passed the number. "I'll be there as quickly as I can find a flight."

"Charter a jet, Jay," John Harris said.

"If I can't find a commercial flight, I will," Jay said, "as long as it has a minimum of two engines and all the instruments money can buy."

"I take it there's a story there," the President said.

"I'm not sure you want to know," Jay replied. "I'll call you back when I've arranged a flight to Dublin."

Jay disconnected and dialed the Savoy Hotel, arranging to have his bag put in a taxi and sent immediately to Heathrow and the private terminal.

A quick call to Aer Lingus reservations turned up a departure to Dublin in less than an hour from Heathrow. Relieved, he decided against booking a seat under his name and called the hotel back to redirect his bag to the Aer Lingus ticket counter.

"Just in time, sir," the concierge said. "I have it in my hand and the driver is waiting."

"How long, do you suppose?"

"This time of evening, thirty minutes, if we're lucky."

One of the ramp attendants from the Metro facility agreed to shuttle him to Terminal 4, and Jay slipped into the car quietly, wanting to avoid the possibility of being seen by Stuart Campbell or his people.

"Aer Lingus terminal, please."

The driver nodded and accelerated away, obscuring Jay's view of a man in a dark business suit who had been watching from a dark corner of the entryway. As the car carrying Jay disappeared, the man quickly returned to the lobby.

The fact that the taxi carrying his bag actually arrived when and where it was supposed to at the curb of Terminal 4 surprised Jay. He thanked and paid the driver before racing through security and an interminable series of concourses to board the Dublin flight with ten minutes to spare. The possibility that Campbell already knew his plan flitted across his mind, but it made little difference. Thanks to the holiday, he knew they'd be okay in Dublin until Thursday regardless of when Campbell showed up, as he ultimately would.

The lights of Heathrow were falling away from the climbing jetliner before he realized that for the second time in his life, a takeoff sequence in a commercial jet had failed to scare him. Jay pulled one of the legal pads out of his briefcase and placed it on his lap, his pen at the ready, before remembering that he hadn't obtained hotel rooms for the crew. Nor had he remembered to alert the Irish customs and immigration officials.

He'd already noticed the lack of in-flight phones on the 737, and he knew the flight crews tried to prohibit the use of cellular phones on the unproven assumption that they could interfere with the aircraft's navigation system—an absurd premise, according to a knowledgeable friend in telecommunications. But in this case he had no choice.

The calls had to be made.

The flight was half full, and he waited until the flight attendants had wheeled their service cart past him before arranging a blanket against the sidewall of his window seat to hide the GSM phone he was leaning against after punching in Michael Garrity's number once more. There was a form of digital static before Garrity answered.

"I hate to bother you again, Mr. Garrity," Jay said.

"For heaven's sake, man, call me Michael!" Garrity replied. "The only person in the world who calls me 'Mister Garrity' is my wife, and then only when she's angry with me."

"I'm sorry, Michael."

"So am I," Garrity said, chuckling. "Seems to happen a lot lately."

"Look, I need to impose on you to get hotel rooms for

the folks on that plane, not just the President, and alert customs and immigration." He passed the basic information.

"I'll take care of it, Jay, provided your credit card lasts," Garrity said cheerfully.

"Okay. I'll be on the ground in an hour."

"I'll be there," Michael Garrity said.

Metro Business Aviation Terminal, Heathrow Airport, London, England

Stuart Campbell had changed his location, appropriating a small conference room as their makeshift command post, and Henri Renoux sat down in one of the swivel chairs, watching him carefully. Background music from recessed ceiling speakers—a Vivaldi concerto—accompanied the elegant decor, and Henri realized the lights had been turned down to half strength, giving the well-appointed room a rich and palatial feel.

Campbell's elbow was placed firmly on the arm of his chair, the bulk of his body balancing easily against the leather of the seat back, his hand supporting his chin and his eyes focused on the wall before him.

"Stuart?" Henri asked tentatively.

"Yes?" Campbell said slowly without turning.

"I think you were right. An intermittent radar target was tracked by London Center for about forty miles heading to the northeast, but then it disappeared in a poor radar coverage area."

"Very well," Stuart said passively, his mind deeply occupied with other thoughts. "Anything more?"

"Yes," Henri responded, drumming his fingers silently on the table. "I think we know where they're heading."

"Dublin, I should think," Stuart said, turning suddenly to look at his associate. "Am I right?"

Henri was nodding and smiling. "How'd you know?"

"It's what I would do, Henri. Who better to run to if you're a beleaguered U.S. President than the country that loves Americans best? I would think less of our good Mr. Reinhart if he'd headed anywhere else."

"He took a flight to Dublin. That's how we knew."

"I suspected that would be the case, and we'll follow in the Lear in the next fifteen minutes," Stuart said, resuming his contemplative posture, his eyes once again staring at a spot on the off-white wall. "Do you know what our esteemed Prime Minister wants to do, Henri?"

"No, sir."

"You're aware I talked with him at length a while ago?"

"I knew he was calling."

Stuart shook his head slightly, almost imperceptibly. "I thought I knew his mind. I knew he was disgusted with Tony Blair's tepid, timid prosecution of the Pinochet debacle. That's why I alerted him from Sicily, to push him a bit, incite him a bit. I knew he'd help smooth the way in pursuit of John Harris."

"I know."

"But I had no idea how virulent he is on this subject. He really wants to ship Harris to Lima, Henri. Can you fancy that?"

"You mean, while the courts . . ."

"No, no. Nothing illegal. He can't rip it away from the judicial process, of course, but he had the Home Secretary and the Secretary of State, the police . . . everyone he could control or influence ready to push the timetable for extradition to its absolute minimum."

"A moot point now, of course," Henri offered. "But you're surprised, Stuart?"

Campbell leaned back to look at Henri. "In fact, I'm stunned. I honestly did not expect that."

"We came very close, then?" Henri asked.

"To what?" Stuart asked, almost absently.

"To succeeding. For our clients."

"Oh. Miraflores the bloodthirsty," Stuart said with a snort, turning back to the wall and leaning back even more. "Yes, I suppose we did. We also put John Harris on a fast track to Lima."

"And this worries you?"

There was silence for a few seconds before Stuart Campbell sighed and nodded.

"Profoundly."

✈ THIRTY-FIVE

**Dublin International Airport, Ireland—
Tuesday—8:40 P.M.**

Michael Garrity waited just outside the customs area holding a small sign with "REINHART" in bold letters. Shorter
than Jay had anticipated, he wore a full head of silver hair
like a Roman emperor, swept forward and partly cropped,
his face deeply lined, and a huge mouth that bisected his
entire face and turned up at each end in a perpetual smile.

They shook hands and Garrity pointed to the front
drive, where a van was waiting to take them to the flight
line.

"It's good to meet you," he said in a deep rumble of a
voice.

"Are they here yet?" Jay asked.

Garrity pushed open the terminal door and moved
toward a passenger van parked by the curb, its flanks carrying the name and logo of Parc Aviation. "No, and as of
ten minutes ago, I'd say Dublin Air Traffic Control had just
about labeled me a crank for calling three times. They had
yet to hear from a EuroAir Ten-Ten."

Jay looked alarmed.

"I wouldn't worry," Garrity said quickly, climbing into the van.

The driver introduced himself and pointed toward a distant exit. "I'll take you out to the ramp to wait for them."

"Your company handles the private jets here?" Jay asked.

"Yes, if they're not too big. We had to get permission to handle your flight, though, since it's a 737."

Jay pulled out his GSM phone and punched a series of numbers into the keypad.

He let the line ring until a woman's voice gently intoned the obvious fact that the party wasn't answering. He punched it off and sighed as Michael spoke.

"By the way, Jay, I rousted one of my secretaries out of bed and she's found the hotel rooms, transportation, and a slightly irritated Immigration inspector who'll meet the airplane."

"Just Immigration?"

"They won't need customs since your people are arriving from another European Union country."

"Oh. Of course. I forgot about that, and I was so busy trying to get on my flight, I forgot to ask."

They passed through several security gates wrapped in their own thoughts before Michael Garrity broke the silence. "You told me on the phone that you had an Irish grandmother, Jay. And you've never been to Ireland?"

"No, I'm sorry to say."

"Well, we've got a bit of work to do tomorrow to get ready for this thing, and your adversary Stuart Campbell will bear close watching, but you must let me show you our fair city at some point."

Jay smiled and shook his head. "I . . . doubt we'll have time for that, Michael."

"Oh, at least a few of the sights the tourists would normally see. You've heard of Molly Malone?"

"Who?"

He sang a few bars of the song, and Jay raised his hand with a laugh. "Oh, yeah. The pretty female fishmonger who died of a fever . . . or 'favor,' as we were taught the song in the States."

" 'Favor' 'tis a bastardized Irish pronunciation of fever." Michael laughed.

"I figured."

"We've a lovely statue of her in the town center. We call her 'The Dish with the Fish.' "

"The Dish . . ."

"Also known as the 'Tart with the Cart.' The statue's not too far from the Four Courts, our rather historic courthouse, where I toil away on most days, and where this matter will be fought."

The van pulled onto the flight line and the driver moved to the edge of a taxiway to wait. Garrity pulled out his cell phone and dialed Dublin Air Traffic Control once again.

"Yes, it's me, the pest. Has he now? Excellent. What time would that be?" Garrity nodded. "Fifteen minutes? Thank you." He replaced the receiver and turned to Jay. "You heard, then?"

Jay smiled and exhaled. "Yeah. Fifteen minutes. That's a relief."

"Where did you gentlemen come in from?" the driver asked.

"London," Jay replied absently, his mind already focused on the next step.

"Oh. You're the second group. If you're looking for the others, by the way, they just left."

Jay looked at him more in irritation than curiosity. "What?"

"The Lear Thirty-five. It came in from London about thirty minutes ago and they mentioned they were expecting some others. I just thought . . . you know, you were part of the same group."

"No," Jay said, shaking his head. "I came in by commercial. From London, you say?"

"Yes, sir. The big fellow and the pilots left a few minutes ago with the people who came to meet them, and I thought they might have just left you behind or something. Sorry."

A ripple of apprehension shot through Jay's middle and caused him to shudder internally.

"Big fellow? Do you have his name?"

The clerk pawed through his shirt pocket for a business card. "I didn't get the man's name, but here's the pilot's information, if that helps. Jean-Paul somebody."

He smiled and handed over the card. "I'll need that back, you know. For our front counter."

Jay looked at the card, his shoulders slumping.

"What is it, Jay?" Michael Garrity asked.

"How in hell . . ." Jay mumbled to himself.

"What?" Michael asked, moving to his side and trying to make out the name on the card.

"William Stuart Campbell," Jay said. "He's already here. The man's either clairvoyant, or he's a one-man CIA."

The Shelbourne Hotel, St. Stephen's Green, Dublin, Ireland

Stuart Campbell felt the weight of his fatigue as the limo sped through the night from the Dublin Airport to his hotel in the heart of the city, but there was too much to be done to succumb to it, and, as leader, he had to set the pace—and the example—for the entire team.

He forced himself to keep a running conversation going with each of the three staff members who'd been waiting for him. With so much to do, their full attention would be vital through the night, and their loyalty would have to be rapidly earned.

Only his firm's Dublin partner had ever met Stuart Campbell before, and Stuart was acutely aware of the halo over his own head, an aura of respect and assumed infallibility that made it difficult for subordinates to speak up and point out mistakes. He was used to building effective teams, though seldom under such time pressure. Establishing friendly, personal bonds with employees and adversaries alike was a practiced technique—one of the many superior habits that had made him consistently successful in negotiations.

Especially with his adversaries.

A familiar building passed the limo's windows and Stuart diverted his attention outside for a few moments as he aligned his memory with a map of Dublin.

The advice of a long-dead mentor—one of the best-known barristers in England through the postwar years—rang through his mind again in a voice he periodically heard in his head, and missed in life.

"Stuart," Sir Henry Delacorte had told him in the infancy of Stuart's practice, "it's hard to say no to a man you really like. Build a bridge to those you deal with, make them like you, and they'll come to you on every discretionary issue in spite of themselves. But never make the mistake of crossing that bridge yourself!"

William Stuart Campbell, the senior lawyer, was unequaled in the art of calculated manipulation, knowing how to gain and use the advantage of an opponent's trust while never letting himself be swayed by such affinities.

But William Stuart Campbell, the man, had always been in minor turmoil over the technique, and that was good, he thought—especially for a man who genuinely liked people. The quiet, internal discomfort never stayed him from the task of influencing someone to do his bidding, but his inner reservations provided a small saving grace—a continuously renewable personal penance for the cynical use of his fellow man. Maintaining that small level of discomfort with his own methods had become a lifeline tied to the anchor of his humanity.

"Are we ready to dive into this thing?" Campbell asked, when he and the three men and two women on his team had reached the opulent old hotel and pulled up chairs around the conference table in the Presidential Suite, informally known as the Princess Grace Room.

There were bobbing heads all around.

"Very well. First, where do we find a district judge?"

"Probably not possible tonight or tomorrow," one of the women answered, explaining the traditional holiday disappearance of most jurists. "But we'll also have to involve the Garda. In fact, they'll have to formally present the Interpol warrant in court or to whatever judge we can find."

"Do we have a list of all the judges?" Stuart asked. "With addresses and telephones and the like?"

"Yes," she answered.

"Then let's start working those telephones and see if someone stayed behind."

"If," the woman replied, "we could find one, I think he might be persuaded to sign the warrant at home so we can get on with the arrest, but I can't guarantee it."

"We don't have much time," Stuart said, leaning back with his hands behind his head and looking at each of them in turn. "Let's remember at all times that the basic mission here is to arrest President Harris and start the legal process against him. That's what our client expects, and what he is paying dearly to have happen."

Patrick Nolan, the firm's partner in Dublin, was nodding. "When you put us on standby, Stuart, I didn't expect this affair would end up here."

"Nor did I," Stuart replied. "I *did* think it possible that Harris might find a way to wiggle out of the net in Athens, but I did not expect him to get away from Italy."

"But, weren't you going to snatch him away right there in Rome?" Nolan asked.

"You mean put him on that jet we chartered to Lisbon?" Stuart replied.

Nolan nodded, watching the senior partner smile and shake his head no.

"That was never a serious possibility, that jet. It was window dressing for President Miraflores. The Italians weren't about to let me do it, and I wasn't about to let it happen, either. Too many damaging consequences in terms of my friendships in official Italy. But then an unexpected opportunity presented itself to more or less herd Harris to London, and I *am* rather surprised that it didn't work."

"Why didn't it?" Nolan asked.

"Because John Harris is a very intelligent man, Paddy. He's somehow gathered a cadre of dedicated people around him," he laughed and shook his head, "including a planeload of geriatric American war veterans who were going to fight me personally if necessary, probably hand-to-hand. Their devotion to Harris was quite impressive."

There were puzzled expressions around the room, and Stuart waved them away. "When this job is all done and we're all up in the hills closing down Johnnie Fox's pub one evening, I'll tell you the story." He sat forward and put his large hands on the table. "Okay. Down to business, and I need the clear thinking of each and every one of you. There's no rank in this room, understood? We're a team, and we need to think like a team, because John Harris will be on the ground here momentarily and the clock is ticking. You can say anything to me without fear of breaching protocol." He paused and smiled for effect. "Well, *almost* anything!"

Stuart could see them visibly relax as they laughed.

"Now, Harris has every reason to simply refuel here in Dublin and get back in the air, but he doesn't have the range on that jet to make it to the States in one jump. That means if they try to fly on, he's got to stop for fuel in either Iceland or Canada, and we've got people in both locales ready to move. Of course, I'd rather not test the Canadians' resolve, considering they've got to sleep with the thirty-thousand-pound gorilla to the south, and the gorilla wants John Harris home free."

"Sir William," one of the women said.

"Stuart," he corrected.

"Yes, sir . . . ah, Stuart. I was going to say, there's no way we're going to get a warrant issued in time if they just refuel and go on."

"I understand, Orla. But his pilots are tired, and I don't think they're going to want to take him anywhere until they've had some rest. And, Mr. Reinhart will hire a local solicitor who will tell him the same thing you've just told me regarding the impossibility of finding a district judge quickly. Harris will calculate quite correctly that we're incapable of clapping the cuffs on him until sometime tomorrow, and therefore he has a few hours of grace. So here's the challenge: how many ways can John Harris leave Ireland other than on that jet, and how do we prevent it without doing something illegal?"

Patrick Nolan looked at the others and pulled a legal pad closer to him to consult his notes before meeting Stuart's gaze. "Well, I'm fairly certain he can't escape by rail."

There was more laughter around the table as Patrick continued. "We know they've made reservations at a hotel, which means, Stuart, that you're right about their wanting rest. But our big worry is the commercial airlines."

Stuart nodded knowingly. "I thought of that. He could simply nick a ticket on Aer Lingus and fly to New York direct."

"As early as seven in the morning," one of the men agreed. "But, no one has booked a reservation for him on any airline with direct service to the States, at least as of two hours ago. That doesn't mean they won't try."

"I know the chairman of Aer Lingus personally," Stuart replied. "Perhaps a call from me concerning the legal and political liability they could be playing with if they provided passage for Harris would be worthwhile. But I'll need the phone numbers quickly."

Notes were scribbled around the table as Nolan raised a finger. "There's one more airline with direct Stateside service, Stuart."

"You mean Delta?"

Patrick nodded.

"They have an Irish manager, do they not?"

Glances were exchanged around the table before Patrick looked back. "I . . . would guess so."

"And they need the government's sanction to fly airplanes in Ireland. Certificates and licenses. If the government were white-hot angry with them for something, it could make their lives fairly difficult, I would think."

One of the men had already left the table and was pulling out his cell phone as Campbell gestured to him to wait. "Bill, we'll need the manager's name, home number, and any personal information you can gather."

"What can you say to him?" Nolan asked.

Stuart Campbell grinned. "Nothing, Paddy, since you're going to call him for me."

"Very well, Stuart, but why me, if I may ask?"

"Well, you're Irish, the man we want to persuade is Irish, and I'm a bleeding British knight. Who's got the better chance?"

Patrick nodded. "Understood."

THIRTY-SIX

On Approach to Dublin International Airport, Ireland—Tuesday—9:05 P.M.

"Outer marker, altitude checks, no flags," Alastair reported as Craig Dayton clicked off the Boeing 737's autopilot and eased the yoke forward to capture the instrument landing system glide path in a steady descent.

"Intercepting glide slope. Flaps twenty-five, landing gear down, Before Landing Checklist," Craig ordered.

"Roger," Alastair echoed. "Flaps coming to twenty-five, and . . . landing gear down." He positioned the landing gear lever to the down position and pulled the laminated checklist into his lap to read through the items, verifying Craig's response to each one.

"Flaps to go, Craig."

"Roger. Field in sight, flaps thirty," Craig reported as the approach lights loomed large four miles ahead of the aircraft.

"Flaps are coming to thirty. Flaps are thirty. Gear and flaps rechecked down, and we're cleared to land. You're on speed, marker plus five, ground speed one hundred twenty-four knots."

The jetliner crossed the threshold of Runway 10 fifty feet above the boundary as Craig flared, stopping the descent with the tires a few inches above the surface before letting the bird gently settle to the concrete with a squeal and a stream of rubber smoke unseen in the darkness.

Craig's hand shot forward to gather the speed brake handle and try to pull it back before the automatic deployment system did the job, a race he never won, but which provided a human backup to the system.

He grabbed the thrust reverse levers, redirecting the air moving through the jet engines and slowing the big Boeing.

"EuroAir Ten-Ten, exit at Taxiway Bravo, contact ground," the tower controller said.

"Ten-Ten, roger, and sir, would you please check to make sure Dublin Center relayed to London Center that we're okay?"

"They already know, Ten-Ten. There's rather considerable commotion about you tonight."

"The subtext," Alastair said as his hands ran through the after-landing sequence, "is: 'You blokes have a whale of a lot of explaining to do.' "

"I'm sure that's true," Craig said, completing the runway turnoff while Alastair switched to the ground control frequency and checked in, turning to Craig after releasing the transit button.

"Our esteemed chief pilot will just love our latest trick," Alastair added.

"Maybe he didn't hear about it," Craig said, smiling, his eyes on the taxiway.

"And maybe tomorrow the sun will rise in the west, Captain, sir. This will be the final straw, I have no doubt."

"Ten-Ten, Dublin Ground. Taxi to the Island, hard stand eighty-three, please. That's off Taxiway Papa."

"Why on earth do they call a simple parking spot with a refueling hydrant a 'hard stand?' " Alastair mumbled to himself.

Craig guided the Boeing to a stop and set the parking

brake. He could see a set of portable stairs approaching the left front as they ran the shutdown checklist and Jillian unlocked the cockpit door.

"May I open the front door, Craig?"

"If it's okay with Matt Ward and Sherry," Craig said.

"It is."

"Then let's get the heck out of here."

Sherry Lincoln stepped into the Irish night at the top of the airstairs and breathed deeply, loving the cool, damp air, and eagerly anticipating the feel of a real bed for the first time in forty-eight hours.

Matt Ward emerged right behind her.

"Beautiful night, huh?" he said.

"Yes. And no sign of police, soldiers, or anything particularly threatening."

"Not yet, at least," Matt added, pointing to four men who were walking around the nose of the Boeing toward the foot of the airstairs. Matt bounded down the stairs and stopped the group. Sherry heard the name "Jay" spoken as Craig Dayton and President Harris emerged, with Jillian, Ursula, and Elle behind them.

Sherry descended the stairs with her eyes on the two men in the front now in conversation with the Secret Service agent, wondering which one owned the steady, metered voice that had been so reassuring during the ordeal.

The first of the two men was fairly short and somewhat rotund with a huge smile under a shock of silver hair, the second athletic and just under six feet in height with a full head of black hair and a well-sculpted face set with large, dark eyes.

Sherry felt a tiny shudder of inner relief when the second one stepped forward with his hand outstretched.

"Miss Lincoln, I presume?"

"Mr. Reinhart?"

"Or should I say 'Ms.'?"

She smiled. "'Miss' is accurate, 'Ms.' is better, and 'Sherry' is preferred."

"It's great to meet you at last, and get you here safely," Jay said, taking her hand gently and looking beyond her as

John Harris reached the bottom of the airstairs and hurried over.

"Jay!"

Jay smiled as he squeezed Sherry's hand and released it to greet Harris. "You're even more trouble than you were as my senior partner, Mr. President."

"At the White House they teach you how to be a burden to everyone simultaneously," the President said, turning to introduce Craig Dayton and Alastair Chadwick.

Jay in turn introduced Michael Garrity before gesturing toward the other two men who had hovered in the background.

"These gentlemen are from Irish Immigration."

One of the officers smiled and pointed to the group. "So, which one of you fine people happens to be a former President of the United States?"

When the formalities and paperwork had been completed, John Harris caught Jay's attention and pointed to another parked aircraft. "I see Campbell's here."

"You . . . recognize the airplane?" Jay asked.

Harris nodded with a frown. "From Sigonella. Yes. It was parked in the distance, but the colors are very distinctive."

"He got here almost an hour ago," Jay said. "I'm completely perplexed how he found out you were coming to Dublin, let alone how he knew you hadn't gone down."

The President began walking the group toward the terminal. "Never underestimate Stuart Campbell, Jay. As trite as that sounds, it's a survival manual in a phrase."

"I believe it," Jay replied. "And I imagine he's hard at work with his people right now trying to find a judge. Michael will fill you in on the realities of that process on the way to the hotel, but the bottom line is, I think we're reasonably secure until morning. In fact, they might be incapable of perfecting their warrant before Thursday morning, since tomorrow's St. Patrick's Day. But, John, if we can get you out of here in the morning on a commercial airline, we need to do it. Urgently."

"Is that possible?" the President said as Jay held the terminal door open for him and Sherry.

"I haven't had time to work on it," Jay said when he caught up with them after handing off the door to Garrity and the others, "and frankly, I was reluctant to make a reservation in your name for fear Campbell's team would be watching."

"You have a list of the flights, though?" Sherry asked.

Jay nodded. "Yes. Aer Lingus and Delta are the direct ones, although Delta makes a stop in Shannon. I was thinking you could use my passport, John . . ."

The President had come through the door and stopped, shaking his head "no" as he cast a sideways glance at Sherry. "I'm not going to do it that way, Jay. I've got to draw the line somewhere. Besides, my using your passport would be a criminal offense in almost any nation on earth. You know that."

"I . . . yes, but I just want to get you home."

"Well, *I* want to get me home, too, but not by pulling some cheap stunt."

He saw Jay wince and hastened to put his hand on Jay's arm. "That wasn't a shot at you, Jay. You're doing exactly what I need you to do by looking at every option, but I've got to ride herd on my own panic."

Jay nodded. "I understand."

"I'm very concerned," Harris continued, inclining his head toward Craig Dayton and Alastair Chadwick, who were waiting at a respectful distance, "that I've let these two wonderful pilots put themselves in great professional jeopardy for me. If they lose their jobs, I've got to fix it."

"We had to get you out of Italy, John."

"I know. But I'm getting more nervous about this by the hour, because I'm finally beginning to appreciate the gigantic scope of the dragnet Miraflores has cast around the globe to snare me. I'm sure Stuart has unlimited funds and unlimited numbers of people to help him."

Another pulse of self-doubt shot through Jay's head. In contrast to the legal juggernaut captained by Stuart Campbell, John Harris's legal team consisted of a single barrister of unknown capability, a solicitor he had yet to meet, and a failed Texas jurist trying to reclaim his long-dormant stripes as an international lawyer. The odds were shameful, and he would need every minute to prepare for battle in the Irish courts.

Craig Dayton caught Jay just before he climbed into the first of two vans hired to take them to the nearby hotel.

"Where do we go from here, Mr. Reinhart?"

"I'm sorry?"

"Are you going to need us, I mean? My airplane and my crew?"

"I don't know. Can you stand by through tomorrow?"

Craig looked around at Alastair, who was approaching with his bags, then back at Jay. "Look, we're probably about to be fired, and . . . the reason I need to know, is that if the charter is continuing, I can probably get EuroAir to let us keep on going. I know the only reason they agreed to this charter is the pressure the White House put on them, but once it's over, the money's stopped, and the political pressure is off, we'll be ordered to deadhead the bird to Frankfurt."

"Tell them the charter continues and the money won't stop," Jay said immediately.

Craig nodded. "Good. I . . . may need some help from Washington again if the stunt we pulled over the English Channel has too many people calling for our heads. They thought we'd gone down, and there was a rescue effort."

"Let me know. I'll make the calls to D.C. and do my best."

"One other thing. We may need more pressure from D.C. anyway to go back Stateside with the airplane."

"You can *make* it Stateside? Without a fuel stop in Iceland or Canada?" Jay asked, his eyebrows up a notch. "I thought . . ."

Craig nodded as he glanced at Alastair once more. "Let me put it this way. Dublin to Presque Isle, Maine, is about twenty-eight hundred nautical miles, but the maximum range of this airplane is just a tiny bit over three thousand nautical miles. That means that if the headwinds aren't too bad, *and* if we fly at what's called maximum endurance airspeeds, *and* if the airports in Iceland and Greenland and

Canada aren't socked in as alternate fields, we might be able to make it safely, although there's one big legal hitch."

"I should say!" Alastair chimed in.

"What?" Jay asked.

"This isn't an ETOPS bird."

"That's . . . alphabet soup to me," Jay replied, leaning against the van and willing himself to believe he wasn't tired.

"We love esoteric acronyms in aviation," Craig was saying. "ETOPS means extended twin-engine overwater operation, and to reach the U.S. mainland from here we'd be way, way out over the Atlantic, instead of staying within three hundred miles of a suitable airfield, which is the normal limit."

"So . . . you'd be doing something illegal?"

"More . . . against regulations than illegal . . . in a criminal sense," Craig added.

"Mr. Reinhart," Alastair interjected, "what my partner here is trying to say with practiced understatement is that technically we're not allowed to fly passengers straight out over the Atlantic, even though we *are* equipped with all the required overwater gear: life rafts, life jackets, survival gear, and such. You see, there's a certain procedure for officially blessing twin-engine jets for such operations, and this one hasn't yet qualified. We're already in terrible trouble with our company, but even if we weren't, I guarantee you EuroAir would never approve such an illicit route."

"They wouldn't have to," Craig said. "We'll file by way of Keflavík, Iceland, and Gander, Newfoundland, then to Presque Isle, Maine. Only we'll change the routing in flight and go direct, or as close to direct as they'll let us. There is a specific system of tracks across the North Atlantic."

"I think I understand," Jay said.

"I'm assuming you still don't want to touch down in any country other than the U.S., including Canada."

"That's right . . . you can navigate over water?" Jay asked.

"Piece of cake," Craig answered, noticing the pained expression on Alastair's face.

"I *hate* that phrase," Alastair muttered.

"He hates that phrase," Craig repeated, arching a thumb at the copilot. "We've got two GPS's, global positioning satellite systems. We know our position within three feet at every moment."

"Yes, indeed," Alastair said. "For instance, at this moment we know our careers are precisely within three feet of the intersection of Unloved and Unemployed. So why not enjoy the trip and push on some more?"

"In other words . . ." Jay started to say, completely confused.

"In other words," Craig replied, "we can do it if the President needs us. Provided the winds aren't ridiculous."

"Try to arrange it, fellows," Jay said. "If I can't get him out any other way, we'll do it your way."

✈ THIRTY-SEVEN

The Great Southern Hotel, Dublin Airport, Dublin, Ireland—Tuesday—9:50 P.M.

The drive to the midlevel airport hotel was brief, and the restaurant Garrity had lined up to feed them turned out to be a smokey pub with too much noise to permit serious conversation. It was nearly eleven when they returned to the hotel, said goodnight to the two pilots and three flight attendants, and gathered in John Harris's room, with the President, Sherry Lincoln, and Jay sitting on two chairs and an ottoman while Matt Ward and Michael Garrity stood.

"I do hope the accommodations are satisfactory, Mr. President," Garrity said. "Mr. Reinhart wanted to keep you as close to the airport as possible."

"They're fine, Michael," the President said. "I don't always need to be in a six-room suite."

Michael Garrity began laying out the basics of extradition in the Republic of Ireland.

"It's the Garda, our police force, that will have to formally present the Interpol warrant, but they'll probably ac-

cept Campbell's help in finding a judge. Now, if he *can't*
find a district judge, Campbell's team will have one choice
left, and that's the High Court justice who's on standby.
There's always one of them every holiday, either hanging
on his cell phone or actually fooling around at home. The
fact that he's accessible is the good news for Campbell, although it's possible a High Court justice would decide he
didn't have jurisdiction. What's good for us is the fact that
a High Court judge is far more likely to listen to our
protests that the evidence is insufficient to support the
basic charge."

John Harris could see Jay's expression darken, and their
eyes met momentarily as Jay looked at the President, his
mind consumed by a new wave of worry.

"Jay and I need to talk, Mr. Garrity, before we continue," the President said.

"Indeed," Garrity replied, puzzled at the sudden chill in
the room. Sherry, too, looked off-balance.

"John," Jay said. "I think we may need to include
everyone in this." He met John Harris's eyes again as the
President stared at him. "Michael, here, has to defend you,
and Sherry and Matt are integral parts of the team. I think
everyone has a need to know."

"What are you talking about, Jay?" Sherry asked.

The President had begun to get to his feet, but he sank
back onto the edge of the chair with a long sigh and nodded. "Very well, Jay. You're probably right."

"Jay, what's going on?" Sherry pressed, looking from
the President to Jay and back.

"What's going on, Sherry," the President began, "is an
allegation that Stuart Campbell dropped like a small bomb
in the London Magistrate Court. Go on, Jay."

Jay described in detail Campbell's assertion that CIA
covert operations chief Barry Reynolds had briefed the
President in the Oval Office and warned him that the
people they were about to hire to carry out the planned Peruvian drug raid would most likely maim and torture anyone they found before killing them.

"And you approved this as an official act?" Michael
Garrity asked evenly.

"Absolutely not!" John Harris said. "I mean . . . all right, look here. What happened was entirely different. Reynolds had been working the case personally and reporting directly to the DCI, who was reporting to me."

"I'm sorry?" Michael replied.

"DCI. The Director of Central Intelligence," the President responded. "Anyway, I received word that we were at a critical juncture in this search-and-destroy mission, and Reynolds needed to brief me personally. I recall thinking that it was an odd request, since usually the DCI or his direct deputy do such briefings."

"So Mr. Reynolds did come to the Oval Office?" Jay asked.

John Harris sighed and nodded. "Yes, he did. There were times when such off-the-record meetings were necessary. We even have them occasionally with members of the military. No time record kept, no names on the appointment calendar. Nothing to indicate it ever occurred, for national security reasons as well as political reasons."

"I see," Garrity said, his eyes locked on the President. "You call it plausible deniability, if I'm to believe Hollywood."

"That's not too far from the real phrase," Harris continued. "Okay, so I received Reynolds, he was there on schedule, and the Secret Service slipped him in the west door to the Oval. Matt? Were you the agent on duty that day?"

"No, sir. I've . . . brought individuals in through that door, but I don't recall that one," he said with great care, his normal unreadable expression changing ever so slightly.

"Well, that's how it was done. Reynolds . . . and I recall this very, very clearly because of my utter shock when I got the report later on the bloodbath that had transpired . . . Reynolds told me that they had a team ready to go in and raid the drug factory and destroy it. We knew we could not use Americans, expatriates or otherwise. We needed mercenaries, and that's what he had found. I asked him if they were militarily trained, and he assured me that they were trained and disciplined and veterans with formal military experience essentially gone bad. He assured me they would stick to their orders, kill only if unavoidable, and that they would thoroughly understand that their target was the factory, not the people who worked there. I knew there were *campesinos* . . . peasants . . . pressed into service in such places. But we had to stop the flow."

"So you approved the raid?" Jay asked.

"Yes. As Commander-in-Chief, and ultimate head of special operations and every other government function. I had to act. The flow of their heroin into the U.S. was reaching epidemic proportions, and an incredible percentage was coming out of that very facility, *and* the exiting government under Fujimori was doing absolutely nothing."

"But, John," Jay interrupted, "the most important point is this: Did Reynolds in any way, form, or fashion indicate to you that the mercenaries you would be authorizing him to hire would torture or murder the workers?"

"No, he did not. In fact, as I've already said, he assured me they would follow orders. And my orders were to do no harm to the workers and to kill only in self-defense."

"Then," Jay continued, his eyes welded on John Harris, "why does Stuart Campbell allege that Barry Reynolds made a videotape of that meeting, a tape that shows the opposite?"

John Harris thrust his arms wide open in a sweeping gesture of frustration.

"I DON'T KNOW! Dammit, Jay, do you have any idea what an accusation like that does to me? I *know* I'm not suffering from Alzheimer's like poor Ronnie Reagan. So far I remember things clearly, thank the Lord, and I know for an absolute fact that there can be no such video or audio evidence because this President never . . . repeat, never . . . listened to any such representations from Reynolds. I mean, you couldn't even read that into his words between the lines, because I specifically asked him if he was *sure* they wouldn't go overboard!"

Jay was nodding. "I demanded a copy of the tape."

"And?" John Harris snapped, his breathing accelerated and his face reddened.

"And Campbell never delivered it, which was in part,

I'm sure, because neither of us stayed in London long enough."

"We need a copy of that tape, I'm afraid," Michael Garrity said.

"Damn right we do!" John Harris said. "I mean, in the first place, the incredible act of claiming to have taped a conversation in the Oval with the President of the United States is ridiculous enough."

"You know, when . . . people were brought in that way," Matt interjected, "we usually knew precisely who they were, and although we would pat them down, we wouldn't run them through the metal detector."

"Meaning?" Jay asked.

"Meaning, it's not impossible that a known CIA chief could come through the door with a hidden camera wired to him. It's not something you'd expect."

John Harris looked Jay in the eye, speaking slowly. "If there is a tape that has any words spoken by Reynolds or myself that vary from what I just told you, it has been electronically fabricated or altered."

Jay nodded slowly. "It's entirely possible. But how do we prove it?"

"Indeed," Michael Garrity said, his eyes on the far wall as he stroked his chin. "A tape like that at a full-blown trial can be challenged, but in a hearing like this . . ."

"It *can* be challenged here," Sherry said, coming partially out of her chair, her eyes wide. "Remember the Rodney King thing? Those police officers were beating the hell out of the man on camera, in living color, and the defense team somehow fuzzed it up to the point of an acquittal. Who's going to believe a ridiculous fake like this?"

"That's loyalty talking, Sherry, for which I'm grateful," the President said sadly.

"He's right, Miss Lincoln," Garrity added. "A tape like that in front of a judge at this stage is going to be very difficult to challenge."

"Can't we attack it as illegally made and therefore inadmissible?" Jay asked.

"Perhaps, but that's entirely up to the judge, and you're dealing with a bizarre combination of things, a U.S. President, the White House, a CIA chief, and I'm not certain that even a U.S. court could so easily declare such a tape patently inadmissible. Keep in mind that you told me Reynolds was a respected senior officer of Central Intelligence."

"So, if Campbell produces it in court in Dublin, it would be a problem?" Jay asked.

"No," Michael Garrity said, carefully choosing his words. "No, Jay, it wouldn't be a problem. For what we're trying to do, it would be a disaster."

The Shelbourne Hotel, St. Stephen's Green, Dublin, Ireland

Stuart Campbell finished the last call he had to make and opened the window overlooking St. Stephen's Green to clear his head.

The temperature was moderate, if not balmy, and a light breeze rustled the curtains. He could almost feel the presence of the Four Courts building on Inns Quay bordering the River Liffey, unseen but less than a mile distant. There was something in the history of the structure that always affected him, a symbol of defiance on a level that his native Scotland had never achieved. The building had been left barely standing in the ruins of the Irish Civil War in April of 1922, a victim of shelling by pro-treaty forces that had all but collapsed the dome. The steely determination of the Irish had rebuilt it to be as much a symbol of the rule of law as the rule of the Republic, and the Four Courts had become the center of justice in the Republic.

It would be the situs of the battle to come, and not the first for him. With the British and Irish legal systems essentially identical in form, he had been—as they expressed it—"called" before the Irish bar as a barrister many years back in a case representing U.K. interests. It had been a thrill he would never discuss with his fellow English barristers, many of whom delighted in rolling their eyes at anything Irish.

Campbell turned for a moment to watch the beehive of

activity behind him. The Presidential Suite was only his central command post. Across the city, the main Dublin office of his law firm was ablaze with lights and a team of sixteen lawyers, secretaries, and clerks working feverishly on the sweeping assignment they'd been given: prepare every possible order for every possible court for every possible contingency.

For the past hour, between his own phone calls to the home numbers of various highly placed individuals, Stuart had received disappointing progress reports on the quest for a judge. As he had feared, there seemed to be no district judge anywhere in the Republic of Ireland who could be persuaded to consider the warrant at home.

"I thought we had it at one point," Patrick had told him twenty minutes before. "Mr. Justice O'Mally, it was, and I caught him by cell phone in his backyard. He said we could bring the case to his home, and then he discovered the warrant concerned one John Harris, former President of the U.S."

"What happened?" Stuart asked.

"Well, the exact words escape me because there was some sputtering and laughing on the other end . . . and a few epithets . . . but the gist of it was that I was certifiably crazy if I thought he was going to issue from home an arrest warrant against a past President of the United States, quote, 'the greatest friend Ireland has ever had.' At the minimum, he said, it would take a full-blown hearing and all the protections possible under Irish law, along with full statutory notice to the other party, and he would accept no waivers of the time requirements for notifying Harris's team."

"That's all?" Stuart laughed.

"No, he was also personally incensed that I was trying to allege that a former U.S. President could really present a risk of flight. After that, Stuart, I bade him good night, since I figured our prospects for a favorable decision from him were, shall we say, somewhat reduced."

"I think the phrase you're searching for, Paddy, is 'snowball's chance in hell.'"

"Right. At best."

The search had continued, but the few who could be located were not interested in holding court in their parlor, with one judge unconvinced that a former president would try to sneak away, and another of the opinion that an escape would be the best possible solution.

"It's almost eleven," Campbell announced as he walked back into the reception area of the suite that already resembled a war room. "I think we should suspend calling judges for tonight and concentrate on strategy until about two A.M., then all get some sleep and get started again around eight." He sat down at the table, watching the faces around him. "Any thoughts?"

"Good idea. We've accomplished nothing, sir," one of the men said, looking at the senior partner. "Did you get anywhere?"

"Yes," Stuart replied, glancing at his notes before looking up. "And I wager that Mr. Harris and Mr. Reinhart are going to be in for a rather rude surprise in the morning if they do what I fully expect them to do."

✈ **THIRTY-EIGHT**

The Great Southern Hotel, Dublin Airport, Dublin, Ireland—Wednesday—12:20 A.M.

It was past midnight when Jay Reinhart, Sherry Lincoln, and Michael Garrity left the President in his room, with Secret Service Agent Matt Ward camped out in a connecting room.

In the hallway, Garrity bade them goodnight and headed for the stairway and his car, leaving Jay and Sherry to walk to the elevator alone.

"I'm going to recheck those flights before going to sleep," she said.

Jay nodded. "The first one's at ten?"

"Yes. That's the Aer Lingus flight."

"If they can't get the warrant for an arrest here in Dublin, they're not going to manage it by the time he gets to Shannon. We just need to get him to the airport around nine, not too early, not too late. We can buy the ticket quietly at that point. In theory, it should work. Without an arrest warrant, neither the Garda nor immigration has any justification for refusing him access to the flight."

"That makes sense," she said. "I'll wake him on time."

There was a bench seat opposite the elevators and they both sank onto it.

"You look exhausted, Jay," she said with a weary smile.

He smiled back. "I am, but it's as much from worry as real fatigue, I think. I . . . .I just don't want to screw this up."

"Me either," she said, pausing awkwardly to look away at the elevators. "He's a good man, Jay."

"I know."

"I've worked for him for four years, and he's one of the most decent, thoughtful . . ."

"Let me stop you, Sherry. I know all the superlatives, and I agree with all of them. We should . . . spend some time together telling each other John Harris stories when this is over," he said with a laugh.

She nodded. "I'd like that. It was a real comfort, by the way, hearing your voice so reassuring on the other end of the phone, especially during the first hours of this mess."

He laughed. "You wouldn't have been reassured if you'd seen my alleged command post in Laramie, Wyoming."

"Oh?"

"How about a kitchen counter with a land line and a cell phone and a bathrobe?"

"A bathrobe?" she smiled, cocking her head.

He hesitated, looking more directly into her eyes than he'd done before.

She's really beautiful, he thought, validating the first impression he'd refused to let himself pursue.

"Yeah. A bathrobe," he said. "It's a long story."

"I may want to hear that story. Sounds edgy, practicing law in your bathrobe."

"Keeps the judges completely off-balance," he chuckled, remembering the nearly fatal flight to Denver. "That was perhaps the most surreal experience I've ever had, trying to get on top of this situation for John from Laramie, trying to stay in touch, dealing with people at a level I'd never experienced." The memory of his front door slamming when Linda left replayed momentarily, but he chased it from his thoughts.

"You mean at the White House?"she asked.

"Yes, and the State Department, and the Justice Department, not to mention the later encounter with the British Government. I'm still not so sure this isn't some wild nightmare induced by an evening of debauchery at a Mexican restaurant."

"They have Mexican restaurants in Laramie?" she asked.

"They think they do. Actually, it's pretty good Tex-Mex."

"How is this going to end, Jay?"

He locked eyes with her again, feeling another small flutter before realizing she was focused on John Harris, not him.

"I wish I knew. If we can get him on the way home, you've got a public relations battle ahead as to why and how he left Ireland, I suppose."

"We can handle it. John Harris is well loved back home."

Jay nodded. "But if we can't get him out of Dodge, this could end up an extended stay in Ireland, although I'm very confident Peru isn't going to shoehorn him out of here."

"I guess that's what I wanted to hear," she said. "That you're confident about the ultimate outcome."

"I had some momentary doubt in that London court-room when Campbell dropped the bombshell about the tape, but I kept telling myself that John Harris's character didn't change in the Oval Office. I couldn't imagine his accepting such a proposition."

"Torture and killing, in other words?"

"Absolutely," Jay said. "This is a man who believes in the death penalty only to rid society of the most evil of two-footed animals, even though morally it hurts him to the core that taking life is the only rational solution in extreme cases. He cares so much . . ."

She raised her hand. "Now *you're* playing *my* song."

He laughed easily, aware of how very relaxed he felt in

her presence. "I am at that." He looked at his watch. "Sherry, I think . . ."

She was already getting to her feet and reaching out to take his hand in what began as a perfunctory handshake and became something else when he reached for her other hand, holding both of them, their eyes meeting for a few seconds.

Reluctantly, he let go of her hands to punch the elevator button. The doors opened almost immediately, and they walked in a little awkwardly, Jay bidding her good night on the second floor as he continued to the third and his room, his thoughts temporarily sidetracked from matters of law and treaties.

And, for some reason he couldn't pinpoint, all efforts to find a mental image of Linda back in Laramie were failing, as was his usually well-tuned capacity for guilt when he thought about Karen.

For the first time since his wife's death, the familiar, gut-wrenching pain that hit him every time he thought about her had disappeared. In its place was a simple, sweet sadness. Why? Maybe he was just too tired, or too wrapped up in the problem at hand. Or maybe he was ready to take the advice he'd been so tired of hearing, that it was time to get on with his life.

Jay put his suit on a hanger, pulled off the rest of his clothes, and brushed his teeth before falling into bed. He was sleepily luxuriating in the feel of the sheets when he remembered he had one final item of unfinished business to complete.

He forced himself back up, sitting naked sideways on the bed as he pulled out a Dublin phone book and looked for hotel listings.

None of the names jumped out at him.

He called the night clerk at the front desk.

"I need to know which Dublin hotel is the best, most plush, most expensive, and best thought of in Ireland."

"Good heavens, sir, you're not happy with us then?"

He laughed as he rubbed his eyes. "No, no, no! I've got to locate someone who would only look for the most expensive lodging. This is a lovely hotel."

"Well that's a relief, that is. You have to be talking about the Shelbourne Hotel, and it is lovely. Is your friend American?"

"British."

"Oh, then most certainly he'd be there. Hang on and I'll ring them."

When the Shelbourne's operator answered, Jay asked for Stuart Campbell's room, unsurprised when there was no hesitation. An unfamiliar voice answered and he could hear more voices in the background, a fact that instantly reignited the earlier gnawing feeling that he was shirking his duties to be considering sleep.

"This is Stuart Campbell."

"Jay Reinhart, Sir William."

"Ah, yes! Mr. Reinhart. Some impressive footwork tonight, eh?"

"Look, we're both preparing for battle, but I have one official notification I must give you. Actually, two."

"Go ahead."

"First, I formally request that you notify me immediately if you in any way arrange contact with a judge regarding any aspect of this matter, and certainly I demand to be present at any hearing, formal or informal, concerning the same, and I'll pass you both my cellular GSM number and the hotel I'm in."

"Of course, Mr. Reinhart. There was never any question of that. I shall notify you in accordance with the rules, have no fear."

"I have a lot of fear, Sir William, because of the nature of your client, but the other matter is . . . and I realize neither of us had time to connect in London . . . but I need a copy of that tape, and I shall object vociferously and loudly in every possible forum if you do not provide me with a copy for advance scrutiny."

"Actually, I've had a little time to consider the matter, and I'm inclined to agree that you *should* see it. Give me your hotel information and I'll have a copy delivered tomorrow afternoon or evening."

"The earlier the better."

"Mr. Reinhart, the format of the tape is very specialized, and it takes special equipment to dub it. I have a camera that can play it, but I'm not sure I can dub tapes with it. However, I'm confident you shall have a copy by tomorrow evening at the latest. Shall we say in standard VHS format?"

"Yes."

"Very well. Burning the midnight oil there, too, are you?"

Jay hesitated, irritation fighting guilt over the truth of the answer. "Absolutely. Goes with the territory."

"Indeed. Well, good night to you, such as it is."

Jay replaced the receiver carefully, replaying the words in his mind and searching for second and third levels of meaning. Perhaps he should stay up and study, but study what? It all came down to what was on that tape, and until he could view it for himself, all he could do was let Garrity and the as yet unseen solicitor take the lead. Besides, he needed the physical strength and renewed mental energy a few hours' sleep would give him.

He set the nightstand alarm for 6 A.M. and turned out the light, falling asleep almost instantly.

✈ THIRTY-NINE

**Dublin International Airport, Ireland—
Wednesday—9:05 A.M.**

The Aer Lingus agent handed a set of tickets over the counter and motioned to Jay, who was next in line.

"I understand you still have seats available on the non-stop to New York at ten?" Jay asked.

"Yes, sir, I believe we do. I'll check. Just a moment."

The agent pecked away at her computer keyboard for nearly a minute before looking back up at him. "Yes, we have seats in both coach and first class."

"I'll need two tickets, one way, first-class, please."

"Your name, please?"

"J. Harris," Jay said.

More pecking.

"Very good, Mr. Harris, and I'll need to see your passport and a credit card."

Jay handed over the credit card before turning to catch Sherry's eye where she stood by the terminal entrance. She nodded and disappeared for nearly a minute, returning with the President in tow. They came up quietly by Jay's side.

"They need your passports," Jay said.

Harris smiled as he and Sherry handed over the blue-cover American passports, and all three watched as the agent flipped them open before looking up with an unreadable smile.

"Just a moment, please. I'll be back straightaway." She left the counter area, which was in the middle of the terminal floor, and entered a door off to one side.

"Oh, boy," Jay muttered.

"I know. She took my passport with her," John Harris said.

The agent emerged a minute later with a man trailing her. She resumed her position behind the counter as he circled around the front to where they were standing, and handed back the President's passport.

"Good morning. I'm Richard Lacey, the station manager," he began, his eyes darting nervously from John Harris to Jay Reinhart to Sherry and back. "Would you be good enough to come with me for a moment?"

"Mr. Lacey," Jay said, "we're trying to complete a transaction here and get on a flight. What's wrong?"

"I'd . . . appreciate it if you would follow me," Lacey said, ushering them away from the counter and through a series of doors to a small conference room.

"What's this about?" John Harris asked when they'd shut the door behind them.

"Please, have a seat, sir."

"I'm not interested in sitting, Mr. Lacey," Harris said. "I am interested in getting on your flight."

"I know that, Mr. President," Lacey replied, his eyes on the table as he took a deep breath.

"All right," Jay began, stepping forward. "If you know who President Harris is, then you've got a specific purpose in pulling us off the floor. What is it?"

Lacey looked up at last. "I'm terribly sorry, but we cannot offer you passage on our airline today."

"And why would that be, Mr. Lacey?" Jay asked, struggling unsuccessfully to keep an acidic edge from his voice. "Has any official agency of the Irish government given you a directive? Because if they have, I can assure you it's not legal."

"Not the government."

"Who, then?"

Lacey was perspiring and obviously nervous. "Won't you please sit a minute?"

"No," Jay snapped. "You're running an airline here and President Harris is attempting to pay you several thousand dollars for passage as a member of the public, and you possess no legal right to deny that passage. You're playing with the potential for a massive lawsuit, sir."

"I'm not making the decisions here, Mr. . . ."

"Reinhart. Jay Reinhart. I'm the President's lawyer."

"Yes. Of course, Mr. Reinhart." He extended his hand but Jay refused to take it, and Lacey lowered it in embarrassment.

"Well, you see, the bottom line is, the chairman of my company has instructed me that regardless of threats or consequences, I may not sell any tickets to President Harris today."

"Or tomorrow?" Jay asked.

"Until further notice. I do not know why."

"Very convenient," Jay snapped.

John Harris gently put a hand on Jay's arm.

"We understand this is out of your discretion, Mr. Lacey," the President said. "But you are telling us that you are not authorized to give me an explanation?"

Lacey pulled a piece of note paper from a suit coat pocket and handed it over with a slightly shaking hand. "I was told to ask you to call Mr. O'Day at this number, sir. That's our chairman, and he will explain."

"Very well."

"Wait a minute, John. It's not all right! I'll get an injunction against this and . . ."

"No, Jay. Let's go. Thank you, Mr. Lacey."

"You're welcome to use the phone in here," Lacey said.

John Harris shook his head. "I fail to see the point, sir, of talking to your chairman or anyone else at this airline. I'm either welcome on your airline or I'm not, and clearly you've established the latter, and clearly you've accepted all the potential liability that may be attached thereto."

"I . . . suppose so," Lacey stammered. He led them

back to the main terminal floor and departed with another mumbled apology. Sherry had waited by the door she'd seen them enter earlier. Jay heatedly explained the situation.

"I'm going to talk to Delta. Wait here," he said.

He returned fifteen minutes later, red-faced and angry. "Delta's Dublin manager claims Irish immigration will fine them if they allow you to leave while a criminal matter is pending, but the local manager can't give me a name or number of any immigration personnel he's talked to, nor will he give me the number of anyone in Atlanta at their company headquarters. That's garbage, of course."

"I rather expected this, Jay," John Harris said quietly.

"I didn't, and it's outrageous!"

John Harris motioned to Jay and Sherry to follow him and they walked to an alcove near the front of the terminal, where the President turned and leaned close to them.

"Yes, it's outrageous, but we all know this is Stuart's doing, and we knew we could expect something like this. He's managed to intimidate them with thinly veiled threats of litigation or potential government sanctions and, of course, they're going to do what any doubtful company would do, which is: err on the side of caution."

"Sounds like you're excusing them, John," Jay said.

The President shook his head. "As I told you last night, never underestimate Stuart Campbell. He's a genuine Lamont Cranston, with the ability to cloud men's minds."

Jay looked puzzled. "Who?"

John Harris smiled. "Lamont Cranston. You have to be over fifty to remember the name, Jay. An old radio show."

"Oh."

John Harris looked over his shoulder at the front drive, then back at them. "Let's get back to the hotel. We can sort out the next move from there."

"I'm glad you're taking this calmly, Mr. President," Jay said.

Harris met his eyes. "Only on the surface, Jay. Inside is a different matter."

**The Great Southern Hotel, Dublin Airport,
Dublin, Ireland**

Alastair Chadwick was sipping a glass of orange juice when he spotted Craig Dayton walking into the hotel restaurant in jeans and a white shirt, looking smug.

"You're smiling," he pointed out.

"Yes," Craig agreed, offering no other explanation.

"Are Jillian, Ursula, and Elle going to join us?"

"Jillian will be down in a few minutes," Craig said. "I don't know about the other two."

"So, do I detect canary feathers around the corners of your mouth?" Alastair asked, as dryly as possible.

Craig sat down and motioned to a nearby waiter, pointing to his coffee cup before looking at Alastair.

"Canary feathers?"

"As in, the cat that ate the canary. In other words, you seem insufferably pleased with yourself."

"I do? Well, I just had a very strange conversation with our chief pilot."

"Really? Strange? Craig, *any* conversation with Herr Wurtschmidt is, by definition, strange. The man's a raving paranoid with delusions of adequacy."

"Maybe, but he told me to carry on, and said he'd fax me the charter papers for customs in Iceland, Canada, and the U.S., if our client decides to go."

Alastair looked stunned. "Just like that?"

"Just like that."

The copilot shifted in his seat and cleared his throat. "Craig, last night we cost the British government a few quid, to say the least, by sending them on a wild goose chase for a missing aircraft that wasn't. He doesn't know?"

"Oh, he knows, but he accepted my explanation," Craig said, stealing a piece of Alastair's toast and dumping a small pitcher of cream into his freshly poured coffee.

"Aha!" Alastair said, raising his remaining slice of toast for emphasis. "Now we get to the truth! You flummoxed him once more!"

"I'm sorry, *what*? Oh! You're into Britspeak again, aren't you?"

"Flummoxed. Bamboozled. Pulled the wool. Messed with his mind."

"Oh, yeah. Mind messing. That one I got."

"Craig, what in heaven's name *did* you tell him?"

"I simply told him . . ." Craig began, as he searched the menu and drew out the suspense.

"Yes? What?"

"I told him that we'd cancelled our instrument clearance in order to stay in international airspace to prevent diplomatic problems, and for some reason London Center couldn't hear our subsequent radio calls."

"That's all?"

"Well . . . I might have told him . . . or might have somehow suggested . . . that we were operating on direct orders from the Royal Air Force and the White House."

"Direct . . . ?"

"Direct orders. I told him it was classified. He said he didn't want to know."

"Yes, I imagine. Nor would I."

"He's beginning to act like Schultz, in *Hogan's Heroes*. Did you ever see that show? Remember old Schultz? Whenever Hogan or his guys would pull something, Schultz would scream: I know *nothing!*"

"I think I envy Schultz. So . . . we're still employed for a few more hours?"

"For a few more hours. Wanna go to Maine?"

"Do I have a choice?"

"No."

"So . . . what's the determining factor for a 'go, no-go' decision?"

"Primarily, whether or not President Harris is able to get out of here on a commercial flight. If he can't, then the decision depends on the weather, the upper-level winds, careful flight planning, and the possibility that someone will find a way to refuse us departure clearance."

"That's a serious threat?"

"Yeah, it is. I haven't heard from them, whether the flight's on or not, but we have to use the North Atlantic Track System to make it direct, and they could refuse us the clearance just like that, and for no apparent reason."

Alastair was nodding as Craig continued.

"It'd be as easy as intimidating the average FAA inspector with a call from a U.S. senator. One call from Mr. Campbell to the right people, and we'd never get off the ground."

London, England

Secretary of State Joseph Byer hung up the telephone and sat back with his arms behind his head as an aide sat in a nearby chair with a questioning look. Byer ignored him for well over a minute, carefully marking the time necessary to reinforce the reality that he was the head wolf, as he was fond of describing himself.

"Wondering what the President wanted this time, Andrew?" he asked at last, his eyes carefully focused on the opposite wall.

"Yes, sir."

"He wanted to know why, if we'd determined that Harris and Reinhart are in Dublin, weren't we in Dublin, too, holding their hands."

"Yes, sir."

"Know why?"

"No, sir. I mean, I think I do, but I didn't hear what you told him."

"I told him that Harris's lawyer insists on running the show, and Harris insists on letting him, so we'll just wait until Harris gets himself arrested and then we'll fly over and offer to help pick up the pieces. And if they don't want our help, so be it. We'll just monitor the situation. Let Harris twist in the wind awhile."

"Yes, sir."

"Meantime, get the others in here. We've got some official channels to engage in Ireland."

"You're not fond of Harris, are you, sir?"

"Has nothing to do with politics, Andrew. I heard about the allegations Mr. Campbell made in that hearing, that Harris knowingly approved torture and murder. I'm deeply worried there could really be such a tape."

"And if there is?"

Byer lowered his arms and turned to look at his aide. "If there is, John Harris is in far more trouble than even he knows, and he's going to drag us into a terrible debacle. The harm he could do to American foreign policy cannot be overstated."

Dun Laoghaire, Ireland—South Dublin

Mr. Justice Gerald O'Connell had slapped his tiny electronic alarm clock across the room for the offense of waking a High Court judge before he was ready to regain consciousness.

That was thirty minutes before he admitted to himself that the hour of ten o'clock was not a respectable time to be in bed alone, even on a holiday.

The judge rolled to a sitting position and sampled his mood, finding it unusually sour. Sleeping alone was an agony and an ecstasy. With his wife on holiday in the States, he could hog the bed and the covers, but the unavailability of feminine comfort was an irritant. *Mrs.* Justice O'Connell—Elizabeth by given name—was still lovely and sexy and desirable and, dammit, he wanted her right now. And where was she? Instead of tending to her womanly duties, she was gallivanting halfway around the globe with her loony sister.

I'll hold her in contempt, I will! he thought, thankful she couldn't read such thoughts from afar. She didn't need red hair to be fearsome when angered, and his demands sometimes infuriated her.

"So you want me now, do you, Your Lordship?" she'd screamed at him one morning several months before, pulling her gown off and standing in all her glory before the large bedroom window for the neighbors to see. "Take me, damn you! Right here, right now! Or would you rather do it in your courtroom on the bench?"

He rubbed his eyes and remembered the equally irritating fact that he was the standby judge for this holiday, available to any rotten barrister or incompetent progenitor of Irish law who couldn't handle the tide of crime and punishment without a bewigged jurist to bless the process.

"Dammit!" he muttered aloud, just to hear the protest echo off the walls.

He almost dared the phone to ring as he boiled a couple of eggs and burned some toast for breakfast in the downstairs kitchen, and ring it did.

"Yes?"

"Mr. Justice O'Connell?"

"Who else do you think would be answering his phone on a holiday?"

"I'm sorry, Judge. I thought you were the standby . . ."

"Yes, I am, dammit. Who's this?"

"Patrick Nolan, sir, of the firm of McCullogh, Malone, and Bourke. I'm afraid we have an urgent matter involving a former U.S. President, and we've exhausted all possibilities of securing a district judge."

He snorted. "That figures. They're all slacking. A U.S. President? Is this a joke?"

"No, My Lord, it isn't." Nolan explained the basics of the case as O'Connell sat down at his kitchen table.

"So the application is for issuance of an arrest warrant based on the Interpol warrant, is that correct?"

"Yes, My Lord."

"So where are the Garda? Such a warrant has to be presented by them, not by a private firm."

"It will be, My Lord. I'm merely assisting them."

"Will the application be opposed by Mr. Harris's counsel?"

"We're certain it will be, and we're ready to notify them when you're ready to receive us, Judge."

"Why on earth would you think I have jurisdiction of a case like this? It's just a warrant!"

Carefully and quickly, Patrick Nolan laid out his argument. "Bottom line, My Lord, in the absence of a District Court and the presence of an emergency, you may assert jurisdiction, if you so desire."

"Well, I may hear it, but get it out of your head that you're coming to my house today."

"Begging your pardon, Judge, but there is a distinct danger of flight."

"From Ireland?"

"Yes."

O'Connell thought it over for a few seconds. "You say this man is a former President of the United States. I do recognize the name."

"Yes, Judge."

"Is there some *serious* worry that he's going to go forth and reoffend somewhere?"

"No, Judge, but we might lose jurisdiction over him."

"What? You said the alleged crimes were committed in Peru, isn't that correct?"

"Yes, My Lord."

"Peru, as in South America, llamas, and halfway around the bleeding globe?"

"Yes, My Lord."

"And, this *is* still the Republic of Ireland, like it was when I went to bed last night, correct?"

"Ah . . . yes, My Lord."

"Then WHY IN BLOODY HELL ARE YOU WOR-RIED?"

"Well . . ."

"I mean, has he threatened to torture anyone here, other than me, that is?"

"No, Judge, of course not, but . . ."

"Tomorrow morning, then, counsel! I'll hear this case promptly at eleven. No. At ten A.M. You'll provide notification to Harris's solicitor?"

"Yes, My Lord."

"Good. Now leave me alone."

"Yes, My Lord. Thank you."

He replaced the receiver and sat in thought as he munched his toast. Anything involving such a high-ranking personage would draw considerable attention. Media coverage, government officials, diplomatic corps, and a thundering herd of interested parties.

I wonder if there's any substance to this? he mused, suppressing his long-held antipathy for the posturing of the American government on so many issues.

This could be bloody interesting!

FORTY

Dublin, Ireland—Wednesday—11:00 A.M.

The appointment to meet at the solicitor's office at eleven had been made with an awareness that the entire issue would be moot if John Harris was already on his way to New York. Now, with the hopes of a commercial escape dashed, Jay was determined to keep the appointment on time. If they had to fight, being as prepared as possible was vital.

He and Sherry Lincoln had spent the hours before the appointment trying to charter a smaller transoceanic business jet to carry the President to New York, but the effort had failed. No one could react on such short notice to a new customer. The only alternative, Sherry was told, involved deadheading a long-range Gulfstream in from Chicago at incredible cost, but even then, the earliest wheels-up time out of Dublin would be late Thursday morning.

"I'm out of tricks," Jay told John Harris at a quarter past ten. "We either get the damn thing quashed here, or fly you out on the 737."

"The crew's still willing?" the President asked.

Jay nodded. "I talked to them fifteen minutes ago. They're rested and can leave whenever we decide to. It's risky, of course. They might have to turn around if the headwinds are too strong, and there's always the chance they might have to divert to Iceland or Canada, which then opens up an entirely new series of challenges."

John Harris was silent for nearly a minute before shaking his head and sighing. "No, Jay, I want to wait right here, I think. I like your man Garrity, and from what he was saying . . . *and* the fact that I would really rather attack this head-on than run . . . perhaps I should simply send those fellows back to Frankfurt. I'll get plenty of protection here."

"We don't know that, John! We don't even have a court or a judge yet."

"Nonetheless, I know what did and did not happen in the Oval, and I trust the Irish judge to sort it out and give me an adequate opportunity to prove that the tape is a fake."

Jay stood and stared at the President for a few uncomfortable seconds as John Harris sat on the side of his bed, keeping his eyes on the carpet.

"John, it's your money, but I want to keep those guys on standby until we know what's happening."

Harris nodded slowly. "Very well. But my intention is not to use them."

The offices of Seamus Dunham of Dunham and McBride, the firm of solicitors Jay had retained on Michael Garrity's recommendation, were in a working-class neighborhood in a nondescript building several miles from the heart of town.

Michael Garrity was waiting as Jay, Sherry, and the President assembled in the small, somewhat shabby conference room and Matt Ward stood guard in the hallway.

When the introductions were complete, Garrity outlined the case against John Harris once more, with emphasis on the alleged existence of the video. He was surprised to hear that Campbell had agreed to deliver a copy to Jay by evening.

Seamus Dunham took over discussion of the strategy when a phone call pulled Garrity away. The barrister returned several minutes later, ashen-faced and exceptionally quiet. He slipped into a chair at the end of the table, saying nothing, but noticed by them all.

"Michael?" Seamus Dunham queried. "Are you ill?"

Garrity glanced up and tried to smile.

"That's a good word for it, I think."

"What's wrong?" Jay asked from the far corner of the table.

"That was Stuart Campbell. We have a judge."

"How did he know to call here?" Jay asked.

"Campbell apparently has every phone number in the Western world," Garrity replied. "It's the High Court, which I expected. The time is ten A.M. tomorrow morning in the Four Courts complex."

"And the judge?" Dunham prompted.

Garrity drummed his fingers against his chin for a few seconds before answering, his eyes on the opposite wall. "I truly did not know he was on standby this weekend. Never thought about it, not that I could have changed anything . . ."

"What are you talking about?" Jay asked, a bit too sharply.

Garrity looked up at Jay. "Only the worst judge we could get for a case like this. Mr. Justice O'Connell." He watched Seamus Dunham's jaw drop slightly.

"Mr. Justice O'Connell," Michael Garrity continued, "who has no love for the United States, and no tolerance for anyone except God, whom he rather imagines himself to be."

"Can't we . . . recuse him?" Jay asked. "If that's the appropriate word over here . . . request that he remove himself for being biased against Americans?"

"Oh, he's not biased against Americans per se, Jay," Garrity said. "He's just institutionally ticked off at the U.S. government for all sorts of things. I'm not so sure he isn't still angry with JFK for getting shot."

"But, John Harris *was* the U.S. government, so to speak," Jay said. "That makes it even more important that he stand down."

"Jay, Mr. Justice O'Connell has yet to disqualify himself on any case I know about. You might say he's biased about his impartiality. We could file a challenge, but inevitably it would fail without some particularly outrageously prejudicial statement from him, and he's much too careful for that."

Seamus Dunham was nodding. "That's a blow, for certain. He's been a strong proponent of the Treaty Against Torture. He's even written a few articles. He was furious that Washington tried to sit on the fence in the Pinochet matter."

"We can't forum shop?" Jay asked. "We can't get another judge?"

"We don't do it like that here," Michael explained. "You're stuck with what you've got, and we've got a major problem right out of the starting gate."

John Harris leaned forward, catching Michael Garrity's eyes.

"What do you expect him to do that you wouldn't expect another judge to do?"

Michael began shaking his head sadly. "He's a tyrant in the courtroom, Mr. President. He's very hard to predict, and very hard to work with. Anything irritates the man, and he'll destroy a perfectly good argument or train of thought by bellowing at you for no apparent reason. In other words, his temper and his antics tend to foul up the barrister's ability to try any case brought before him."

"Is he reversed very often by your Supreme Court?" Jay asked.

Garrity and Dunham both shook their heads no. "Seldom."

"Which tells me," John Harris replied, "that tyrant or not, he knows the law."

"It's not interpreting the law I'm worried about," Michael Garrity said. "It's exercising the broad discretion he'll have in this case."

"So what do you recommend?" John Harris asked.

"I recommend," Michael began, "that we spend the rest of the afternoon trying to build a body of case law to refute the idea that either an unproven videotape or a single allegation can constitute a reasonable basis for this warrant."

"And the prospect for success?" the President asked, his eyes firmly tracking both lawyers.

Seamus Dunham sighed and looked at Michael Garrity before meeting the President's gaze.

"Mr. President, I would strongly advise you to be prepared for anything. What we have here is a stacked deck."

The Shelbourne Hotel, St. Stephen's Green, Dublin, Ireland

Stuart Campbell excused himself from the beehive of activity in the Presidential Suite and adjourned to his bedroom, taking along the videocassette recorder he needed to make a copy of the tape for Reinhart.

"No one else is to have access to that taped evidence but me," Stuart had warned his team. "I have the equipment to make the dub, and I'll do it myself."

It was 4:30 P.M. by his bedroom clock when he opened his briefcase and removed a small item in bubble wrap. He laid it on the bed, pulled a tiny digital video camera free of the wrapping, and removed a tiny tape cassette. He turned on the camera and inserted the tape, settling on the edge of the bed and watching the black screen suddenly come alive with black-and-white images of the back of a man's suit coat. The man disappeared out of the frame behind a desk. Then the camera-bearing individual apparently sat on a couch and readjusted himself and the focus of the camera to a recognizable image: the familiar interior of the best-known office on earth.

The sound quality was poor but serviceable, and as Campbell had done with the first copy of the tape in Lima, he watched it from beginning to end, making absolutely certain that the words he had heard spoken were precisely as he recalled.

At the tape's end, it appeared that Reynolds had turned

off the camera just as he departed the Oval Office, leaving as the last image a bouncing shot of a long hallway outside the eastern entrance with a uniformed officer visible, standing by a mirror to one side.

Stuart had long since prepared the basic legal brief on the tape. Having met Reynolds and recorded his voice in a sworn, witnessed statement, he had evidence that the voice on the Oval Office tape and Reynolds's voice were the same.

Campbell fumbled through his briefcase to verify the presence of the other tape, the one containing numerous network television clips of John Harris and his voice, ample proof for a cursory comparison of Harris's voice and image on the Reynolds tape. He pulled out the transcript of the conversation, wondering if John Harris really recalled the words that had been spoken, or if he'd heard only what he'd expected to hear that day. In any event, the transcript would be devastating to Harris.

Stuart carefully put the transcript and supporting tapes away.

It had been wise, he thought, to insist that Barry Reynolds turn over the original tape. A copy would carry much less weight if examined by experts.

He thought back to his brief meeting in Baltimore with Reynolds and his surprise at Reynolds's belief that President Miraflores had ordered him killed in retaliation for the Peruvian raid.

"Miraflores knew I had been the bag man for the operation," Reynolds had said. "But he didn't realize I was acting under presidential orders."

"Who told him?" Stuart had asked.

"I did," Reynolds had replied quietly as he sat in his living room with the drapes drawn. "Before I left the Company, we confirmed the contract on my head. I knew his death squads would get me sooner or later if he didn't cancel the contract, but I also knew he'd never attempt to assassinate an ex-President."

"And, even though you technically commissioned the raid, you thought he'd forgive you?"

"I knew Miraflores hated John Harris, because his

brother was killed in that raid. I knew he'd trade my scalp
for Harris's."

"So you gave him the tape you'd made for insurance."

"I sent him a copy of the tape," Reynolds had confirmed, "and agreed to testify if Harris was brought to trial
under international law, and if he'd call off his dogs. So
far, so good."

That had been two months ago.

Campbell looked at the video camera again, a late-
nineties model. He'd had no idea such technology existed
before Harris's presidency, especially in the form of a tiny
camera worn concealed in something as small as a tie clip
with the recorder itself in a briefcase. But Reynolds had
shown him the camera in Baltimore. It seemed a little
crude, but it worked.

Dublin, Ireland

John Harris had been standing at the window of Seamus
Dunham's office only half listening to the intense legal
analysis being discussed behind him while his mind drifted
half a world away.

He thought of Alice, as he did so many times a day. Her
loss three years ago to something as simple and devastating as a medical error would always haunt him, along with
the wholly illogical feeling that if he'd been at her side in
the operating room, the wrong medication would not have
been administered.

The images of her triggered the usual struggle to stem
the tears. Outwardly, he had handled her death with the
dignity that defined her life, refusing to sue a devastated
medical team, forgiving the surgeon and anesthesiologist
and the three nurses both in public and in private, trying to
help them through the hell of public outrage and misunderstanding. There had already been a national focus on
preventable medical error, but Alice's death—the death of
a former First Lady—provided a catalyst, and she would
be proud . . . no, she *was* proud, he corrected himself, of
the progress that had come from her loss, and the lives that

had been saved in the years since with so many improve-ments in healthcare safety.

And now, he thought, *here I am with another challenge of character. And how should I handle this, honey? Run? Stay? Fight? Fold?* The options had become so terribly confusing, the black hole of fear in his middle rising up every few hours to engulf him and confuse his decisions. *I was the President of the United States of America,* he told himself. *I have a duty to stand and fight with dignity.*

But did he have a duty to submit to a thinly disguised assassination attempt wrapped disingenuously in the robes of the law?

He ached with the pain of needing her now, at this mo-ment, to nudge him in the right direction again, as she had so many pivotal times during those incredible four years in the White House. The night he'd reached his wits' end over the issue of running again, for instance. How, he'd asked her, could he possibly let his party down with reelection virtually guaranteed? Yet, hadn't he placed the marrow of his credibility behind the concept of a single, six-year term, a change that would require a constitutional amend-ment, but benefit the nation greatly? That was a major campaign promise to the American people. How could he walk away from that?

Alice had joined him quietly in the Oval after chasing out the Chief of Staff and shutting the door. Together they had stood at the window overlooking the Rose Garden for the longest time, watching the fountain in the distance and the Washington Monument as she squeezed his arm and said nothing.

"What do I do?" he asked her at last. "How can I walk away from this responsibility?"

She had smiled at him and pointed to the lighted spire of the monument.

"George set the example, didn't he?" she said. "His greatness was teaching us by example that principles would guide and protect this nation when the politics of the moment had been long forgotten."

He remembered the weight that had lifted from his shoulders then, and the ease of making the announcement that shocked the nation and made him an outcast in his own party.

The job was still undone, he reminded himself. There was still no single six-year term. Perhaps living to keep fighting that battle justified turning tail and running. Perhaps not.

But there was one thing that loomed always in his mind, accepted and unquestioned and unquenchable: how empty the world was without her.

I miss you, honey! he thought, almost losing the battle to fight back the tears.

✈ FORTY-ONE

Dublin, Ireland—Wednesday—5:30 P.M.

The sun was hanging low in the western sky when Jay Reinhart emerged from Seamus Dunham's building with the others close behind. He forced himself to be aware of the beauty before him: the diffused red hues of the angled sunlight igniting the glow of reddish masonry, firing the reflective street signs, and forcing the hapless westbound drivers to navigate with hands held tenuously before their eyes. The city was shifting from the lethargy of a lazy afternoon to the energy of a St. Patrick's Day celebration, its people charging about to various purposes with an infectious optimism that seemed wholly undampened by the inherent knowledge that not every human circumstance within Dublin's fair city was positive. There was to be a grand and lengthy fireworks display after dark at the east end of the city where the River Liffey empties into the bay, and the traffic in the heart of Dublin was already building.

Jay loved sunsets, but there was a limit to what one could enjoy when the thunderheads of circumstance loomed large on the horizon. Yet the ruddy resonance of a city at sunset somehow demanded appreciation, even if it was an item of faith to be stored and valued later in the hoped-for absence of challenge and peril.

The President turned down Garrity's invitation to watch the fireworks, electing to return to the airport hotel to order a sandwich through room service, while a relieved Matt Ward feigned delight in doing the same thing as he continued his vigil over the man.

Seamus Dunham had a wife and child to attend to, which left Sherry and Jay in the effusively resilient hands of Michael Garrity, for whom the word *no* apparently held little meaning.

"Nonsense!" he had replied heartily when Jay tried to beg off what was increasingly sounding like an impending pub crawl. "Regardless of what happens tomorrow, there's a local law requiring me to show you some of Dublin, and I shan't be cited for contempt of tourism."

"Really, Michael, I appreciate it but . . ."

"I'll hear no objections," he roared, "and that goes for you, too, young lady!" he said, nodding to Sherry.

The protests were obviously in vain, so they had reluctantly agreed to a quick swing around the city, with a quick bite at one of Michael's favorite watering holes.

But that was all, Jay had cautioned. Neither of them was in a celebratory mood.

Michael Garrity's car proved to be a trial in itself. The car was an expensive model, but too small for Jay to be comfortable in front or back, so he tried to be gallant and take the rear seat. But he ended up sitting sideways, his legs too long to fit in the miniature space behind the front seat, even when Sherry moved the front passenger seat fully forward.

She insisted on switching at their first stop and he agreed, reluctantly. Michael stopped the car and Sherry relocated, catching Jay's appreciative eyes before he slid into the front seat. Michael accelerated away again with the verve of a Mario Andretti blowing the pace car off the track.

"Do you folks always drive like this?" Jay managed

after a close encounter with a passing truck had raised his heart rate.

"Like what, Jay?" Michael asked with complete innocence, prompting Jay to drop the subject.

The Four Courts was a required stop on any tour, though the front doors were closed. "You'll be seeing enough of it tomorrow," Michael intoned, as if the prospect was joyous instead of ominous. He catapulted the car into motion again for a high-speed pass at Trinity College, Dublin Castle, and O'Connell Street, "named for the patriot, not our bloody judge," he said, negotiating another turn at several times the force of gravity, by Jay's calculation.

"Now, see that bronze statue there?" he asked, wagging an index finger a dangerous distance out of the driver's window as he whizzed past the oversized figure of a comely mermaid sans clothing, lying blissfully in a cascading fountain.

"Most Dubliners won't show visitors the touristy sights like this, but I think they're a part of our culture. That's supposed to be the goddess of the Liffey, Dublin's central river, or somesuch nonsense. I can never remember the full story. We just call her the 'Floozy in the Jacuzzi.'"

He reversed course with the subtlety of a fighter pilot pulling 7 G's and shot south toward the center of the city again, diverting to the right along the south bank of the river and rocketing past a railway station with his arm and index finger once again waving in the breeze.

"That would be more or less a Mecca for us Dubliners," he said, pointing to the Guinness brewery. "They don't give tours of the main brewery anymore," he said sadly, "but they'll still give you a taste for free at their little store. And you know, it really does taste better right near the gates of the place than anywhere else on earth."

"I've heard that," Jay managed, holding onto the armrest with a death grip as he looked back to see Sherry doing the same, her eyes one dimension wider than normal.

"Well, it's true. I've had that elixir just about everywhere, and I swear you could navigate back to Dublin by following the trail of the ever-sweeter pints."

Michael turned for a moment to make sure they'd been listening.

"Is it true, Michael," Jay asked in response, "that they used to run ads alleging Guinness was as good as a medicine?"

Michael turned to grin at him. "What do you mean 'alleging,' my boy? It *is* good for you. Doctors here in Ireland even prescribe it for lactating mothers."

"What," Sherry laughed, "feed your newborn a pint a day?"

"No, no, Sherry. Feed *yourself* a pint a day and you'll give better milk."

"Only in Ireland." She laughed.

They zoomed into a garage west of the Temple Bar district and Jay unfolded himself from the front and helped Sherry from the back before following Michael to a pub called the Brazer Head, across the Liffey from the Four Courts. Smoky, loud, and small inside, the pub was filled with members of the legal profession. Michael turned before pushing open the door and proclaimed it one of the oldest pubs in Dublin and the alternate "library" for Dublin's barristers. "This old establishment has been plying its trade since the seventeenth century," he said.

"Library?"

"Oh, I didn't mention the Library before, did I? Our office at the Four Courts is really the main law library. I'll show you tomorrow. It's very historic. Only barristers are allowed inside, and you can stand outside and look in, watching us trying to keep our wigs on as the solicitors call for us at the front desk."

They found a small table toward the back, and Michael ordered a round of Guinness Stout, proclaiming it the national drink as the three pints arrived bearing perfect heads of tan foam.

"Now, we'll have an agreement, we will, if you don't mind. No talk of tomorrow."

"Fine with me," Jay said, letting himself almost relax. His eyes drank in Sherry's soft smile across the table as she nodded in mutual assent.

"You really love this town, don't you, Michael?" Sherry said, having to repeat herself over the din in the pub.

"I do indeed, especially since the world has changed so much here. Less than fifteen years ago, we were the same poor little country of fact and fable, stout of heart and empty of pocket until the dot-coms of the world found us. Now . . . well, look around you. These days we call ourselves the Celtic Tiger. Actually, we say the Celtic Tiger has arrived. Prosperity's flowing in, and we're all pinching ourselves and getting used to the idea of an Ireland that's economically robust. Imagine that! We've actually got people immigrating *to* Ireland if you can believe it!"

"I'm pleased to hear it," she said.

"Jay, you told me some of your people are Irish," Michael said. "What do you think of us so far?"

Jay smiled at their host. "I haven't had a lot of time to evaluate what I think, Michael, but . . ."

"But . . . if you weren't so worried about John Harris, you'd like us a lot, and you'll like us better if we let your client go, right?"

"Something like that."

"Fair enough." He raised his glass of stout. "Slainte!"

Jay and Sherry both echoed the word and the gesture as Jay watched Michael down half the pint in one easy motion.

"I was told you didn't drink, Michael," Jay said, watching Michael's eyebrows flutter up in surprise before he could extricate his mouth from the glass.

"*What?* Who on earth told you such a scandalous lie?" he asked, smiling skeptically.

"The solicitor in London who recommended you. Geoffrey Wallace."

"Oh, Wallace! That was the meeting in Edinburgh. I don't drink much, Jay, but that was just a windup."

"A joke?"

"Yes. The bloody Brit was going on about how all Irishmen were drunkards, which is scandalously wrong, and so I thought I'd disappoint him. Apparently it worked."

"Michael!" someone called across the pub, and Michael

Garrity raised his hand and waved heartily, then motioned whoever it was to come over.

"This is great," Michael said, as the individual began weaving through tables to comply. "This fellow's Byrne McHenry, and probably the best comedian in Ireland, and the best impressionist. He does a Ronald Reagan that would seriously confuse Nancy."

McHenry arrived at the table and pumped Michael's hand as he tossed a few insults at the barrister, who introduced him to Jay and Sherry in turn.

"So, are y'all from Texas?" McHenry said in a surprisingly good George Bush imitation.

"How have you been, Byrne?" Michael asked.

They talked on a personal basis for a few minutes before McHenry looked at his watch. "I've got a show in an hour, folks, out at Jury's, so I'd better go. Nice to meet you."

He was replaced at tableside by two other barristers coming over to greet Garrity, and a waitress bringing sandwiches and another round of stout.

Jay munched on his sandwich and nursed the second pint as he drifted away from the intense conversation Sherry and Michael were having over Celtic art. The details of the old pub's interior and the stories of its customers were far more interesting, he thought. The woodwork had probably been in place since the mid-nineteenth century, since there were tell-tale characteristics in the way the cornices had been joined and the care with which the crown molding had been mitered.

The bar itself was not as elaborate or ornate as many he'd seen in the eastern U.S. or Britain, but it had a distinctive character about it, a pride of workmanship, that shone through what had to have been over a century and a half of continuous use.

Jay smiled at the memory of seeing an operating harness shop nearby when they entered. In the back, arrayed on a workbench, had been the same tools of the trade and raw leather that once kept the carriages of Dublin powered and the horses harnessed.

Jay realized he might have heard his name spoken above the din.

"I'm sorry, what?"

"Are you still with us, Jay?" Michael asked, laughing.

Jay smiled and nodded as he slowly began pushing back from the table. "Just thinking, Michael, and worrying that we need to get back to the hotel."

"Ah, you'll miss the show," Michael protested. "And the fireworks are truly spectacular. Every year they get more impressive, though the crowd's a bit of a pain. Really, lad, the evening's young."

"But I'm not, anymore," Jay said with a smile as he got to his feet, appreciative of the fact that Michael was following without further protest. "I have a lot to do, Michael, and I'm still time-zone challenged."

"Oh! Of course. I should have thought of that. I apologize." He scooped up the bill and motioned for the waitress as they headed for the door.

Michael dropped Jay and Sherry at the front door of the hotel forty-five minutes later and the two of them stood in amusement watching the rotund barrister career off into the night.

"He's a good fellow," Jay said.

"You done good finding him, counselor," Sherry confirmed. "What time did he say to meet him in the morning?"

"Half nine, which I think means nine-thirty, at the Four Courts."

She laughed. "I appreciate, perhaps more than you know, the fact that you refused Michael's offer to come pick us up in the morning."

Jay stopped chuckling long enough to pause at the front desk to ask if anything had been left for him.

The clerk handed over a sealed manila envelope.

"What's that, Jay?" Sherry asked.

"That," he replied, scrutinizing the address label, "is Stuart Campbell's dub of the videotape CIA operative Barry Reynolds is supposed to have made."

"How do we play it?"

"I rented a VCR from the hotel earlier today and had them send it to my room. You . . . want to see this?" he asked as he punched the elevator call button.

She nodded.

"If you don't mind being in my room, that is."

The elevator opened and Sherry walked in and turned with the most provocative over-the-shoulder look she could manage, using a poor excuse for a German accent. "So, you sink we need a chaperone, Herr Reinhart?"

"Ah, no . . . I mean . . ."

"Weren't your intentions honorable after all?" she teased.

"My intentions?"

"Sure. Said the fly to the spider, what, exactly, do you mean, 'I'd like to have you for dinner'?"

An embarrassed grin suddenly took over Jay's face, causing him to blush slightly in the time it had taken to catch on.

"Oh. OH! No, I mean . . ."

She smiled. "It's okay, Jay, I'm just joking with you. I'm not trying to get frisky."

He shook his head in confusion, the possibilities belatedly cascading into his head. "This wasn't a ploy to get you in bed, Sherry."

"Darn," she said with a grin, stopping him cold.

"What?" he managed, again thrown off balance.

"Jay, *hello?* I'm really just joking around here, not that I . . . I mean, not that I wouldn't be . . ." Suddenly Sherry began blushing, too.

"Okay," he said, instantly angry with himself for being unable to think of anything smarter to say as the elevator doors opened on the third floor and they moved into the corridor.

"We're quite a pair, huh?" she said with a laugh as they walked toward his door. "I doubt the Army Signal Corps could unsnarl the hurricane of mixed signals we just gave each other."

"You're right," he chuckled, as he unlocked his door and held it open for her.

Instead she turned to him. "Okay. Let's restart." She

reached out and took his hand and shook it. "Hi there, handsome legal man. I'm Sherry, and I'd like to go into your room and sit at a discreet distance from you and watch this very businesslike videotape, then leave for my own room before anything familiar or amorous gets started, without reference to whether it would . . . or not."

Jay looked in her eyes and smiled. "In broader terms, I think you just encapsulated it perfectly."

✈ FORTY-TWO

The Great Southern Hotel, Dublin Airport, Dublin, Ireland—Wednesday—8:15 P.M.

Nearly a minute of empty videotape passed before an image flashed on the screen. The picture was black-and-white and grainy, and the tiny portable camera was obviously being worn on Reynolds's clothing, producing a bouncing, lurching picture. It was mostly a blur as Reynolds walked in, but there were some items and features in the background that looked fleetingly familiar before the picture steadied. Reynolds had seated himself on one of the facing couches, pointing his hidden camera toward the east door, which was being closed by an unseen hand.

Suddenly the picture shifted to take in the figure of a man leaning back against the front of the presidential desk in what was now unmistakably the Oval Office, bright light streaming in the windows behind him.

The only sound so far had been cloth scratching against a microphone, muffled voices, and the noise of footsteps and cushions as Reynolds sat.

A familiar voice rang out as the picture steadied on the President's legs.

"Okay, Barry, where are we? Are we set?"

Jay glanced at Sherry in mild alarm, and she nodded. The tone, the accent, and the meter were all too familiar. John Harris's voice was very distinctive, though some of the words were distant and hard to understand.

"Well, sir," a voice closer to the microphone and correspondingly louder began, "we're ready to go, but it's . . . costly."

"How much . . . want?" was the reply, broken by the sound of cloth scraping the microphone again.

"You really want to know, Mr. President?"

"This . . ." More scraping. ". . . never happened, Barry, so I want to know now, since officially I never will."

"Very well, sir. They want a million, U.S."

The first of the reply was lost. ". . . bargain, if they can do the job."

"Yes, Mr. President, they can do it. But I have to warn you about something."

"Now . . ." The voice faded, then came back clearly. ". . . different matter. Do I want to know whatever you're going to warn me about? Even off the record?"

There was a hesitation before Reynolds spoke again.

"Sir, *I* need to tell you, because I don't want to trigger this thing unless I know you understand the possibilities and are ready to accept them. I don't want to decide this myself. And, in fact, I'm strongly recommending against this operation."

The President sighed and crossed his arms, saying, "Very well. Go ahead."

"There are likely to be sixty or seventy people in that factory and in the compound, and some of them will be civilian."

"The workers?" the President asked.

"Yes, sir. If we commission this so-called army we're ready to hire—these mercenaries who are ex–Shining Path, ex–Peruvian Army, and a real ragtag bunch—if we commission them, they'll go in with the intention to leave no one alive, regardless of who they find. They won't do it without that understanding."

"As far as . . . concerned, Barry, anyone in that factory is forfeit, regardless. They're killing Americans with . . . poison they make . . ." The voice faded to incoherence again.

"Yes, sir. But it will almost certainly be a bloodbath, and the government is certain to be outraged, especially if they can prove the Company was behind it. That's why I'd say we shouldn't do it. Too much risk. I need to make sure you understand."

"I understand, Barry."

"These are real cutthroats, sir, as I say, on a level you may not be ready to believe really exists in this world. These vermin would just as soon dismember you alive for the fun of it as to decide to have dinner. They're the closest thing to pure two-footed animals I think I've ever met, and . . . frankly . . . we can be certain that they're going to enjoy this job."

The President asked something in a muffled voice.

"Meaning torture," Reynolds replied. "We're authorizing torture. They'll have themselves a playground with a license to kill, and they'll very likely kill slowly and painfully for the fun of it."

Reynolds hesitated, then got to his feet and walked back toward the fireplace before turning, the camera catching the President in full view at the other end of the office.

"Sir, these guys would frighten the SS in Nazi Germany. And I need you to know that the Peruvian peasants working there may well have family members with them."

"Family . . ." The President's voice was too far away from the microphone to be heard.

"Could be," Reynolds replied to the unheard question. "I can't guarantee who'll be there. But if they're there, they'll be eliminated."

There was more incoherent comment from the President, followed by the word *recommendation*.

"Depends on what you want to accomplish, sir," Reynolds replied. "If you want to shut down that factory once and for all, devastate the leadership, frighten away anyone else who would set up such a large drug-making facility, and massively impact the heroin flow all at once, then there's probably no other way to get it done. But there will be a terrible cost in lives."

The President pushed away from his desk and disappeared out of the frame. Reynolds apparently sat back down on the couch and swiveled toward the desk again, raising the level of the frame and revealing the chief executive with his back to the camera standing at the window overlooking the Rose Garden.

The frame lowered once more as the President turned, his head just out of the shot at the top as he turned toward Reynolds. ". . . no choice," he said, the words barely understandable. "You've . . . green light. But you never told me this, and . . ." The words faded momentarily. "Don't try to limit or warn them in any way. Don't tell them 'no torture,' or you'll poison our ability to say we never knew."

"Understood, sir."

"Now. Bring . . . over here and show me the details."

The rest of the tape was a recitation of the logistics of the plan, a handshake, and Reynolds's exit through the east door.

The screen had been black for many seconds before Jay reached out and stopped the videocassette player. He sat quietly for nearly a minute before drawing a deep breath and shaking his head.

"Oh my God."

Sherry Lincoln sat stunned and immobile in her chair, her eyes still on the darkened screen. Jay heard her swallow hard, but she said nothing as he got to his feet and leaned on the television.

"Sherry . . . I cannot believe what I just heard."

"Nor can I," she said quietly.

"That was . . . to the best of my knowledge . . . John Harris's voice," he said. "I mean, I don't know Reynolds or his voice, but I spent years around John, and . . ."

"It's him, Jay. No one else. I recognize the phraseology, the meter, everything."

Jay sat again, shaking his head, his hands out in a helpless gesture. "I . . . have no way to fight this tomorrow, except, maybe, just try to harp on the fact that you can fake tapes."

"It's not a fake," Sherry said.

Jay turned to her. "You saw something or heard something that convinced you?"

She looked up at him, true pain filling her eyes. "I know what the Oval looks like. I never saw his face closely enough, but that was his voice, and everything else is exactly right, and after all, there's only one damn Oval Office!" A hint of anger was creeping into her voice, but Jay spoke the words.

"Then . . . he lied to us, Sherry."

"He did that, all right."

"I . . . would never, ever have believed . . . but there it is. And there was one moment you could see his face when Reynolds was at the other end."

"I hadn't noticed that," she said. "I just know his voice."

They sat in stunned silence for a few minutes before Sherry got to her feet.

"What are you thinking?" Jay asked as she picked up the phone and punched in a few numbers.

"I'm calling him. I want him up here. I want an explanation, although I can't see how one could exist."

Her words to the President were short and to the point, undoubtedly leaving him puzzled. She replaced the receiver and turned to Jay with tears glistening in her eyes.

"He'll be up in ten minutes, as soon as he gets dressed," she said, sitting again. "What do we do, Jay? I assume they'll make mincemeat of him when this is shown tomorrow."

"Yes. I can't defend this. It clearly establishes sufficient cause."

"So what do we do? I think he's finished in Ireland."

Jay sighed again and reached for the phone. "There's only one option left. We've got to risk a direct flight to Maine."

The fact that Craig Dayton and lead flight attendant Jillian Walz had been lovers for the past year was standard knowledge at EuroAir, but their practiced discretion on the road usually obscured the liaison, even when Craig answered the room phone with a husky, distracted voice at what would otherwise be the mid-evening hour.

Jay Reinhart was on the other end, his voice and demeanor very grave, and they kept the conversation brief.

Craig replaced the receiver after an economy of words and snuggled back against Jillian in the spoon position, stroking her silken hair as he related the call.

She turned her head toward him slightly. "You sure this flight is safe, Craig?"

"Not a problem, honey. Alastair and I've looked at it very carefully, and what we'll do, as I just told him, is we'll go to the halfway point and look at the winds, and if there's any question that we're getting too close on projected reserve fuel at Presque Isle, we'll turn around and come back."

"I wish I could release my two girls."

He shook his head slightly. "Can't do it and be legal unless we removed a lot of seats. If we have that many seats, we have to have three of you."

"I know, I know."

"You want to go home?"

"I want you to stay employed, and I'm very afraid. You're about to go pressing the rules again."

"I actually think I've got them buffaloed in Frankfurt, Jill."

"There'll be no fuel slips from Iceland or Canada. They'll know you went direct."

"They'll think the U.S. government told me to do so. Anyway, John Harris is still free because of what we've done, and I'm not abandoning him now."

"Rats," she said. "So what time?"

"Wheels up at seven A.M., babe. That means we should be out of here no later than four-thirty."

His hand began running lightly along her thigh and she turned in his arms and held his face. "We have to sleep fast, Craig."

"Aw . . ." he whined.

"No more tonight!" she replied.

"What if I beg real nice?"

"No. You already did that," Jillian said. "Begging only works once . . . every few hours."

She kissed him. "Call Alastair. Set the alarm. Sleep. In that order!"

"Yes, ma'am."

Twenty-five minutes after the call to Craig Dayton, Jay Reinhart stood in silence beside a seated John Harris and turned off the videocassette player after showing the same sequence.

"My God in heaven," the President managed.

"I think those were roughly my words, John. What's going on here?"

Sherry was sitting in stony silence in the corner, watching John Harris as he slowly shook his head. "Jay . . ." He turned toward her. "Sherry . . . I want you to listen to me very closely. I have either suffered a major mental breakdown and lost a substantial portion of my memory and my grip on reality, or . . . what you've just shown me is a flat-out fake."

"John, that's *your* voice!" Jay said more sharply than he'd intended.

"And that's the Oval, sir," Sherry added.

John Harris licked his lips, his eyes on the dark screen. "I know what we've just seen looks like the real thing, but I ... did ... NOT ... speak those words. I did not *hear* those words from Reynolds. I'm not even sure I ever saw my face on there."

"It's there, John, in one shot," Jay said quietly.

The President looked up at him, his face betraying pain. "You don't believe me, do you, Jay?"

"I honestly don't know what to believe, John. I want to believe you, and I want to believe this is a fake, but ... and maybe I do, personally, but I'm dead in the morning in court with this. Campbell will play this and even a U.S. judge would have to find a prima facie case against you."

"There will be time to fight this, Jay," Harris said. "We'll need to get expert analysis and show how it was fabricated. I don't know precisely where I was in the office ... I mean, the visual image is probably real, but somehow they've faked the voices. After all, there are people out there who do very good imitations of presidents."

"We don't have time to do any sort of research or scientific analysis by tomorrow!" Jay answered. "I mean, we could do a digital voice analysis later and prove it isn't you, but that takes time, and first I have to convince the judge that he can't rely on this tape in any way. You can be sure Stuart Campbell's got a carefully manicured pedigree for this thing: chain of possession, affidavits, everything needed to convince. That means an arrest for certain and the beginning of a long, bloody process, and I can't be sure—with Garrity's being spooked over the judge—that we won't be facing a faster extradition track than normal."

John Harris exhaled a long and ragged breath, shaking his head. "This is one of those never-ending nightmares, isn't it, Jay?"

"Apparently."

They all fell quiet for more than a minute.

"Sir?" Sherry said from the corner, emotion constricting her voice.

"Yes, Sherry?"

"I want you to tell me the absolute truth."

"I always have, Sherry," he said with palpable sadness.

"I know . . . as far as I know . . . and I've always believed that. Tell me the words on that tape were never spoken by you, if that's the truth."

The President got to his feet and moved to her, placing a hand on her shoulder and the other under her chin, raising her eyes to him.

"Sherry, I swear to you, what you heard was not my voice, nor my words. The conversation you heard was faked somehow."

She nodded as she blinked back tears and stood to hug him silently, leaving the President off balance until she sat down and he returned to sit on the end of the bed.

"All right, Jay. What do we do?"

"We fly. You fly. Seven A.M. departure. Captain Dayton has agreed to fly to the halfway point and if the winds and his fuel are okay, take you on to Presque Isle, Maine, and the airfield there. It's literally the closest suitable U.S. airport."

"And you?"

"I'll . . . stand and fight as best I can. I have to anyway, because you may be back."

"Understood." The President got to his feet and patted Jay's shoulder. "If it helps, try to think how you could fake something like this, Jay."

"I am, sir. What scares me is that someone may have perfectly matched your voice digitally so that even if you didn't say the words in that sequence, they could still be your words and your voice rearranged."

"Don't lose faith in me, Jay. Things are seldom what they appear."

Jay looked up at him for several very long moments before replying. "That's precisely what worries me," he said.

John Harris returned to his room and Sherry bade Jay good-bye with confirmation that she would leave with the President on the 737. They hesitated at his door, holding hands briefly as she promised to call the second they landed in the United States.

Jay returned to the empty room in turmoil, desperate for sleep, feeling the effect of the two pints of stout, and determined to figure out a way around the inevitable. He turned on the TV and VCR and reran the tape, looking for something that had bothered him earlier, a fleeting glimpse of something he now couldn't place. Whatever it was now eluded him.

He sat on the edge of the bed in deep thought, regretting the time spent at the pub, though Michael and his friends were delightful company.

His friends.

Jay yanked a sheaf of business cards from his pocket and lunged for the phone to get Michael Garrity on the line.

"What is it, lad?" Michael asked.

Jay related the details of what he'd seen on the tape Stuart Campbell had provided.

"Oh, me. That will make things very difficult indeed."

"Can we block admission of the tape?"

"Yes and no. Remember, we're dealing with Justice O'Connell, and he'll do whatever he'll do without benefit of counsel. Under our Criminal Procedure Acts, it's really up to the trial judge. There's no automatic exclusion just because the evidence—the video—might have been obtained contrary to U.S. law," Michael said, pausing. "All I can do is fight a good fight to keep it out by persuading him that it's terribly prejudicial to President Harris."

"Michael," Jay said, "I've got an idea how we can convince him—if you're willing to lose a night of sleep, and if you can get one of your friends to help us tonight."

✈ FORTY-THREE

**Dublin International Airport, Ireland—Thursday—
5:45 A.M.**

Alastair Chadwick had been gathering weather reports and
studying the flight plan for nearly a half hour when Craig
swung into the flight planning room of the aeronautical information services office in the lower level of the main terminal.

"Okay, Magellan, what's the word?"

Alastair peered at Craig over his reading glasses.
"Smashing, I should think."

"Not . . . the best of words to use in aviation, old
friend," Craig replied, scanning the weather depiction on
the computer terminal.

Alastair pointed to the papers. "Basically, Craig, we've
got two weather systems moving around that we need to be
aware of, and a rapidly changing jet stream." He used his
index finger to trace the serpentine wave of the jet stream,
the high speed river of stratospheric air depicted as flowing from eastern Canada across the Atlantic in a great arc.
Along the expanse of Canada's Hudson's Bay it roared to

the northeast, but south of Greenland it flowed south, and at a right angle across their westbound route to Maine.

"How fast?" Craig asked.

"The core is moving about eighty to ninety knots, but it pretty much stays out of the way, *unless* that upper curve around Greenland starts to come south and, well, flatten. Then we could be facing it on the nose, and we couldn't make it to Maine with safe fuel reserves if that happens."

"And the forecast?"

"They don't expect that much movement, but it's not impossible in three hours for it to become a problem. We'll have to keep close tabs on it."

"Okay. By the way, I know I've hogged the last two legs, but would you mind if I flew this one, too?"

"Of course not." Alastair grinned. "The fact that I'm rapidly forgetting how to fly because my captain won't let me handle the aircraft is wholly immaterial, I should think. I'll just save my pennies and take flight lessons at a local aeroclub when I get home. Maybe I can afford time in a Piper Cub."

"And you think *I'm* good at generating guilt!" Craig laughed.

"Now," Alastair continued, ignoring the comment, "pay attention, Mr. Bond."

"Certainly, Q."

"There's a deep low over Iceland, and Keflavík is very marginal . . . just barely legal for our flight plan. We've also got to consider that the winds behind us could change in computing our equal-time decision point."

"Understood," Craig said, moving closer to study the chart, his mind completely focused.

"Gander, Newfoundland, is a decent alternative, and the weather all across the Maritimes is good, and the weather back here should hold through late afternoon, in case we have to come back."

"In other words, you can't think of any meteorological reason not to do this?"

"Nothing compelling," Alastair said with a smile. "Aside from the basic insanity of it all, we're fine."

• • • •

Despite the weather, Craig had fully expected something to go wrong. There were simply too many ways the flight of newly named EuroAir Charter 1020 could be blocked. It was overly optimistic, he thought, to believe they were really going to get airborne or be issued their clearance to Maine, some 2,800 nautical miles distant. Considering what had already happened, he expected the opposition would know their plans and would somehow find a way to interface, either through EuroControl in Brussels or through pressuring the appropriate companies to refuse fuel for their aircraft.

Yet, the pre-departure tasks had been completed on schedule and their plane had been serviced, fueled, ground-checked, and readied for flight by 6:15 A.M. By 6:25 A.M., John Harris, Sherry Lincoln, and Matt Ward had joined the three flight attendants and two pilots aboard.

Craig was mildly shocked when they actually received the air traffic control clearance to the United States, something he had fully expected to be withheld. But there was still the matter of a takeoff clearance, and when the tower issued it routinely, he found himself in total disbelief.

Craig hesitated and looked at Alastair. "*Really?* Did I hear that right?"

"The tower sayeth, and I quote, 'EuroAir Ten-Twenty, cleared for takeoff.'"

"I can't believe it!"

"I suppose," Alastair added, "since they've been kind enough to give us the clearance, we ought to commit an act of aviation about now."

Craig nudged the throttles forward to taxi the 737 onto the runway. "How do we do this again?" Craig asked.

"Do what?"

"Take off."

"You've forgotten that, too? Boy, am I glad we don't allow outsiders in the cockpit to hear these comments."

"Okay, check my memory, Alastair. When I pull the yoke, the houses get smaller, when I push, the houses get larger."

"Provided, that is, you first push the throttles up and provide a little forward momentum."

"Oh. Yeah. It's all coming back to me now. I'm supposed to say, 'Set power, engage autothrottles.' "

"By George, I think you've got it."

"Alastair!" Craig said with mock surprise as the engines came up to full thrust and they began rolling forward. "I'm impressed you would cite the name of America's founding father, President Washington."

Craig reached up to confirm the landing lights were on as Alastair snickered. "That reference, I'll have you know, was to England's esteemed King George."

"Sure it was. Eighty knots," Craig said.

" 'Eighty knots' is *my* bloody line!"

"So, *say* it."

"Eighty knots."

"Feel better?"

"Much," Alastair said, watching the airspeed climb steadily to the computer flying speed of 138 knots. "Vee One, Vee R," he said.

Craig brought the yoke back smoothly, lifting the 737 into the air, his thoughts already turning to the impending receipt of their oceanic clearance across the Atlantic and the task of monitoring the winds and weather ahead.

"Positive rate, gear up," Craig ordered.

"Roger, gear up," Alastair replied, raising the landing-gear lever.

"What time is it, local?" Craig asked.

"Six fifty A.M. We beat our schedule by ten minutes."

Craig nodded. "I just hope it's not wasted effort."

The Great Southern Hotel, Dublin Airport, Dublin, Ireland

The alarm jolted Jay awake at 8:10 A.M. after less than three hours of sleep. He imagined Michael Garrity would be feeling just as groggy across town, provided he'd made it back to his house. The prospect of fighting the courtroom battle ahead when he could barely keep his eyes open was already worrying Jay, but it was a comforting thought that the night's work might have given them a weapon against Stuart Campbell's well-oiled machine.

He rocked to a vertical position and staggered to the bathroom for a shower, wishing he could stand under the hot water for at least an additional month or two.

He was having trouble keeping his mind off the EuroAir 737. He'd phoned the FBO around 7:30 A.M. for confirmation that they'd lifted off, and so far the lack of a call from Sherry meant that they were proceeding on schedule.

Jay stuck his head out of the shower and tried to focus on his watch on the counter. *8:23 a.m.!* Craig had warned him that the decision point would come some three hours after departure, or just about the time the hearing got underway.

He returned to the hot water and stood with his eyes closed for a moment, luxuriating in the memory of Sherry Lincoln's laugh and smile.

Maybe the attraction is a rebound kind of thing, he thought.

Or maybe not. In any event, I'd . . . like to . . . well, see if . . .

Jay shook his head vigorously and forced his mind back to the task at hand. Michael Garrity would do the talking in court, but it would be up to Jay to help direct him, and he had to stay focused. If John Harris ended up back on Irish soil, it would be around 1 P.M., and if they failed in court, the Garda would be waiting with a freshly issued arrest warrant.

A fleeting memory of something he'd dreamed crossed his mind. Was it a question, or a fantasy? Whatever it was hovered just out of reach until he closed his eyes and concentrated.

Jay left the shower, dried himself, and moved quickly to the phone as he retrieved a slip of paper from his shirt pocket in search of a London phone number. With any luck, the Secretary of State would still be there.

Alastair punched the transmit switch on his control yoke. "Roger, Shanwick, EuroAir Ten Twenty level at flight level three seven zero." He glanced at the altimeter, confirming that Craig had leveled the 400 model Boeing 737 at its maximum operational altitude.

Alastair punched some numbers in the small handheld GPS unit in his lap and stuck a suction cup–mounted antenna on the side window.

"What?" Craig asked. "You don't trust the flight computer or the onboard navigation system?"

"I like plenty of backups, Captain, sir," Alastair said. "And I like playing with my new toy."

There was a click behind them as Jillian Walz opened the cockpit door to hand Alastair the Coke he'd ordered, then disappeared for a moment and returned with coffee for Craig. She hesitated with the cup in hand and turned to Alastair. "Since . . . this is a charter and . . . you know about us, Ali, do you mind very much if I kiss your captain?"

Alastair raised his eyebrows and tried to look shocked.

"And where, exactly, were you planning to kiss him, young lady?" he asked in as stilted a voice as he could manage.

"On the flight deck."

"The *flight deck*? Only a shameless hussy would do such a thing."

"Okay. I'm a shameless hussy. *Now* may I kiss him?"

Alastair held his right hand up, fanning his fingers as if tapping a cigar while he cycled his eyebrows and tried a strange, British-accented impression of Groucho Marx. "As long as that's all you do in the presence of a lonely copilot!"

Jillian kissed Craig's cheek and handed him the coffee before patting Alastair's shoulder.

"Poor, poor Ali! No love, no companionship, no women."

"How're our passengers doing?" Craig asked.

"Sherry Lincoln and Matt Ward are both snoozing, but

the President is awake and pacing around like a caged tiger."

"How about Elle and Ursula?"

"Doing what we flight attendants do best in flight."

"Talking?"

"Talking. See you boys later. Ring if you need anything . . . within reason, of course."

When Jillian had left, Alastair took a long drink of the Coke as he pulled a notebook from his flight kit.

"Okay. Here's the situation. I compute our decision point as being right at three hours, twenty-four minutes into the flight. We go westbound beyond that time, we'd best keep on going. Right now we're right on predicted maximum endurance fuel burn, on speed, and the winds have been cooperating bang on to prediction so far."

Craig nodded. "What do you estimate we'll have on arrival at Presque Isle?"

"Let's see . . . ah, three thousand pounds of jet fuel. Not a lot, but not an emergency, either."

"But almost no margin for higher winds."

"That's the bad news," Alastair said.

"And how long have we been motoring in this general direction?"

Alastair checked one of the displays. "We've been airborne two hours and forty-eight minutes. In other words, I need to wring the latest winds and weather from the radio so my courageous captain can conclude whether it'll be a gallon of Guinness in Galway, or a bucket of Bud near Bangor."

Craig looked at him wide-eyed for several seconds before speaking. "Promise me, Alastair, *please*, for the good of mankind . . . that you'll never, *ever* try writing poetry!"

The Four Courts, Dublin, Ireland

Jay's taxi braked to a halt in front of the Four Courts just as Michael Garrity was climbing the steps.

Jay paid the driver and hurried to catch up with him as he pushed through the large doors.

"Michael!"

"Ah. There you are. All rested and ready?" Michael asked with a wink.

"Yeah, sure."

They entered the Round Hall and Michael stopped to point out the entrances to the four courtrooms that radiated from the rotunda.

"Come on. We've got a few minutes. Let me show you the library, then we'll find out which courtroom we're in."

EuroAir 1020, in Flight

John Harris paced to the front of the first-class cabin and turned again, as he'd done a dozen times in the past half hour. He glanced at his watch, which was still on Dublin time.

9:48 A.M.

He could imagine the lawyers beginning to assemble for the 10 A.M. hearing, and the thought of their battling it out while he essentially sneaked out of town under the cover of darkness was eating at him.

You panicked, John, he told himself. *When faced with that tape, you panicked. You should never have run like this!*

He glanced over at Sherry, her head gently lolled on a pillow wedged against the window. Her help over the last four years had been of incalculable value, he thought, and he felt guilty for not giving her more time to live her life. She rarely dated. He'd kept her too busy with work, and the paternalistic feeling that had grown on his part had led him to worry lately that he eventually should urge her to look for a better job, and one that made a social life possible.

But it was hard to envision facing the task of being an ex-President without her.

One thing's for certain, he told himself. *Life is going to change now. No matter what happens back there in Dublin.*

• • •

In the cockpit of EuroAir 1020, Alastair suddenly yelped and looked up from his notebook.

"What?" Craig asked.

"We're at the decision point. Turn it around, Craig."

"What?"

"Turn this bloody craft around. We can't make it."

"Wait a minute. What do you mean, we can't make it?"

Alastair was shaking his head. "The jet stream has moved south! Look at our ground speed. It's down another forty knots, and the wind direction is coming around on our nose."

"The wind speed's increased?"

"Yes! Suddenly, on this forecast, the damn figures are all different and . . . and much worse. Also, Gander's suddenly below minimums with fog! At this rate, we not only can't make Presque Isle with running engines, we're in potential trouble this far south getting to Gander with sufficient reserves. If we could have flown a true great circle instead of the North Atlantic Track System . . ."

"How about the winds behind us?"

Alastair shook his head. "They're calling them the same, and what we've experienced is on prediction, but that low over Iceland is in motion southbound, so we'd better move now."

"Call them," Craig said.

"Shanwick, EuroAir Ten-Twenty. We need immediate clearance to reverse course and return to Dublin due to deteriorating winds and fuel."

"Stand by, Ten-Twenty."

"Negative, Shanwick. We've no time to stand by. We're going to need to descend to a safe altitude and turn immediately while you're coordinating."

"Are you declaring an emergency, Ten-Twenty?"

"Not unless you force us to, sir."

"If you reverse course without clearance and without an emergency declaration, that will be a violation, sir."

Craig nodded. "Declare it! I'm turning and coming down a thousand feet."

Alastair nodded as he pressed the transmit button. "EuroAir Ten-Twenty is declaring a Pan Pan Pan, potential fuel emergency at this time. We're reversing course and descending to flight level three six zero pending clearance, and we request to leave the NatTracks and proceed direct Dublin."

"Roger, Ten-Twenty, copy your emergency. Keep your same transponder code for now and make your turn. I copy flight level three six zero. Report reaching."

Craig had already turned the heading knob on the auto-flight panel, bringing the Boeing back to an easterly heading as he moved the altitude selector and began the descent. He stopped the magnetic heading at 085 degrees as Shanwick Control formally approved the new course and altitude.

"Alastair, are we okay to Dublin?"

"I'm looking. We're going to be tight, but if the tail-wind holds . . . we're okay."

"Dammit! It was looking so good!"

"I've seldom seen a reversal this severe, or I screwed up the figures, or both. The headwinds we calculated were a minus forty maximum, and the average was minus thirty-two. Suddenly with that new information, it would have been a minus one hundred thirty!"

"We screwed something up! They can't change that fast!"

"They did. But you're right, somewhere in our figuring . . ."

"Damn!"

"I know it. I'm sorry, Craig."

"Forget it. We're human. Now let's just get this old girl on the ground safely."

"Should I tell Jillian?"

Craig nodded. "Yes. And make sure she tells the President. It looks like we're bringing him right back to the frying pan."

✈ FORTY-FOUR

**The Four Courts, Dublin, Ireland—Thursday—
9:50 A.M.**

"And this would be the lion's den," Michael Garrity said, leaning close to Jay's ear as they walked into courtroom three.

Only one of the court staff—the registrar—was in position beneath the bench at the head of the courtroom, arranging papers and fussing with her files. Stuart Campbell was still outside the courtroom in the Round Hall in animated discussion with no fewer than seven other support solicitors, barristers, and staff.

Jay looked at his watch with eyes rendered bleary by less than four hours of sleep. *9:50 a.m. I've got to focus.*

"Now, Jay," Michael was saying, "Judge O'Connell is well known for temper tantrums when people talk in his courtroom. You'll be sitting just behind me, so you can lean forward and whisper in my ear, but two warnings, if you please."

"Sure."

"First, make absolutely certain no living soul can hear

any sound from the whisper beyond the radius of a foot or two, or he'll surely bellow at us."

"Okay."

"Second, please don't knock my wig off."

Jay laughed. "That happens?"

"Oh, it's very embarrassing to have a client lean over to whisper something to you, and pull back, taking your wig along with him, or leave it at an odd angle on your head. The judge will definitely comment."

"I'll be careful."

"He won't let you speak, as we've discussed, although Campbell will be a full participant, since he's already been called before our bar at least once in the past."

"I understand."

"Also, I am what we call an SC, or senior counsel, so I'll be assisted by another barrister from my office, Tom Duggan, who had better be here pretty soon. I'll introduce you."

"SC is like QC, Queen's counsel?"

Michael smiled wryly. "We have no queen, lad. This is the Republic of Ireland."

"Sorry."

"Mind you, we think Liz is a dandy old girl, we just have no allegiance to her, let alone any desire to be her lawyers."

A male staff member wheeled a large television set on a metal stand into the courtroom and placed it near the end of the jury box, plugging in the TV and the video equipment below it. Both Michael and Jay watched the adjustments without comment, knowing full well what Stuart Campbell would be using it to show. The ominous presence of the TV left a cold, black feeling of apprehension in Jay's gut.

EuroAir 1020, in Flight

"How are the winds holding, Alastair?" Craig asked.

The copilot had been chewing his lip as he scribbled

calculations and used a pocket flight calculator to double-check the aircraft's flight management computer.

"The tailwind's almost gone, Craig, and the latest weather report has that low really galloping south."

"Should we consider Reykjavík, Iceland?"

Alastair shook his head no. "We'd be right into another monstrous headwind at this altitude, and we don't dare descend into higher fuel consumption rates."

"We're right on maximum endurance?"

"Right on. It's all a function of winds right now, but . . ." He looked up at Craig and sighed. "I have to tell you, Craig, I'm not showing us arriving in Dublin with much fuel. We may want to consider Galway."

Craig shook his head and laughed ruefully. "You had to go and tempt Murphy a while ago by mentioning Galway, didn't you?"

"I'm sorry," Alastair said, lowering his head into his calculations again. Craig realized with a small jolt of adrenaline that Alastair had met a joking comment with a sincere apology. That wasn't like Alastair, which meant, Craig decided, that the copilot was really scared.

And that fact alone raised Craig's apprehension to a new level.

"Better get Galway weather just in case," Craig suggested.

Alastair nodded. "I am. In the meantime, don't change those throttles from maximum endurance. We need to stretch every drop of fuel we have."

The Four Courts, Dublin, Ireland

Jay glanced nervously at his watch again and tried to force himself to calm down. He looked around, recording the details of the ornate old courtroom that had obviously seen much wear and tear over the years.

The rug, to begin with, intrigued him. It was a heavily faded green with white dots, or what might have been meant to resemble small flowers. There were no pathways worn into the fabric, but the rug was at least a decade beyond its useful life.

The shape of the courtroom was generally rectangular and approximately fifty feet in depth from the back doors to the bench. The woodwork in the chamber was ornate, but worn as well, with heavy use of molding known as dental work on the many layers and courses of crown molding overhead. The bench, as well as all the other fixtures and furniture in the room, was stained a dark fruitwood. The judge's seat was elevated above the registrar and stenographer, backed by a faded burgundy curtain that cascaded down from an elaborate paneled header some twenty feet above the bench crowned with a harp in carved relief, the symbol of the Irish Republic.

The witness stand was a simple chair to the judge's right, more in keeping with an American court than a British one, and the jury box ran along the wall to the judge's left, with benches provided behind the tables used by the instructing solicitors. Opposing counsel—the barristers—sat opposite their respective solicitors. The bench for the public was in the back.

The courtroom was heated with old-style radiators, and a recessed series of glass panels, some artificially lighted from above, adorned the middle of the ceiling twenty-five or thirty feet overhead.

A door opened loudly in the rear of the court, and Jay turned to see Sir William Stuart Campbell and his entourage enter, Campbell already wearing his barrister's robe and wig, accompanied by two other barristers among his group. He moved to his chair and turned briefly to smile and nod at Jay and Michael as more people trooped in the back and took their places on the various benches.

And suddenly the clerk was calling the case, and Judge O'Connell had swept in from his chambers to convene the court.

"Mr. Campbell, I recognize you, sir, with pleasure," Justice O'Connell said as he sat down. "I have been continuously impressed with your tireless efforts on behalf of international jurisprudence and the writing and acceptance of the Treaty Against Torture over the years."

Campbell bowed slightly in pleasant surprise. "I thank you, My Lord, for your gracious words."

"And Mr. Garrity, welcome back. I certainly recognize you."

"Not with displeasure, I hope, My Lord," Michael said with a smile.

"Certainly not," O'Connell said, adding no more.

Campbell took the floor first, laying out the pedigree of the Interpol warrant as Michael Garrity and Jay Reinhart listened and made notes, waiting for the chance to counter him.

"Mr. Campbell," O'Connell asked, "is President Harris, the defendant, present in the Republic of Ireland currently, or do you have reason to believe he will be in the immediate future?"

"The answer to both questions is 'yes,' My Lord. Mr. Harris arrived Tuesday night in Dublin."

EuroAir 1020, in Flight

The President had decided to let Sherry sleep a bit longer, but she stirred now and opened her eyes, smiling as she stretched, before noticing the dour expression on his face.

"What's going on, John?"

He sighed. "We're going back, Sherry. The winds were too high." He relayed what Craig and Alastair had told him when he came to the cockpit after Jillian relayed the message.

"Oh, Lord."

"It's okay, Sherry. It's probably for the best. I've been having great doubts about this escape attempt anyway."

"I haven't," she said.

"Well . . . we've no choice now."

She stood up and pointed to the cockpit. "I'm going to have to use the satellite phone. I promised to let Jay know if this happened."

The Four Courts, Dublin, Ireland

The realization that Stuart Campbell might not know that John Harris was airborne and streaking away from Ireland was a surprise. Surely, Jay had assumed, Campbell would have arranged for someone to monitor the EuroAir 737. Was he really unaware, or was he going to officially ignore it to keep it from becoming an issue?

Jay leaned over to whisper directly in Michael Garrity's ear. *"Michael, should we admit he's not here? Would that delay things?"*

Michael shook his head and whispered back. *"Not unless we're one hundred percent sure John Harris is not coming back. If we raise the issue, he'll question us, and we'll have to admit there's a chance the plane could turn around. There's nothing to be gained."*

"There's everything to be gained if we can avoid showing that tape," Jay whispered back.

"Mr. Garrity!" Judge O'Connell snapped.

"Yes, My Lord?" Michael replied, startled.

"Would you care to join us in this action, or would you prefer to take your client outside and have a jolly chat where you're not interrupting these proceedings?"

"My Lord, I beg your pardon, but this gentleman is Mr. Jay Reinhart, the American lawyer representing Mr. Harris, and it is proper, I believe, for me to converse with him quietly, is it not?"

"The key word is *quietly*, Mr. Garrity! I don't like a lot of whispering in my court. I have sharp ears, sir. I can hear that disgusting *psst psst psst* sound from yards away, and I will not have it!"

"Yes, My Lord."

"Proceed, Mr. Campbell," O'Connell ordered.

Jay knew the dangers of challenging Campbell's assertion that the warrant was valid on its face. Campbell would immediately offer the videotape of John Harris into evidence, a tape that would prove, Campbell would say, that the charges against Harris were obviously substantial enough to justify an Irish warrant and an order to send John Harris to Lima for trial.

But if Michael didn't challenge the validity of the charges, the Irish warrant would be granted almost automatically. It was a form of catch-22 that Michael and he had discussed carefully, and he was thinking about that discussion as Michael Garrity rose to his feet.

"My Lord, may it please the court . . ."

"Proceed, Mr. Garrity," the judge said.

"Thank you, My Lord. Mr. Campbell asserts that the Peruvian Interpol warrant seeking the arrest of a former President of the United States of America is valid simply because it was issued through normal legal process in Peru. I say that this High Court should have full jurisdiction over the simple and vital question: is the Interpol warrant based on real, rational, and reliable prima facie charges? Or, are the charges underlying this warrant a sham, as we maintain? What if the warrant was issued without justification simply because the government of Peru illegally directed a judge to do so? If there is any possibility whatever of that, My Lord, you must require proof that the charges are more than a fantasy, and that proof should be beyond question."

Justice O'Connell literally snorted and leaned toward Michael.

"Mr. Garrity, I love a good flowery rhetorical dance as much as the next overburdened judge with time to burn, but stick to the point and state it in plain English."

"Indeed, I am attempting to do exactly that, My Lord."

"You're not succeeding."

"Then I shall try again. My Lord, this court must examine the sufficiency of the evidence, not just rely on the Interpol warrant, before issuing an Irish warrant," Michael replied.

"Good!" O'Connell replied sarcastically. "See there? You can do it if you try to get to the blasted point. Very well. You are challenging Mr. Campbell, here, to provide some reliable proof that the Interpol warrant is based on substance, and I happen to agree with you. Mr. Campbell? What evidence exists that would justify an Irish arrest warrant and extradition order, beyond the fact that an unknown Peruvian judge wants Harris arrested?"

Stuart Campbell rose smoothly to his feet, his six-foot-four frame towering over the table and dominating Jay's field of vision. He introduced the existence of the video-tape, where and how it had been made, and offered document after document to validate it with sworn statements from Barry Reynolds, along with evidence of who physically possessed it and how it had been kept under tight control.

Jay scribbled notes furiously during the presentation and passed them in a constant stream to Michael Garrity as copies of each document were handed over by Campbell's staff. He could feel the GSM phone vibrating at one point, but he had no time to answer it, and the subsequent small vibrations told him a message was waiting, which he'd have to get to later.

Mike . . . pls object to this!!! The tape was illegally obtained.

This sworn statement he's offering merely states that he swears he's making the statement, not that it's true!

B.S.! He wants the judge to accept the idea that the technology for this kind of tape existed during John Harris's term. He needs an expert for that! We don't know if it did or not, and the presumption should not be our burden.

Michael objected repeatedly to every document, and he was overruled every time.

"Sit down, Mr. Garrity," O'Connell finally barked. "I am going to receive any and all documents that even appear to be genuine, and *then* I will decide whether they should be considered real. I'll hear no more objections on that point."

"My Lord," Campbell said at last, "with your permission, I should like to show the court the videotape in question."

Michael was on his feet instantly. "My Lord, please."

"What now, Mr. Garrity? Surely you're not going to risk a contempt citation by entering yet another objection contrary to my orders?"

"My Lord, the truth regarding the inadmissibility of this proffered videotape is being wrongly sequestered by My Lord's orders forbidding me to object. I would beg the court's leave to apply for a writ of habeas corpus to release that truth."

O'Connell shook his head in disgust. "Good heavens, Mr. Garrity! That's a precious and somewhat entertaining attempt, but the process of habeas corpus, as you well know, for approximately six hundred years, has been used to release human beings, not the truth as *you* see it. Overruled."

"My Lord," Michael continued, "had you not banned me from objecting to the showing of this tape, I would be pointing out at this moment that our code of criminal procedure prohibits the use of illegally collected evidence, and this tape under U.S. law is illegally made, and thus inadmissible in Irish proceedings."

"But, in fact," O'Connell said, leaning partially over the bench and shaking a gavel at him, "I *have* banned you from doing so, and thus I've heard not a syllable of what you're not supposed to have said in the first place. Now SIT DOWN, Mr. Garrity, so I can view this tape before we all die of old age."

✈ FORTY-FIVE

EuroAir 1020, in Flight—Thursday—10:40 A.M.

While Sherry Lincoln had been in the cockpit using the satellite phone, neither Craig nor Alastair said anything about the tight fuel status or their return to Dublin. She spoke a few words into the phone, sighed, and handed it back to Craig.

"Couldn't get through?"

"He's in court. I'm sure he can't answer it. I left a message."

"Come back up anytime if you want to try again."

"Thanks, fellows," she said, moving out of the cockpit and closing the door behind her.

Alastair had been working a separate air-to-air radio frequency and quietly polling other aircraft flying the North Atlantic Track System for the latest winds displayed on their onboard flight computers, precisely accurate readouts not immediately available to weather forecasters. Craig was monitoring Shanwick Control and listening as well to the other frequency Alastair was on. He heard the copilot thank another flight crew, then sit up and look left.

"I think we'd better try flight level three one zero," Alastair said quietly.

"Why?"

"That was an eastbound flight about two hundred miles ahead of us. A seven forty-seven. He's at three one now and getting winds of zero six five true at thirty knots. There's an Airbus A340 at three seven zero just twenty ahead of him bucking headwinds of zero six six at fifty-four knots."

The expression on Craig's face was one Alastair did not want to see, but it was clear that the captain understood.

"Alastair, we had a *tailwind* coming out here! We still have . . ." Craig looked at the wind display on his flight computer. "Uh, oh . . . almost zero wind."

"The low is coming south, Craig, and we're flying into the counterclockwise flow."

"My God, how fast is it moving?"

"Fifty to sixty knots at least, maybe faster. This wasn't forecast."

There was an eternity of silence before Craig spoke again. "So, what does this do to our fuel projections?"

"Nothing pretty. If those winds are correct, we can't make it back to Dublin, even with dry tanks."

"It really is Galway, then?"

Alastair nodded. "And getting a bit tight at that."

Craig's face turned dead serious. "Alastair, you're not telling me we're going to have trouble making the coast of Ireland now, are you?"

The absence of an immediate demur froze Craig's blood as he watched the copilot sigh and hold a hand out, palm up. "I think we'll make Galway, but without a lot of reserves. We . . . turned around a little late."

"Oh my Lord!" Craig said, almost under his breath.

"That's why we should go down to flight level three one zero, Craig. We gain more speed than we lose fuel economy."

Craig nodded. "Call Shanwick Control. Let's do it. We have to make this work, old buddy."

The Four Courts, Dublin, Ireland

Stuart Campbell had already connected his video camera to the television monitor. At a nod from Mr. Justice O'-Connell he pressed the "play" button, just as several reporters filed into the back of the court to watch the black-and-white images of the Oval Office unfold on the screen.

Jay sat in painful silence and endured the replaying of the exchange between Reynolds and the President, glancing at his watch as surreptitiously as possible.

They should be past the halfway point by now, he calculated. He could imagine Sherry's relief at the thought of actually touching down on U.S. soil.

When the tape ended, Campbell carefully pressed the "stop" button and turned to face the judge.

"My Lord, based on the sworn statements of Mr. Reynolds as to how this tape was made and whose voices and images are on it, I submit to you that the words of President John Harris himself irrefutably establish a prima facie case that not only fully supports the issuance of the Peruvian Interpol warrant, but mandates under the Treaty Against Torture that this court must issue an immediate arrest warrant under Irish jurisdiction, and must enter an immediate order of extradition of the defendant to Peru, subject to the normal appeals process."

"My Lord," Michael Garrity said, getting to his feet.

"Mr. Garrity," Judge O'Connell said in a more subdued fashion. "What could you possibly say to refute what we just saw?"

Michael glanced down at the lengthy note Jay was pushing across to him and read it quickly before continuing.

"My Lord, I'll readily admit that what we have just seen purports to be a scene in the Oval Office of the White House in Washington and a scandalous exchange between President Harris and Mr. Reynolds. I'll also admit that the possessory chain of this tape from Mr. Reynolds's hands to the present moment has been clearly and satisfactorily established. But in this day and age, not all that we see and hear can be believed. Electronic means exist to alter images and sound, and I submit to you that a very real possibility exists that the sound track on this tape is not the original sound track, but a substitute, carefully and cynically dubbed onto this tape cassette for the purpose of railroading an ex-President. After all, My Lord, we have the government of Peru directly involved in seeking to secure John Harris for purposes of criminal prosecution. With the power and resources of a sovereign nation involved, anything that is electronically possible could have been used to alter this tape."

"Do you have evidence of alteration, Mr. Garrity?" O'-Connell asked.

"No, My Lord. But the defendant should not bear the burden of proving that this tape is false. It is Mr. Campbell who should bear the burden of proving that it is authentic, yet he offers the tape with no firsthand witnesses and no means by which we can be sure whose voices we have heard."

Stuart Campbell rose to his feet. "My Lord, as to the matter of who has the burden of proof, I beg the court recognize that this is but a hearing on the sufficiency of the warrant. The opportunity for President Harris to contest in detail or even wholly impeach the validity of this videotape will be afforded in the criminal trial in Lima. This is not the forum for testing the tape, but merely for showing that there is a prima facie reason to believe that Mr. Harris may have committed the crime as charged."

"My Lord," Michael countered, "are you prepared to rule, as Mr. Campbell desires, that the authenticity of this tape may not be questioned in this forum?"

"No, Mr. Garrity, I am not," Mr. Justice O'Connell replied. "I'm reserving that judgment for the moment."

"Then, My Lord," Michael continued, taking a breath, "I offer into evidence what may well be the real videotape taken clandestinely, and illegally, by Mr. Barry Reynolds on the date in question."

The judge looked confused for a moment as Stuart Campbell turned with a blank expression.

"I'm sorry, Mr. Garrity, I don't understand," O'Connell said.

Jay pushed the videotape cassette across the table to Michael, who held it up.

"We have here a videotape of the same encounter, and I request My Lord's leave to play it."

"The same tape?" O'Connell replied with ill-disguised irritation. "Why?"

"My Lord, the reason for this will become very clear if you'll grant leave to present it."

"Have you any documentation supporting the authenticity of *this* tape?"

"Indeed, I do, My Lord," Michael said, following the script they'd agreed to. "This tape was delivered to Mr. Reinhart last evening, and we have the affidavit of the hotel desk clerk bridging the possessory chain between Mr. Campbell's people and Mr. Reinhart. Mr. Campbell represented that this tape was identical to one he just displayed in this court."

"It *is* the same tape, then?" O'Connell said.

"Well, yes and no, My Lord."

"Enough games, Mr. Garrity! Is the bloody thing the same or not?"

"My Lord, the videocassette is precisely the same one provided by Mr. Campbell and his team, and the images are the same, but there is another sound track of which Mr. Campbell is undoubtedly unaware, and by using a different format, we can play that sound track."

"A different sound track? I see," O'Connell said, his irritation suddenly subsiding into puzzlement. "I am aware, Mr. Garrity, that in some cases there are multiple sound tracks on videotapes."

"My Lord!" Stuart Campbell said in a pained voice. "This is nonsense. I have played for you the original tape, and there is but one sound track on it."

"Are you certain of that, Mr. Campbell?" O'Connell asked. "Are you an expert in the electronics of such instruments?"

"Well, no, My Lord, but . . ."

"Then I'm sufficiently curious to want to see and hear this. Proceed, Mr. Garrity."

Michael handed the tape to Jay, who came forward and inserted it into the larger videocassette player hooked to the television. He pressed the "play" button and returned to the table as the screen came alive again with the same images.

EuroAir 1020, in Flight

"It's getting better, Craig," Alastair said after a flurry of new calculations at thirty-one thousand feet.

"Thank God!"

"We're not out of the woods yet, but I'm estimating arrival at Galway with one thousand five hundred pounds of fuel remaining, and that's in . . . an hour and ten minutes."

"The winds are holding, then?"

Alastair nodded. "So far, so good. The problem is the weather at Galway. There's an ILS, but right now the field is beset by fog and it's right at minimums."

"Galway's on the coast, right?"

He nodded. "On Galway Bay. They get sea fog."

"If we have to bust minimums to get in, we'll bust minimums."

"The decision height is two hundred feet above the surface."

"Roger that. If necessary, we'll take it all the way to the surface, provided we're precisely on centerline," Craig said. "We'll use category three-A procedures as if the field was good to fifty feet. We'll use both autopilots, brief a monitored approach, you'll fly the approach, and I'll take over to do the landing."

"Instead of my doing a missed approach at fifty feet if we can't see the runway?"

"At fifteen hundred pounds remaining, we won't have the fuel for a safe go around. We'll get one shot at it."

The Four Courts, Dublin, Ireland

Jay Reinhart pushed the "play" button, sending the voice of President John Harris over the TV's speakers against a scratchy background of ambient noise, the words seeming to be the same at first, but then becoming markedly different, even though the pictures on the screen were identical.

"Okay, Barry, where are we? Are we set?"

"Well, sir," a voice closer to the microphone and correspondingly louder began, "we're ready to go, but it's going to be costly."

"How much . . . want?"

"They're asking for a million dollars in U.S. funds."

". . . already agreed to that."

"Yes, Mr. President. I remember the instructions."

"Now, Barry . . . critical question to ask you. Are these people controllable?"

"Yes, sir."

"Are you absolutely sure that they understand . . . orders here, that there be no excessive force . . . absolutely no violence beyond the minimum necessary to destroy the factory?"

"They do, sir."

"I'm . . . concerned . . . harm no innocent civilians. I don't care how many witnesses there are, I don't want the workers harmed unless . . . shooting, that sort of thing."

"Understood, sir."

Stuart Campbell was shaking his head in amazement with his hands held out in frustration as he queried his team and came up with no explanations.

On the tape, the President sighed and crossed his arms with his head still not in view.

". . . go ahead."

"We expect there will be sixty or seventy people

in that factory and in the compound, and some of them will be civilian."

"The workers?" the President asked.

"Yes, sir. It's heavily defended outside, and that's where most of the combat will likely occur. If we commission this force we're ready to hire—these mercenaries who are ex–Shining Path, ex–Peruvian Army—they should be able to neutralize resistance rapidly and then empty the facility before they blow it up."

"My Lord," Campbell protested, but O'Connell waved him down as he kept his eyes on the screen.

"Sit, please, Mr. Campbell."

On the TV set, the same shot as before played out, the hidden camera riding Reynolds's coat as he got to his feet and walked back toward the fireplace before turning, showing the President in full form at the other end of the office.

"Sir," Reynolds's voice intoned, "these guys are good. They'll get the job done, without question, and they'll follow orders."

". . . vital, Barry. I won't authorize this unless . . . surgical as we can make it."

"It will be, sir."

". . . recommendation?"

"Depends on what you want to accomplish, sir. If you want to shut down that factory once and for all, devastate the leadership, frighten away anyone else who would set up such a large drug-making facility, and massively impact the heroin flow all at once, then I'd say let's pay them and get it done. Seems a small sacrifice to make."

As before, the President pushed away from his desk and disappeared out of the frame. Reynolds apparently sat back down on the couch and swiveled toward the desk, raising the level of the frame and revealing the chief executive with his back to the

camera standing at the window overlooking the Rose
Garden.

The frame lowered once more as the President
turned, his head just out of the shot at the top, his
voice suddenly clearer as he faced Reynolds. "Okay,
Barry. You've got the green light. Officially this
meeting never occurred, of course."

"Understood, sir."

"Now. Bring . . . over here and show me the details."

The rest of the tape was an identical recitation of the logistics of the plan, a handshake, and Reynolds's exit back
through the west door of the Oval with a brief shot of the
hallway beyond.

Jay stopped the tape, ejected it, and returned to his seat
wholly distracted by the final frames of the tape, the same
fleeting scene that had snagged his interest on the first
viewing. He now recognized it.

Michael Garrity rose slowly to his feet, gesturing in the
direction of the television.

"My Lord, this recording is obviously in direct opposition in meaning and import to the one Mr. Campbell first
played. In Mr. Campbell's version, President Harris is
clearly guilty of ordering an act of torture and murder in
his official capacity as President. In our version, he is
clearly concerned about making certain no such actions are
taken. Which one is correct, then?"

"Indeed, Mr. Garrity," O'Connell said, "that appears to
be the question."

"Both of them," Michael continued, "contain the very
identifiable voice of the President, and both of them have
the same voice identified as Mr. Reynolds, and therefore,
it would seem, one must be real, and one must be fake. The
point is, however, if *one* can be fabricated, so can the
other. It is not a matter, My Lord, of which one is the real
one so much as it is a matter of the demonstrated reality
that *either* could be faked that should be important to the
court. The extremely serious nature of what this Interpol
warrant seeks to accomplish . . . namely the arrest of a for-

mer president . . . demands that supporting evidence be beyond serious question, and yet we have a clear demonstration that the voices can be faked, and thus neither can be accepted as conclusive without independently verifiable evidence."

Mr. Justice O'Connell's eyebrows suddenly came together as a flash of anger clouded his face.

"Mr. Garrity! Are you saying, sir, that the tape you've just shown this court *was* a fake?"

Michael hesitated, not expecting the onslaught.

"Yes, My Lord. My legal team retained last night the services of perhaps the best impressionist in Ireland, Mr. Byrne McHenry, a professional entertainer, and in only a few hours of work with an ordinary tape recorder he produced the sound track you heard in order to demonstrate . . ."

The explosion of sound from the judge startled everyone in the courtroom.

"THAT," he sputtered, his eyes flaring, "is perhaps the most despicable act of purposeful misleading of a court I have ever experienced as a judge! Mr. Garrity, you may well stand to charges before the bar as a result of this dishonorable stunt. You've wasted the time of this court and attempted to use false evidence to sway us. SIT DOWN!"

Michael Garrity faced the judge calmly, still on his feet.

"No, My Lord, I will not sit down with your verbal indictment ringing in my ears."

"YOU WILL SIT DOWN, SIR, OR BE HELD IN CONTEMPT!"

"I did not use *false* evidence, My Lord. I used evidence of *falsity*. There is a substantial difference."

O'Connell had his gavel pointed at Garrity again, but he stopped short of verbalizing the blast he had planned, and instead replaced the gavel on the bench and sat back, shaking his head.

"Very well, Mr. Garrity, stand or sit or do whatever you like, but you're little trick has backfired on you and your client. You have done precisely the opposite of what you intended, sir, because I shall now disregard your offered evidence as non-credible."

Michael sat down slowly, his eyes tracking the judge.

"Mr. Garrity, this is very serious business, this action for perfection of a warrant and an order of extradition. It is serious business because of several factors. First, the Treaty Against Torture demands the faithful adherence of every signatory nation, and after dragging our lazy feet for over a decade, Ireland has finally ratified it as well. That means, sir, that no extradition treaty with Peru is needed. We have the treaty's provisions for extradition, and they will suffice. It also means that a matter of a U.S. President ordering the killing and torture of individuals sets up without question a prima facie case for issuance of a corresponding Irish warrant for the arrest of the accused party. The treaty requires that the complained of action, in this case premeditated torture and murder by proxy, be a violation of the criminal law of the country considering extradition. Clearly these acts are crimes in Ireland. In addition, it is reprehensible that this involves a former U.S. President, since the United States bears much shame for dragging its feet for years on these matters even after it ratified the treaty. Its conduct during the Pinochet matter in England was unforgivable in my view. Washington sat by in stony silence when they should have been actively supporting immediate extradition. Why do I say this from the bench? Because it is the duty of each signatory nation to deal with matters under the treaty very rapidly. We must avoid even the appearance of foot-dragging or delayed compliance if international law is to have real meaning. Therefore, if I had the power to do so, I would not only order Mr. Harris arrested today, I would order him placed within that hour on the next transport to Lima, Peru, for trial. Unfortunately, our extradition procedures require additional steps, including a certification from the Peruvian government that there be no imposition of a death penalty. But, I am going to call a brief recess and study whether or not I can accelerate those procedures and extradite the man immediately through denial of appeal and perhaps some other legal method."

Michael jumped to his feet. "Mr. Justice O'Connell, I object . . ."

"SIT DOWN, Mr. Garrity! Of course you object, and the record will carry your objections, and I fully expect you to appeal on the grounds that I'm biased, or prejudging the case, or whatever. I expect you'll challenge my assertion of jurisdiction, the driver's license I used to get here this morning, and perhaps even what I ate for breakfast. And if our Supreme Court wants to reverse me, so be it. But in the meantime, I will rule in my court the way I see fit, without the interference of the likes of *you,* sir!"

Stunned to silence, Michael sank slowly into his chair.

✈ FORTY-SIX

EuroAir 1020, in Flight—Thursday—11:05 A.M.
Dublin Time

Sherry Lincoln caught the ashen expression on Jillian
Walz's face as Jillian left the cockpit. Sherry got to her
feet, cornering Jillian in the forward galley.

"What's wrong up there?"

"Oh, nothing. Just technical . . ."

"Jillian! I know I'm a civilian and not one of your crew,
but I can tell B.S. when it's thrown at me. What's going
on? If it's a personal thing, I'll back off, but if it has to do
with the operation of this flight, you're going to tell me."

Jillian looked away and pursed her lips for a second,
then met Sherry's eyes and tried, unsuccessfully, to smile.
"We have a small problem. The winds are far worse than
planned, and . . . and . . ."

"You're . . . not telling me we're going somewhere else
but Ireland?"

Jillian exhaled sharply. "Ah . . . *no* . . . I'm not.
We're . . . going to be landing at Galway because we're
very short of fuel."

"How short?"

"One approach only, and there's fog, and since you must know, I'm scared to death."

It was Sherry's turn to swallow hard. "But we *are* going to make it?"

"Craig says yes, but it will be close. I know these fellows, and what's scaring me is that I've never seen them this quiet."

The Four Courts, Dublin, Ireland

Before Mr. Justice O'Connell could formally declare the brief recess he had decided to take, Michael Garrity jumped to his feet. "My Lord . . ."

"Sit down, Mr. Garrity, you have no credibility before this court! You shall not speak."

"Then perhaps you'll hear *me*, judge."

Even though Mr. Justice O'Connell had seen Jay Reinhart get to his feet, the fact that someone not a member of the bar had dared address his court momentarily stopped him.

"What?"

"Your honor . . . I'm sorry, My Lord . . ."

"You have no standing to address this court, Mr. Reinhart."

"Judge, if you have disqualified our barrister, and the defendant is not here to speak for himself, then I am the only voice left."

"SIT DOWN, SIR!"

"No, My Lord . . ."

"YOU DO NOT CALL ME 'MY LORD'! You are not a barrister before this bar!"

"True, but I am a lawyer, sworn to the law, and able to speak for my client if no one else can. And I will call you whatever you deem appropriate, Mr. Justice O'Connell."

The judge sat back heavily in his chair, his eyes flickering to Campbell, then back to Jay.

"What, exactly, do you have to say, Mr. Reinhart?"

"Just this, Judge. It was *I* who conceived the idea of

fabricating the new sound track, merely to demonstrate clearly the point Michael Garrity made, that either sound track could have been fabricated. Never was there any intention to mislead this court. Quite the contrary. There was no way, I felt, to properly demonstrate this point by merely stating it. We had to show you it could be done. We had to show you that a good imitator could do a convincing version of John Harris's very distinctive voice. And we established that. We also demonstrated that a talented mimic could even fabricate Mr. Reynolds's voice. No matter how angry you may be, sir, at the tactic, it did, in fact, make that critical point. Without the supporting evidence that his tape's sound track is real . . . and clearly Mr. Campbell simply cannot provide such evidence today in this forum . . . there is no way for him, for us, or for this court to know the truth. Absent that truth, his tape cannot be used as prima facie support of the charges against John Harris."

"Are you through, sir?" O'Connell said in an acidic tone.

"Yes, Judge. Thank you." Jay sat down.

"The recorder will strike that entire speech from the record," the judge directed. "Nothing in it has in any way changed my opinion of the circus you've tried to make of my court, Mr. Garrity, although . . . I am constrained to consider this anew. We'll take a fifteen-minute recess, and then I shall rule on both the warrant and the order of extradition."

EuroAir 1020, in Flight

The sudden ringing of the satellite phone caused both pilots to jump slightly, so intense was their concentration on the unfolding battle between remaining fuel and remaining distance.

Alastair answered, almost not recognizing Jay Reinhart's strained voice.

"I just got Sherry's message that you've turned around! Tell me it's not so."

"It is, I'm afraid," Alastair said. "In fact, it appears

we're going to have to land in Galway for fuel because we're a bit short."

"Galway?"

"Yes."

"Could you . . . refuel there and try it again?"

Alastair shook his head no without even glancing at Craig. "No way. The winds have gone to hades in a handbasket."

There was a brief pause on the other end. "I see. Ah, I need to speak to Sherry."

Craig picked up the PA microphone and paged her to the cockpit, and she responded within ten seconds.

"It's Jay, Sherry. I told him we were returning to Ireland," Alastair said, handing her the phone.

"Jay! You heard we're coming back."

"It's all backfired, Sherry. Everything we've tried. This judge is hell-bent to send John packing to Lima, and he's off on a recess right now trying to figure out if he can bypass the normal appeals and slam him on a plane immediately."

"Oh my Lord."

"Your returning here couldn't come at a worse time."

"So what do we do, Jay?"

His voice was dejected but the instructions he gave were firm. "Just get yourselves safely on the ground wherever and call me. Leave a message if I don't answer immediately, then sit tight. I . . . think I'm out of options here, but until I'm sure, I'd rather keep you aboard."

"I understand. Good luck."

The Four Courts, Dublin, Ireland

More than forty minutes had elapsed when Mr. Justice O'-Connell reentered his court.

"My Lord," Stuart Campbell said, rising slowly.

O'Connell looked slightly startled.

"Yes, Mr. Campbell?"

"Before you rule in this matter, My Lord, there is one additional point I need to make regarding our videotape."

Mr. Justice O'Connell hesitated, then let out a slightly exasperated sigh.

"Is this truly necessary, Mr. Campbell? You'll be gilding the lily."

"It is necessary for the record, My Lord."

"Very well. Proceed."

Jay had selected the vibrate function on his GSM phone before walking into the courtroom hours before, but he'd forgotten it through the proceedings. The insistent vibrations now coursing through his coat pocket finally reached his conscious mind, and he pulled the phone out and triggered the "on" button as he quietly got to his feet to step outside the courtroom.

"Mr. Reinhart?" a familiar voice asked. "This is Secretary Byer."

"Yes, sir," Jay replied.

"I'm going to patch you back to Washington, Mr. Reinhart, where one of my people has an answer for you. We'll be there in a half hour, but you may need to hear this now. In a nutshell, you were right."

When Secretary Byer had finished, Jay stopped him from disconnecting.

"I have a question, Mr. Secretary. You're intimately familiar with the Oval Office. Would you describe for me what's outside the door on the western wall? I need to check my memory, and trust me, this is very important."

In the courtroom, Campbell had hit the "play" button on his camera, starting the tape toward the end of the sequence when the President and Reynolds were apparently leaning over a map discussing the impending raid.

Campbell pressed the "pause" button then and turned to O'Connell.

"My Lord, as to the authenticity of this recording, I call your attention to the small item visible on the desk. You see there the Great Seal of the United States in the form of a medallion encased in what appears to be Lucite, and just to the right you can see several papers bearing John Harris's signature."

Campbell returned to his table and selected a piece of

paper that he handed to the clerk before handing a copy to Michael Garrity.

"I would enter into evidence at this time a personal item from my own collection of mementos, a letter from John Harris dated in 1985, which bears his signature. You can see that his signature on those letters on the screen, and the one in this exhibit, are identical."

Michael thought of objecting on the grounds that it wasn't the opinion of a graphology expert, but the gesture would be futile at best.

"I'll admit that, Mr. Campbell."

Jay had returned and was sliding back into his chair as Stuart Campbell turned the camera off. Jay began whispering urgently to Michael Garrity.

"Mr. Garrity?" the judge asked. "Do you rest, sir?"

"Just a second, My Lord," Michael answered, ignoring the scowl on the judge's face. In a few moments he stood up and gestured toward Jay.

"My Lord, we have received additional evidence that is extremely material to this case, and I ask you to permit Mr. Reinhart to recite it as he has just recited it to me."

"No."

"My Lord . . ."

"If you've something to say, Mr. Garrity, *you* will say it. You are the barrister before this court."

"Very well, My Lord, although I was afraid I had no further credibility before you."

O'Connell looked at Garrity as if he were seeing him for the first time.

"Mr. Garrity . . . I have reflected on my previous comments, and they were, perhaps, a bit hasty. I shall not cite you for contempt for your . . . your show earlier."

"Thank you, My Lord."

"State your new evidence."

"As your Lordship knows, the Treaty Against Torture, otherwise known as the United Nations Convention Against Torture, under Article Three specifically prohibits any member state from sending, by extradition or otherwise, any person to a country in which there is a reasonable possibility that prohibited acts of torture or infliction of pain without coloration of law may be inflicted. Mr. Reinhart has just received confirmation from the Secretary of State of the United States, and from Washington, that the United States government has new evidence that the government of Peru is about to be cited by a section of the United Nations for human rights abuses, specifically for the systematic torture of political prisoners, including the infliction of torture and unusually harsh punishment against two former Peruvian legislators. Placing Peru on such a list formally declares that until removed by the U.N., Peru is to be considered as a matter of law to have a demonstrated propensity for torturing any prisoner of former political standing. This information meets the applicable definitions of the Treaty Against Torture wherein it prohibits extradition of any person to a state that may reasonably be expected to use prohibited methods of torture or unusual punishment against such a person. Clearly, a former President of the United States fits this category, and since Peru may be said to have a clear intention to inflict torture and unlawful pain on the person of John Harris, any request for his extradition to Peru must be summarily denied."

"Mr. Garrity," the judge replied, "have you anything but verbal statements to make to support this charge?"

"Yes, My Lord, but it will take several days to physically receive the certification from the United Nations Directorate involved."

"Then your motion to vacate the application for extradition is denied."

"My Lord, I then move to adjourn this matter for ten days, or in the alternative, if the court proposes to issue orders, I move to stay execution of any such arrest or extradition order, for ten days. We must have time to produce those instruments."

"I imagine," the judge said, "that Mr. Campbell will have a rather impassioned response to that motion, Mr. Garrity."

Stuart Campbell remained seated, his face impassive as O'Connell looked at him with increasing puzzlement. "What say you, Mr. Campbell?"

"My Lord?"

"I assume you have an objection to Mr. Garrity's motion?"

"No, My Lord. I do not."

"No?" O'Connell asked, his face betraying complete confusion.

"No."

"Mr. Campbell, Mr. Garrity is asking to adjourn these proceedings for ten days, and you are not objecting?"

"No, My Lord."

The judge sat in confused silence for a few seconds before sighing and shaking his head.

"Very well, then. I am going to consider granting the motion. We'll take a momentary recess."

✈ FORTY-SEVEN

"How far out?" Craig asked, his voice crisp but more strained than Alastair had ever heard it.

"One hundred forty miles from the airport. About ninety from land."

Craig studied the fuel gauges over his head, his lips almost white.

"How much left?" Alastair asked.

"Not enough. We're under six hundred, if I can believe the gauges."

"Six hundred per side?"

"No. Total."

"Oh, Lord," Alastair said.

"I don't want to descend down at the normal point," Craig said. "Let's wait until we're within fifty miles of the field, just in case."

"Agreed."

Craig punched the interphone button and waited for Jillian to come on the line.

"Jillian, I want you to get Elle and Ursula briefed and

strapped in with life jackets on. Get Sherry, the Secret Service guy, and the President in life jackets as well as yourself, and get everyone seated about midway back in aisle seats. Review where the life rafts are. And hurry. I don't think we're going in the water, but I want to take no chances."

"Okay," she said and was gone.

"EuroAir Ten-Twenty, contact Galway Approach now, one twenty two point four. He understands your fuel emergency."

"Roger, Shanwick Control. Thank you."

"Good luck, sir."

Alastair switched the frequency and punched the transmit rocker switch.

"Galway Approach, EuroAir Ten-Twenty, level flight level three one zero. We have ATIS information Bravo."

"Roger, Ten-Twenty, radar contact one hundred twenty-six miles from Galway Airport. I'll provide you with radar vectors to the ILS approach runway zero nine at Galway."

"Roger."

Craig was looking up at the fuel gauges again.

"What?" Alastair said.

Craig diverted his gaze back to the forward instrument panel. "You don't want to know. Just do a little praying, please."

"Roger."

Alastair passed the request to remain at altitude until fifty miles out to the controller.

"How far?" Craig asked.

"One hundred and five miles," Alastair said, at the exact moment the gauges for engine number two on the right wing began winding back toward zero thrust and temperature.

"All right, we've lost number two," Alastair said in a matter-of-fact voice.

"And there goes one," Craig replied.

"Try a restart?" Alastair asked.

"With what? We're out of gas."

"I'll get the APU . . . damn, no gas for the aux power unit either."

"We'll keep the speed up enough for windmilling hydraulics but . . ."

The electrical power died at the same moment.

"Damn!" Craig threw the appropriate switches on the overhead panel. "Okay, I've got my side powered from the battery."

"I've got emergency lights and my battery GPS over here. No instruments," Alastair said.

"We'll have to make a no-flap approach," Craig added. "Hydraulics should last, and we should have standby rudder. VHF radio number one and VHF navigation radio number one and the transponder should work, but the computer's gone."

Alastair was already reaching for the transmit switch. "Galway Approach, EuroAir Ten-Twenty has a dual engine flameout. No possibility of restart. We'll need sharp vectoring right onto the localizer."

The controller's voice came back on a wave of audible alarm. "Ah . . . roger, ah, Ten-Twenty . . . you're one hundred nautical miles from the end of the runway. Can . . . you make it?"

Craig was running a high-speed calculation in his head, factoring in the winds as he slowed the jet to its most efficient no-flap airspeed.

Alastair watched his lips move, and his head begin to move side to side.

"No."

"No?" Alastair asked.

"Ask him if there's a closer field. We can't make Galway."

The Four Courts, Dublin, Ireland

Mr. Justice O'Connell sat in thought for several minutes before looking up suddenly. "Very well. We're back on the record, and I am ready to rule on Mr. Garrity's motion."

"Justice O'Connell?"

The judge sighed loudly but without sarcasm as he picked up his gavel. "Are you attempting to address this court again, Mr. Reinhart? Are you unaware that I'm provisionally ruling in your client's favor?"

"Yes, sir, but in one respect your ruling will still deny him justice."

O'Connell replaced the gavel on the bench and swallowed.

"Explain yourself, sir."

"There is more evidence on that tape, Judge. Please wait, and let me instruct Mr. Garrity."

Jay turned to Michael, but O'Connell's voice cut through the attempt.

"I'll hear you very briefly, Mr. Reinhart. To save time. Tell me directly."

Jay got to his feet and looked at Stuart Campbell. "Mr. Campbell, would you please rewind that tape in your camera to the end of the original section, where Reynolds leaves the Oval Office?"

Campbell nodded and moved to the camera, deftly manipulating the controls before turning to Jay.

"What would you like to see?" Campbell asked.

Jay came around the table. "May I?"

"By all means," Campbell said as he backed away from the screen.

Jay pushed the "play" button and let the picture continue until the last few frames of the alcove and the hallway outside the west door came into view.

He pushed "pause," then leaned in close to the picture to verify what he thought he'd seen.

"What are we looking at, Mr. Reinhart?" O'Connell asked.

Jay sighed as he turned toward the bench. "Judge O'-Connell, it is very important to my client that the world not erroneously believe the implications of this tape. *I* firmly believed as I came into this court this morning that John Harris was innocent, and that this tape had been tampered with, and that the conversation Mr. Campbell presented was false. I believe we successfully demonstrated how that could be done. But there was something bothering me when I first saw this, and I now know what it is. I wasn't sure until Mr. Campbell played it a second time. Then I remembered a small, inconsequential item from a recent article in the American press."

"Mr. Reinhart, get to the point. What do you see on this screen that I do not?"

Jay pointed to the hallway visible through the western wall door of the Oval Office.

"This video clearly shows a long hallway that extends at a ninety-degree angle to the western wall of the office. But in the real White House, there is no such hallway. Merely a small alcove. I can testify to this directly since I've been in the office and out that door. Can you see this, Judge?"

O'Connell left the bench and descended the steps to look closely at the screen.

"I do see a hallway, yes. But how am I to know your memory is correct? How long ago were you there, Mr. Reinhart?"

Jay hesitated. "Over ten years ago, I'll admit. But one does not forget that office."

The judge walked back around and regained his bench as Jay decided to chance a direct request.

"Your Honor, if I may have a ten-minute recess, the Secretary of State of the United States is on his way here. He is in the Oval Office on a weekly basis and can testify firsthand as to whether this hallway really exists or not."

The judge sat down, saying nothing. He scratched his face and glanced at Stuart Campbell, who was silent, then leaned forward.

"Ten-minute recess it shall be, Mr. Reinhart."

Joe Byer took the stand when Mr. Justice O'Connell reconvened the court, making fast work of the confirmation that the hallway shown in the video did not exist in the real White House.

"Thank you Mr. Byer, you may step down," the judge said, focusing on Jay. "Mr. Reinhart, if not the White House . . . and I am satisfied about that . . . then what are we looking at?"

Jay got to his feet. "There are, Judge, a total of five different fully furnished mockups of the Oval Office available for the rental of film makers in the U.S. One of them is a permanent set used in the production of a popular television series about the White House. Others have been used constantly in a long procession of feature films or made-for-TV films. These sets can be shipped by truck anywhere in North America and set up in less than a week, and the interiors are essentially indistinguishable from the real office. What we see on this video are pictures made on an artificial set, a mock-up of the Oval Office."

The judge looked at Stuart Campbell, who shook his head and raised the palm of one hand to indicate he had nothing to add or object to.

Jay had moved closer to the video screen and toggled the video forward and backward, seemingly absorbed in the picture.

"Mr. Reinhart, if you're through, sir . . ."

Jay's eyes had grown wider as he held an index finger in the air. "Wait . . . wait just a second, Your Honor . . ."

"Mr. Reinhart . . ."

Jay turned to the bench. "Judge O'Connell, would you consider coming down here again? There's something else I've just found that absolutely proves my point."

Mr. Justice O'Connell shook his head as he got to his feet and moved around to the screen once again.

"Here, sir. On that angled wall, you see that mirror, on the side of the alleged hallway just outside the door?"

"Yes?"

"Look in the mirror."

"I see some vertical lines, not quite vertical," he said. "What are they?"

"Those, Judge, are some of the two-by-fours holding up the backside of the set."

EuroAir 1020, in Flight

"Ten-Twenty, turn right now to a heading of zero nine five degrees. I'm taking you to a closer airport at Connemara. Twenty-one miles closer. There's one runway, runway two seven, and there's an ILS for that one. It's twenty-two hundred meters . . . ah, over sixty-five hundred feet in length."

"What's the designator?" Alastair asked quickly, receiving the four-letter code and punching it rapidly into his handheld GPS. "I show sixty-two miles, Galway."

"Roger. Sixty-one miles now," the controller said.

"Tell him we can do that, Alastair, but we'll have only one chance at it. How's the weather there? If it's good enough, maybe we can land straight in to the east."

Alastair passed the question.

"I have the weather for Connemara Regional," the controller said. "The ceiling is indefinite at one hundred fifty feet, visibility a half mile and fog, winds are two seven zero at twelve knots. The ILS is up for runway two seven. Just tell me what you want."

Alastair turned to Craig, who was licking his lips and mentally racing through more calculations.

"I think," Craig said, without turning his head, "that we have no choice but to fly the instrument approach to runway two seven, even though that means we have to fly past the airport and turn around. We've got enough altitude to pass the runway a mile and a half to the south as we're going eastbound, then make a tight left one-hundred-eighty-degree turn back west on instruments and find the localizer for runway two seven, and just . . . come down to the glide slope."

"Fly *by* the airport? Hell, Craig, he can vector us right to it!"

Craig looked at Alastair with a rapid glance. "But we can't see it! What if we're displaced a quarter mile to one side of the runway when we break out? We'll sit down on a building or worse with no chance of going around."

"We have no go-around potential if we fly by and turn, either!"

"Alastair, we've flamed out both engines. We have *no* go-around capability period! But, if we keep the speed up, we'll still have the hydraulics for the flight controls and landing gear and maybe flap extension, and we'll have the ILS on my side to get down the centerline. All we need is enough altitude. Get your flashlight out, just in case."

"I have it." Alastair scanned the situation again on his GPS and on the captain's panel to his left. Fifty miles from Connemara, speed two hundred ten knots, altitude twenty-one thousand feet and descending steadily with the head-wind gone and a tailwind beginning to improve their chances of reaching the airport with enough altitude left to maneuver for landing. As long as they kept the airspeed high enough, the wind flowing through the unpowered jet engines would keep them rotating fast enough to keep pumping hydraulic pressure into the aircraft systems. The battery would be good for thirty minutes, and they'd be on the ground long before that. As soon as they slowed under a hundred eighty knots, however, the hydraulic power would die and the only flight controls left would be the standby rudder system, manual pitch trim, and a hard-to-handle system called "manual reversion" for keeping the wings level.

"Okay," Alastair said. "The way I see it, we'll pass south of the runway at . . . about three thousand feet. A tight left turn at, ah . . . fifteen-hundred, no, twelve-hundred-feet-per-minute descent rate should put us on final approach at six hundred feet above the ground with a little energy to spare."

"Tight, but okay. Alastair, tell the controller that, and also tell him we need to begin our turn not an inch farther than one mile east of the approach end of the runway, displaced exactly one and a half miles south."

"You're sure?"

"Check me, Alastair, but I think that'll give us wiggle room. I can always slip it to a landing as long as we have some hydraulics left, which means I've got to keep the speed up, which means I'll have to dive it down final."

"How about the gear?"

"We'll put the gear down as I start the turn to final. Use it as a speed brake. Be ready to yank the manual releases if we don't have enough hydraulic pressure. And . . . keep your left leg clear, but on short final, pull out the manual crank on the pitch trim wheel and stand by to help me flare."

"Roger."

"I'm gonna hold two hundred knots until we're lined up fat on final, and I may try to extend some flaps at that point to slow us down. If we touch down at two hundred, we'll never get her stopped."

"Got it. We're thirty-nine miles out."

Alastair relayed the plan carefully to the controller, watching the unfolding flight path on the flight computer and the horizontal situation indicator in front of him to verify they were being aimed ever so slightly to the south of the airport.

"They know we're coming?" Alastair asked the controller.

"Yes, sir. Crash equipment is standing by. You're cleared to land. Verify you've got no engine power?"

"We're flamed out. No fuel."

"Roger."

"Twenty-eight miles to go, Craig," Alastair said, yanking his flight manual out of his flight bag and wildly leafing through to check the speed figures for final approach at their weight.

"Since we're so light, she's going to want to float when you flare, and we won't have speed brakes, and of course, there are no reversers without . . . you know . . ."

"Engines running," Craig finished.

"Yeah."

"Got it."

"Twenty miles," Alastair said.

"Okay . . . look . . . get me set up now for the ILS, double check I have the right frequency in the radio, and make sure we've got the right inbound course set in . . . that's a heading of two seven zero."

"Already done."

"When . . . when we break out, we take whatever we've got. I'm going to have to plunk it down and get on the brakes to get stopped."

"Understood, Craig. You won't have antiskid, you know, and if you blow the tires . . ."

"I know . . . we'll never stop. I'll be careful."

"Twelve miles."

"Roger. Altitude?"

"We're good. Coming through six thousand feet. I wish we could see something besides gray out there."

"We will. Lock your shoulder harness."

"Okay."

"Get on the PA. Tell them in the back to get in a brace position."

"I can't. No electrical."

"Roger," Craig said.

"I show your heading dead-on to pass one and a half miles south. Weather information remains the same. The tower reports the ceiling is a bit better than the hundred fifty feet, and all approach lights are on."

"Roger," Craig said.

"We're four miles from the airport, Craig, heading zero nine zero degrees, one point five miles south."

"Okay. Call me perfectly abeam the end of the runway, then give me mileage increments east of that point."

"Will do."

"Altitude's . . . three thousand five hundred," Craig said to himself, pushing the jet's nose down slightly to reach three thousand as they passed abeam the end of the runway.

"Abeam, Craig. Speed two hundred twenty. Zero visibility."

"Roger."

The controller repeated the same information.

"Stand by, now, sir," Alastair said. "No more transmissions while we're working this." He glanced at the left seat. "Okay, Craig, we're one half mile east, twenty-eight hundred feet above the ground, speed two hundred knots."

"Roger."

"Coming up on one mile east, speed two hundred, altitude twenty-six hundred."

"Keep calling it. Not turning yet."

"One point one miles, one point two, one point three . . ."

"Okay!" Craig said. "Now. Landing gear down!" He rolled the 737 into a forty-five-degree left bank, beginning the turn back to the runway.

"Gear down," Alastair repeated, working the handle and

checking the gear as it fell into place and rewarded him with three green lights.

"Gear down and locked, Craig, coming through heading of north, forty-degree bank, speed two hundred, altitude two thousand one hundred, and we're one point nine miles from the end of the runway. We're high and fast. I see no lights out there, no glow through the fog, nothing."

"Okay. Have faith."

"Localizer alive, Craig. Coming fast."

"Steepening . . . the . . . bank!" Craig said, rolling the 737 into a nearly fifty-degree left bank angle to catch the ILS inbound course. He rolled out of the turn precisely on course and perfectly aligned with the unseen runway ahead and reached for the speed brake handle, pulling it to the deployed position. The windmilling hydraulic pressure dutifully raised the speed brake panels on both wings, steepening the descent and slowing them.

"Bang on course, one point two miles out, altitude one thousand six hundred. We're a thousand higher than we should be."

"Flaps straight down to fifteen!"

"Flaps? Craig, the speed brakes are out! No speed brakes with flaps, remember?"

"Can't help it. I've got to slow!"

"Roger." Alastair moved the flap handle quickly as Craig pushed forward to increase the descent rate with the flaps beginning to come out on the residual hydraulic pressure.

"Point nine from the end, way above glide slope, speed one ninety, we're one thousand two hundred."

"Dumping it! Flaps thirty!"

Alastair complied, his left hand moving the lever almost instantly.

"Flaps are coming through fifteen on the way to thirty. Half mile, Craig, eight hundred feet, two thousand feet per minute down and one eighty on the speed."

"Call the glide slope when you see it! We'll intercept it from above."

"Sink two thousand, quarter mile out, four hundred feet, speed one seventy-five."

"I'm gonna hold the sink rate until I see it!"

"Sink two thousand, three hundred feet, speed one seventy-five. Remember the hydraulics may die! Don't wait too long to pull!"

A galaxy of fuzzy lights swam into view just ahead, coming up at them fast as Craig began hauling back on the yoke.

"Sink twelve hundred, two hundred feet, speed one sixty. PULL, CRAIG!"

Craig yanked the yoke almost back in his lap, feeling the nose coming up but with greater sluggishness each passing second as the airspeed slowed the turning of the engines and the hydraulic pressure bled away.

"One hundred feet! Sinking too fast!" Alastair said, the runway under them now but the sink rate still excessive.

Craig had unfolded the manual handle on the pitch trim on his side, as had Alastair, and suddenly they were both rotating the wheel backwards at a blinding rate to the nose-up position. They felt the nose respond at the last second as the 737 settled into ground effect, killing off the remainder of the sink rate as the tires kissed perfectly onto the surface with a moderate plunk.

"Reverse it! Rotate nose down!" Craig barked as Alastair complied, both of them cranking the pitch trim in the opposite direction, lowering the nosewheel to the runway.

"Brakes, Craig!" Alastair called as Craig's right hand left the manual trim and yanked the speed brake handle back, momentarily startled to find it already deployed. He'd forgotten.

There was only emergency brake pressure now to stop them. The normal antiskid protection had died with the electrical system, leaving only the glow of the battery-powered flight instruments on Craig's side as the runway lights flashed by. "Airspeed one hundred twenty, Craig!"

If he pressed the brake pedals too hard, he'd blow the tires and doom them to run off the far end of the runway.

There were red lights visible now through the mist marking the end of the runway several thousand feet ahead. They were coming fast. Craig metered the braking, feeling the disks grab, slowing them as he used the same rudder pedals to steer between the gradually slowing blur of runway lights.

"Ninety knots!" Alastair called out. "Eighty . . . seventy . . ."

The end-of-the-runway red lights loomed closer.

The brakes felt mushy, as if they were fading, and possibly overheating.

"Fifty knots, forty!" Alastair called as Craig pressed harder on the brakes, gambling against a blown tire.

The red lights were just ahead as Alastair called them through 20 knots. Craig jammed on the remaining brakes, feeling the 737 shudder and skid to a halt just as the red lights slowed and disappeared beneath the nose.

For perhaps thirty seconds the two pilots sat in shocked silence, barely daring to believe they were alive and intact.

Alastair reached for the transmit button, relying on the battery power for the remaining radio.

"Galway Approach, Ten-Twenty is down safely at . . . wherever this is. Thank you, sir."

"Jesus, Mary, and Joseph!" the controller said, emotion overwhelming the cool professionalism that had marked his previous transmissions. "Now I can restart me heart. Well done, lads!"

The Four Courts, Dublin, Ireland

Mr. Justice O'Connell had reclaimed his seat on the bench and taken the time to make several notes as he composed his response, then looked up.

"Very well. I find the videotape evidence as submitted here today to be inadmissible in the extreme due to the inability of Mr. Campbell to override the evidence that it was faked. We are essentially back precisely where we were two hours ago when this hearing began. And so, Mr. Campbell, I turn to you with one question, sir. Have you any evidence to present to this court to support the Peruvian Interpol warrant, or the application for extradition, other than the fact that it was issued by a Peruvian court of competent jurisdiction?"

Stuart Campbell got to his feet slowly and cleared his throat, his eyes on the papers before him until he looked up at the judge.

"My Lord, without the efficacy of that videotape, I possess no such supporting evidence. And, I should like to state that I anticipate I will need to take instructions from my client, and that possibly, in due course, an application may need to be made on behalf of my instructing solicitor to come off the record."

Jay leaned forward to whisper in Michael's ear. "What the heck does that mean?"

Michael scratched the answer on his legal pad. "It means he's about to dump Peru as a client and get out of this."

"I will not ask your grounds, Mr. Campbell," O'Connell answered. "I believe they're all too obvious. So noted. And, for want of sufficient supporting evidence to sustain this request against the challenge of the defendant, the warrant is quashed in the Republic of Ireland, and the motion to extradite is denied."

This time the gavel came down with finality.

✈ **EPILOGUE**

Dublin International Airport, Ireland—Thursday— 3:20 P.M.

Jay slid the door of the Parc Aviation van open and stepped onto the ramp, preferring to wait by himself for the EuroAir 737, just now touching down.

He glanced at his watch, which was showing 3:20 P.M., and wondered how pilots achieved the level of composure necessary to survive a near-death experience, then fly the airplane back to Dublin as if nothing extraordinary had happened.

"They'll probably strike a hero's medal for us, and pin it on just before we're executed," Alastair had quipped by phone when Jay had reached them after the verdict.

A blue and white Boeing 757 from Andrews Air Force Base in Washington sat on another hard stand several hundred yards to the south. Jay glanced over his shoulder to make sure the Secretary of State and his people were still inside a waiting limousine several hundred yards away.

The 737 was coming up the taxiway toward the pre-appointed parking stand as a marshaller wearing an orange safety vest held up his arms to guide them in. Jay watched with his mind on Sherry. Her voice had been composed on the phone from Connemara, but he'd heard the residual tension as she talked and asked her about it.

"I'm okay. I mean, we knew there was something wrong when the crew told us to put on our life jackets, but it was all right."

It was telling, Jay thought, that she responded to his news of the extraordinary events in court with a single "Good!" before returning to the subject of the pilots' incredible performance.

"They were magnificent," she had said.

"But they miscalculated their fuel, Sherry," Jay had countered.

"True, but they pulled it out. That's the important thing. They got us here safely, even if my hair is now completely silver!"

Only John Harris had seemed unaffected by the aeronautical drama, focusing instead on what had transpired in Mr. Justice O'Connell's court.

"A movie set of the Oval Office! I never thought of that, Jay," he'd said. "I knew my words on that tape were false, but . . . even *I* would have sworn that was me on the screen in the Oval."

Jay pulled his attention back to the oncoming 737. The EuroAir jet was turning onto the hard stand, the noise forcing his fingers in his ears. As soon as the pilots brought the craft to a halt and cut the engines, the internal airstairs began to descend.

Jay walked toward the front entrance, waving to the attractive flight attendant who was standing in the doorway. She motioned to him to come aboard and he bounded up the steps.

Sherry was waiting at the top with a bear hug, and John Harris was right behind, his handshake progressing to a hug and a hand on Jay's shoulder.

"Well done, Jay! Very well done!"

"Thank you, John, but . . ."

"No 'buts.' You did it!"

The pilots emerged from the cockpit, their faces reflecting the strain of the past few hours, as Matt Ward slipped into the doorway to scrutinize the ramp beyond, noting the approach of a limousine.

"Joe Byer is here to greet you, too," Jay said, as he ran a hand through his hair to control an unruly forelock. "He got the information to me just in time this morning about the U.N.'s findings . . . about Peru torturing political prisoners. And then he flew over here in time to help me prove we were dealing with an artificial set and actors, not you and the Oval Office. He's been very helpful."

Matt Ward left the doorway and moved to the President's side.

"Secretary Byer and three others are on their way to the plane, Mr. President."

"See them in, please, Matt," Harris responded, turning to the captain. "Craig? You remember when we were headed to Rome and I said I wanted to take you and your crew to dinner?"

Craig Dayton looked cornered. "Ah, I think so, sir."

"Well, tonight's the night, provided you'll stay over."

"Thank you, Mr. President, but . . ."

The President raised the palm of his hand. "No objections, Craig, I've got some work to do on your behalf, and it'll be easier if you're still here and I'm still paying for the charter."

Craig glanced at Alastair. "I'll be real surprised, Mr. President, if they ever let us fly on EuroAir again, even as passengers."

"Give me a few hours," John Harris said, "and we'll see about that. By the way, I need that list of EuroAir personnel and phone numbers we talked about."

"Okay," Craig managed, noting that the Secretary of State was already halfway up the stairs.

"So," John Harris said, "tonight we're all going to debrief over the best food I can find in Dublin, and I've reserved rooms for everyone at the Shelbourne Hotel. No arguments. I'm buying."

He turned, then, extending his hand just as Joe Byer stepped through the entry door.

**The Shelbourne Hotel, St. Stephen's Green,
Dublin, Ireland**

With Matt Ward and Sherry Lincoln dispatched on various errands, John Harris had the two-room suite to himself, which was just what he wanted.

A knock on the door came as expected, and he greeted the visitor with a correct handshake.

"I thought it was time for some hatchet burying," Harris said as he motioned the man toward the couch and sat in an opposite chair.

"I agree," William Stuart Campbell replied with a neutral expression.

"We've never talked about the U.N. negotiations back in the eighties, Stuart, and . . . it occurred to me that I never explained or apologized for what happened."

"No," Stuart said. "But I assumed you achieved exactly what you wanted to achieve."

John Harris shook his head. "I did not intend to kill your amendment."

"Then why did you do it? Just what *was* your intention?"

John Harris studied the carpet for a few seconds before replying. "There you were in the limelight, Stuart, the engine behind the convention. Pearls of wisdom cascaded from your mouth with every speech. You'd done a masterful job of gathering the entire international community around you . . ."

"And your client," Stuart interrupted, "was determined to have you kill my offered amendment on sovereign immunity, the amendment that would have everyone in agreement that butchers like Pinochet could never hide behind the concept."

"I didn't have a client, Stuart," John Harris said.

"What?" Stuart Campbell's eyebrows came together. "But . . . you were there representing the Saudis . . ."

"I was there representing myself. You only assumed I was representing the Saudis because you knew I'd been doing a lot of recent work for them."

"But . . . *why,* John? You convinced the entire Third

World that I was somehow going to kidnap and try all their leaders when all I was trying to do was keep the true criminals from slipping away."

"I know."

"And . . . you believed, personally, that this was the right thing to do?"

Harris shook his head slowly. "I wish I could claim noble purpose."

"But, why? You cost us a year of angst while Britain grappled with the archaic concept of sovereign immunity for that bloody bastard Pinochet!"

"Was this personal, Stuart?" John Harris asked without warning. "This little action against me on Peru's behalf?"

"Personal?"

"Did you take this case because I blocked you in New York?"

Stuart looked at John Harris for several moments. "Yes and no."

Harris laughed. "The perfect lawyer's answer! I overuse it myself."

Stuart was not laughing. "I didn't create the opportunity, John. I was shown the tape by President Miraflores, and I believed it was real."

Harris nodded. "Well, even I was fooled. Not by the words, which I knew weren't mine, but by the images."

"I chose to believe it was real," Stuart continued, "because I thought it was the best of poetic justice."

"Poetic . . . ?"

"Yes! Have you forgotten the other provision that went along with that amendment of mine regarding sovereign immunity?"

"I . . . guess I have."

"It was a procedure, John, for quickly trying the evidence of an Interpol warrant in order to protect former presidents and prime ministers against frivolous actions. Each nation would be required to hold an immediate and honest hearing on whether the charges were backed by real evidence or not, and whether the complaining country was competent to hold a fair trial. In other words, John, precisely what you needed in this case."

"So, you thought . . ."

"I thought, what a marvelous opportunity! John Harris, the high and mighty, is going to rue the day he killed that amendment."

"Did you know the charges were false?"

"Of course not. Good heavens, man, I do have some standards!"

"But . . . you were willing to send me to Lima?"

"I knew it would never come to that, John. President Cavanaugh couldn't permit it. I knew he'd intervene."

"Stuart, you're not telling something here. You had an ace up your sleeve somewhere, because you had to know there was still a chance some judge would grant extradition and the Italian government would comply."

Campbell nodded. "Very well. I knew your legal team would eventually realize that with Peru failing all the tests for humane treatment of prisoners, you could hardly be sent there. And Reinhart did catch on . . . with a little help from your State Department."

John Harris studied the carpet and took a deep breath. "Well, Stuart, in the interest of full disclosure, what I did to block you at the U.N. was personal for me, too. Someone had to cut you down a notch."

Stuart Campbell looked startled. "Simple jealousy, then?"

John Harris nodded. "When you take away all the justifications and excuses, yes. And I regretted it through every day of the Pinochet circus. And I humbly apologize to you now."

Stuart Campbell nodded his head slowly. "I accept your apology, John, and add one of my own."

They sat in silence for the better part of a minute before John Harris shook his head. "We're quite a pair, huh, Stuart?"

"Sorry?"

"Two legal titans involving the world in our private little shoving contest. Like two brothers fighting on the street corner, blissfully unaware that we're upsetting the neighbors."

For the first time, Campbell's expression softened to a

smile. "Yes, I suppose there's some truth to that. Our motivations were hardly pure and lofty."

Stuart Campbell let his gaze wander to the windows and the lengthening, reddening rays of the late afternoon sun, his thoughts soaring back to Scotland and his own boyhood, memories of the good battles of the brothers Campbell flashing in his mind. Harris's analogy was closer to the truth than he wanted to admit.

"John, have you ever given a speech to some important world function, and found yourself mentally standing in the wings watching yourself, and wondering why all those important people were listening to the likes of you, because, in your mind, you're still a pimply-faced fifteen-year-old?"

John Harris was nodding. "More times than I'll ever admit." He sat forward. "See, Stuart, when we strip away all the veneer and the fancy jargon and the cloak of noble purpose and official position, we *are* just a couple of overgrown boys doing a pretty good job of acting out our respective roles."

Stuart nodded. "Which is a pretty apt description of life in general."

The Commons Restaurant, Dublin

From the moment Craig Dayton had walked into the restaurant, he'd tried to focus on enjoying the extraordinary company and the once-in-a-lifetime circumstance of dining with a grateful former world leader and a sitting cabinet secretary whom Harris had invited as well. That, coupled with Jillian sitting across from him looking incredibly beautiful in a shimmering white dress that traced and caressed the magnificent femininity of her body, gave him every reason to ignore whatever professional disaster tomorrow was going to bring.

Or so he kept telling himself.

But the effort was failing, and he could no longer hide his depression, so before the main course arrived, President Harris excused himself and asked Craig and Alastair to follow.

He led them to a corner of an empty banquet room.

"This is bad news, isn't it?" Craig asked, unable to suppress the sick feeling inside.

"Well, that all depends," John Harris said, his expression betraying nothing.

Alastair was trying to smile. "It's certainly all right, sir. We didn't expect you'd be able to influence a bunch of hard-nosed German managers to forgive such a stunt."

"And what stunt would that be, Alastair?"

"Well . . ."

"You aren't referring, are you, to the brave and heroic acts of a couple of airline pilots whose timely actions prevented the putative kidnapping of a former U.S. President?"

"And . . . who almost cashiered that same former President by running an airliner out of gas? Yes, that would be the stunt," Alastair said, laughing ruefully.

"Well," the President continued, "I guess we do have a problem if you want to see it that way, because I'll need to call EuroAir's chairman back and ask him to cancel the parade."

"I'm sorry . . . what?" Craig asked.

John Harris smiled. "Relax, both of you. The airline you're working for has just landed a brand-new contract for U.S. military charters, subject to passing the scrutiny of the air safety inspection people at Scott Air Force Base in Illinois. EuroAir seems rather ecstatic about that. And, after a serious chat with the Secretary of Defense *and* the Secretary of State, EuroAir has come to understand that it is in their best interests to be very proud of you, and very quiet about the magnificent demonstration of airmanship that followed a somewhat less laudatory fuel event."

"Mr. President! You did *that?* I can't believe it! You bloody well pulled it off!" Alastair said, his face ablaze with amazement as Craig grabbed John Harris's hand and began to shake it.

"Thank you, sir! Thank you! Are you sure? I . . . I just . . ."

"Hey, take it easy fellows!" John Harris said, smiling. "The truth is, I'm the one who owes the thanks to both of *you*, and this was the absolute minimum I wanted to do. Now, let's get back in there and enjoy the evening."

It was nearly 9:30 p.m. when the President bade good night to Michael Garrity, Craig Dayton, and the rest, and walked in a different direction with Joe Byer.

"You said you'd heard from Washington about Reynolds," John Harris probed.

"Yes, I did hear, and it's pretty tawdry, Mr. President."

"Tell me."

"In brief? Reynolds was promised all the protection he needed, but he decided to make a side deal with Miraflores. It wasn't just about delivering you; it was about money as well. In effect he sold out the Company and his President for the proverbial thirty pieces of silver, and he paid to have that tape made to perfect his scam by indicting you. I'm told he had it shot in Los Angeles."

"Is Langley going to go after Reynolds legally?"

"I don't know," Byer said. "The spook business is a little out of my element, Mr. President. I'm just relaying what the CIA told us."

After leaving the restaurant, Jay walked with Sherry Lincoln back to the Shelbourne a few blocks away.

"May I buy you a drink, kind sir?" she joked, gesturing to the hotel bar.

He checked his watch and smiled. "Sure. As long as I pay for it."

"I guess that can be arranged," she said, her eyes following his to the watch. "You're going somewhere?" she asked.

"In a little while."

"What's her name?"

Jay laughed and shook his head. "No. Nothing like that. A cleanup professional matter is all."

"Okay. Now I'm burning with curiosity."

"What would you like to drink?"

"Nothing creative. A glass of some naive white zinfandel, I suppose," she said. "And you?"

"Zinfandel is good." He retrieved the wine and joined Sherry at a small table.

"When are you going back, Sherry?" he asked.

"To the U.S.? I don't know. John hasn't said, but I suspect he'll want to wait a few days and decompress . . . since all of you seem very sure there's no more legal danger in staying here."

"Not in Ireland, at least."

"Why were you asking?" she said, smiling.

Jay tried to feign innocence. "Oh, no reason."

"I see."

"Other than an idea that, maybe, I'd like to rent a car and see some of this beautiful country."

"They drive on the wrong side of the road here, Jay."

"I know. That's why I need a copilot. You interested?"

Sherry smiled again, sending a warm wave of anticipation through him. "Oh, I'm interested, if the schedule permits. We're talking two rooms for any overnights, right?"

"Of course, Sherry," he said quickly. "I am a gentleman, you know."

"Like I've never heard that line before." She laughed. "Okay. Let me talk to the President in the morning and we'll see. Maybe I could break loose for a few days. I'd like that, if John can spare me."

"I really hope you can," Jay said, looking directly into her eyes.

Sherry hesitated, her smile broadening as she replied softly, "So do I."

The River Liffey, Dublin

The pedestrian-only bridge just west of the famous Ha'penny Bridge was only a short walk from the hotel. Jay had left Sherry at the door to her room just half an hour before, his mind consumed with conflicting thoughts—including the need to finish a heartfelt letter to Linda he had begun to write that afternoon.

He hated the pain he'd caused Linda, and hated the abrupt way he'd slapped her with the news that he was leaving Laramie. She was right, he thought, about Karen's memory holding him away from life and commitment, and he would change all that. Maybe it had been the near-death experience getting to Denver that had suddenly jarred him from the grip of Karen's memory, or maybe time was finally dulling the intense pain. He could actually think of her now with more sadness than grief, and that was amazing.

Thinking of Linda, however, triggered nothing but guilt. He should have told her months ago that love wasn't growing like it should, but it was easier to submerge in *her* love night after night, just taking the moment. He hoped they could remain friends, hoped she'd forgive him, but time would tell.

I'll finish the letter as soon as I get back, Jay thought, wondering again why he'd agreed to this meeting.

He reached the metal bridge and walked to mid-span before turning to watch the light show of nighttime Dublin reflect on the dark silver of the river's surface. He enjoyed the light breeze at his back and the constant passage across the bridge of individuals and strolling couples who formed a pleasant crosscurrent to the water below.

Jay saw someone lean on the railing to his right, and he looked over, instantly recognizing the man before he spoke.

"Thank you for meeting me here, Mr. Reinhart," Stuart Campbell's resonant voice announced as the senior attorney leaned forward, breathing deeply and examining the night.

"You understand that I'm still John Harris's lawyer," Jay said, his curiosity still overriding the caution of being asked by opposing counsel for a private meeting in the dead of night.

"Of course. I just wanted you to know that you fought an excellent battle today."

"Thank you, Sir William," Jay said hesitantly, wondering what would follow.

Campbell remained quiet as he leaned on the railing, scanning the dark water below.

Jay broke the silence. "May I ask *you* a question?"

"By all means."

"Why did you do it?"

Stuart Campbell glanced at him again with an even expression. "Not object to your motion for adjournment, you mean?"

"Exactly. We had nothing but verbal representations about a phone call to Washington. You could have easily overridden it."

"Yes, but I had no choice," Stuart said.

"I don't understand."

"I already knew Peru's record on prisoner abuse. You'd found the key, and one way or another you would prevail against extradition when you obtained proof of the U.N.'s actions. Why prolong the agony?"

"I see, I guess."

Stuart Campbell looked at him again. "That ploy of yours was brilliant, you know."

"I'm sorry?"

"Doing the alternative audio track to demonstrate that the tape could have been staged. Impeccable logic."

"Thank you."

"So, where are you going professionally, former District Judge Jay Reinhart? As you see, I know your history."

Jay shook his head. "I don't know, really. Probably back to Wyoming." He began to smile skeptically and turned to look at Campbell. "Why? Are you offering me a job or something?"

"Good heavens, no!" Campbell laughed, falling silent just as rapidly. "But, on the other hand, you never know. If you start practicing over here, I might just have to hire you to keep from having to meet you on the battlefield."

Jay snorted. "Yeah, as if I'm a threat to Sir William Stuart Campbell."

"Don't sell yourself short, Mr. Reinhart. Were I your senior partner, I would be heaping praise and reward on your shoulders this minute for your handling of this matter."

Jay pushed away from the railing and turned toward the senior lawyer.

"Well, you know something, Sir William? This may all be a game to you, but to me the law is a very serious thing, especially when someone's life hangs in the balance. It matters a lot to me. So I'm very thankful I'm not your partner. Now, what's the *real* reason you asked me to meet you here?"

Stuart Campbell smiled and reached in his inside coat pocket to pull out a small audiocassette tape.

"What's that?" Jay asked.

"The openly taped record of a phone call between myself and President Miraflores several weeks ago. I thought you might like to have it."

"What's . . . on it?" Jay asked.

"President Miraflores's angry voice as he quakes with anticipation of John Harris's handcuffed arrival in Lima and makes plans for trying, convicting, sentencing . . . and burning John Harris alive. You see, one of Miraflores's brothers was a drug dealer, and the brother's death in that raid was the main source of his fury against John Harris. The stated intentions on this tape would have instantly prevented extradition, if needed."

"You held that tape back!"

"Of course I did. I assumed it was protected under attorney-client privilege."

"Okay, but then . . . then it's still privileged . . ."

Stuart smiled and shook his head, his eyebrows flaring in mock surprise. "Apparently I was wrong. I checked my phone log and discovered this conversation predated my taking the case. So you're welcome to use it any way you see fit. Mr. Miraflores is no longer my client."

Jay took the offered tape and balanced it in his hand. "Why now, Sir William?"

Stuart Campbell chuckled and stood away from the railing, ready to depart. "Because, Mr. Reinhart, the law and justice matter a lot to me, too. They always have."

Jay watched in mild shock as the big lawyer turned and walked away.

So, Sir William Stuart Campbell had controlled it all

from the beginning, Jay thought. Even Campbell's defeat before Mr. Justice O'Connell had been consonant with his plan to drag an ex-President to the brink and yank him to safety just in time. He'd been John Harris's prosecutor and savior rolled into one, and, as always, master of the game.

Jay quietly slipped the audiocassette into his pocket and turned back toward the river to lean on the railing, his mind furiously working on the question Campbell had asked him.

So where am *I going professionally? Where* should *I go?* He thought about Sherry and the trip they'd be taking together the next day if her schedule worked out.

Something else Sir William had said flashed across his mind, a comment about legal battlefields with Jay on the front lines.

Maybe I should *think about resuming an international practice,* Jay thought. It was a possibility he'd have to explore, and Ireland might just be a pretty good place to start.

JOHN J. NANCE

TURBULENCE

A NOVEL

PUTNAM